A BEAST

had thrown a challenge to Tarl Cabot. It came in the form of a bloody armlet that had graced the arm of Telima, once Tarl's beloved.

The story was that this monstrous beast-like creature, riding a mighty winged tarn, had plunged from the sky, destroyed Telima and thrown back the armlet.

Tarl knew it meant defiance and scorn for him, once an agent of the priest-kings. The Others—those vicious enemies of men— were daring him to respond.

But Tarl Cabot was no longer an Earth-man, weighing his chances with logic and calm. He felt himself Gorean, and in the Gorean code there could be but one reply: to gird on his weapons and avenge his honor as a man.

The beasts had calculated correctly. But they had underrated the full extent of their human foeman's cunning.

Marauders
of
GOR

John Norman

DAW BOOKS, INC.
DONALD A. WOLLHEIM, PUBLISHER

1301 Avenue of the Americas
New York, N. Y.　　　10019

First printing, March 1975

1 2 3 4 5 6 7 8 9

Printed in U.S.A.

Contents

Marauders
of
GOR

1

THE HALL

I sat alone in the great hall, in the darkness, in the Captain's Chair.

The walls of stone, some five feet in thickness, formed of large blocks, loomed about me. Before me, over the long, heavy table behind which I sat, I could see the large tiles of the hall floor. The table was now dark, and bare. No longer was it set with festive yellow and scarlet cloths, woven in distant Tor; no longer did it bear the freight of plates of silver from the mines of Tharna, nor of cunningly wrought goblets of gold from the smithies of luxurious Turia, Ar of the south. It was long since I had tasted the fiery paga of the Sa-Tarna fields north of the Vosk. Now, even the wines from the vineyards of Ar seemed bitter to me.

I looked up, at the narrow apertures in the wall to my right. Through them I could see certain of the stars of Gor, in the tarn-black sky.

The hall was dark. No longer did the several torches, bristling and tarred, burn in the iron rings at the wall. The hall was silent. No musicians played; no cup companions laughed and drank, lifting their goblets; on the broad, flat tiles before me, under the torches, barefoot, collared, in scarlet silks, bells at their wrists and ankles, there danced no slave girls.

The hall was large, and empty and silent. I sat alone.

Seldom did I have my chair carried from the hall. I remained much in this place.

I heard footsteps approaching. I did not turn my head. It caused me pain to do so.

"Captain," I heard.

It was Luma, the chief scribe of my house, in her blue robe and sandals. Her hair was blond and straight, tied behind her head with a ribbon of blue wool, from the bounding Hurt, dyed in the blood of the Vosk sorp. She was a scrawny girl, not attractive, but with deep eyes, blue; and she was a superb scribe, in her accounting swift, incisive, accurate, brilliant; once she had been a paga slave, though a poor one; I had saved her from Surbus, a captain, who had purchased her to slay her, she not having served him to his satisfaction in the alcoves of the tavern; he would have cast her, bound, to the swift, silken urts in the canals. I had dealt Surbus his death blow, but, before he had died, I had, on the urging of the woman, she moved to pity, carried him to the roof of the tavern, that he might, before his eyes closed, look once more upon the sea. He was a pirate, and a cutthroat, but he was not unhappy in his death; he had died by the sword, which would have been his choice, and before he had died he had looked again upon gleaming Thassa; it is called the death of blood and the sea; he died not unhappy; men of Port Kar do not care to die in their beds, weak, lingering, at the mercy of tiny foes that cannot see; they live often by violence and desire that they shall similarly perish; to die by the sword is regarded as the right, and honor, of he who lives by it.

"Captain," said the woman, standing back, to one side of the chair.

After the death of Surbus, the woman had been mine. I had won her from him by sword right. I had, of course, as she had expected, put her in my collar, and kept her slave. To my astonishment, however, by the laws of Port Kar, the ships, properties and chattels of Surbus, he having been vanquished in fair combat and permitted the death of blood and sea, became mine; his men stood ready to obey me; his ships became mine to command; his hall became my hall, his riches mine, his slaves mine. It was thus that I had become a captain in Port Kar, jewel of gleaming Thassa.

"I have the accounts for your inspection," said Luma.

Luma no longer wore her collar. After the victory of the 25th of Se'Kara, over the fleets of Tyros and Cos, I had freed her. She had much increased my fortunes. Freed, she took payment, but not as much as her services, I knew, warranted. Few scribes, I expected, were so skilled in the supervision and management of complex affairs as this light, unattractive, brilliant girl. Other captains, other merchants, seeing the waxing of my fortunes, and understanding the commercial complexities involved, had offered this scribe considerable emoluments to join their service. She, however, had refused to do so. I expect she was pleased at the authority, and

2

the trust and freedom, which I accorded her. Too, perhaps, she had grown fond of the house of Bosk.

"I do not wish to see the accounts," I told her.

"The Venna and Tela have arrived from Scagnar," she said, "with full cargoes of the fur of sea sleen. My information indicates that highest prices currently for such products are being paid in Asperiche."

"Very well," I said, "give the men time for their pleasures, eight days, and have the cargoes transferred to one of my round ships, whichever can be most swiftly fitted, and embark them for Asperiche, the Venna and Tela as convoy."

"Yes, Captain," said Luma.

"Go now," I said. "I do not wish to see the accounts."

"Yes, Captain," she said.

At the door, she stopped. "Does the captain wish food or drink?" she asked.

"No," I told her.

"Thurnock," she said, "would be pleased should you play with him a game of Kaissa."

I smiled. Huge, yellow-haired Thurnock, he of the peasants, master of the great bow, wished to play Kaissa with me. He knew himself no match for me in this game.

"Thank Thurnock for me," said I, "but I do not wish to play."

I had not played Kaissa since my return from the northern forests.

Thurnock was a good man, a kind man. The yellow-haired giant meant well.

"The accounts," said Luma, "are excellent. Your enterprises are prospering. You are much richer."

"Go," said I, "Scribe. Go, Luma."

She left.

I sat alone in the darkness. I did not wish to be disturbed.

I looked about the hall, at the great walls of stone, the long table, the tiles, the narrow apertures through which I could glimpse the far stars, burning in the scape of the night.

I was rich. So Luma said, so I knew. I smiled bitterly. There were few men as helpless, as impoverished as I. It was true that the fortunes of the house of Bosk had waxed mightily. I supposed there were few merchants in known Gor whose houses were as rich, as powerful, as mine. Doubtless I was the envy of men who did not know me, Bosk, the recluse, who had returned crippled from the northern forests.

I was rich. But I was poor, because I could not move the left side of my body.

3

Wounds had I at the shore of Thassa, high on the coast, at the edge of the forests, when one night I had, in a stockade of enemies, commanded by Sarus of Tyros, chosen to recollect my honor.

Never could I regain my honor, but I had recollected it. And never had I forgotten it.

Once I had been Tarl Cabot, in the songs called Tarl of Bristol. I recalled that I, or what had once been I, had fought at the siege of Ar. That young man with fiery hair, laughing, innocent, seemed far from me now, this huddled mass, half paralyzed, bitter, like a maimed larl, sitting alone in a captain's chair, in a great darkened hall. My hair was no longer now the same. The sea, the wind and the salt, and, I suppose, the changes in my body, as I had matured, and learned with bitterness the nature of the world, and myself, and men, had changed it. It was now, I thought, not much different from that of other men, as I had learned, too, that I was not much different, either, from others. It had turned lighter now, and more straw colored. Tarl Cabot was gone. He had fought in the siege of Ar. One could still hear the songs. He had restored Lara, Tatrix of Tharna, to her throne. He had entered the Sardar and was one of the few men who knew the true nature of Priest-Kings, those remote and extraordinary beings who controlled the world of Gor. He had been instrumental in the Nest War, and had earned the friendship and gratitude of the Priest-King, Misk, glorious, gentle Misk. "There is Nest Trust between us," Misk had told him. I recalled that once I, in the palms of my hands, had felt the delicate touch of the antennae of that golden creature. "Yes, there is Nest Trust between us," Tarl Cabot had told him. And he had gone to the Land of the Wagon Peoples, to the Plains of Turia, and had obtained there the last egg of Priest-Kings and had returned it, safe, to the Sardar. He had well served Priest-Kings, had Tarl Cabot, that young, brave, distant man, so fine, so proud, so much of the warriors. And he had gone, too, to Ar, and there had defeated the schemes of Cernus and the hideous aliens, the Others, intent on the conquest of Gor, and then the Earth. He had well served Priest-Kings, that young man. And then he had ventured to the delta of the Vosk, to make his way through it, to make contact with Samos of Port Kar, agent of Priest-Kings, to continue in their service. But in the delta of the Vosk he had lost his honor. He had betrayed his codes. There, merely to save his miserable life, he had chosen ignominious slavery to the freedom of honorable death. He had sullied the sword, the honor,

4

which he had pledged to Ko-ro-ba's Home Stone. By that act he had cut himself away from his codes, his vows. For such an act there was no atonement, even to the throwing of one's body upon one's own sword. It was in that moment of his surrender to his cowardice that Tarl Cabot had gone, and, in his place, knelt a slave contemptuously named Bosk, for a great, shambling oxlike creature of the plains of Gor.

But this Bosk, forcing his mistress, the beautiful Telima, to grant him his freedom, had come to Port Kar, bringing her with him as his slave, and had there, after many adventures, earned riches and fame, and the title even of Admiral of Port Kar. He stood high in the Council of Captains. And was it not he who had been victor on the 25th of Se'Kara, in the great engagement of the fleets of Port Kar and Cos and Tyros? He had come to love Telima, and had freed her, but she, when he had learned the location of his former Free Companion, Talena, once daughter of Marlenus of Ar, and resolved to free her from slavery, had left him, in the fury of a Gorean female, and had returned to the rence marshes, her home in the Vosk's vast delta.

A true Gorean, he knew, would have gone after her, and brought her back in slave bracelets and a collar. But he, in his weakness, had wept, and let her go.

Doubtless she despised him now in the marshes.

And so, Tarl Cabot gone, Bosk, Merchant of Port Kar, had gone to the northern forests, to free Talena, once his Free Companion.

There he had encountered Marlenus of Ar, Ubar of Ar, Ubar of Ubars. He, though only of the Merchants, had saved Marlenus of Ar from the degradation of slavery. That one such as he had been of service to the great Marlenus of Ar doubtless was tantamount to insult. But Marlenus had been freed. Earlier he had disowned his daughter, Talena, for she had sued for her freedom, a slave's act. His honor had been kept. That of Tarl Cabot could not be recovered.

But I recalled that I had, in the stockade of Tyros, recollected the matter of honor. I had entered the stockade alone, not expecting to survive. It was not that I was the friend of Marlenus of Ar, or his ally. It was rather that I had, as a warrior, or one once of such a caste, set myself the task of his liberation.

I had accomplished this task. And, in the night, under the stars, I had recollected a never-forgotten honor.

But wounds had I to show for this act, and a body heavy with pain, whose left side I could not move.

I had recollected my honor, but it had won for me only the chair of a cripple. To be sure, carved in wood, high on the chair, was the helmet with crest of sleen fur, the mark of the captain, but I could not rise from the chair.

My own body, and its weakness, held me, as chains could not.

Proud and mighty as the chair might be, it was the throne only of the maimed remains of a man.

I was rich!

I gazed into the darkness of the hall.

Samos of Port Kar had purchased Talena, as a mere slave, from two panther girls, obtaining her with ease in this manner while I had risked my life in the forest.

I laughed.

But I had recollected my honor. But little good had it done me. Was honor not a sham, a fraud, an invention of clever men to manipulate their less wily brethren? Why had I not returned to Port Kar and left Marlenus to his fate, to slavery, and doubtless, eventually, to a slave's death, broken and helpless, under the lashes of overseers in the quarries of Tyros?

I sat in the darkness and wondered on honor, and courage. If they were shams, I thought them most precious shams. How else could we tell ourselves from urts and sleen? What distinguishes us from such beasts? The ability to multiply and subtract, to tell lies, to make knives? No, I think particularly it is the sense of honor, and the will to hold one's ground.

But I had no right to such thoughts, for I had surrendered my honor, my courage, in the delta of the Vosk. I had behaved as might have any animal, not a man.

I could not recover my honor, but I could, and did upon one occasion, recollect it, in a stockade at the shore of Thassa, at the edge of the northern forests.

I grew cold in the blankets. I had become petulent, bitter, petty, as an invalid, frustrated and furious at his own weakness, does.

But when I, half paralyzed and crippled, had left the shore of Thassa I had left behind me a beacon, a mighty beacon formed from the logs of the stockade of Sarus, and it had blazed behind me, visible for more than fifty pasangs at sea.

I did not know why I had set the beacon, but I had done so.

It had burned, long and fiery in the Gorean night, on the stones of the beach, and then, in the morning it would have been ashes, and the winds and rains would have scattered them, and there would be little left, save the stones, the sand and the prints of the feet of sea birds, tiny, like the thief's brand, in the sand. But it would once have burned, and that was fixed, undeniable, a part of what had been, that it had burned; nothing could change that, not the eternities of time, not the will of Priest-Kings, the machinations of Others, the willfullness and hatred of men; nothing could change that it had been, that once on the beach, there, a beacon had burned.

I wondered how men should live. In my chair I had thought long on such matters.

I knew only that I did not know the answer to this question. Yet it is an important question, is it not? Many wise men give wise answers to this question, and yet they do not agree among themselves.

Only the simple, the fools, the unreflective, the ignorant, know the answer to this question.

Perhaps to a question this profound the answer cannot be known. Perhaps it is a question too deep to be answered. Yet we do know there are false answers to such a question. This suggests that there may be a true answer, for how can there be falsity without truth?

One thing seems clear to me, that a morality which produces guilt and self-torture, which results in anxiety and agony, which shortens life spans, cannot be the answer.

Many of the competitive moralities of Earth are thus mistaken.

But what is not mistaken?

The Goreans have very different notions of morality from those of Earth.

Yet who is to say who is the more correct?

I envy sometimes the simplicities of those of Earth, and those of Gor, who, creatures of their conditioning, are untroubled by such matters, but I would not be as either of them. If either should be correct it is for them no more than a lucky coincidence. They would have fallen into truth, but to take truth for granted is not to know it. Truth not won is not possessed. We are not entitled to truths for which we have not fought.

Do we not learn to live by doing, as we learn to speak by speaking, to paint by painting, to build by building?

Those who know best how to live, sometimes it seems to me, are those least likely to be articulate in such skills. It is not that they have not learned but, having learned, they find they cannot tell what they know, for only words can be told, and what is learned in living is more than words, other than words, beyond words. We can say, "This building is beautiful," but we do not learn the beauty of the building from the words; the building it is which teaches us its beauty; and how can one speak the beauty of the building, as it is? Does one say that it has so many pillars, that it has a roof of a certain type, and such? Can one simply say, "The building is beautiful"? Yes, one can say that but what one learns when one sees the beauty of the building cannot be spoken; it is not words; it is the building's beauty.

The morality of Earth, from the Gorean point of view, is a morality which would be viewed as more appropriate to slaves than free men. It would be seen in terms of the envy and resentment of inferiors for their superiors. It lays great stress on equalities and being humble and being pleasant and avoiding friction and being ingratiating and small. It is a morality in the best interest of slaves, who would be only too eager to be regarded as the equals of others. We are all the same. That is the hope of slaves; that is what it is in their interest to convince others of. The Gorean morality on the other hand is more one of inequalities, based on the assumption that individuals are not the same, but quite different in many ways. It might be said to be, though this is oversimple, a morality of masters. Guilt is almost unknown in Gorean morality, though shame and anger are not. Many Earth moralities encourage resignation and accomodation; Gorean morality is bent more toward conquest and defiance; many Earth moralities encourage tenderness, pity and gentleness, sweetness; Gorean morality encourages honor, courage, hardness and strength. To Gorean morality many Earth moralities might ask, "Why so hard?" To these Earth moralities, the Gorean *ethos* might ask, "Why so soft?"

I have sometimes thought that the Goreans might do well to learn something of tenderness, and, perhaps, that those of Earth might do well to learn something of hardness. But I do not know how to live. I have sought the answers, but I have not found them. The morality of slaves says, "You are equal to me; we are both the same"; the morality of masters says, "We are not equal; we are not the same; become equal to me; then we will be the same." The morality of slaves reduces all to bondage; the morality of masters encourages all to attain, if they can, the heights of freedom. I know of no prouder, more self-reliant, more magnificent creature than the free Gorean, male or female; they are often touchy, and viciously tempered, but they are seldom petty or small; moreover they do not hate and fear their bodies or their in-

8

stincts; when they restrain themselves it is a victory over titanic forces; not the consequence of a slow metabolism; but sometimes they do not restrain themselves; they do not assume that their instincts and blood are enemies and spies, saboteurs in the house of themselves; they know them and welcome them as part of their persons; they are as little suspicious of them as the cat of its cruelty, or the lion of its hunger; their desire for vengeance, their will to speak out and defend themselves, their lust, they regard as intrinsically and gloriously a portion of themselves as their hearing or their thinking. Many Earth moralities make people little; the object of Gorean morality, for all its faults, is to make people free and great. These objectives are quite different it is clear to see. Accordingly, one would expect that the implementing moralities would, also, be considerably different.

I sat in the darkness and thought on these things. There were no maps for me.

I, Tarl Cabot, or Bosk of Port Kar, was torn between worlds.

I did not know how to live.

I was bitter.

But the Goreans have a saying, which came to me in the darkness, in the hall. "Do not ask the stones or the trees how to live; they cannot tell you; they do not have tongues; do not ask the wise man how to live, for, if he knows, he will know he cannot tell you; if you would learn how to live do not ask the question; its answer is not in the question but in the answer, which is not in words; do not ask how to live, but, instead, proceed to do so."

I do not fully understand this saying. How, for example, can one proceed to do what one does not know how to do? The answer, I suspect, is that the Gorean belief is that one does, truly, in some way, know how to live, though one may not know that one knows. The knowledge is regarded as being somehow within one. Perhaps it is regarded as being somehow innate, or a function of instincts. I do not know. The saying may also be interpreted as encouraging one to act, to behave, to do, and then, in the acting, the doing, the behaving, to learn. These two interpretations, of course, are not incompatible. The child, one supposes, has the innate disposition, when a certain maturation level is attained, to struggle to its feet and walk, as it did to crawl, when an earlier level was attained, and yet it truly learns to crawl, and to walk, and then to run, only in the crawling, in the walking and running.

9

The refrain ran through my mind. "Do not ask how to live, but, instead, proceed to do so."

But how could I live, I, a cripple, huddled in the chair of a captain, in a darkened hall?

I was rich, but I envied the meanest herder of verr, the lowest peasant scattering dung in his furrows, for they could move as they pleased.

I tried to clench my left fist. But the hand did not move. How should one live?

In the codes of the warriors, there is a saying: "Be strong, and do as you will. The swords of others will set you your limits."

I had been one of the finest swordsmen on Gor. But now I could not move the left side of my body.

But I could still command steel, that of my men, who, for no reason I understood, they Goreans, remained true to me, loyal to a cripple, confined to a captain's chair in a darkened hall.

I was grateful to them, but I would show them nothing of this, for I was a captain.

They must not be demeaned.

"Within the circle of each man's sword," say the codes of the warrior, "therein is each man a Ubar."

"Steel is the coinage of the warrior," say the codes. "With it he purchases what pleases him."

When I had returned from the northern forests I had resolved not to look upon Talena, once daughter of Marlenus of Ar, whom Samos had purchased from panther girls.

But I had had my chair carried to his hall.

"Shall I present her to you," asked Samos, "naked, and in bracelets?"

"No," I had said. "Present her in the most resplendent robes you can find, as befits a high-born woman of the city of Ar."

"But she is a slave," he said. "Her thigh bears the brand of Treve. Her throat is encircled in the collar of my house."

"As befits," said I, "a high-born woman of the city of glorious Ar."

And so it was that she, Talena, once daughter of Marlenus of Ar, then disowned, once my companion, was ushered into my presence.

"The slave," said Samos.

"Do not kneel," I said to her.

"Strip your face, Slave," said Samos.

Gracefully the girl, the property of Samos, first slaver of

Port Kar, removed her veil, unfastening it, dropping it about her shoulders.

We looked once more upon each other.

I saw again those marvelous green eyes, those lips, luscious, perfect for crushing beneath a warrior's mouth and teeth, the subtle complexion, olive. She removed a pin from her hair, and, with a small movement of her head, shook loose the wealth of her sable hair.

We regarded one another.

"Is master pleased?" she asked.

"It has been long, Talena," said I.

"Yes," she said, "it has been long."

"He is free," said Samos.

"It has been long, Master," she said.

"Many years," said I. "Many years." I smiled at her. "I last saw you on the night of our companionship."

"When I awakened, you were gone," she said. "I was abandoned."

"Not of my own free will did I leave you," said I. "That was not of my will."

I saw in the eyes of Samos that I must not speak of Priest-Kings. It had been they who had returned me then to Earth.

"I do not believe you," she said.

"Watch your tongue, Girl," said Samos.

"If you command me to believe you," she said, "I shall, of course, for I am slave."

I smiled. "No," I said, "I do not command you."

"I was kept in great honor in Ko-ro-ba," she said, "respected and free, for I had been your companion, even after the year of the companionship had gone, and it had not been renewed."

At that point, in Gorean law, the companionship had been dissolved. The companionship had not been renewed by the twentieth hour, the Gorean Midnight, of its anniversary.

"When Priest-Kings, by fire signs, made it clear Ko-ro-ba was to be destroyed, I left the city."

No stone would be allowed to stand upon a stone, no man of Ko-ro-ba to stand by another.

The population had been scattered, the city razed by the power of the Priest-Kings.

"You fell slave," I said.

"Within five days," she said, "as I tried to return to Ar, I was sheltered by an itinerant leather worker, who did not believe, of course, that I was the daughter of Marlenus of Ar. He treated me well the first evening, with gentleness and

11

honor. I was grateful. In the morning, to his laughter, I awakened. His collar was on my throat." She looked at me, angrily. "He then used me well. Do you understand? He forced me to yield to him, I, the daughter of Marlenus of Ar, he only a leather worker. Afterwards he whipped me. He taught me to obey. At night he chained me. He sold me to a salt merchant." She regarded me. "I have had many masters," she said.

"Among them," I said, "Rask of Treve."

She stiffened. "I served him well," she said. "I was given no choice. It was he who branded me." She tossed her head. "Until then many masters had regarded me as too beautiful to brand."

"They were fools," said Samos. "A brand improves a slave."

She put her head in the air. I had no doubt this was one of the most beautiful women on Gor.

"It is because of you, I gather," said she to me, "that I have been permitted clothing for this interview. Further, I have you to thank, I gather, that I have been given the opportunity to wash the stink of the pens from my body."

I said nothing.

"The cages are not pleasant," she said. "My cage measures four paces by four paces. In it are twenty girls. Food is thrown to us from above. We drink from a trough."

"Shall I have her whipped?" asked Samos.

She paled.

"No," I said.

"Rask of Treve gave me to a panther girl in his camp, one named Verna. I was taken to the northern forests. My present master, noble Samos of Port Kar, purchased me at the shore of Thassa. I was brought to Port Kar chained to a ring in the hold of his ship. Here, in spite of my birth, I was placed in a pen with common girls."

"You are only another slave," said Samos.

"I am the daughter of Marlenus of Ar," she said, proudly.

"In the forest," I said, "it is my understanding that you sued for your freedom, begging in a missive that your father purchase you."

"Yes," she said. "I did so."

"Are you aware," I asked, "that against you, on his sword and on the medallion of Ar, Marlenus swore the oath of disownment?"

"I do not believe it," she said.

12

"You are no longer his daughter," I said. "You are now without caste, without Home Stone, without family."

"You lie!" she screamed.

"Kneel to the whip," said Samos.

Piteously she knelt, a slave girl. Her wrists were crossed under her, as though bound, her head was to the floor, the bow of her back was exposed.

She shuddered. I had little doubt but what this slave knew well, and much feared, the disciplining kiss of the Gorean slave lash.

Samos' sword was in his hand, thrust under the collar of her garment, ready to thrust in and lift, parting the garment, causing the robes to fall to either side, about her then naked body.

"Do not punish her," I told Samos.

Samos looked at me, irritably. The slave had not been pleasing.

"To his sandal, Slave," said Samos.

I felt Talena's lips press to my sandal. "Forgive me, Master," she whispered.

"Rise," I said.

She rose to her feet, and stepped back. I could see she feared Samos.

"You were disowned," I told her. "Your status now, whether you know this or not, is less than that of the meanest peasant wench, secure in her caste rights."

"I do not believe you," she said.

"Do you care for me," I asked, "Talena."

She pulled the robes down from her throat. "I wear a collar," she said. I saw the simple, circular, gray collar, the collar of the house of Samos, locked about her throat.

"What is her price?" I asked Samos.

"I paid ten pieces of gold for her," said Samos.

She seemed startled that she had sold for so small a sum. Yet, for a girl, late in the season, high on the coast of Thassa, it was a marvelous price. Doubtless she had obtained it only because she was so beautiful. Yet, to be sure, it was less than she would have brought if expertly displayed on the block in Turia or Ar, or Ko-ro-ba, or Tharna, or Port Kar.

"I will give you fifteen," I said.

"Very well," said Samos.

With my right hand I reached into the pouch at my belt and drew out the coins.

I handed them to Samos.

"Free her," I said.

13

Samos, with a general key, one used for many of the gray collars, unlocked the band of steel which encircled her lovely throat.

"Am I truly free?" she asked.

"Yes," I said.

"I should have brought a thousand pieces of gold," she said. "As the daughter of Marlenus of Ar my companion price might be a thousand tarns, five thousand tharlarion!"

"You are no longer the daughter of Marlenus of Ar," I told her.

"You are a liar," she said. She looked at me, contemptuously.

"With your permission," said Samos, "I shall withdraw."

"Stay," said I, "Samos."

"Very well," said he.

"Long ago," said I, "Talena, we cared for one another. We were companions."

"It was a foolish girl who cared for you," said Talena. "I am now a woman."

"You no longer care for me?" I asked.

She looked at me. "I am free," she said. "I can speak what I wish. Look at yourself! You cannot even walk. You cannot even move your left arm! You are a cripple, a cripple! You make me ill! Do you think that one such as I, the daughter of Marlenus of Ar, could care for such a thing? Look upon me. I am beautiful. Look upon yourself. You are a cripple. Care for you? You are a fool, a fool!"

"Yes," I said, bitterly, "I am a fool."

She turned away, robes swirling. Then she turned and faced me. "Slave!" she sneered.

"I do not understand," I said.

"I took the liberty," said Samos, "though at the time I did not know of your injuries, your paralysis, to inform her of what occurred in the delta of the Vosk."

My right hand clenched. I was furious.

"I am sorry," said Samos.

"It is no secret," I said. "It is known to many."

"It is a wonder that any man will follow you!" cried Talena. "You betrayed your codes! You are a coward! A fool! You are not worthy of me! That you dare ask me if I could care for such as you is to me, a free woman, an insult! You chose slavery to death!"

"Why did you tell her of the delta of the Vosk?" I asked Samos.

"So that if there might have been love between you, it would no longer exist," said Samos.

"You are cruel," I said.

"Truth is cruel," said Samos. "She would have to know sooner or later."

"Why did you tell her?" I asked.

"That she might not care for you and lure you from the service of those whose names we shall not now speak."

"I could never care for a cripple," said Talena.

"It remained yet my hope," said Samos, "to recall you to a lofty service, one dignified and of desperate importance."

I laughed.

Samos shrugged. "I did not know until too late the consequences of your wounds. I am sorry."

"Now," said I, "Samos, I cannot serve even myself."

"I am sorry," said Samos.

"Coward! Traitor to your codes! Sleen!" cried Talena.

"All that you say is true," I told her.

"You did well, I understand," said Samos, "in the stockade of Sarus of Tyros."

"I wish to be returned to my father," said Talena.

I drew forth five pieces of gold. "This money," said I to Samos, "is for safe passage to Ar, by guard and tarn, for this woman."

Talena drew about her face her veil, refastening it. "I shall have the moneys returned to you," she said.

"No," I said, "take it rather as a gift, as a token of a former affection, once borne to you by one who was honored to be your companion."

"She is a she-sleen," said Samos, "vicious and ignoble."

"My father would avenge that insult," she said, coldly, "with the tarn cavalries of Ar."

"You have been disowned," said Samos, and turned and left. I held still the five coins in my hand.

"Give me the coins," said Talena. I held them in my hand, in the palm. She came to me and snatched them away, as though loath to touch me. Then she stood and faced me, the coins in her hand. "How ugly you are," she said. "How hdieous in your chair!"

I did not speak.

She turned and strode toward the door of the hall. At the portal she stopped, and turned. "In my veins," she said, "flows the blood of Marlenus of Ar. How revolting and incredible that one such as you, a coward and betrayer of codes, should have aspired to touch me." She lifted the

15

coins in her hand. It was gloved. "My gratitude," said she, "Sir," and turned away.

"Talena!" I cried.

She turned to face me once more.

"It is nothing," I said.

"And you will let me go," she said. She smiled contemptuously. "You were never a man," she said. "Always you were a boy, a weakling." She lifted the coins again in her hand. "Farewell, Weakling," said she, and left the room.

I now sat in my own hall, in the darkness, thinking on many things.

I wondered how to live.

"Within the circle of each man's sword," say the codes of the warrior, "therein is each man a Ubar."

"Steel is the coinage of the warrior," say the codes. "With it he purchases what pleases him."

Once I had been among the finest swordsmen on the planet Gor. Now I was a cripple.

Talena would now be in Ar. How startled, how crushed would she have been, to learn at last, incontrovertibly, that her disownment was true. She had begged to be purchased, a slave's act. Marlenus, protecting his honor, on his sword and upon the medallion of the Ubar, had sworn her from him. No longer had she caste, no longer a Home Stone. The meanest peasant wench, secure in her caste rights, would be more than Talena. Even a slave girl has her collar. I knew that Marlenus would keep her sequestered in the central cylinder, that her shame not reflect upon his glory. She would be in Ar, in effect, a prisoner. She was no longer entitled even to call its Home Stone her own. Such an act, by one such as she, was subject to public discipline. For it she might be suspended naked, bound by the wrists, on a forty foot rope from one of the high bridges, to be lashed by tarnsmen, sweeping past her in flight.

I had watched her go.

I had not attempted to stop her.

And when Telima had fled my house, when I had determined to seek Talena in the northern forests, I had, too, let her go. I smiled. A true Gorean, I knew, would have followed her, and brought her back in bracelets and collar.

I thought then of Vella, once Elizabeth Cardwell, whom I had encountered in the city of Lydius, at the mouth of the Laurius River, below the borders of the forests. I had once loved her, and had wanted to return her safe to Earth. But she had not honored my will, but, that night, had saddled my tarn, great Ubar of the Skies, and fled the Sardar. When the bird had returned I, in fury, had driven it away. Then I had encountered the girl in a paga tavern in Lydius; she had fallen slave. Her flight had been a brave act. I admired her, but it was an act not without its consequences. She had gambled; she had lost. In an alcove, after I had used her, she had begged me to buy her, to free her. It was a slave's act, like that of Talena. I had left her slave in the paga tavern. Before I had left I had informed her master, Sarpedon of Lydius, that, as he did not know, she was an exquisitely trained pleasure slave, and a most stimulating performer of slave dances. I had not returned that night to see her dance in the sand to please his customers. I had matters of business to attend to. She had not honored my will. She was only a female. She had cost me a tarn.

She had told me that I had become harder, more Gorean. I wondered if it were true or not. A true Gorean, I speculated, would not have left her in the paga tavern. A true Gorean, I speculated, would have purchased her, and brought her back, to put her with his other women, a delicious new slave for his house. I smiled to myself. The girl Elizabeth Cardwell, once a secretary in New York City, was one of the most delicious little wenches I had ever seen in slave silk. Her thigh bore the brand of the four bosk horns.

No, I had not treated her as would have a true Gorean. I had not brought her back in my collar, to serve my pleasures.

And, too, I knew that I had, in the fevered delirium attendant on my wounds, when I lay in the stern castle of the Tesephone, cried out her name.

This had shamed me, and was weakness. Though I was half motionless, though I could not close the fingers of my left hand, I resolved that I must burn from myself the vestiges of weakness. There was still much in me that was of Earth, much shallowness, much compromise, much weakness. I was not yet in my will truly Gorean.

I wondered how to live. "Do not ask how to live, but, instead, proceed to do so."

I wondered, too, on the nature of my affliction. I had had the finest wound physicians on Gor brought to attend me, to inquire into its nature. They could tell me little. Yet I had learned there was no damage in the brain, nor directly to the spinal column. The men of medicine were puzzled. The wounds were deep, and severe, and would doubtless, from

17

time to time, cause me pain, but the paralysis, given the nature of the injury, seemed to them unaccountable.

Then one more physician, unsummoned, came to my door.

"Admit him," I had said.

"He is a renegade from Turia, a lost man," had said Thurnock.

"Admit him," I had said.

"It is Iskander," whispered Thurnock.

I knew well the name of Iskander of Turia. I smiled. He remembered well the city that had exiled him, keeping still its name as part of his own. It had been many years since he had seen its lofty walls. He had, in the course of his practice in Turia, once given treatment outside of its walls to a young Tuchuk warrior, whose name was Kamchak. For this aid given to an enemy he had been exiled. He had come, like many, to Port Kar. He had risen in the city, and had been for years the private physician of Sullius Maximus, who had been one of the five Ubars, presiding in Port Kar prior to the assumption of power by the Council of Captains. Sullius Maximus was an authority on poetry, and gifted in the study of poisons. When Sullius Maximus had fled the city, Iskander had remained behind. He had even been with the fleet on the 25th of the Se'Kara. Sullius Maximus, shortly after the decision of the 25th of Se'Kara, had sought refuge in Tyros, and had been granted it.

"Greetings, Iskander," I had said.

"Greetings, Bosk of Port Kar," he had said.

The findings of Iskander of Turia matched those of the other physicians, but, to my astonishment, when he had replaced his instruments in the pouch slung at his shoulder, he said, "The wounds were given by blades of Tyros."

"Yes," I said, "they were."

"There is a subtle contaminant in the wounds," he said.

"Are you sure?" I asked.

"I have not detected it," he said. "But there seems no likely alternative explanation."

"A contaminant?" I asked.

"Poisoned steel," he said.

I said nothing.

"Sullius Maximus," he said, "is in Tyros."

"I would not have thought Sarus of Tyros would have used poisoned steel," I said. Such a device, like the poisoned arrow, was not only against the codes of the warriors, but, generally, was regarded as unworthy of men. Poison was regarded as a woman's weapon.

Iskander shrugged.

"Sullius Maximus," he said, "invented such a drug. He tested it, by pin pricks, on the limbs of a captured enemy, paralyzing him from the neck down. He kept him seated at his right side, as a guest in regal robes, for more than a week. When he tired of the sport he had him killed."

"Is there an antidote?" I asked.

"No," said Iskander.

"Then there is no hope," I said.

"No," said Iskander. "There is no hope."

"Perhaps it is not the poison," I said.

"Perhaps," said Iskander.

"Thurnock," said I, "give this physician a double tarn, of gold."

"No," said Iskander. "I wish no payment."

"Why not?" I asked.

"I was with you," he said, "on the 25th of Se'Kara."

"I wish you well, Physician," I said.

"I wish you well, too, Captain," said he, and left.

I wondered if what Iskander of Turia had conjectured was correct or not.

I wondered if such a poison, if it existed, could be overcome.

There is no antidote, he had informed me.

The refrain ran through my mind: "Do not ask how to live, but, instead, proceed to do so."

I laughed bitterly.

"Captain!" I heard. "Captain!" It was Thurnock. I could hear running feet behind him, the gathering of members of the household.

"What is it?" I heard Luma ask.

"Captain!" cried Thurnock.

"I must see him, immediately!" said another voice. I was startled. It was the voice of Samos, first slaver of Port Kar.

They entered, carrying torches.

"Put torches in the rings," said Samos.

The hall was lit. Members of the house came forward. Samos appeared before the table. At his side was Thurnock, a torch still uplifted in his hand. Luma was present. I saw, too, Tab, who was captain of the Venna. Clitus, too, was there, and young Henrius.

"What is wrong?" I asked.

Then one other stepped forward. It was Ho-Hak, from the marshes, the rencer. His face was white. No longer about his throat was clasped the collar of the galley slave,

19

with short, dangling chain. He had been a bred slave, an exotic. His ears were large, bred so as a collector's fancy. But he had killed his master, breaking his neck, and escaped. Recaptured, he had been sentenced to the galleys, but had escaped, too, from them, killing six men in his flight. He had, finally, succeeded in making his way into the marshes, in the Vosk's vast delta, where he had been taken in my rencers, who live on islands, woven of rence reeds, in the delta. He had become chief of one such group, and was much respected in the delta. He had been instrumental in bringing the great bow to the rencers, which put them on a military par with those of Port Kar, who had thitherto victimized and exploited them. Rencer bowmen were now used by certain captains of Port Kar as auxiliaries.

Ho-Hak did not speak but cast on the table an armlet of gold.

It was bloodied.

I knew the armlet well. It had been that of Telima, who had fled to the marshes, when I had determined to seek Talena in the northern forests.

"Telima," said Ho-Hak.

"When did this happen?" I asked.

"Within four Ahn," said Ho-Hak. Then he turned to another rencer, one who stood with him. "Speak," said Ho-Hak.

"I saw little," he said. "There was a tarn and a beast. I heard the scream of the woman. I poled my rence craft toward them, my bow ready. I heard another scream. The tarn took flight, low, over the rence, the beast upon it, hunched, shaggy. I found her rence craft, the pole floating nearby. It was much bloodied. I found there, too, the armlet."

"The body?" I asked.

"Tharlarion were about," said the rencer.

I nodded.

I wondered if the beast had struck for hunger. Such a beast in the house of Cernus had fed on human flesh. Doubtless it was little other to them than venison would be to us.

It was perhaps just as well that the body was not recovered. It would have been half eaten, torn apart. It was just as well that the remains had been given to the tharlarion.

"Why did you not kill the beast, or strike the tarn?" I asked.

The great bow was capable of such matters.

"I had no opportunity," said the rencer.

"Which way did the tarn take flight?" I asked.

"To the northwest," said the rencer.

I was certain the tarn would follow the coast. It is extremely difficult, if not impossible, to fly a tarn from the sight of land. It is counterinstinctual for them. In the engagement of the 25th of Se'Kara we had used tarns at sea, but they had been kept below decks in cargo ships until beyond the sight of land. Interestingly, once released, there had been no difficulty in managing them. They had performed effectively in the engagement.

I looked at Samos. "What do you know of this matter?" I asked.

"I know only what I am told," said Samos.

"Describe the beast," I said to the rencer.

"I did not see it well," he said.

"It could only have been one of the Kurii," said Samos.

"The Kurii?" I asked.

"The word is a Gorean corruption of their name for themselves, for their kind," said Samos.

"In Torvaldsland," said Tab, "that word means 'beasts'."

"That is interesting," I said. If Samos were correct that 'Kurii' was a Gorean corruption of the name of such animals for themselves, and that the word was used in Torvaldsland as a designation for beasts, then it seemed not unlikely that such animals were not unknown in Torvaldsland, at least in certain areas, perhaps remote ones.

The tarn had flown northwest. It would, presumably, follow the coast north, perhaps above the forests, perhaps to the bleak coasts of forbidding Torvaldsland itself.

"Do you surmise, Samos," I asked, "that the beast killed for hunger?"

"Speak," said Samos to the rencer.

"The beast," he said, "had been seen earlier, twice, on abandoned, half-rotted rence islands, lurking."

"Did it feed?" I asked.

"Not on those of the marshes," said the man.

"It had opportunity?" I asked.

"As much or more as when it made its strike," said the man.

"The beast struck once, and once only?" I asked.

"Yes," said the man.

"Samos?" I asked.

"The strike," said Samos, "seems deliberate. Who else in the marshes wore a golden armlet?"

"But why?" I asked. "Why?"

21

He looked at me. "The affairs of worlds," said Samos, "apparently still touch you."

"He is crippled!" cried Luma. "You speak strangely! He can do nothing! Go away!"

I put down my head.

On the table I felt my fists clenched. I suddenly felt a hideous exhilaration.

"Bring me a goblet," I said.

A goblet was fetched. It was of heavy gold. I took it in my left hand. Slowly I crushed it.

I threw it from me.

Those of my house stood back, frightened.

"I will go," said Samos. "There is work to be done in the north. I will seek the vengeance."

"No, Samos," I said. "I will go."

There were gasps from those about.

"You cannot go," whispered Luma.

"Telima was once my woman," I said. "It is mine to seek the vengeance."

"You are crippled! You cannot move!" cried Luma.

"There are two swords over my couch," said I to Thurnock. "One is plain, with a worn hilt; the other is rich, with a jewel-encrusted hilt."

"I know them," whispered Thurnock.

"Bring to me the blade of Port Kar, swift, fit with in-hilted jewels."

He sped from the room.

"I would have paga," I said. "And bring me the red meat of bosk."

Henrius and Clitus left the table.

The sword was brought. It was a fine blade. It had been carried on the 25th of Se'Kara. Its blade was figured, its hilt encrusted with jewels.

I took the goblet, filled with burning paga. I had not had paga since returning from the northern forests.

"Ta-Sardar-Gor," said I, pouring a libation to the table. Then I stood.

"He is standing!" cried Luma. "He is standing!"

I threw back my head and swilled down the paga. The meat, red and hot, was brought, and I tore it in my teeth, the juices running at the side of my mouth.

The blood and the paga were hot and dark within me. I felt the heat of the meat.

I threw from me the goblet of gold. I tore the meat and finished it.

I put over my left shoulder the scabbard strap.

"Saddle a tarn," said I to Thurnock.

"Yes, Captain," he whispered.

I stood before the captain's chair. "More paga," I said. Another vessel was brought. "I drink," said I, "to the blood of beasts."

Then I drained the goblet and flung it from me.

With a howl of rage I struck the table with the side of my fists, shattering the boards. I flung aside the blanket and the captain's chair.

"Do not go," said Samos. "It may be a trick to lure you to a trap."

I smiled at him. "Of course," I said. "To those with whom we deal Telima is of no importance." I regarded him. "It is me they want," I said. "They shall not fail to have their opportunity."

"Do not go," said Samos.

"There is work to be done in the north," I said.

"Let me go," said Samos.

"Mine," I said, "is the vengeance."

I turned and strode toward the door of the hall. Luma fell back before me, her hand before her mouth.

I saw that her eyes were deep, and very beautiful. She was frightened.

"Precede me to my couch," I said.

"I am free," she whispered.

"Collar her," I said to Thurnock, "and send her to my couch."

His hand closed on the arm of the thin blond scribe.

"Clitus," I said, "send Sandra, the dancer, to my couch as well."

"You freed her, Captain," smiled Clitus.

"Collar her," I told him.

"Yes, Captain," he said. I well remembered Sandra, with her black eyes, brownish skin and high cheekbones. I wanted her.

It had been long since I had had a woman.

"Tab," said I.

"Yes, Captain," said he.

"The two females," I told him, "have recently been free. Accordingly, as soon as they are collared, force them to drink slave wine."

"Yes, Captain," grinned Tab.

Slave wine is bitter, intentionally so. Its effect lasts for more than a Gorean month. I did not wish the females to conceive. A female slave is taken off slave wine only when it is her master's intention to breed her.

"The tarn, Captain?" asked Thurnock.

"Have it saddled," I told him. "I leave shortly for the north."

"Yes, Captain," he said.

2

THE TEMPLE
OF KASSAU

The incense stung my nostrils.

It was hot in the temple, close, stifling. There were many
bodies pressed about. It was not easy to see, for the clouds
of incense hung heavy in the air.

The High Initiate of Kassau, a town at the northern brink
of the forest, sat still in his white robes, in his tall hat, on
the throne to the right, within the white rail that separated
the sanctuary of Initiates from the common ground of the
hall, where those not annointed by the grease of Priest-
Kings must stand.

I heard a woman sobbing with emotion to my right.
"Praise the Priest-Kings," she repeated endlessly to herself, nodding her head up and down.

Near her, bored, was a slender, blondish girl, looking
about. Her hair was hung in a snood of scarlet yarn, bound
with filaments of golden wire. She wore, over her shoulder,
a cape of white fur of the northern sea sleen. She had a
scarlet vest, embroidered in gold, worn over a long-sleeved
blouse of white wool, from distant Ar. She wore, too, a
long woolen skirt, dyed red, which was belted with black,
with a buckle of gold, wrought in Cos. She wore shoes of
black, polished leather, which folded about her ankles, laced
twice, once across the instep, once about the ankle.

She saw me regarding her, and looked away.

Other wenches, too, were in the crowd. In the northern
villages, and in the forest towns, and northward on the coast
the women do not veil themselves, as is common in the
cities to the south.

Kassau is the seat of the High Initiate of the north, who
claims spiritual sovereignty over Torvaldsland, which is

25

commonly taken to commence with the thinning of the trees northward. This claim, like many of those of initiates, is disputed by few, and ignored by most. The men of Torvaldsland, on the whole, I knew, while tending to respect Priest-Kings, did not accord them special reverence. They held to old gods, and old ways. The religion of the Priest-Kings, institutionalized and ritualized by the caste of Initiates, had made little headway among the primitive men to the north. It had, however, taken hold in many towns, such as Kassau. Initiates often used their influence and their gold, and pressures on trade and goods, to spread their beliefs and rituals. Sometimes a chieftain, converted to their ways, would enforce his own commitments on his subordinates. Indeed, this was not unusual. Too, often, a chief's conversion would bring with it, even without force, those of his people who felt bound to him in loyalty. Sometimes, too, the religion of the Priest-Kings, under the control of the initiates, utilizing secular rulers, was propagated by fire and sword. Sometimes those who insisted on retaining the old ways, or were caught making the sign of the fist, the hammer, over their ale, were subjected to death by torture. One that I had heard of had been boiled alive in one of the great sunken, wooden-lined tubs in which meat was boiled for retainers. The water is heated by placing rocks, taken from a fire, into the water. When the rock has been in the water it is removed with a rake and then reheated. Another had been roasted alive on a spit over a long fire. It was said that he did not utter a sound. Another was slain when an adder forced into his mouth tore its way free through the side of his face.

I looked at the cold, haughty, pale face of the High Initiate on his throne.

He was flanked by minor initiates, in their white robes, with shaven heads.

Initiates do not eat meat, or beans. They are trained in the mysteries of mathematics. They converse among themselves in archaic Gorean, which is no longer spoken among the people. Their services, too, are conducted in this language. Portions of the services, however, are translated into contemporary Gorean. When I had first come to Gor I had been forced to learn certain long prayers to the Priest-Kings, but I had never fully mastered them, and had, by now, long forgotten them.

Still I recognized them when heard. Even now, on a high

platform, behind the white rail, an Initiate was reading one aloud to the congregation.

I was never much fond of the meetings, the services and the rituals of initiates, but I had some special interest in the service which was being held today.

Ivar Forkbeard was dead.

I knew this man of Torvaldsland only by reputation. He was a rover, a great captain, a pirate, a trader, a warrior. It had been he, and his men, who had freed Chenbar of Tyros, the Sea Sleen, from a dungeon in Port Kar, breaking through to him, shattering his chains from the walls with the blunt, hammerlike backs of their great, curved, single-bladed axes. He was said to be fearless, and mighty, swift with sword and ax, fond of jokes, a deep drinker, a master of pretty wenches, and a madman. But he had taken in fee from Chenbar Chenbar's weight in the sapphires of Shendi. I did not think him too mad.

But now the Forkbeard was dead.

It was said that he wished, in regret for the wickedness of his life, to be carried in death to the temple of Priest-Kings in Kassau, that the High Initiate there might, if it be his mercy, draw on his bones in the sacred grease the sign of the Priest-Kings.

It would thus indicate that he, Forkbeard, if not in life, had in death acknowledged the error of his ways and embraced the will and wisdom of the faith of Priest-Kings.

Such a conversion, even though it be in death, would be a great coup for the initiates.

I could sense the triumph of the High Initiate on his throne, though his cold face betrayed little sign of his victory.

Now initiates to one side of the sanctuary, opposite the throne of the High Initiate, began to chant the litanies of the Priest-Kings. Responses, in archaic Gorean, repetitive, simple, were uttered by the crowd.

Kassau is a town of wood, and the temple is the greatest building in the town. It towers far over the squalid huts, and stabler homes of merchants, which crowd about it. Too, the town is surrounded by a wall, with two gates, one large, facing the inlet, leading in from Thassa, the other small, leading to the forest behind the town. The wall is of sharpened logs, and is defended by a catwalk. The main business of Kassau is trade, lumber and fishing. The slender, striped parsit fish has vast plankton banks north of the town, and may there, particularly in the spring and fall, be taken in great numbers. The smell of the fish-drying sheds of Kassau carries far out to sea. The trade is largely in furs from the north, exchanged for weapons, iron bars, salt and luxury goods, such as jewelry and silk, from the south, usually brought to Kassau from Lydius by ten-oared coasting vessels. Lumber, of course, is a valuable commodity. It is generally milled and taken northward. Torvaldsland, though not treeless, is bleak. In it, fine Ka-la-na wood, for example, and supple temwood, cannot grow. These two woods are prized in the north. A hall built with Ka-la-na wood, for example, is thought a great luxury. Such halls, incidentally, are often adorned with rich carvings. The men of Torvaldsland are skilled with their hands. Trade to the south, of course, is largely in the furs acquired from Torvaldsland, and in barrels of smoked, dried parsit fish. From the south, of course, the people of Kassau obtain the goods they trade northward to Torvaldsland, and, too, of course, civilized goods for themselves. The population of Kassau I did not think to be more than eleven hundred persons. There are villages about, however, which use Kassau as their market and meeting place. If we count these perhaps we might think of greater Kassau has having a population in the neighborhood of some twenty-three hundred persons.

The most important thing about Kassau, however, was that it was the seat of the High Initiate of the north. It was, accordingly, the spiritual center of a district extending for hundreds of pasangs around. The nearest high initiate to Kassau was hundreds of pasangs south in Lydius.

The initiates are an almost universal, well-organized, industrious caste. They have many monasteries, holy places and temples. An initiate may often travel for hundreds of pasangs and, each night, find himself in a house of initiates. They regard themselves as the highest caste, and, in many cities, are so regarded generally. There is often a tension between them and the civil authorities, for each regards themselves as supreme in matters of policy and law for their districts. The initiates have their own laws, and courts, and certain of them are particularly versed in the laws of initiates. Their education, generally, is of little obvious practical value, with its attention to authorized exegeses of dubious, difficult texts, purporting to be revelations of Priest-Kings, the details and observances of their own calendars, their interminable, involved rituals, and so on, but, paradoxically, this sort of learning, impractical though it appears, has a subtle practical aspect. It tends to bind initiates together, making them

28

interdependent, and muchly different from common men. It sets them apart, and makes them feel important and wise, and specially privileged. There are many texts, of course, which are secret to the caste, and not even available to scholars generally. In these it is rumored there are marvelous spells and mighty magic, particularly if read backward on certain feast days. Whereas initiates tend not to be taken with great seriousness by the high castes, or the more intelligent members of the population, except in matters of political alliance, their teachings and purported ability to intercede with Priest-Kings, and further the welfare of their adherents, is taken with great seriousness by many of the lower castes. And many men, who suspect that the initiates, in their claims and pretensions, are frauds, will nonetheless avoid coming into conflict with the caste. This is particularly true of civic leaders who do not wish the power of the initiates to turn the lower castes against them. And, after all, who knows much of Priest-Kings, other than the obvious fact that they exist. The invisible barrier about the Sardar is evidence of that, and the policing, by flame death, of illegal weapons and inventions. The Gorean knows that there are Priest-Kings. He does not, of course, know their nature. That is where the role of the initiates becomes most powerful. The Gorean knows there are Priest-Kings, whoever or whatever they might be. He is also confronted with a socially and economically powerful caste that pretends to be able to intermediate between Priest-Kings and common folk. What if some of the claims of Initiates should be correct? What if they do have influence with Priest-Kings?

The common Gorean tends to play it safe and honor the Initiates.

He will, however, commonly, have as little to do with them as possible.

This does not mean he will not contribute to their temples and fees for placating Priest-Kings.

The attitude of Priest-Kings toward Initiates, as I recalled, having once been in the Sardar, is generally one of disinterest. They are regarded as being harmless. They are taken by many Priest-Kings as an evidence of the aberrations of the human kind.

Incidentally, it is a teaching of the initiates that only initiates can obtain eternal life. The regimen for doing this has something to do with learning mathematics, and with avoiding the impurities of meat and beans. This particular teaching of the initiates, it is interesting to note, is that taken least seriously by the general population. No one, except possibly, initiates, takes it with much seriousness. The Gorean feeling generally is that there is no reason why initiates, or only initiates, should live forever. Initiates, though often feared by the lower castes, are also regarded as being a bit odd, and often figure in common, derisive jokes. No female, incidentally, may become an Initiate. It is a consequence, thusly, that no female can obtain eternal life. I have often thought that the Initiates, if somewhat more clever, could have a much greater power than they possess on Gor. For example, if they could fuse their superstitions and lore, and myths, with a genuine moral message, of one sort or another, they might appeal more seriously to the general population; if they spoke more sense people would be less sensitive to, or disturbed by, the nonsense; further, they should teach that all Goreans might, by following their rituals, obtain eternal life; that would broaden the appeal of their message, and subtly utilize the fear of death to further their projects; lastly, they should make greater appeal to women than they do, for, in most Gorean cities, women, of one sort or another, care for and instruct the children in the crucial first years. That would be the time to imprint them, while innocent and trusting, at the mother's or nurse's knee, with superstitions which might, in simpler brains, subtly control them the length of their lives. So simple an adjustment as the promise of eternal life to women who behaved in accordance with their teachings, instructing the young, and so on, might have much effect. But the initiates, like many Gorean castes, were tradition bound. Besides, they were quite powerful as it was. Most Goreans took with some seriousness their claim to be able to placate and influence Priest-Kings. That was more than they needed for considerable power.

There had been much fear in Kassau when the ship of Ivar Forkbeard had entered the inlet. But it had come at midday. And on its mast, round and of painted wood, had hung the white shield. His men had rowed slowly, singing a dirge at the oars. Even the tarnhead at the ship's prow had been swung back on the great wooden hinges. Sometimes, in light raiding galleys, it is so attached, to remove its weight from the prow's height, to ensure greater stability in high seas; it is always, however, at the prow in harbor, or when the ship enters an inlet or river to make its strike; in calm seas, of course, there is little or no danger in permitting it to surmount the prow generally. That the tarnhead was hinged

30

back, as the ship entered the inlet, was suitable indication, like the white shield, that it came in peace.

The ship was a beautiful ship, sleek and well-lined. It was a twenty bencher, but this nomenclature may be confusing. There were twenty benches to a side, with two men to each bench. It carried, thus, forty oars, with two men to each oar. Tersites of Port Kar, the controversial inventer and shipwright, had advocated more than one man to an oar but, generally, the southern galleys utilized one man per oar, three oars and three men on a diagonal bench, facing aft, the oars staggered, the diagonality of the bench permitting the multiplicity of levers. The oars were generally some nineteen feet in length, and narrower than the southern oars, that they might cut and sweep with great speed, more rapidly than the wider bladed oar; and with two men to each oar, and the lightness of the ship, this would produce great speed. As in the southern galleys the keel to beam ratio was designed, too, for swiftness, being generally in the neighborhood of one to eight. Forkbeard's ship, or serpent, as they are sometimes called, was approximately eighty feet Gorean in length, with a beam of some ten feet Gorean. His ship, like most of the northern ships, did not have a rowing frame, and the rowers sat within the hull proper, facing, of course, aft. The thole ports, I noted, had covers on the inside, on swivels, which permitted them to be closed when the ship was under sail. The sail was quite different from the southern ships, being generally squarish, though somewhat wider at the bottom. The mast, like that of the southern ships, could be lowered. It fitted into two blocks of wood, and was wedged in the top block by means of a heavy, diagonal wooden plug, driven tight with hammers. The northern ship carries one sail, not the several sails, all lateens, of the southern ships, which must be removed and replaced. It was an all-purpose sail, hung straight from a spar of needle wood. It can be shortened or let out by reefing ropes. At its edges, corner spars can hold it spread from the ship. I doubted that such a ship could sail as close to the wind as a lateen-rigged ship but the advantages of being able to shorten or let out sail in a matter of moments were not inconsiderable. The sail was striped, red and white. The ship, like most of the northern ships, was clinker built, being constructed of overlapping planks, or strakes, the frame then fitted within them. Between the strakes tarred ropes and tar served as calking. Outside the planks, too, was a coating of painted tar, to protect them from the sea, and the depredations of ship worms. The tar was painted red and black, in irregular lines. The ship, at night, mast down, with such colorings, moving inland on a river, among the shadows, would be extremely difficult to detect. It was a raider's ship. The clinker-built construction, as opposed to the carvel construction of the south, with flush planking, is somewhat more inclined to leak, but it is much stronger in the high waters of the north. The clinker construction allows the ship to literally bend and twist, almost elastically, in a vicious sea; the hull planking can be bent more than a foot Gorean without buckling. The decking on the ship is loose, and may be lifted or put to one side, to increase cargo space. The ship, of course, is open. To protect goods or men from the rain or sun a large rectangle of boskhide, on stakes, tentlike, stretched to cleats on the gunwales, is sometimes used. This same rectangle of boskhide may be used, dropped between the gunwales, to collect rain water. At night the men sleep on the deck, in waterproof bags, sewn from the skins of the sea sleen; in such a bag, also, they store their gear, generally beneath their bench. In some such ships, the men sit not on benches but on their own large, locked sea chests, fixed in place, using them as benches. When, in the harbor, the ship rested on its moorings, the shields, overlapping, of its men were hung on the sides; this was another indication of peaceful intent. The shields were round, and of wood, variously painted, some reinforced with iron bands, others with leather, some with small bronze plates. In battle, of course, such shields are not hung on the side of the ship; they would obstruct the thole ports; but even if oars were not used, they would be within the hull, at hand; why should a crewman expose himself to missile fire to retrieve a shield so fastened? Also, of course, when the ship is under sail they are not carried on the side, for the waves, always a menace in a ship with a low freeboard, would strike against them, and perhaps even tear them from the ship. But now they hung at the ship's sides, tied by their straps to the wooden bars inside the gunwales. The men did not carry their shields. They came in peace.

I had turned away and walked to the temple, for I wished to have a place to stand.

Another feature of the northern ships is that they have, in effect, a prow on each end. This permits them to be beached, on rollers, more easily. They can be brought to land in either direction, a valuable property in the rocky, swift northern waters. Furthermore this permits the rowers, in reversing position on the benches, to reverse the direction of the ship. This adds considerably to the maneuverability of the craft. It is almost impossible to ram one of the swift ships of the north.

The procession, I knew, must now be on its way to the temple.

Within the temple the incense hung thick about the rafters. It smarted my eyes, it sickened me.

The litany and responses of the congregation were now completed and the initiates, some twenty within the rail, began to sing in archaic Gorean. I could make out little of the wording. There was an accompaniment by sistrums. Portions of the hymn were taken up by four delicate boys, standing outside the white rail on a raised platform. Their heads were shaved and they wore robes resembling those of the initiates. Choirs of such boys often sang in the great temples. They were young male slaves, purchased by initiates, castrated by civil authorities and, in the monasteries, trained in song. I supposed, to one versed in music, their soprano voices were very beautiful. I did not much care for them. Here in the far north, of course, in Kassau, to have any such boys, properly trained in the archaic hymns, indicated some wealth. I did not think such singers existed even in Lydius. The High Initiate of Kassau obviously was a man of expensive tastes.

I looked about myself. Most of the people seemed poor, fishermen, sawyers, porters, peasants. Most wore simple garments of plain wool, or even rep-cloth. The feet of many were bound in skins. Their backs were often bowed, their eyes vacant. The furnishings of the temple were quite splendid, gold hangings, and chains of gold, and lamps of gold, burning the finest of imported tharlarion oils. I looked into the hungry eyes of a child, clinging in a sack to its mother's back. She kept nodding her head in prayer. The temple itself is quite large. It is some one hundred and twenty feet in length, and forty feet in width and height. Its roof, wooden-shingled, is supported on the walls, and two rows of squared pillars. On these pillars, and at places on the walls, were nailed sheets of gold. On these were inscribed prayers and invocations to the Priest-Kings. There were many candles in the sanctuary. They made the air even closer, burning the oxygen. The high altar, of marble, setting on a platform, also marble, of three broad steps, was surmounted by a great rounded circle of gold, which is taken often as a symbol of Priest-Kings. It is without beginning or end. It stands, I suppose, for eternity. At the foot of the altar beasts were sometimes sacrificed, their horns held, their heads twisted, the blood from their opened throats caught in shallow golden bowls, to be poured upon the altar; too, choice portions of their flesh would be burnt upon the altar, the smoke escaping through a small hole in the roof. The temple, incidentally, is oriented to the Sardar. When the high initiate stands facing the altar, before the circle of gold, he faces the distant Sardar, the abode of Priest-Kings. He bows and prays to the Sardar and lifts the burned meat to the remote denizens of those mysterious mountains.

These are no pictures or representations of Priest-Kings within the temple, incidentally, or, as far as I know, elsewhere on Gor. It is regarded as blasphemy to attempt to picture a Priest-King. I suppose it is just as well. The Initiates claim they have no size or shape or form. This is incorrect but the Initiates are just as well off, I expect, in their conjectures. I speculated what a great picture of Misk might look like, hanging at the side of the temple. I wondered what might become of the religion of Priest-Kings if Priest-Kings should ever choose to make themselves known to men.

I would not prophesy for it a bright future.

I looked again upon the slender, blondish girl, bored in the crowd. Again she looked at me, and looked away. She was richly dressed. The cape of white fur was a splendid fur. The scarlet vest, the blouse of white wool, the long woolen skirt, red, were fine goods. The buckle from Cos was expensive. Even the shoes of black leather were finely tooled. I supposed her the daughter of a rich merchant. There were other good looking wenches, too, in the crowd, generally blond girls, as are most of the northern girls, many with braided hair. They were in festival finery. This was holiday in Kassau. Ivar Forkbeard, in death, if not in life, was making pilgrimage to the temple, that his bones might be annointed at the hands of the high initiate, would he so graciously deign to do so. This word had been brought from the wharves to the High Initiate. He had, in his mercy, granted this request. The hollow bars on their great chains, hanging from timber frames outside the temple, had been struck. Word had been spread. Ivar Forkbeard, the unregenerate, the raider, the pirate, he who had dared to make the fist of the hammer over his ale, would come at last, in death if not in life, humbly to the temple of Priest-Kings. There was much rejoicing in Kassau.

In the crowd, with the poor, there were many burghers of

34

Kassau, stout men of means, the pillars of the town, with their families. Several of these stood on raised platforms, on the right, near the front of the temple. I understood these places to be reserved for dignitaries, men of substance and their families.

I examined the younger women on the platform. None, it seemed to me, was as excellent as the slender blond girl in the cape of white sea-sleen fur and scarlet vest. One was, however, not without interest. She was a tall, statesque girl, lofty and proud, gray-eyed. She wore black and silver, a full, ankle-length gown of rich, black velvet, with silver belts, or straps, that crossed over her breasts, and tied about her waist. From it, by strings, hung a silver purse, that seemed weighty. Her blond hair was lifted from the sides and back of her head by a comb of bone and leather, like an inverted isoceles triangle, the comb fastened by a tiny black ribbon about her neck and another such ribbon about her forehead. Her cloak, of black fur, from the black sea sleen, glossy and deep, swirled to her ankles. It was fastened at the left shoulder by a large circular brooch of silver, probably from Tharna. She was doubtless the daughter of a very rich man. She would have many suitors.

I looked again to the High Initiate, a cold, stern, dour man, hard faced, who sat in his high, white hat in his robes upon the throne within the white rail.

Within that rail, about the altar, some in chests, others displayed on shelvings, was much rich plate, and vessels of gold and silver. There were the golden bowls used to gather the blood of the sacrificed animals; cups used to pour libations to Priest-Kings; vessels containing oils; lavers in which the celebrants of the rites might cleanse their hands from their work; there were even the small bowls of coins, brought as offerings by the poor, to solicit the favor of initiates that they might intercede with Priest-Kings on their behalf, that the food roots would not fail, the suls not rot, the fish come to the plankton, the verr yield her kid with health to both, the vulos lay many eggs.

How hard to me, and cruel, even, seemed the face of the High Initiate. How rich they were, the initiates, and how little they did. The peasant tilled his fields, the fisherman went out in his boat, the merchant risked his capital. But the initiate did none of these things. Rather he lived by exploiting the superstitions and fears of simpler men. I had little doubt but that the High Initiate had long ago seen through his way of life, if he had not at first. Surely now he

35

was no simple novice. But he had not changed his way of life. He had not gone to the fields, nor to the fishing banks, nor to the market. He had remained in the temple. I studied his face. It was not that of a simple man, or that of a fool. I had little doubt but what the initiate knew full well what he was doing. I had little doubt but what he knew that he knew as little as others of Priest-Kings, and was as ignorant as they. And yet still he sat upon his throne, in the gilded temple, amid the incense, the ringing of the sistrum, the singing of boys.

The child in the sack on the mother's back whimpered. "Be silent," she whispered to it. "Be silent!"

Then, from outside, rang once the great hollow bar, hanging on its chain.

Inside the initiates, and the boys, at a sign from the High Initiate, a lifted, clawlike hand, were silent.

Then the initiate rose from his throne, and went slowly to the altar and climbed the steps. He bowed thrice to the Sardar and then turned to face the congregation.

"Let them enter the place of Priest-Kings," he said.

I now heard the singing, the chanting, of initiates from outside the door. Twelve of them had gone down to the ship, with candles, to escort the body of Ivar Forkbeard to the temple. Two now entered, holding candles. All eyes craned to see the procession which now, slowly, the initiates singing, entered the incense-filled temple.

Four huge men of Torvaldsland, in long cloaks, clasped about their necks, heads down, bearded, with braided hair, entered, bearing on their shoulders a platform of crossed spears. On this platform, covered with a white shroud, lay a body, a large body. Ivar Forkbeard, I thought to myself, must have been a large man.

"I want to see him," whispered the blond girl to the woman with whom she stood.

"Be silent," hushed the woman.

I am tall, and found it not difficult to look over the heads of many in the crowd.

So this is the end, I thought to myself, of the great Ivar Forkbeard.

He comes in death to the temple of Priest-Kings, that his bones may be annointed with the grease of Priest-Kings.

It was his last will, now loyally, doggedly, carried out by his saddened men.

Somehow I regretted that Ivar Forkbeard was dead.

The initiates, chanting, now filed into the temple with

their candles. The chant was taken up by the initiates, too, within the sanctuary. Behind the platform of crossed spears, heads down, filed the crew of Forkbeard. They wore long cloaks; they carried no weapons; no shields; they wore no helmets. Weapons, I knew, were not to be carried within the temple of Priest-Kings.

They seemed beaten, saddened dogs. They were not as I had expected the men of Torvaldsland to be.

"Are those truly men of Torvaldsland?" asked the blond girl, of the older woman, obviously disappointed.

"Hush," said the older woman. "Show reverence for this place, for Priest-Kings."

"I had thought they would be other than that," sniffed the girl.

"Hush," said the older woman.

"Very well," said the girl, irritably. "What weaklings they seem."

To the amazement of the crowd, at a sign from the High Initiate of Kassau, two lesser initiates opened the gate to the white rail.

Another initiate, sleek, fat, his shaved head oiled, shining in the light of the candles, carrying a small golden vessel of thickened chrism went to each of the four men of Torvaldsland, making on their foreheads the sign of the Priest-Kings, the circle of eternity.

The crowd gasped. It was incredible honor that was being shown to these men, that they might, themselves, on the platform of crossed spears, carry the body of Ivar Forkbeard, in death penitent, to the high steps of the great altar. It was the chrism of temporary permission, which, in the teachings of initiates, allows one not consecrated to the service of Priest-Kings to enter the sanctuary. In a sense it is counted an annointing, though an inferior one, and of temporary efficacy. It was first used at roadside shrines, to permit civil authorities to enter and slay fugitives who had taken sanctuary at the altars. It is also used for workmen and artists, who may be employed to practice their craft within the rail, to the enhancement of the temple and the Priest-Kings' glory.

Ivar Forkbeard's body was not annointed as it was carried through the gate in the rail.

The dead need no annointing to enter the sanctuary. Only the living, it is held, can profane the sacred.

The four men of Torvaldsland carried the huge body of Ivar Forkbeard up the steps of the altar, on the crossed spears. Then, still beneath its white shroud, they laid it gently on the highest step of the altar.

Then the four men fell back, two to each side, heads down. The High Initiate then began to intone a complex prayer in archaic Gorean, to which, at intervals, responses were made by the assembled initiates, those within the railing originally and now, too, those twelve, still carrying candles, who had accompanied the body from the ship through the dirt streets of Kassau, among the wooden buildings, to the temple. When the initiate finished his prayer, the other initiates began to sing a solemn hymn, while the chief initiate, at the altar, his back turned to the congregation, began to prepare, with words and signs, the grease of Priest-Kings, for the annointing of the bones of Ivar Forkbeard.

Toward the front of the temple, behind the rail, and even at the two doors of the temple, by the great beams which close them, stood the men of Forkbeard. Many of them were giants, huge men, inured to cold, accustomed to war and the labor of the oar, raised from boyhood on steep, isolated farms near the sea, grown strong and hard on work, and meat and cereals. Such men, from boyhood, in harsh games, had learned to run, to leap, to swim, to throw the spear, to wield the sword, to wield the ax, to stand against steel, even bloodied, unflinching. Such men, these, would be the hardest of the hard, for only the largest, the swiftest and finest might win for themselves a bench on the ship of a captain, and the man great enough to command such as they must be first and mightiest among them, for the men of Torvaldsland will obey no other, and that man had been Ivar Forkbeard.

But Ivar Forkbeard had come in death, if not in life, to the temple of Priest-Kings, betraying the old gods, to have his bones annointed at last with the grease of Priest-Kings. No more would he make over his ale, with his closed fist, the sign of the hammer.

I noted one of the men of Torvaldsland. He was of incredible stature, perhaps eight feet in height and broad as a bosk. His hair was shaggy. His skin seemed grayish. His eyes were vacant and staring, his lips parted. He seemed to me in a stupor, as though he heard or saw nothing.

The High Initiate now turned to face the congregation. In his hands he held the tiny, golden, rounded box in which lay the grease of Priest-Kings. At his feet lay the body of the Forkbeard.

The congregation tensed and, scarcely breathing, lifting their heads, intent, observed the High Initiate of Kassau. I saw the blond girl standing on her toes, in the black shoes, looking over the shoulders of the woman in front of her. On the platform the men of importance, and their families, observed the High Initiate, among them, craning her neck, looking over her father's shoulder, was the large blond girl, in her black velvet and silver.

"Praises be unto the Priest-Kings!" called out the High Initiate.

"Praises unto the Priest-Kings," responded the initiates.

It was in that moment, and in that moment only, that I detected on the thin, cold face of the High Initiate of Kassau, a tiny smile of triumph.

He bent down, on one knee, the tiny, rounded, golden box containing the grease of Priest-Kings in his left hand, and drew back with his right hand the long, white shroud concealing the body of Ivar Forkbeard.

Doubtless it was the High Initiate of Kassau who first knew. He seemed frozen. The eyes of the Forkbeard opened, and Ivar Forkbeard grinned at him.

With a roar of laughter, hurling the shroud from him, to the horror of the High Initiate, and other initiates, and the congregation, Ivar Forkbeard, almost seven feet in height, leaped to his feet, in his right hand clutching a great, curved, single-bladed ax of hardened iron.

"Praise be to Odin!" he cried.

Then he with his ax, with a single swing, spattering blood on the sheets of gold, cut the head from the body of the High Initiate of Kassau, and leaped, booted, to the height of the very altar of the temple itself.

He threw back his head with a wild roaring laugh, the bloody ax in his hand.

I heard the beams of the two doors of the temple being thrown in place, locking the people within. I saw the cloaks of the men of Torvaldsland hurled from them and saw, gripped in their two hands, great axes. I suddenly saw the large man of Torvaldsland, he of incredible stature, seem to come alive, eyes wild, screaming, veins prominent on his forehead, mouth slobbering, striking about himself almost blindly with a great ax.

Ivar Forkbeard stood on the high altar. "The men of Torvaldsland," he cried, "are upon you!"

3

I MAKE THE ACQUAINTANCE OF IVAR FORKBEARD AND BOOK PASSAGE ON HIS SHIP

Screaming pierced my ears.

I was almost thrown from my feet by the buffeting, shrieking bodies.

I strained my eyes to see through the clouds of incense hanging in the temple.

I smelled blood.

A girl cried out.

People, merchants, the rich, the poor, fishermen, porters, fled toward the great doors, there to be cut down with axes. They fled back to the center of the temple, huddled together. Axes began to cut through their midst. I heard shouts. I heard the harsh war cries of Torvaldsland. I heard golden sheets of metal being pried from the square pillars of the temple. The interior of the sanctuary was strewn with dead initiates, many hacked to pieces. Others, crowding together, knelt against the walls. The four boys who had sung in the services held to one another, crying, like girls. From the high altar, standing upon it, Ivar Forkbeard directed his men. "Hurry!" he cried. "Gather what you can!"

"Kneel beneath the ax!" cried out one of the burghers of Kassau, who wore black satin, a silver chain about his neck. I gathered he might be administrator in this town.

The people, obediently, began to kneel on the dirt floor of the temple, their heads down.

I saw two men of Torvaldsland loading their cloaks with golden plate and vessels from the sanctuary, hurling them like tin and iron into the furs.

A fisherman cringed near me. One of the men of Torvaldsland raised his ax to strike him. I caught the ax as it descended and held it. The warrior of Torvaldsland looked at me, startled. His eyes widened. At his throat was the point of the sword of Port Kar.

Weapons are not to be carried in the temple of Priest-Kings but I had been taught, long ago, by Kamchak of the Tuchuks, at a banquet in Turia, that where weapons may not be carried, it is well to carry weapons.

"Kneel beneath the ax," I told the fisherman.

He did so.

I released the ax of the man of Torvaldsland, and removed my blade from his throat. "Do not strike him," I told the man of Torvaldsland.

He drew back his ax, and stepped away, regarding me, startled, wary.

"Gather loot!" cried Forkbeard. "Are you waiting for the Sa-Tarna harvest!"

The man turned away and began to pull the gold hangings from the walls.

I saw, twenty feet from me, screaming, the giant, he of incredible stature, striking down at the kneeling people, who were crying out and trying to crawl away. The great blade dipped and cut, and swept up, and then cut down again. I saw the wild muscles of his bare arms bulging and knotted. Slobber came from his mouth. One man lay half cut through.

"Rollo!" cried out Forkbeard. "The battle is done!"

The giant, with the grayish face and shaggy hair, stood suddenly, unnaturally, quiet, the great, curved blade lifted over a weeping man. He lifted his head slowly, and turned it, slowly, toward the altar.

"The battle is done!" called out Forkbeard.

Two men of Torvaldsland then held the giant by the arms, and lowered his ax, and, gently, turned him away from the people. He turned and looked back at them, and they cowered away. But it did not seem he recognized them. It seemed he did not know them and had not seen them before. Again his eyes seemed vacant. He turned away, and walked slowly, carrying his ax, toward one of the doors of the temple.

"Those who would live," called out Forkbeard, "lie on your stomachs."

The people in the temple, many of them spattered with the blood of their neighbors, some severely wounded, threw themselves, shuddering, man and woman, and child, to their stomachs. They lay among many of their own dead.

I myself did not lie with them. Once I had been of the warriors.

I stood.

The men of Torvaldsland turned to face me.

"Why do you not lie beneath the ax, Stranger?" called out Forkbeard.

"I am not weary," I told him.

Forkbeard laughed. "It is a good reason," he said. "Are you of Torvaldsland?"

"No," I told him.

"You are of the warriors?" asked Forkbeard.

"Perhaps once," I told him.

"I shall see," said Forkbeard. Then to one of his men, he said, "Hand me a spear." One of the spears which had formed the platform on which he had been carried, gaining entrance to Kassau and the temple, was handed to him.

Suddenly behind me I heard a war cry of Torvaldsland.

I turned and swept to the guard position, in the instant seeing the man's distance, and spun again to strike from my body, before it could penetrate it, the hurled spear of Ivar Forkbeard. It must be taken behind the point with the swift blow of the forearm. The spear caromed away and struck the wall of the temple, fifty feet behind me. In the same instant I had spun again, in the guard position, to stand against the man with his ax. He pulled up short, and looked to Ivar Forkbeard. I turned again to face the Forkbeard.

He grinned. "Yes," he said, "once perhaps you were of the warriors."

I looked to the man behind me, and to the others. They lifted their axes in their right hand. It was a salute of Torvaldsland. I heard their cheers.

"He remains standing," said Ivar Forkbeard.

I sheathed my sword.

"Hurry!" called the Forkbeard to his men. "Hurry! The people of the town will gather!"

Swiftly, tearing hangings from the walls, prying loose sheets of gold, pulling down even lamps from their chains, filling their cloaks with cups and plates, the men of Torvaldsland stripped the temple of what they could tear loose and carry. Ivar Forkbeard leaped down from the altar and began, angrily, to hurl vessels of consecrated oils against the walls behind the sanctuary. Then he took a rack of candles and hurled it against the wall. Fire soon bit into the timbers behind the sanctuary.

The Forkbeard then leaped over the rail of the sanctuary and strode among the people lying on their stomachs, the wall facing the Sardar being eaten by fire, illuminating the interior of the temple.

He reached down, here and there, to rip a purse from one of the richer townsfolk. He took the purse of the burgher in black satin, and took, too, from his neck the silver chain of his office, which he slung about his own neck.

He then drew with the handle of his ax a circle, some twenty feet in diameter, in the dirt floor of the temple.

It was a bond-maid circle.

"Females," he cried out, gesturing with the great ax toward the wall opposite the doors, "swiftly! To the wall! Stand with your backs against it!"

Terrified, weeping, the men groaning, the females fled to the wall. I saw, standing there, terrified, their backs against it, the blond girl in the scarlet vest and skirt, her hair in the snood of scarlet yarn, tied with filaments of golden wire; and the large, statesque girl, too, in black velvet, with the silver straps crossed over her breasts, and tied about her waist, with the purse. Ivar Forkbeard, in the light of the burning wall of the temple, quickly examined the line of women. From some he took jewelry, bracelets, necklaces and rings. From others he took purses, hanging at their belts. He tore away the purse from the large blond girl, and the silver straps, too, which had decorated the black velvet of her gown. She shrank back against the wall. She was large breasted. The men of Torvaldsland are fond of such women. The jewelry and coins which he took he hurled into a golden sacrificial bowl, which one of his men carried at his side. As he went down the line, too, he freed certain women of the wall, telling them to swiftly return to their places, and lie beneath the ax. Gratefully they fled to their former places.

This left nineteen girls at the wall. I admired the taste of Forkbeard. They were beauties. My choices would have been the same.

Among them, of course, were the slender blond girl in the red vest and skirt, and the larger one, now in black velvet, torn, stripped of its silver straps, its brooches, the purse.

He ripped the snood of scarlet yarn from the slender blond girl's hair. Her hair, now loose, fell behind her to the small of her back. He then tore away the ribbons and comb of bone and leather that had so intricately held the hair of the larger blond girl, she in black velvet. Her hair was even longer than that of the more slender girl.

The nineteen girls regarded him, terrified, eyes wide, their faces lit on the left side by the flames of the burning wall.

"Go to the bond-maid circle," said Ivar Forkbeard, indicating the circle he had drawn in the dirt.

The women cried out in misery. To enter the circle, if one is a female, is, by the laws of Torvaldsland, to declare oneself a bond-maid. A woman, of course, need not enter the circle of her own free will. She may, for example, be thrown

44

within it, naked and bound. Howsoever she enters the circle, voluntarily or by force, free or secured, she emerges from it, by the laws of Torvaldsland, as a bond-maid.

Seventeen of the girls, weeping, fled to the circle, and huddled within it.

Two did not, the slender blond girl and the larger one, in black velvet.

"I am Aelgifu," said the large girl. "I am the daughter of Gurt of Kassau. He is administrator. There will be ransom money for me."

"It is true!" cried a man, the burgher in black satin, whose chain of office Forkbeard had torn from his neck.

"One hundred pieces of gold," said Forkbeard to him, observing the girl.

She stiffened.

"Yes," cried the man. "Yes!"

"Five nights from this night," said Ivar Forkbeard, "on the skerry of Einar by the rune-stone of the Torvaldsmark."

I had heard of this stone. It is taken by many to mark the border between Torvaldsland and the south. Many of those of Torvaldsland, however, take its borders to be much farther extended than the Torvaldsmark. Indeed, some of the men of Torvaldsland regard Torvaldsland to be wherever their ships beach, as they took their country, and their steel, with them.

"Yes!" said the man. "I will bring the money to that place."

"Go to the bond-maid circle," said Ivar Forkbeard to the large girl, "but do not enter it."

"Yes," she said, hurrying to its edge.

"The wall of the temple will not last much longer," said one of the men of the Forkbeard.

Forkbeard looked then at the younger, blond, more slender girl, she with her hair now loose, the snood of scarlet yarn ripped away, in her red vest and skirt, and black shoes. She looked up at him, boldly. "My father is poorer than Aelgifu's," she said, "but for me, too, there will be a ransom."

He looked down at her and grinned. "You are too pretty to ransom," he said.

She looked at him with horror. In the crowd I heard a man and a woman cry out with misery.

"Go to the circle and enter it," said Ivar Forkbeard to the girl.

She held up her head. "No," she said. "I am free. Never

45

will I consent to be a bond-maid. I shall first choose death!"

"Very well," laughed the Forkbeard. "Kneel."

Startled, she did so, uncertainly.

"Put your head down," he said, "throw your hair forward, exposing your neck."

She did so.

He lifted the great ax.

Suddenly she cried out and thrust her head to his boot. She held his ankle.

"Have mercy on a bond-maid!" she wept.

Ivar Forkbeard laughed and reached down and pulled her up by the arm, his great fist closed about her arm within the white woolen blouse, and thrust her stumbling well within the circle.

"The wall will soon fall," said one of the men.

I could see the fire creeping now, too, to the roof.

"Bond-maids," ordered Ivar Forkbeard harshly, "strip!"

Crying out the girls removed their garments. I saw that the weeping, slender blond-haired girl was incredibly beautiful. Her legs and belly, and breasts, were marvelous. And her face, too, was beautiful, sensitive and intelligent. I envied the Forkbeard his catch.

"Fetter them," said Ivar Forkbeard.

"I hear the townsfolk gathering," said one of the men at the door.

Two of the men of Torvaldsland had, from their left shoulder to their right hip, that their right arms be less impeded, a chain formed of slave bracelets; each pair of bracelets locked at each end about one of the bracelets of another pair, the whole thus forming a circle. Now they removed this chain of bracelets, and, one by one, removed the pairs, closing them about the small wrists, behind their backs, of the female captives, now bond-maids. These bracelets were of the sort used to hold women in the north. They are less ornate and finely tooled than those available in the south. But they are satisfactory for their purpose. They consist of curved, hinged bands of black iron, three quarters of an inch in width and a quarter inch in thickness. On one of each of the two curved pieces constituting a bracelet there is a welded ring; the two welded rings are joined by a single link, about an inch in width, counting both sides, each of which is about a quarter of an inch in diameter, and three inches long. Some of the girls cried out with pain as the fetters, locking, bit into their wrists.

I saw the slender girl's wrists pulled behind her and

snapped in the fetters. She winced. They were rough, plain fetters, but they would hold her well, quite as well as the intricately wrought counterparts of the south.

Ivar Forkbeard regarded Aelgifu. "Fetter her, too," he said. She was fettered.

The fire had now climbed well unto the roof and had taken hold on another wall, near the railing, against which the women, earlier, had stood.

It was growing hard to breathe in the temple.

"Coffle the females," said Forkbeard.

With a long length of binding fiber the nineteen girls were swiftly fastened throat to throat.

Aelgifu, clothed, led the coffle. She was free. The others were only bond-maids.

The beams which secured the doors were thrown back, but the doors were not opened.

The men of Torvaldsland struggled to lift their burdens. Gold is not light.

"Utilize the bond-maids," said the Forkbeard, angrily. Swiftly, about the necks of the bond-maids were tied strings of cups, candlesticks and sacks, improvised from cloaks, of plate. Soon, they, too, were heavily burdened. Several staggered under the weight of the riches they bore.

"In the north, my pretty maids," Ivar assured them, "the burdens you carry will be more prosaic, bundles of wood for the fires, buckets of water for the hall, baskets of dung for the fields."

They looked at him with horror, understanding then what the nature of their life would be.

And at night, of course, they would serve the feasts of their masters, carrying and filling the great horns, and delighting them with the softness of their bodies in the furs.

"We are ready to depart," said one of the men.

I could hear angry townspeople outside.

"You will never get us to the ship," said the slender blond girl.

"Be silent, bond-maid," said Ivar Forkbeard.

"My bondage will not last long," she laughed.

"We shall see," laughed Ivar Forkbeard.

He then ran, almost through the flames to the high altar of the temple of Kassau. With a single leap he attained its summit. Then, with his boot and shoulder, he tottered the great circle of gold which surmounted it. It moved unsteadily, rocking back and forth, and then rolled from the altar, struck the steps and broke apart.

It was only golden sheathing on a wheel of clay.

The people of Kassau, within the burning temple, cried out, startled.

They had understood the circle to be of solid gold.

Standing on the broken fragments of the circle, Ivar Forkbeard cried out, his ax lifted, and his left hand, too, "Praise be to Odin!" And then, throwing his ax to his left shoulder, holding it there by his left hand he turned and faced the Sardar, and lifted his fist, clenched. It was not only a sign of defiance to Priest-Kings, but the fist, the sign of the hammer. It was the sign of Thor.

"We can carry no more," cried one of his men.

"Nor shall we," laughed Ivar.

"The circle?" cried one.

"Leave it for the people to see," laughed Ivar. "That it is only gold on a wheel of clay!"

He turned to face me.

"I want passage to Torvaldsland," I said. "I hunt beasts."

"Kurii?" he asked.

"Yes," I said.

"You are mad," he said.

"Less mad I expect than Ivar Forkbeard," I said.

"My serpent," said he, "is not a vessel on which one may book passage."

"I play Kaissa," I said.

"The voyage north will be long," he said.

"I am skilled at the game," I said. "Unless you are quite good, I shall beat you."

We heard the people screaming outside. I heard one of the beams in the ceiling crack. The roar of the flames seemed deafening. "We shall die in the temple if we do not soon flee," said one of his men. Of all those in the temple, I think only I, and Ivar Forkbeard, and the giant, he of incredible stature, who had fought with such frenzy, did not seem anxious. He did not seem even aware of the flames. He carried a sack of plate at his back, heavy and bulging, which had been given to him by other men, that he might carry it.

"I, too, am skilled at the game," said Ivar Forkbeard. "Are you truly good?"

"I am good," I said. "Whether I am as good as you, of course, I shall not know until we play."

"True," said Forkbeard.

"I shall join you at your ship," I said.

"Do so," said he.

Then he turned to one of his men. "Keep close to me the coins brought as offerings by the poor to the temple of Kassau," he said. These coins had now been placed in a large, single bowl.

"Yes, Captain," said the man.

The rear wall, too, of the temple now caught afire. I heard another beam in the ceiling crack.

There were sparks in the air. They stung my face. The bond-maids, their bodies exposed to them, cried out in pain.

"Open the other gate!" cried Ivar Forkbeard. Two of his men threw open the other door of the temple. Hysterically, crowding, those citizens of Kassau who had, weeping, terrified, been lying on their stomachs in the dirt, beneath the burning roof, leapt to their feet and fled through the door.

Ivar permitted them to leave the temple.

"They are coming out!" cried a voice from the outside. We heard angry men running to the door, people turning, the movements of chains, flails and rakes.

"Now let us leave," said Ivar Forkbeard.

"You will never get us to the ship," said the slender girl.

"You will hurry, pretty little bond-maids, and you, too, my large-breasted lovely," said Ivar, indicating black-velveted Aelgifu, "or you will be cut out of the coffle by your heads."

"Open the door," he said.

The door was swung open. "To the ships," he cried. "Hurry, my pretties," he laughed, striking the slender blond girl, and others of them, sharply with the palm of his hand. His men, too, the girls between them, pushed through the door.

"They are coming out here!" cried a voice, a man in the crowd of the poor, a peasant, turning about, seeing us. But many of those in the crowd were clasping loved ones, and friends, as they escaped from the other door. Swiftly, down the dirt street to the wharves from the temple, striding, but not running, moved Ivar Forkbeard with his men, and his loot, both that of female flesh and gold. Many of the peasants, and fishermen, and other poor people, who had not found places in the temple, turned about. Several of them began to follow us, lifting flails and great scythes. Some carried chains, others hoes.

They had no leadership.

Like wolves, crying out, shouting, lifting their fists, they ran behind us as we made our way toward the wharves. Then a rock fell among us, and another.

None of them cared to rush upon the axes of the men of Torvaldsland.

"Save us!" cried the slender blond girl. "You are men! Save us!"

At her cries many of the men seemed emboldened and rushed more closely about us, but swings of the great axes kept them back.

"Gather together!" we heard. "Charge!" We saw Gurt, in his black satin, rallying them.

They had lacked a leader. They had one now.

Ivar Forkbeard then took Aelgifu by the hair and turned her, so that those following might see.

"Stop!" cried Gurt to them.

The single-bladed edge of the great ax lay at Aelgifu's throat; her head was bent back. The Forkbeard, his left hand in her hair, his right hand just below the head of the ax, grinned at Gurt.

"Stop," said Gurt, moaning, crushed. "Do not fight them! Let them go!"

Ivar Forkbeard released Aelgifu and thrust her rudely, stumbling, ahead of him.

"Hurry!" called Ivar Forkbeard to his men. "Hurry, bright-fleshed ones," called he to the fettered, burdened, coffled bond-maids.

Behind us, we heard the roof of the temple collapse. I looked back. Smoke stained the sky.

A hundred yards from the wharves we saw a crowd of angry men, perhaps two hundred, blocking the way. They held gaffs, harpoons, even pointed sticks. Some carried crate hooks and others chisels, and iron levers.

"You see," cried the blond girl, delightedly, "my bondage is short!"

"Citizens of Kassau!" called out Ivar Forkbeard cheerily. "Greetings from Ivar Forkbeard!"

The men looked at him, tense, hunched over, weapons ready, angry.

Forkbeard then, grinning, slung his ax over his left shoulder, dropping it into the broad leather loop by which it may be carried, its head behind his head and to the left. This loop is fixed in a broad leather belt worn from the left shoulder to the right hip, fastened there by a hook, that the weight of the ax will not turn the belt, which fits into a ring in the master belt. All men of Torvaldsland, incidentally, even if otherwise unarmed, carry a knife at their master belt. The sword, when carried, and it often is, is commonly supported

50

in its own belt, looped over the left shoulder, which is, it might be mentioned, the common Gorean practice. It can also, of course, be hung, by its sheath and sheath straps, from the master belt, which is quite adequate, being a stout, heavy belt, to hold it. It is called the master belt, doubtless, to distinguish it from the ax belt and the sword belt, and because it is, almost always, worn. A pouch, of course, and other accouterments may hang, too, from it. Gorean garments, generally, do not contain pockets. Some say the master belt gets its name because it is used sometimes in the disciplining of bond-maids. This seems to be a doubtful origin for the name. It is true, however, questions of the origin of the name aside, that bond-maids, stripped, are often taught obedience under its lash.

Ivar Forkbeard reached out his hands and took from one of his men the bowl of coins which the poor had brought as their pitiful offerings to the temple of Kassau.

Then, smiling, by handfuls he hurled the coins to the right and to the left.

Tense, the men watched him. One of those coins, of small denomination though they might be, was a day's wages on the docks of Kassau.

More coins, in handfuls, showered to the street, to the sides of the men.

"Fight!" screamed the blond girl. "Fight!"

One of the men, suddenly, reached down and snatched one.

Then, with a great, sweeping gesture, Ivar Forkbeard emptied the bowl of coins, scattering them in a shower of copper and iron over the men.

Two more men reached down to snatch a coin.

"Fight!" screamed the blond girl. "Fight!"

The first man, scrabbling in the dirt, picked up another coin, and then another.

Then the second and third man found, each, another coin.

Then the others, agonized, unable longer to resist, scurried to the left and right, their weapons discarded, and fell to their knees snatching coins.

"Cowards! Sleen!" wept the blond girl. Then she cried out in misery, half choked by the coffle loop on her throat, as she found herself hurried, fettered and burdened with the others, through the workers of Kassau.

We brushed through the scrabbling workers and saw before us the wharf, and the serpent, sleek and swift, of Ivar Forkbeard, at its moorings. Ten men had remained at the

51

ship. Eight held bows, with arrows at the string; none had dared to approach the ship; the short bow of the Gorean north, with its short, heavy arrows, heavily headed, lacks the range and power of the peasant bow of the south, that now, too, the property of the rencers of the delta, but, at short range, within a hundred and fifty yards, it can administer a considerable strike. It has, too, the advantage that it is more manageable in close quarters than the peasant bow, resembling somewhat the Tuchuk bow of layered horn in this respect. It is more useful in close combat on a ship, for example, than would be the peasant bow. Too, it is easier to fire it through a thole port, the oar withdrawn. The two other men stood ready with knives to cut the mooring ropes.

The men of Ivar Forkbeard threw their bulging cloaks, filled with gold and plate, into the ship.

Ivar Forkbeard looked back.

We heard, in the distance, a muffled crash. A wall of the temple had fallen. Then, a moment later, we heard the falling of another wall.

Smoke, in angry billows, black and fiery, climbed the sky above Kassau.

"I shall fetch a belonging or two," I said, "and be with you presently."

"Do not delay overlong," suggested Ivar Forkbeard.

"Very well," I said.

I ran to the yard of a tavern near the docks. There I unsaddled, unbridled and freed the tarn I had ridden north. "Fly!" I commanded it. It smote the air with its wings, and beat its way into the smoky skies of Kassau. I saw it turn toward the southeast. I smiled. In such a direction, I knew, lay the mountains of Thentis. In those mountains had the forebearers of the bird been bred. I thought of the webs of spiders and turtles running to the sea. How fantastic, how strange, I thought, is the blood of beasts, and I realized, too, that I was a beast, and wondered on what might be the nature of those instincts which must be my own.

I hurled a golden tarn disk to the ground, to pay for my lodging in Kassau, and the care of the bird.

I would leave the saddle.

But from it I took the saddlebags, containing some belongings, and some gold, and, too, the bedroll of fur and boskhide. From it, too, I took, in its waterproof sheath, the great bow, and its arrows, forty arrows, both flight and sheaf.

I looked after the tarn. Already it had gone, disappearing in the smoking sky above Kassau.

I did not, however, regret its departure.

I had booked better passage to Torvaldsland.

I turned and ran back to the wharf.

Eight bows were trained on me; eight arrows lay ready at the taut string.

"Do not fire," called Ivar Forkbeard to his bowmen. He grinned. "He plays Kaissa."

I threw my gear into the ship, and, bow in hand, leaped into the serpent.

"Cast off," said Ivar Forkbeard.

The two mooring ropes were flung free of the mooring cleats. They were not cut. The bowmen took their places, with their fellows, on the benches.

The serpent backed from the pier and, in the harbor, turned.

The red-and-white striped sail, snapping, unfolding, was dropped from the spar.

Between the benches, amidships, among piles of loot, their wrists fettered behind them, sat the naked bond-maids, and Aelgifu, in her torn, black velvet. They were still in throat coffle. Their ankles had been crossed, and lashed tightly with binding fiber. Aelgifu's shoes, I noted, had been removed, and her woolen hose; this was done that her ankles and feet, bared now like those of the bond-maids, might be as securely tied. No Gorean puts binding fiber over shoes or hose. It seemed Aelgifu, proud and rich, would go barefoot, like a peasant wench or a stripped bond-maid, by the will of Ivar Forkbeard, until her ransom was paid on the skerry of Einar five nights from this night, by the rune-stone of the Torvaldsmark. She alone of the women, though fettered and bound, and in coffle, did not seem unduly upset.

Ivar Forkbeard went to the bond-maids. He looked down on the blond, slender girl. The coffle loop was on her throat. She sat, with her legs drawn up, her ankles crossed and fastened with binding fiber. She looked up at him. She moved her wrists in the fetters; there was a small sound as the three-inch joining link moved in the welded rings of the fetters.

"It seems your bondage," said he, "pretty maid, will not be as short as you had hoped."

She looked down.

"There is no escape," he told her.

She sobbed.

The men of Torvaldsland began to sing at the oars.

Ivar Forkbeard reached down to the planking on the deck and picked up Aelgifu's shoes and hose, where they had been discarded when they had been removed and her ankles bound. He threw them over the side.

Then he joined me at the stern. We could see men at the docks. Some were even attempting to rig a coasting vessel, to pursue the serpent. But they would not rig it.

It was pointless.

The men of Torvaldsland sang with great voices. The oars, two men to an oar, lifted and dipped. The helmsman leaned on the tiller of the great steering oar.

Behind us we could see the smoke of the burning temple. Too, it seemed, the fires had spread elsewhere in Kassau, doubtless carried by the wind.

We could now see those at the dock, and even those who had been bestirring themselves with the coasting vessel, returning to the town. We heard the ringing of the great bar which hung on its timber frame outside the temple. The town was afire. The men of Kassau left the docks, hurrying up the dirt streets, to take up their new labors.

Behind us, amidships, we heard the weeping of women, fettered bond-maids being carried north to serve harsh masters.

The smoke billowed high in the sky above Kassau. We could hear, clearly, carrying over the water, the ringing of the great bar outside the temple.

The men of Torvaldsland singing, the oars lifting and dipping, the serpent of Ivar Forkbeard took its way from the harbor of Kassau.

4

THE FORKBEARD AND I
RETURN TO·OUR GAME

Ivar Forkbeard, leaning over the side of his serpent, studied the coloring of the water. Then he reached down and
scooped up some in the palm of his hand, testing its temperature.

"We are one day's rowing," said he, "from the skerry of
Einar and the rune-stone of the Torvaldsmark."

"How do you know this?" I asked.

We had been out of sight of land for two days, and, the
night preceding, had been, with shortened sail, swept eastward by high winds.

"There is plankton here," said Ivar, "that of the banks
south of the skerry of Einar, and the temperature of· the
water tells me that we are now in the stream of Torvald,
which moves eastward to the coast and then north."

The stream of Torvald is a current, as a broad river in
the sea, pasangs wide, whose temperature is greater than
that of the surrounding water. Without it, much of Torvaldsland, bleak as it is, would be only a frozen waste. Torvaldsland is a cruel, harsh, rocky land. It contains many
cliffs, inlets and mountains. Its arable soil is thin, and found
in patches. The size of the average farm is very small. Good
soil is rare and highly prized. Communication between farms
is often by sea, in small boats. Without the stream of Torvald it would probably be impossible to raise cereal crops
in sufficient quantity to feed even its relatively sparse population. There is often not enough food under any conditions,
particularly in northern Torvaldsland, and famine is not unknown. In such cases men feed on bark, and lichens and
seaweed. It is not strange that the young men of Torvaldsland often look to the sea, and beyond it, for their fortunes.

The stream of Torvald is regarded by the men of Torvalds-land as a gift of Thor, bestowed upon Torvald, legendary founder and hero of the land, in exchange for a ring of gold.

Ivar Forkbeard went to the mast. Before it sat Aelgifu. She was chained to it by the neck. Her wrists, in the black, iron fetters of the north, were now fastened before her body, that she could feed herself. There was salt in her hair. She still wore her black velvet but now it was stained with sea water, and salt, and was discolored, and stiff, and creased. She was barefoot.

"Tomorrow night," said Ivar Forkbeard to her, "I shall have your ransom money."

She did not deign to speak to him, but looked away. Like the bond-maids, she had been fed only on cold Sa-Tarna porridge and scraps of dried parsit fish.

The men of Torvaldsland sometimes guide their vessels by noting the direction of the waves, breaking against the prow, these correlated with prevailing winds. Sometimes they use the shadows of the gunwales, falling across the thwarts, judging their angles. The sun, too, of course, is used, and, at night, the stars give them suitable compass, even in the open sea.

It is a matter of their tradition not to rely on the needle compass, as is done in the south. The Gorean compass points always to the Sardar, the home of Priest-Kings.

The men of Torvaldsland do not use it. They do not need it.

The sextant, however, correlated with sun and stars is not unknown to them. It is commonly relied on, however, only in unfamiliar waters.

Even fog banks, and the feeding grounds of whales, and ice floes, in given seasons, in their own waters, give the men of Torvaldsland information as to their whereabouts, they utilizing such things as easily, as unconsciously, as a peasant might a mountain, or a hunter a river.

The ships of the men of Torvaldsland are swift. In a day, a full Gorean day of twenty Ahn, with a fair wind they can cover from two hundred to two hundred and fifty pasangs.

I studied the board before me.

It was set on a square chest. It was a board made for play at sea, and such boards are common with the men of Torvaldsland. In the center of each square was a tiny peg. The pieces, correspondingly, are drilled to match the pegs, and fit over them. This keeps them steady in the movements at sea. The board was of red and yellow squares. The Kaissa of the men of Torvaldsland is quite similar to that of the south, though certain of the pieces differ. There is, for example, not a Ubar but a Jarl, as the most powerful piece. Moreover, there is no Ubara. Instead, there is a piece called the Jarl's Woman, which is quite powerful, more so than the southern Ubara. Instead of Tarnsmen, there are two pieces called the Axes. The board has no Initiates, but there are corresponding pieces called Rune-Priests. Similarly there are no Scribes, but a piece, which moves identically, called the Singer. I thought that Andreas of Tor, a friend, of the caste of Singers, might have been pleased to learn that his caste was represented, and honored, on the boards of the north. The Spearmen moved identically with the southern Spearmen. It did not take me much time to adapt to the Kaissa of Torvaldsland, for it is quite similar to the Kaissa of the south. On the other hand, feeling my way on the board, I had lost the first two games to the Forkbeard. Interestingly, he had been eager to familiarize me with the game, and was abundant in his explanations and advice. Clearly, he wished me to play him at my full efficiency, without handicap, as soon as possible. I had beaten him the third game, and he had then, delighted, ceased in his explanations and advice and, together, the board between us, each in our way a warrior, we had played Kaissa.

The Forkbeard's game was much more varied, and tactical, than was that of, say, Marlenus of Ar, much more devious, and it was far removed from the careful, conservative, positional play of a man such as Mintar, of the caste of Merchants. The Forkbeard made great use of diversions and feints, and double strategies, in which an attack is double edged, being in effect two attacks, an open one and a concealed one, either of which, depending on a misplay by the opponent, may be forced through, the concealed attack requiring usually only an extra move to make it effective, a move which, ideally, threatened or pinned an opponent's piece, giving him the option of surrendering it or facing a devastating attack, he then a move behind. In the beginning I had played Forkbeard positionally, learning his game. When I felt I knew him better, I played him more openly. His wiliest tricks, of course, I knew, he would seldom use, saving them for games of greater import, or perhaps for players of Torvaldsland. Among them, even more than in the south, Kaissa is a passion. In the long winters of Torvaldsland, when the snow, the darkness, the ice and wintry winds are upon the land, when the frost breaks open the

rocks, groaning, at night, when the serpents hide in their
roofed sheds, many hours, under swinging soapstone lamps,
burning the oil of sea sleen, are given to Kaissa. At such
times, even the bond-maids, rolling and restless, naked, in
the furs of their masters, their ankles chained to a nearby
ring, must wait.

"It is your move," said Forkbeard.

"I have moved," I told him. "I have thrown the ax to Jarl
six."

"Ah!" laughed the Forkbeard. He then sat down and
looked again at the board. He could not now, with impunity, place his Jarl at Ax four.

The sun, for Torvaldsland, was hot. In the chronology of
Port Kar, it was early in Year 3 of the Sovereignty of the
Council of Captains. In the chronology of Ar, which serves,
generally, to standardize chronology on Gor, it was 10,122
C.A., or Contasta Ar, from the founding of Ar. The battle
of the 25th of Se'Kara had taken place in 10,120 C.A. In
that same year, in its spring, in Port Kar, the Council of
Captains had assumed its sovereignty, thus initiating Year 1
of its reign. Most Gorean cities use the Spring Equinox as
the date of the New Year. Turia, however, uses the Summer
Solstice. The Spring Equinox, incidentally, is also used for
the New Year by the Rune-Priests of the North, who keep
the calendars of Torvaldsland. They number years from the
time of Thor's gift of the stream of Torvald to Torvald,
legendary hero and founder of the northern fatherlands. In
the calendars of the Rune-Priests the year was 1,006.

Forkbeard and I sat in the shade, under a tented awning
of sewn boskhides, some thirty-five feet in length. It begins
aft of the mast, which is set forward. It rests on four poles,
with two long, narrow poles, fixed in sockets, mounted in
tandem fashion, serving as a single ridge pole. These poles
can also be used in pushing off, and thwarting collisions on
rocks. The bottom edges of the tented awning are stretched
taut and tied to cleats in the gunwales. There is about a foot
of space between the gunwales and the bottoms of the tented
awnings, permitting a view to sea on either side.

Somewhat behind us, between the benches, in the shade
of the awning, among other riches taken in the sack of the
temple of Kassau, were the bond-maids. They, loot, too,
knelt, or sat or laid among golden plate, and candlesticks
and golden hangings. Their ankles were no longer bound;
their wrists, now, those of most of them, were fettered before their bodies; about their necks, now, however, they wore

not simple binding fiber; it had been replaced the first evening out of Kassau; they wore now, knotted about their
throats, a coffle rope of the north, about a half inch in
thickness, of braided leather, cored with wire. At night they
slept with their hands fettered behind them. Some of the
girls slept, some curled on the golden hangings of the temple; some sat or knelt, heads down; of the girls, four of
them, though still held in the coffle, were no longer fettered.
They knelt, with soft cloths and polishes, cleaning and rubbing to a high shine, which must please the Forkbeard, the
golden trove of the looted temple of Kassau.

The men of Forkbeard, their oars inboard, the ship under
sail, amused themselves as they would. Some slept on the
benches or between them, some under the awning and some
not, or on the exposed, elevated stem deck. Here and there
some sat in twos or threes, talking. Two, like Forkbeard and
myself, gave themselves to Kaissa. Two others, elsewhere,
played Stones, a guessing game. The giant, he who might
have been nearly eight feet in height, and had in the temple
wrought such furious slaughter, sat now, almost somnolently,
on a rowing bench, sharpening, with slow, deliberate movements, with a circular, flat whetstone, the blade of his great
ax. Three other men of the Forkbeard attended to fishing,
two with a net, sweeping it along the side of the serpent, for
parsit fish, and the third, near the stem, with a hook and
line, baited with vulo liver, for the white-bellied grunt, a
large game fish which haunts the plankton banks to feed on
parsit fish. Only two of the Forkbeard's men did not rest,
he at the helm, bare-headed, looking to sea, and the fellow
at the height of the mast, on lookout. The helmsman studies
the sky and the waters ahead of the serpent; beneath clouds
there is commonly wind; and he avoids, moving a point
or more to port or starboard, areas where there is little wave
activity, for they betoken spots in which the serpent might,
for a time, find itself becalmed. The lookout stood upon a
broad, flat wooden ring, bound in leather, covered with the
fur of sea sleen, which fits over the mast. It has a diameter of
about thirty inches. It sets near the top of the mast, enabling
the man to see over the sail, as well as to other points. He,
standing on this ring, fastens himself by the waist to the mast
by looping and buckling a heavy belt about it, and through
his master belt. Usually, too, he keeps one hand on or about
the mast. The wooden ring is reached by climbing a knotted
rope. The mast is not high, only about thirty-five feet Gorean,
but it permits a scanning of the horizon to some ten pasangs.

Forkbeard put his First Singer to his own Ax four, threatening my Ax. I covered my piece with my own First Singer, moving it to my own Ax five. He exchanged, taking my Ax at Jarl six, and I his First Singer with my First Singer. I now had a Singer on a central square, but he had freed his Ax four, on which he might now situate the Jarl for an attack on the Jarl's Woman's Ax's file.

The tempo, at this point, was mine. He had played to open position; I had played to direct position.

The Ax is a valuable piece, of course, but particularly in the early and middle game, when the board is more crowded; in the end game when the board is freer, it seems to me the Singer is often of greater power, because of the greater number of squares it can control. Scholars weight the pieces equally, at three points in adjudications, but I would weight the Ax four points in the early and middle game, and the Singer two, and reverse these weights in the end game.

Both pieces are, however, quite valuable. And I am fond of the Ax.

"You should not have surrendered your Ax," said Forkbeard.

"In not doing so," I said, "I would have lost the tempo, and position. Too, the Ax is regarded as less valuable in the end game."

"You play the Ax well," said Forkbeard. "What is true for many men may not be true for you. The weapons you use best perhaps you should retain."

I thought on what he had said. Kaissa is not played by mechanical puppets, but, deeply and subtly, by men, idiosyncratic men, with individual strengths and weaknesses. I recalled I had, many times, late in the game, regretted the surrender of the Ax, or its equivalent in the south, the Tarnsman, when I had simply, as I thought rationally, moved in accordance with what were reputed to be the principles of sound strategy. I knew, of course, that game context was a decisive matter in such considerations but only now, playing Forkbeard, did I suspect that there was another context involved, that of the inclinations, capacities and dispositions of the individual player. Too, it seemed to me that the Ax, or Tarnsman, might be a valuable piece in the end game, where it is seldom found. People would be less used to defending against it in the end game; its capacity to surprise, and to be used unexpectedly, might be genuinely profitable at such a time in the game. I felt a surge of power.

Then I noted, uneasily, the Forkbeard moving his Jarl to the now freed Ax four.

The men with the net drew it up. It it, twisting and flopping, silverish, striped with brown, squirmed more than a stone of parsit fish. They threw the net to the planking and, with their knives, began to slice the heads and tails from the fish.

"Gorm," said the Forkbeard. "Free the first bond-maid on the coffle. The lazy girl has rested too long. and send her to me with a bailing scoop."

Gorm was bare-chested and barefoot. He wore trousers of the fur of sea sleen. About his neck was a golden chain and pendant, doubtless taken once from a free woman of the south.

As he approached the bond-maids they shrank back from him, fearing him, as would any bond-maid one of the men of Torvaldsland. I looked upon the eyes of the first girl on the coffle, who was the slender, blondish girl, who had worn the red vest and jacket. I recalled how disappointed she had been in the men of Torvaldsland, when, heads hanging, they had accompanied the Forkbeard to the temple at Kassau. She had then, with amusement, regarded them with contempt. But it was neither amusement nor contempt which shone in her eyes now as she, shrinking back from him, looked upon Gorm. She now saw the men of Torvaldsland in their mightiness, in their freedom, and strength and power, and she, a stripped, fettered bond-maid, coffled, feared them. She knew that she belonged to them, such fierce and mighty beasts, and that she, and her beauty, lay at their mercy, that she, and her beauty, were theirs to do with as they pleased. Roughly Gorm unknotted the coffle rope from her neck. He then gestured that she, kneeling, should lift her fettered wrists to him; she did so; he, with a key from his belt, opened the fetters which held her; he thrust them in his belt; he then pulled her by the arm roughly to her feet and thrust her toward the Forkbeard. She stumbled across the loose deck planking and stood, hair before her face, before us. She thrust her hair back with her right hand, and stood well. A bailing scoop was thrust into her hands. It has four sides. It is made of wood. It is about six inches in width. There is a diagonally set board in its bottom, and the back and two sides are straight. It has a straight, but rounded handle, carved smaller at the two ends, one where it adjoins the scoop, the other in back of the grip.

Gorm moved aside eight narrow planks from the loose

decking. Below, some two inches deep, about a foot below the deck planking, about two inches over the keel beam, black and briny, shifted the bilge water. There was not much water in the bilge, and I was surprised. For a clinker-built ship, the serpent of Ivar Forkbeard was extraordinarily tight. The ship, actually, had not needed to be bailed at all. Indeed, it had not been bailed since Kassau. The average ship of Torvaldsland is, by custom, bailed once a day, even if the bilge water does not necessitate it. A ship which must, of necessity, be bailed three times in two days is regarded as unseaworthy. Many such ships, however, are sailed by the men of Torvaldsland, particularly late in the season, when the ship is less tight from months of the sea's buffeting. In the spring, of course, before the ships are brought from the sheds on rollers to the sea, they are completely recalked and tarred.

"Bail," said the Forkbeard.

The girl went to the opened planking and fell to her knees beside it, the wooden scoop in her hands.

"Return to me," said the Forkbeard, harshly.

Frightened the girl did so.

"Now turn about," said he, "and walk there as a bond-maid."

Her face went white.

Then she turned and walked to the opened planking as a bond-maid.

The other bond-maids gasped. The men watching her hooted with pleasure. I grinned. I wanted her. "Bond-maid!" scorned Aelgifu, from where she was fettered and chained to the mast. I gathered that these two, in Kassau, had been rival beauties.

Then, sobbing, the blondish girl, who had been forced to walk as a bond-maid, fell to her knees beside the opened planking. Once she vomited over the side. But, on the whole, she did well.

Once the Forkbeard went to her and taught her to check the scoop, with her left hand, for snails, that they not be thrown overboard.

Returning to me he held one of the snails, whose shell he crushed between his fingers, and sucked out the animal, chewing and swallowing it. He then threw the shell fragments overboard.

"They are edible," he said. "And we use them for fish bait."

We then returned to our game.

Once the blond girl cried out, the scoop in her hand. "Look!" she cried, pointing over the port gunwale.

A hundred yards away, rolling and sporting, were a family of whales, a male, two females, and four calves.

Then she returned to her bailing.

"Your hall is taken," said the Forkbeard. His Jarl had moved decisively.

The taking of the hall, in the Kaissa of the North, is equivalent to the capture of the Home Stone in the south.

"You should not have surrendered your ax," said the Forkbeard.

"It seems not," I said. The end game had not even been reached. The hall had been taken in the middle game. I would think more carefully before I would surrender the ax in the future.

"I am finished," said the slender girl, returning to where we sat, and kneeling on the deck.

She had performed her first task for her master, the Forkbeard, drying, as it is said, the belly of his serpent. It had been the first of her labors, set to her by her master in her bondage.

"Give Gorm back the scoop," said the Forkbeard, "and then carry water to my men."

"Yes," she said.

The Forkbeard looked at her.

"Yes," she said "—my Jarl." To the bond-maid the meanest of the free men of the North is her jarl.

We heard Aelgifu laugh from the mast.

The blond-haired girl rose to her feet and surrendered the scoop to Gorm, who put it away, and then closed the deck planking. She then went to one of the large, wooden, covered water buckets, roped to the deck, and in it submerged a water-skin. I heard the bubbling as the skin filled.

The men of Torvaldsland had not sought the whales. They had meat enough. They had barely taken notice of them.

It was now late in the afternoon.

I noted the blondish girl, the water bag now, wet and heavy, over her shoulder, going to the men of the Forkbeard, to offer them drink.

She was quite beautiful.

The men who had fished with the net had now cleaned the catch of parsit fish, and chopped the cleaned, boned, silverish bodies into pieces, a quarter inch in width.

Another of the bond-maids was then freed to mix the

63

bond-maid gruel, mixing fresh water with Sa-Tarna meal, and then stirring in the raw fish.

"Let us have another game," said the Forkbeard.

I set up the pieces.

He went to Aelgifu, who sat before the mast, her wrists fettered before her, her neck chained to the mast.

He lifted her black, velvet dress up a little, revealing her ankle. She shrank back against the mast.

"Tomorrow night," he said, "I will have your ransom money."

"Yes," she said.

With his two large hands, he held her right ankle. She could not draw it away.

"I am free," she whispered.

Holding her ankle with his left hand he, with the fingers of his right hand, caressed, gently, her instep. She shuddered.

"I am free," she said. "Free!"

"Would you not, my large-breasted beauty," said he, "like to spend the night with me in my bag of the skin of the sea sleen?"

"No!" she cried. "No!" Then she said, "If I am violated, he will not pay the ransom! Too he will bring with him a woman, that determination on this matter be made! Surely you wish my ransom!"

"Yes," said the Forkbeard, putting down her ankle, "I do indeed want your ransom, and I shall have it."

"Then, Beast," said she, "do not touch me!"

"I am not touching you," said he, and got to his feet.

She turned away, and would not look at him. But she said to him, "Give me a covering for the night, that I may not be wet and cold."

"Go lie with the bond-maids," said he.

"Never!" she said.

"Then stay where you are," said the Forkbeard.

She looked up at him, her hair bedraggled, her eyes flashing. "Very well," said she, "I shall endure the night cheerfully. It will be my last in your bondage!"

The girl who had prepared the bond-maid gruel had now been refettered and placed again in the coffle.

The slender blond girl, who had been giving the men water from the skin bag, was now given the work of filling small bowls from the large wooden bowl, for the bondmaids. She used a bronze ladle, the handle of which was curved like the neck and head of a lovely bird. About the handle was a closed bronze ring, loose. It formed a collar for the bird's neck. The bond-maids did not much care for their gruel, unsweetened, mudlike Sa-Tarna meal, with raw fish. They fed, however. One girl who did not care to feed was struck twice across her back by a knotted rope in the hand of Gorm. Quickly then, and well, she fed. The girls, including the slender blondish girl, emptied their bowls, even to licking them, and rubbing them with their saliva-dampened fingers, that no grain be left, lest Gorm, their keeper in the ship, should not be pleased. They looked to one another in fear, and put down their bowls, as they finished, fed bond-wenches.

"Come here, Wench," called the Forkbeard.

The slender blondish girl quickly approached him, and knelt before him on the deck.

"Feed her," said the Forkbeard, gesturing over his shoulder.

The girl rose, and went to fill one of the small bowls for Aelgifu. Soon, she brought it to her.

As she approached Aelgifu, Aelgifu called out to her, "You walk well, Thyri. You walk as a bond-maid."

The slender, blondish girl, called Thyri, though now, actually, she had no name, not having been given one by the Forkbeard, did not respond to Aelgifu's taunt.

"Kneel," said Aelgifu.

The girl knelt.

"What have you there?" asked Aelgifu.

"Gruel," said the girl.

"Taste it," said Aelgifu.

Obediently, angrily, the girl did so.

"It is bond-maid gruel, is it not?" asked Aelgifu.

"Yes," said the girl.

"Why then," asked Aelgifu, "have you brought it to me?"

The girl put her head down.

"I am free," said Aelgifu. "Take it away. It is for such as you."

The girl did not respond.

"When my ransom is paid, and I return," said Aelgifu, "there will no longer be dispute as to who is the most beautiful in Kassau."

"No," said the girl.

"But I was always the most beautiful," said Aelgifu.

The blond girl's eyes flashed.

"Take this gruel away," said Aelgifu. "It is for bond-maids such as you."

The blond girl rose to her feet and left Aelgifu. The Forkbeard looked up from his game. He reached out and took the bowl from the blond girl. He said to Gorm, "Return her to the coffle." He took the blond girl back to the coffle. He made her kneel and again snapped on her wrists the iron, single-linked fetters of the north, and then he tied her by the neck at the end of the coffle.

The Forkbeard was using the Jarl's Ax's gambit, a powerful opening.

I studied the board with care.

Ivar Forkbeard approached Aelgifu with the small bowl of gruel. He crouched down beside her.

"When your father sees you tomorrow night," said he, "you must not be weak, but rosy-cheeked and bright-eyed. What otherwise would he think of the hospitality I extend to my prisoners?"

"I will not eat the gruel of bond-maids," said Aelgifu.

"You will eat it," said the Forkbeard, "or you will be stripped and put to the oar."

She looked at him with horror.

"That will not violate you, my pretty," said the Forkbeard. In this punishment, the girl, clothed or unclothed, is bound tightly on an oar, hands behind her, her head down, toward the blade. When the oar lifts from the water she gasps for breath, only in another moment to be submerged again. A recalcitrant girl may be kept on the oar for hours. There is also, however, some danger in this, for sea sleen and the white sharks of the north occasionally attempt to tear such a girl from the oar. When food is low it is not unknown for the men of Torvaldsland to use a bond-maid, if one is available on the ship, for bait in such a manner. The least pleasing girl is always used. This practice, of course, encourages bondmaids to vie vigorously to please their masters. An Ahn on the oar is usually more than sufficient to make the coldest and proudest of females an obedient, eager-to-please bondmaid. It is regarded as second only to the five-lash Gorean slave whip, used also in the south, and what among the men of Torvaldsland is called the whip of the furs, in which the master, with his body, incontrovertibly teaches the girl her slavery.

"Open your mouth, my large-breasted beauty," said the Forkbeard.

Eyes wide, she did so. He thrust the contents of the small bowl into her mouth. Choking, the proud Aelgifu swallowed the thick gruel, that of dampened Sa-Tarna meal and raw fish, the gruel of bond-maids.

"Tomorrow night I shall have your ransom," he said.

"Tomorrow night," she cried, "I shall be free of you!"

He threw the cup back to the stern of the ship, and returned to sit down with me.

"I think I may have devised a plan," I said, "to meet the Jarl's Ax's gambit."

"Good," said the Forkbeard, studying the board.

We heard sobbing from the bond-maids. We looked and saw the slender, blondish girl weeping, her body shaken by sobs, head down.

"Be silent!" said one of the other girls. "They will beat us!"

Gorm was then at her, and struck her five times with his knotted rope.

The slender blond girl stifled her sobs. "Yes, my Jarl!" she wept.

Then she put her head down, and was silent, though her body still shook.

The Forkbeard and I returned to our game.

5

FEED HER ON THE
GRUEL OF BOND-MAIDS

It was at noon of the following day that the lookout cried out, "Serpent to starboard!"

The Forkbeard looked up from the board, swiftly. The men of Ivar Forkbeard, too, suddenly came alive. They rushed to the starboard gunwales. Still they could see nothing. "Benches!" called the Forkbeard. Swiftly his men took their places; I heard the oars slide half outboard.

"Do not disturb the arrangement of the pieces," said Ivar Forkbeard, leaving the board. He climbed halfway up the knotted rope, halfway up the mast.

I stood up. The day was cloudy. The awning had not been stretched this day. It lay rolled between the benches. I could see nothing.

The bond-maids looked about themselves, frightened. Gorm was suddenly among them. He began, one by one, fettering their hands behind their backs. When he had done this, he knelt among them, crossing their ankles, tying them, too, tightly. If there was to be battle, they would be utterly helpless, completely unable to interfere in the least way. They would await the battle's result, and their disposition; they were females. At the mast, Aelgifu stood, still chained to it by the neck, her wrists still fettered before her.

"It is the serpent of Thorgard of Scagnar," cried out Forkbeard, much pleased.

"Is he an ally?" I asked.

"No," laughed the Forkbeard, delighted, "an enemy!"

I saw the men of the Forkbeard grinning, one to the other. The huge fellow, with grayish face, who seemed generally much in lethargy, who had slaughtered with such frenzy in the temple of Kassau, slowly lifted his head. I thought I saw his nostrils flare. His mouth opened slightly, and I saw his teeth.

The Forkbeard then ordered the sail high reefed, set even to the spar.

"Keep her stern to the wind," he said. The oars slid outboard. Let free the ship will swing prow to the wind.

"We have time," said Ivar Forkbeard, "for another move or two."

"I am still attempting to break the Jarl's Ax's gambit," I said.

"Singer to Ax two is not a strong move," said the Forkbeard.

Twice yesterday, in long games, until the Torvaldsland gulls had left the sea and returned inland, I had failed to meet the gambit.

"You intend to follow it, of course," said the Forkbeard, "with Jarl to your Ax four."

"Yes," I admitted.

"Interesting," said the Forkbeard. "Let us play that variation."

It was a popular variation in the south. It is seen less frequently in the north. In the south, of course, the response is to the Ubar's Tarnsman's gambit. I could see that the Forkbeard, though expecting the variation, given the preceding four moves, was delighted when it had materialized. He had, perhaps, seldom played it.

"The serpent of Thorgard has seen us!" called the lookout, not at all dismayed.

"Excellent," said Ivar Forkbeard. "Now we will not be forced to wind the signal horns across the water."

I grinned. "Tell me about Thorgard of Scagnar," I said.

"He is an enemy," said Ivar Forkbeard, simply.

"The ships of this Thorgard," I said, "have often preyed on the shipping of Port Kar."

"The shipping of Port Kar," smiled Ivar Forkbeard, "is not uniquely distinguished in this respect."

"He is, therefore," said I, "my enemy as well as yours."

"What is your name?" had asked the Forkbeard.

"Call me Tarl," I said.

"It is a name of Torvaldsland," he said. "Are you not of Torvaldsland?"

"No," I had told him.

"Tarl what?" he had asked.

"It is enough that you call me Tarl," I said, smiling.

"Very well," said he, "but here, to distinguish you from others in the North, we must do better than that."

"How is that?" I asked.

He looked at my hair, and grinned. "We will call you Tarl Red Hair," he said.

"Very well," I said.

"Your city," he asked, "what is it?"

"You may think of me," I had said, "as one of Port Kar."

"Very well," said he, "but I think we shall not make a great deal of that, for the men of Port Kar are not overly popular in the north."

"The men of Torvaldsland," I assured him, "are not overly popular in the south."

"The men of Port Kar, however," said the Forkbeard, "are respected in the north."

"The men of Torvaldsland," I told him, "are similarly respected in the south."

Gorean enemies, if skilled, often hold one another in high regard.

"You play Kaissa well," had said Ivar Forkbeard. "Let us be friends."

"You, too, are quite skilled," I told him. Indeed, he had much bested me. I still had not fathomed the devious variations of the Jarl's Ax's gambit as played in the north. I expected, however, to solve it.

We had shaken hands over the board.

"Friend," he had said.

"Friend," I had said.

We had then tasted salt, each from the back of the wrist of the other.

"The serpent of Thorgard wheels upon us!" called the lookout cheerily.

"Shall I get the great bow from my belongings?" I asked Ivar Forkbeard.

I knew its range well exceeded that of the shorter bows of the north.

"No," said the Forkbeard.

"Eight pasangs away!" called the lookout. "The serpent hunts us!"

The Forkbeard and I played four more moves. "Fascinating," he said.

"Four pasangs away!" called the lookout.

"What shield is at his mast?" called the Forkbeard.

"The red shield," called the lookout.

"Raise no shield to our own mast," said the Forkbeard.

His men looked at him, puzzled.

"Thorgard is quite proud of his great longship," he said, "the serpent called Black Sleen."

I had heard of the ship.

"It has a much higher freeboard area than this vessel," I told Ivar Forkbeard. "It is a warship, not a raider. In any engagement you would be at a disadvantage."

The Forkbeard nodded.

"It is said, too," said I, "to be the swiftest ship in the north."

"That we will find out," said the Forkbeard.

"Two pasangs away!" called the lookout.

"It has forty benches," said Ivar Forkbeard. "Eighty oars, one hundred and sixty rowers." The benches on only one side, I recalled, are counted. "But her lines are heavy, and she is a weighty ship."

"Do you intend to engage her?" I asked.

"I would be a fool to do so," said the Forkbeard. "I have with me the loot of the temple of Kassau, and eighteen bond-maids, and lovely Aelgifu. I would have much to lose, and little to gain."

"That is true," I said.

"When I engage Thorgard of Scagnar," said Ivar Forkbeard, "I shall do so to my advantage, not his."

"One pasang!" called the lookout.

"Do not disturb the pieces," said Ivar, getting up. He said to Gorm, "Take the first bond-maid and draw her up the mast." Then he said to two others of his men, "Unbind the ankles of the other bond-maids and thrust them to the rail, where they may be seen." Then he said to the rowers on the starboard side, "When I give the signal, let us display to Thorgard of Scagnar what we can of the riches of the temple of Kassau!"

The men laughed.

"Will we not fight?" asked the giant, slowly.

Ivar Forkbeard went to him, as might have a father, and took his head in his hands, and held it against his chest. "No battle now," said he, "Rollo. Another time."

"No—battle—now?" asked the giant.

"No battle now," repeated the Forkbeard, shaking the giant's head. "Another time. Another time."

There was an agony of disappointment in the large eyes of the huge head.

"Another time!" laughed the Forkbeard, giving the great

head a shake, as though it might have been that of a pet hound or bear.

"A half pasang and slowing!" called the lookout. "She will approach astern!"

"Swing to face her amidships," laughed the Forkbeard. "Let them see what riches we carry!"

The blond, slender girl's wrists were now fettered before her body, and a rope attached to the fetters. It was thrown over the spar. Her hands were jerked over her head. Then, by her fettered wrists, she moaning, her naked body twisting against the mast, foot by foot, she was drawn to five feet below the spar. She dangled there, in pain, her body that of a stripped bond-maid, exquisite, tempting, squirming, a taunt to the blood of the men of Thorgard of Scagnar.

"That will encourage them to row their best," said Ivar Forkbeard.

Then the other bond-maids, seventeen of them, were thrust to the rail, and, steadied by the hands of rowers, stood upon it, wrists fettered behind them, in coffle.

The ship of Thorgard was now little more than a quarter of a pasang away. I could detect its captain, doubtless the great Thorgard himself, on its stern deck, above the helmsman, with a glass of the builders.

What marvelous beauties he saw, seventeen naked prizes, fettered and coffled, that might be his, could he but take them, and, dangling from the mast, perhaps the most exquisite of all, the slender, blond girl, perhaps herself worth five bond-maids of the more common sort. Aelgifu, too, of course, might be seen, chained to the mast, her wrists fettered before her. That she was clothed would indicate to Thorgard that she was free, and might bring high ransom.

"Throw the bond-maids between the benches and secure them," said Ivar, to those steadying them at the rail. Quickly the miserable bond-wenches were pulled back and flung, belly down, some lying on others, between the benches. Gorm quickly bent to them, lashing their ankles together. "Lower the wench from the spar!" called the Forkbeard. "You on the starboard side, display now the loot of Kassau's temple!"

Rowers of Ivar Forkbeard now took their place at the port side. Some waved the golden hangings of the temple over their heads, as though they might have been banners. Others, jeering across the water, lifted up plates and candlesticks. The blond, slender girl, lowered from the mast, collapsed at its foot. She was pulled to her feet by the arm and thrust running, stumbling, to Gorm. He fettered her hands behind her body, and thrust her to her belly, face down, among the other girls. He then fastened her again in the coffle and, swiftly, lashed together her ankles.

The ship of Thorgard was now only some hundred yards away.

An arrow cleft the air, passing over the gunwales.

"Throw the loot over the bond-maids," called the Forkbeard. This would provide the miserable wenches, terrified and fettered, some measure of protection from missiles, stones and darts. "The awning!" called Forkbeard. Some of the girls looked up, the slender, blond girl among them, and saw the darkness of the awning, unrolled, quickly cast over the loot. Some of them screamed, being suddenly plunged in darkness.

More arrows slipped past. One struck in the mast. Aelgifu knelt behind it, still chained to it by the neck, her head in her fettered hands. A javelin struck in the deck. A stone bounded from the rail at the top of the port gunwale, splintering it.

The ship of Thorgard, Black Sleen, was no more than some fifty yards away. I could see helmeted men at its gunwales, some five feet above the water line. The helmets of the north are commonly conical, with a nose-guard, that can slip up and down. At the neck and sides, attached by rings, usually hangs a mantle of linked chain. The helmet of Thorgard himself, however, covered his neck and the sides of his face. It was horned. Their shields, like those of Torvaldsland, are circular, and of wood. The spear points are large and heavy, of tapered, socketed bronze, some eighteen inches in length. Many, too, carried axes.

"Benches!" laughed Ivar Forkbeard. "Sail!"

In my opinion he had waited too long.

His men leaped to their benches and seized their oars. At the same time the sail, with its red and white stripes, in its full length, fell snapping from the yard.

"Stroke!" called Ivar. A javelin hissed past him.

The wind, like a hammer, took the sail.

The oars bit the water.

The prow of the serpent of Ivar Forkbeard leaped from the water and its stern went almost awash.

"Stroke!" called the Forkbeard.

I laughed with pleasure. The serpent of Ivar Forkbeard leaped toward the line of the horizon.

There was consternation on the deck of Black Sleen. I

could see Thorgard of Scagnar, in the horned helmet, bearded, crying orders.

The prow of Black Sleen, sluggishly, I thought, turned in our wake.

I saw men rushing to their benches. I saw the long oars lift, and then fall.

A javelin, and four more arrows struck the deck of Ivar's ship. Two of the arrows struck the plate of the temple of Kassau, and hung, broken, in the boskhide awning that covered the Forkbeard's loot, both that of gold and flesh, and then another javelin fell behind us, into the sea, and the bowmen returned to their benches.

For a quarter of an Ahn the Forkbeard himself held the helm of his ship.

But after a quarter of an Ahn, grinning, the Forkbeard surrendered the helm to one of his men, and came to join me amidships.

We placed the board again between us on the chest. The position of the pieces had not changed, held by the board's pegs.

"A most interesting variation," said Forkbeard, returning his attention to the board.

"It may meet the Jarl's Ax's gambit," I said.

"I think not," said Forkbeard, "but let us see."

After another quarter of an Ahn Forkbeard bade his men rest at their oars.

Far behind us Black Sleen, reputed to be the fastest ship in the north, struggled, under oars and sail, to match our pace. She could not do so. Under sail alone the serpent of Ivar Forkbeard, almost scornfully, sped from her. Soon she had become no more than a speck astern, and was then visible only to the lookout. The awning was drawn back, and rolled, and placed to one side. The bond-maids, their bodies sweaty, broken out from rash and heat, struggled to their knees, their heads back, and drank the fresh air. The litter of gold under which they had been forced to lie was kicked to one side. Gorm then unbound their fair ankles, and, taking their wrists from behind them, once more fettered them before their bodies, at their bellies. Shortly thereafter they were fed, certain of them preparing the food. Life returned to normal aboard the ship. Soon Black Sleen was visible not even to the lookout.

It was growing toward evening.

"Take course," said Ivar Forkbeard, to his helmsman, "for the skerry of Einar."

"Yes, Captain," said the helmsman.

Aelgifu laughed with joy.

It was there, at the rune-stone of the Torvaldsmark, that Ivar Forkbeard would receive her ransom.

I discovered, to my instruction, an Ahn later, that Singer to Ax two, followed by Jarl to Ax four, is insufficient to counter the Jarl's Ax's gambit, as it is played in the north.

"I did not think it would be," said Ivar Forkbeard.

"The name of the ship of Thorgard of Scagnar," I said, "is Black Sleen. What is the name of your ship, if I may know?"

"The name of my ship," said Ivar, "is the Hilda."

"Is it not unusual for a ship of the north to bear the name of a woman?" I asked.

"No," he said.

"Why is she called the Hilda?" I asked.

"That is the name of the daughter of Thorgard of Scagnar," said Ivar Forkbeard.

I looked up at him, astonished.

"The Hilda is my ship," said Ivar Forkbeard, "and the daughter of Thorgard of Scagnar will be my bond-maid."

We lay to, without lights, a pasang from the skerry of Einar.

The wrists of the bond-maids were fettered behind their backs; their ankles were tied; they wore the coffle rope of the north; and their mouths, with waddings of sleen fur, and strappings of leather, were tightly gagged.

There was silence on the ship of Ivar Forkbeard. Ivar, and four men, had taken the longboat, which is tied, keel up, on the decking of the after quarter, and made their way to the skerry. With them, her hair combed, warmed with a broth of dried bosk meat, heated in a copper kettle, over a fire on a rimmed iron plate, legged, set on another plate on the stern quarter, her hands tied behind her with simple binding fiber, had gone Aelgifu.

Gorm, who seemed second to Ivar, and I, stood at the railing near the prow on the port side of the serpent.

I could see, against the night sky, the darker shape, but low in the water, of the skerry. Too, against the sky, I could see the tall rune-stone, looking like a needle against the stars, which forms the Torvaldsmark.

Ivar had left the ship in good humor. "I shall return with Aelgifu's ransom money," he had told us.

With him, in the longboat, in a round, bronze can, with

twist lid, he had taken his scales, collapsible, of bronze and chain, with their weights. I knew that Gurt of Kassau, too, would bring his scales. I hoped that the weights matched, for if they did not, there would be trouble indeed. Gurt, I knew, if wise, would not attempt to cheat the Forkbeard. I had less confidence in the weights of the man of Torvaldsland.

"Have you a coin you wish to check?" had asked Ivar, seriously, of me.

"All right," I had said, sensing his amusement. I had drawn forth from my pouch a golden tarn.

He had placed it on the scale.

"Unfortunately," said he, "this coin is debased. It is only three-quarters weight."

"It bears the stamp," said I, "of the mints of Ar."

"I would have thought better of the mints of Ar," said he.

"If Ar were to produce debased coins," I said, "her trade would be reduced, if not ruined."

"Have you another coin?" he asked.

I put a silver Tarsk, of Tharna, on the scale.

He changed his weight.

"Debased," said he. "It is only three-quarters weight."

"Tharna, too," I said, "is apparently tampering with her coinage."

"The worst," said Ivar Forkbeard, "is likely to be the coinage of Lydius."

"I expect so," I said.

I smiled. The ransom money of Gurt of Kassau would, doubtless, be largely composed of the stamped coin of Lydius. The only mint at which gold coins were stamped within a thousand pasangs was in Lydius, at the mouth of the Laurius. Certain jarls, of course, in a sense, coined money, marking bars of iron or gold, usually small rectangular solids, with their mark. Ring money was also used, but seldom stamped with a jarl's mark. Each ring, strung on a larger ring, would be individually weighed in scales. Many transactions are also done with fragments of gold and silver, often broken from larger objects, such as cups or plates, and these must be individually weighed. Indeed, the men of the north think little of breaking apart objects which, in the south, would be highly prized for their artistic value, simply to obtain pieces of negotiable precious metal. The fine candlesticks from the temple of Kassau, for example, I expected would be chopped into bits small enough for the pans of the northern scales. Of their own art and metalwork, however, it should be mentioned that the men of the north are much more respectful. A lovely brooch, for example, wrought by a northern craftsman, would be seldom broken or mutilated.

"I have two pair of scales," admitted Ivar Forkbeard, grinning. "These are my trading scales," he said.

"Do you think Gurt of Kassau will accept your scales?" I asked.

The Forkbeard fingered the silver chain of office, looped about his neck, which he had taken from the administrator of Kassau. "Yes," he said, "I think so."

We laughed together.

But now, with Gorm, and the men of Ivar Forkbeard, I waited, in silence, on his serpent.

"Should the Forkbeard not have returned by now?" I asked.

"He is coming now," said Gorm.

I peered through the darkness. Some hundred yards away, difficult to see, was the longboat. I heard the oars, in good rhythm, lifting and dipping. The oar stroke's spacing was such that I knew them not in flight.

Then I saw the Forkbeard at the tiller.

The longboat scraped gently at the side of the serpent.

"Did you obtain the ransom money?" I asked.

"Yes," said he, lifting a heavy bag of gold in his hand.

"You were long," I said.

"It took time to weigh the gold," he said. "And there was some dispute as to the accuracy of the scales."

"Oh?" I asked.

"Yes," said the Forkbeard. "The weights of Gurt of Kassau were too light."

"I see," I said.

"Here is the gold," he said, hurling the sack to Gorm. "One hundred and twenty pieces."

"The scales of Gurt of Kassau, I see," I said, "weighed lightly indeed."

"Yes," laughed the Forkbeard. He then threw other purses to Gorm.

"What are these?" I asked.

"The purses of those who were with Gurt of Kassau," he said.

I heard a moan from the longboat, and saw something, under a fur of sea sleen, move.

The Forkbeard threw off the fur, revealing the proud Aelgifu, bound hand and foot, gagged, lying in the bottom of the boat. She still wore her black velvet. She looked up, her eyes terrified. The Forkbeard lifted her up to Gorm. "Put her in the coffle," he told him.

Aelgifu was carried to where the bond-maids, perfectly restrained, lay. The binding fiber on her wrists was removed. Her hands were fettered behind her. The coffle rope was looped about her throat, and knotted. Gorm left her ankles, like those of the bond-maids, securely bound.

I helped the Forkbeard and his men lift the longboat to the deck. It was tied down on the after quarter, keel up.

Suddenly an arrow struck the side of the ship.

"Free the serpent!" called the Forkbeard. "Benches!" The two anchor hooks, fore and aft, were raised. They resemble heavy grappling hooks. Their weight, apiece, is not great, being little more than twenty-five Gorean stone, or about one hundred Earth pounds. They are attached to the ship not by chain but by tarred rope. The men of the Forkbeard scurried to their benches. I heard the thole-port caps turned back, and the oars thrust through the wood.

I could see, from the shore, black and dark, more than a dozen small boats, containing perhaps ten or fifteen men each, moving towards us.

Two more arrows struck the ship. Others slipped past in the darkness, their passage marked by the swift whisper of the feathers and shaft.

"To sea!" called the Forkbeard. "Stroke!"

The serpent turned its prow to sea, and the oars moved down, entered the water, and pulled against it.

"Stroke!" called the Forkbeard.

The serpent slipped away.

The Forkbeard stood angrily at the rail, looking back at the small flotilla of boats, dark in the night.

He turned to his men. "Let this be a lesson to you," he called to them, "never trust the men of Kassau!"

At the oars the men struck up a rowing song.

"And what did you do with Gurt and those with him on the skerry?" I asked.

"We left them naked," said the Forkbeard. Then he looked aft, at the small boats falling behind. "It seems these days," he said, "one can trust no one."

Then he went to the bond-maids. "Remove their gags," he said.

Their gags were removed, but they dared not speak. They were bond-maids. Their bodies, bound, loot, prizes of the Forkbeard, lying in the darkness, among the glint of the gold taken in the sack of Kassau's temple, were very beautiful.

78

The Forkbeard freed Aelgifu of her gag.

"It seems," he said, "that last night was not the last night which you will spend in my bondage."

"You took ransom money!" she cried. "You took ransom!"

"I have taken more than ransom money," said he, "my large-breasted beauty."

"Why did you not free me?" she cried.

"I want you," he said. Then he looked at her. "I said only, you might remember," said he, "that I would take your ransom money. Never did I say that I would exchange you for those paltry moneys. Never did I say, my pretty one, that I would permit you, so luscious a wench as you, to escape my fetters."

She struggled, her head turned to one side, her wrists locked behind her in the black iron of the north.

Her ankles were bound. The coffle rope was on her throat. She was miserable.

"Welcome to the coffle," said he.

"I am free," she cried.

"Now," he said.

She shuddered.

"You are too pretty to ransom," he informed her, and turned away. To Gorm, he said, "Feed her on the gruel of bond-maids."

6

IVAR FORKBEARD'S
LONG HALL

There was a great cheer from the men of Ivar Forkbeard.
The serpent turned slowly between the high cliffs, and entered the inlet. Here and there, clinging to the rock, were
lichens, and small bushes, and even stunted trees. The water
below us was deep and cold.

I felt a breeze from inland, coming to meet the sea.

The oars lifted and fell.

The sail fell slack, and rustled, stirred in the gentle wind
from inland.

Men of Torvaldsland reefed it high to the spar.

The rowing song was strong and happy in the lusty throats
of the crew of the Forkbeard.

The serpent took its way between the cliffs, looming high
on each side.

Ivar Forkbeard, at the prow, lifted a great, curved bronze
horn and blew a blast. I heard it echo among the cliffs.

Amidships, crowded together, standing, facing the starboard side of the vessel, were the bond-maids and Aelgifu.
She wore still her black velvet. They were in throat coffle;
their wrists were fettered before their bodies. They looked
upon the new country, harsh, forbidding, which was to be
their home.

I heard, perhaps from a pasang away, up the inlet, between the cliffs, the winding of a horn.

Soon, I gathered, we would be at Forkbeard's landfall.

"Put her," said Forkbeard, indicating the slender, blond
girl, "at the prow."

She was quickly removed from the coffle and unfettered.
Gorm put a rope on her neck and pulled her to the prow.
There, she held by another crewman, he fastened her at the

prow. Her back was bent over it. Her wrists and ankles, drawn back, were tied at its sides. She was roped to it, too, at the belly and throat.

Again Ivar Forkbeard winded the great bronze horn. In several seconds an answering blast echoed between the cliffs. The oars lifted and dipped. The men sang.

"Hang gold about the ship!" he cried.

Candlesticks and cups were hung on strings from the prow. Plates, with iron nails, were pounded against the mast. Golden hangings were draped like banners at the gunwales.

Then the ship turned a bend between the cliffs, and, to my astonishment I saw a dock, of rough logs, covered with adzed boards, and a wide, sloping area of land, of several acres, green, though strewn with boulders, with short grass. There was a log palisade some hundred yards from the dock. High on the cliff I saw a lookout, a man with a horn. Doubtless it had been he whom we had heard. From his vantage, high on the cliff, on his belly, unseen, he would have been able to see far down the inlet. He stood now and waved the bronze horn in his hand. Forkbeard waved back to him.

I saw four small milk bosk grazing on the short grass. In the distance, above the acres, I could see mountains, snowcapped. A flock of verr, herded by a maid with a stick, turned, bleating on the sloping hillside. She shaded her eyes. She was blond; she was barefoot; she wore an ankle-length white kirtle, of white wool, sleeveless, split to her belly. About her neck I could see a dark ring.

Men were now running from the palisade and the fields down to the dock. They were bare-headed, and wore shaggy jackets. Some wore trousers of skin, others tunics of dyed wool. I saw, too, fields, fenced with rocks, in the sloping area. In them were growing, small at this season, shafts of Sa-Tarna; too, there would be peas, and beans, cabbages and onions, and patches of the golden sul, capable of surviving at this latitude. I saw small fruit trees, and hives, where honey bees were raised; and there were small sheds, here and there, with sloping roofs of boards; in some such sheds might craftsmen work; in others fish might be dried or butter made. Against one wall of the cliff was a long, low shed; in that the small bosk, and the verr, might be housed in the winter, and there, too, would be stored their feed; another shed, thick, with heavy logs, in the shadow of the cliff, would be the ice house, where ice from the mountains, brought down on sledges to the valley, would be kept, covered with chips of wood.

There were only a few bosk visible, and they were milk bosk. The sheds I saw would accomodate many more animals. I surmised, as is common in Torvaldsland, most of the cattle had been driven higher into the mountains, to graze wild during the summer, to be fetched back to the shed only in the fall, with the coming of winter.

Men in the fields wore short tunics of white wool; some carried hoes; their hair was close cropped; about their throats had been hammered bands of black iron, with a welded ring attached. They did not leave the fields; such a departure, without permission, might mean their death; they were thralls.

I saw people running down the sloping green land, toward the water. Several came from within the palisade. Among them, white kirtled, collared, excited, ran bond-maids. These, upon the arrival of their master, are permitted to greet him. The men of the north enjoy the bright eyes, the leaping bodies, the squealing, the greetings of their bond-maids. In the fields I saw an overseer, clad in scarlet, with a gesture of his hand, releasing the thralls. Then, they, too, ran down toward the water.

It would be holiday, I gathered, at the hall of Ivar Forkbeard.

The Forkbeard himself now, from a wooden keg, poured a great tankard of ale, which must have been of the measure of five gallons. Over this he then closed his fist. It was the sign of the hammer, the sign of Thor. The tankard then, with two great bronze handles, was passed from hands to hands among the rowers. The men threw back their heads and, the liquid spilling down their bodies, drank ale. It was the victory ale.

Then the Forkbeard himself drained the remains of the tankard, threw it to the foot of the mast, and then, to my astonishment, leapt from the ship, onto the moving oars. The men sang. The Forkbeard then, to the delight of those on the bank, who cheered him, as the serpent edged into the dock, addressed himself delightedly to the oar-dance of the rover of Torvaldsland. It is not actually a dance, of course, but it is an athletic feat of no little stature requiring a superb eye, fantastic balance and incredible coordination. Ivar Forkbeard, crying out, leaped from moving oar to moving oar, proceeding from the oars nearest the stem on the port side to the stern, then leaping back onto the deck at the stern quarter and leaping again on the oars this time on the starboard side, and proceeding from the oar nearest the stern to that nearest the stem, and then, lifting his arms, he leaped again into the ship, almost thrown into it as the oar lifted. He then stood on the prow, near me, sweating and grinning. I saw cups of ale, on the bank, being lifted to him. Men cheered. I heard the cries of bond-maids.

The serpent of Ivar Forkbeard, gently, slid against the rolls of leather hung at the side of the dock. Eager hands vied on the dock to grasp the mooring ropes.

The oars slid inboard; the men hung their shields at the serpent's flanks.

Men on the dock cried out with pleasure, looking on the harshly roped beauty of the slender, blondish girl, so cruelly fastened, back bent, at the prow of the Forkbeard's serpent.

"I have eighteen others!" called Ivar Forkbeard. His men, laughing, thrust the other girls forward, to the rail, forcing them to stand on the rowing benches.

"Heat the irons!" called the Forkbeard.

"They are hot!" laughed a brawny man, in leather apron, standing on the dock.

The girls shuddered. They would be branded.

"Bring the anvil to the branding log!" said the Forkbeard. They knew then they would wear collars.

"It is there!" laughed the brawny fellow, doubtless a smith.

Gorm had now unbound the slender, blond girl from the prow. He put her at the head of the coffle. Aelgifu, in her black velvet, it creased and stained, discolored, the fabric stiff and separated here and there, brought up the rear. Gorm did not refetter the slender, blond girl, though he tied her by the neck in the coffle. Further, he removed the fetters from the other girls, too, including Aelgifu. All remained, however, coffled.

The gangplank was then thrust over the rail of the serpent and struck on the heavy, adzed boards of the dock.

The slender, blond girl, the hand of Ivar Forkbeard on her arm, was thrust to the head of the gangplank. She looked down at the cheering men.

Gorm then stood beside Ivar Forkbeard. He carried, on a strap over his shoulder, a tall, dark vessel, filled with liquid.

The men on the shore laughed.

Attached to the vessel, by a light chain, was a golden cup. It had two handles.

From a spout on the vessel, grinning, Gorm filled the golden cup. The liquid swirling in the cup was black.

"Drink," said Ivar Forkbeard, thrusting the cup into the hands of the slender, blond girl, she who had, so long ago, in the temple of Kassau, worn the snood of scarlet yarn, with twisted golden wire, the red vest and skirt, the white blouse.

She held the cup. It was decorated; about its sides, cunningly wrought, was a design, bond-maids, chained. A chain design also decorated the rim, and, at five places on the cup, was the image of a slave whip, five-strapped.

She looked at the black liquid.

"Drink," said the Forkbeard.

She lifted it to her lips, and tasted it. She closed her eyes, and twisted her face.

"It is too bitter," she wept.

She felt the knife of the Forkbeard at her belly. "Drink," said he.

She threw back her head and drank down the foul brew. She began to cough and weep. The coffle rope was untied from her throat. "Send her to the branding log," said the Forkbeard. He thrust the girl down the gangplank, into the arms of the waiting men, who hurried her from the dock.

One by one, the prizes of Ivar Forkbeard, even the rich, proud Aelgifu, were forced to down the slave wine. Then they were, one by one, freed from the coffle, and hurried to the branding log.

Ivar Forkbeard then, followed by Gorm, and myself, and his men, descended the gangplank. He was much greeted. Many clasped him, and struck him on the back. And he, too, clasped many of them to himself, and shook the heads of many in his great hands.

"Was the luck good?" asked one man, with a spiral silver ring on his arm.

"Fair," admitted the Forkbeard.

"Who is this?" asked another man, indicating me. "I see his hair has not been cropped, and he does not wear the chains of a thrall."

"This is Tarl Red Hair," said the Forkbeard.

"Whose man is he?" asked the man.

"My own," I said.

"Have you no Jarl?" asked the man.

"I am my own Jarl," I said.

"Can you play with the ax?" he asked.

"Teach me the ax," I said to him.

"Your sword is too tiny," said he. "Is it used for peeling suls?"

"It moves swiftly," I said. "It bites like the serpent."

He reached out his hand to me and then, suddenly,

gripped me about the waist. Clearly it was his intention, as a joke, to hurl me into the water. He did not move me. He grunted in surprise. I took him, too, about the waist. We swayed on the adzed boards. The men moved back, to give us room.

"Ottar enjoys sport," said Ivar Forkbeard.

With a sudden wrench I threw him from his feet and hurled him from the dock into the water.

He crawled, drenched and sputtering, back to the dock. "Tomorrow," he laughed, "I will teach you the ax." We clasped hands. Ottar, in the absence of Ivar Forkbeard, kept his cattle, his properties, his farm and accounts.

"He plays excellent Kaissa," said the Forkbeard.

"I shall beat him," said Ottar.

"We shall see," I said.

A bond-maid thrust through the crowd. "Does my Jarl not remember Gunnhild?" she asked. She whimpered, and slipped to his side, holding him, lifting her lips to kiss him on the throat, beneath the beard. About her neck, riveted, was a collar of black iron, with a welded ring, to which a chain might be attached. "What of Pouting Lips?" said another girl, kneeling before him, lifting her eyes to his. Sometimes bond-maids are given descriptive names. The girl had full, sensuous lips. she was blond; she also smelled of verr; it had doubtless been she whom I had seen on the slope herding verr. "Pouting Lips has been in agony awaiting the return of her Jarl," she whimpered. The Forkbeard shook her head with his great hand. "What of Olga?" whined another wench, sweet and strapping, black-haired; "Do not forget Pretty Ankles, my Jarl," said another wench, a delicious little thing, perhaps not more than sixteen. She thrust her lips greedily to the back of his left hand, biting at the hair there.

"Away you wenches!" laughed Ottar. "The Forkbeard has new prizes, fresher meat to chew!"

Gunnhild, angrily, with two hands, jerked her kirtle to her waist, and stood straight, proudly before the Forkbeard, her breasts, which were marvelous, thrust forward. How magnificent she seemed, the heavy black iron at her throat, riveted. "None of them can please you," she said, "as well as Gunnhild!"

He seized her in his arms and raped her lips with a kiss, his hand at her body, then threw her from him to the boards of the dock.

"Prepare a feast!" he said. "Let a feast be prepared!"

"Yes, my Jarl!" she cried, and leaped to her feet, running

toward the palisade. "Yes, my Jarl!" cried the other girls, hurrying behind her, to begin the preparations for the feast.

Then the Forkbeard turned his attention to the serpent, and the disembarkment of its riches, which, on the shoulders of his men, and others, were carried, amid shouts of joy and wonder from those gathered about, to the palisade.

When this was done, I accompanied the Forkbeard to a place behind, and to one side, of a forge shed. There was a great log there, from a fallen tree. The bark had been removed from the log. It was something in the neighborhood of a yard in thickness. Against the log, kneeling, one behind the other, their right shoulders in contact with it, knelt the new bond-maids, and Aelgifu. Some men stood about, as well, and the brawny fellow, the smith. Nearby, on a large, flat stone, to keep it from sinking into the ground, was the anvil. A few feet away, glowing with heat, stood two canister braziers. In these, among the white coals, were irons. Air, by means of a small bellows, pumped by a thrall boy, in white wool, collared, hair-cropped, was forced through a tube in the bottom of each. The air above the canisters shook with heat.

To one side, tall, broad-shouldered, stood a young male thrall, in the thrall tunic of white wool, his hair cropped short, an iron collar on his throat.

"She first," said the Forkbeard, indicating the slender, blond girl.

She, moaning, was seized by a fellow and thrown on her belly over the peeled log. Two men held her upper arms; two others her upper legs. A fifth man, with a heavy, leather glove, drew forth one of the irons from the fire; the air about its tip shuddered with heat.

"Please, my Jarl," she cried, "do not mark your girl!"

At a sign from the Forkbeard, the iron was pressed deeply into her flesh, and held there, smoking for five Ihn. It was only when it was pulled away that she screamed. Her eyes had been shut, her teeth gritted. She had tried not to scream. She had dared to pit her will against the iron. But, when the iron had been pulled back, from deep within her flesh, smoking, she, her pride gone, her will shattered, had screamed with pain, long and miserably, revealing herself as only another branded girl. She, by the arm, was dragged from the log. She threw back her head, tears streaming down her face, and again screamed in pain. She looked down at her body. She was marked for identification. A hand on her arm, she was thrust, sobbing, to the anvil, beside which she was thrust to her knees.

The brand used by Forkbeard is not uncommon in the north, though there is less uniformity in Torvaldsland on these matters than in the south, where the merchant caste, with its recommendations for standardization, is more powerful. All over Gor, of course, the slave girl is a familiar commodity. The brand used by the Forkbeard, found rather frequently in the north, consisted of a half circle, with, at its right tip, adjoining it, a steep, diagonal line. The half circle is about an inch and a quarter in width, and the diagonal line about an inch and a quarter in height. The brand is, like many, symbolic. In the north, the bond-maid is sometimes referred to as a woman whose belly lies beneath the sword.

"Look up at me," said the smith.

The slender, blond girl, tears in her eyes, looked up at him.

He opened the hinged collar of black iron, about a half inch in height. He put it about her throat. It also contained a welded ring, suitable for the attachment of a chain.

"Put your head beside the anvil," he said.

He took her hair and threw it forward, and thrust her neck against the left side of the anvil. Over the anvil lay the joining ends of the two pieces of the collar. The inside of the collar was separated by a quarter of an inch from her neck. I saw the fine hairs on the back of her neck. On one part of the collar are two, small, flat, thick rings. On the other is a single such ring. These rings, when the wings of the collar are joined, are aligned, those on one wing on top and bottom, that on the other in the center. They fit closely together, one on top of the other. The holes in each, about three-eighths of an inch in diameter, too, of course, are perfectly aligned.

The smith, with his thumb, forcibly, pushed a metal rivet through the three holes. The rivet fit snugly.

"Do not move your head, Bond-maid," said the smith.

Then, with great blows of the iron hammer, he riveted the iron collar about her throat.

A man then pulled her by the hair from the anvil and threw her to one side. She lay there weeping, a naked bond-maid, marked and collared.

"Next," called out the Forkbeard.

Weeping, another girl was flung over the branding log.

In the end only Aelgifu was left.

The Forkbeard, with the heel of his boot on the ground, drew a bond-maid circle.

She looked at it.

Then, to the laughter of the men, her head high, lifting her skirt, she stepped to the circle, and stood, facing him, within it.

"Remove your clothing, my pretty one," said Ivar Forkbeard. She reached behind the back of her neck and unbuttoned the dress of black velvet, and then drew it over her head. She stood then before us in a chemise of fine silk. This, too, she drew over her head, and threw to the ground.

She then stood there, statuesque, proudly.

Ivar licked his lips. Several of his men cried out with pleasure, others struck their left shoulders with the palms of their right hand. Two, who were armed with shield and spear, smote the spear blade on the wooden shield.

"Will she not be a tasty morsel indeed?" Ivar asked his men.

The men cheered, and struck their shoulders, and again, the spear blades smote upon the shields.

Fear entered the eyes of the proud Aelgifu.

"Run to the iron, wench," suddenly commanded Ivar Forkbeard, harshly. Moaning, Aelgifu ran from the circle to the branding log, and was thrown over it, belly down. In a moment the iron had bitten her. Her scream brought laughter from some of the other bond-maids. She was then thrust to the anvil and thrown to her knees beside it.

I saw the young, broad-shouldered thrall, who had been standing to one side, go to the slender blond girl. He lifted her to her feet.

"I see, Thyri," said he, "that you are now a woman whose belly lies beneath the sword."

"Wulfstan," she said.

"I am called Tarsk here," he said.

He fingered the collar on her throat. "The proud Thyri," he said, "a bond-maid!" He smiled. "You refused my suit," said he. "Do you recall?"

She said nothing.

"You were too good for me," he said. He laughed. "Now," said he, "doubtless you would crawl on your belly to any man who would free you."

She looked at him angrily.

"Would you not?" he asked.

"Yes, Wulfstan," she said. "I would!"

He held her by the collar. "But you will not be freed,

Thyri," he said. "You will continue to wear this. You are a bond-maid."

She looked down.

"It pleases me," said he, "to see you here." He stepped back from her. She lifted her eyes, angrily, to look upon him. "A brand," said he, "improves a woman. It improves you, Thyri. Your collar, too, the iron on your neck, it against the softness of your body, is quite becoming."

"Thank you, Wulfstan," said she.

"Women," said he, "belong in collars."

Her eyes flashed.

"Sometimes," said he, "to discipline a bond-maid, she is hurled naked among the thralls." He smiled. "Do not fear. Should this be done to you I, in my turn, shall use you well, Bond-maid. Quite well."

She shrank back from him.

The last blows of the smith's hammer rang out and Aelgifu, by the hair, was pulled from the anvil, wearing a collar of black iron.

"Hurry, Bond-maids!" cried Ivar Forkbeard. "Hurry, lazy girls! There is a feast to be prepared!"

The bond-maids, Thyri and Aelgifu among them, fled, like a frightened herd of tabuk, across the short, turflike green grass, to the gate of the palisade, to be put to work.

Ivar Forkbeard roared with laughter, his head back. On his lap, naked, cuddling, sat she who had been Aelgifu, her arms about his neck, her lips to the side of his head; her name had now been changed; the new name of the daughter of Gurt, Administrator of Kassau, was Pudding. On his other side, stripped, her collar of black iron at her throat, her arms about his waist, rubbing herself against his belt, was the bond-maid Gunnhild.

I held the large drinking horn of the north. "There is no way for this to stand upright," I said to him, puzzled.

He threw back his head again, and roared once more with laughter.

"If you cannot drain it," he said, "give it to another!"

I threw back my head and drained the horn.

"Splendid!" cried the Forkbeard.

I handed the horn to Thyri, who, in her collar, naked, between two of the benches, knelt at my feet.

"Yes, Jarl," said she, and ran to fill it, from the great vat. How marvelously beautiful is a naked, collared woman.

"Your hall," said I to the Forkbeard, "is scarcely what I had expected."

I had learned, much to my instruction, that my conception of the northern halls left much to be desired. Indeed, the true hall, lofty, high-beamed, built of logs and boards, with its benches and high-seat pillars, its carvings and hangings, its long fires, its suspended kettles, was actually quite rare, and, generally, only the richest of the Jarls possessed such. The hall of Ivar Forkbeard, I learned, to my surprise, was of a type much more common. Upon reflection, however, it seemed to me not so strange that this should be so, in a bleak country, one in which many of the trees, too, would be stunted and wind-twisted. In Torvaldsland, fine timber is at a premium. Too, what fine lumber there is, is often marked and hoarded for the use of shipwrights. If a man of Torvaldsland must choose between his hall and his ship, it is the ship which, invariably, wins his choice. Furthermore, of course, were it not for goods won by his ship or ships, it would be unlikely that he would have the means to build a hall and house within it his men.

"Here, Jarl," said Thyri, again handing me the horn. It was filled with the mead of Torvaldsland, brewed from fermented honey, thick and sweet.

The hall of Ivar Forkbeard was a longhouse. It was about one hundred and twenty feet Gorean in length. Its walls, formed of turf and stone, were curved and thick, some eight feet or more in thickness. It is oriented north and south. This reduces its exposure to the north wind, which is particularly important in the Torvaldsland winter. A fire, in a rounded pit, was in its center. It consisted, for the most part, of a single, long room, which served for living, and eating and sleeping. At one end was a cooking compartment, separated from the rest of the house by a partition of wood. The roof was about six feet in height, which meant that most of those within, if male, were forced to bend over as they moved about. The long room, besides being low, is dark. Too, there is usually lingering smoke in it. Ventilation is supplied, as it is generally in Torvaldsland, by narrow holes in the roof. The center of the hall, down its length, is dug out about a foot below the ground level. In the long center are set the tables and benches. Also, in the center, down its length are two long rows of posts, each post separated from the next by about seven feet, which support the roof. At the edges of the hall, at ground level, is a dirt floor, on which furs are spread. Stones mark sections off into sleeping quarters. Thus, in a sense, the hall proper is about a foot below ground level, and the sleeping level, on each side, is at the ground level, where the walls begin. The sleeping levels, which also can accomodate a man's gear, though some keep it at the foot of the level, are about eight feet in length. The hall proper, the center of the hall, is about twelve feet in width.

The two bond-maids, stripped, too, like the others, for the feast, Pretty Ankles and Pouting Lips, struggled down the length of the smoky, dark hall, a spitted, roasted tarsk on their shoulders. They were slapped by the men, hurrying them along. They laughed with pleasure. Their shoulders were protected from the heat of the metal spit by rolls of leather. The roasted tarsk was flung before us on the table. With his belt knife, thrusting Pudding and Gunnhild back, Ivar Forkbeard addressed himself to the cutting of the meat.

He threw pieces down the length of the table.

I heard men laughing. Too, from the darkness behind me, and more than forty feet away, on the raised level, I heard the screams of a raped bond-maid. She was one of the new girls. I had seen her being dragged by the hair to the raised platform. Her screams were screams of pleasure.

"Well," said Ivar Forkbeard to me, "I am an outlaw."

"I did not know that," I said.

"That is one reason," said he, "that my hall is not of wood."

"I see," I said. "But you have at least a palisade," I said.

He threw me a piece of meat.

He cut two small pieces, and thrust them in the mouths of Pudding and Gunnhild.

They ate obediently, his pets.

"The palisade," he said, "is low, and the cracks are filled with daub."

I tore a piece of meat from what Ivar had thrown me and held it to Thyri. She smiled at me. She was trying to learn how to please a man. "Thank you, my Jarl," she said. She took the meat, delicately, in her teeth. I grinned, and she looked down, frightened. She knew that soon she might be taught, truly, how to please men.

"You are rich," I said, "and have many men. Surely you could have a hall of wood, if you wished."

"Why did you come to Torvaldsland?" suddenly asked Ivar Forkbeard.

"On a work of vengeance," I told him. "I hunt one of the Kurii."

91

"They are dangerous," said Ivar Forkbeard.

I shrugged.

"One has struck here," said Ottar, suddenly.

Ivar looked at him.

"Last month," said Ottar, "a verr was taken."

I knew then that it could not be the one of the Kurii I sought.

"We hunted him, but failed to find him," said Ottar.

"Doubtless he has left the district," said Ivar.

"Do the beasts often bother you?" I asked.

"No," said Ivar. "They seldom hunt this far to the south."

"They are rational," I told him. "They have a language."

"That is known to me," said Ivar.

I did not tell Ivar that those he knew as Kurii, or the beasts, were actually specimens of an alien race, that they, or those in their ships, were locked in war with Priest-Kings for the domination of two worlds, Gor and the Earth. In these battles, unknown to most men, even of Gor, from time to time, ships of the Kurii had been shattered and fallen to the surface. It was the practice of Priest-Kings to destroy the wrecks of such ships but, usually, at least, they did not attempt to hunt and exterminate survivors. If the marooned Kurii abided by the weapon and technology laws of Priest-Kings, they, like men, another life form, were permitted to survive. The Kurii I knew were beasts of fierce, terrible instincts, who regarded humans, and other beasts, as food. Blood, as to the shark, was an agitant to their systems. They were extremely powerful, and highly intelligent, though their intellectual capacities, like those of humans, were far below those of Priest-Kings. Fond of killing, and technologically advanced, they were, in their way, worthy adversaries of Priest-Kings. Most lived in ships, the steel wolves of space, their instincts bridled, to some extent, by Ship Loyalty, Ship Law. It was thought that their own world had been destroyed. This seemed plausible, when one considered their ferocity and greed, and what might be its implementation in virtue of an advanced technology. Their own world destroyed, the Kurii now wished another.

The Kurii, of course, with which the men of Torvaldsland might have had dealings, might have been removed by as much as generations from the Kurii of the ships. It was regarded as one of the great dangers of the war, however, that the Kurii of the ships might make contact with, and utilize, the Kurii of Gor in their schemes.

Men and the Kurii, where they met, which was usually

only in the north, regarded one another as mortal enemies. The Kurii not unoften fed on men, and men, of course, in consequence, attempted to hunt and slay, when they could, the beasts. Usually, however, because of the power and ferocity of the beasts, men would hunt them only to the borders of their own districts, particularly if only the loss of a bosk or thrall was involved. It was usually regarded as quite sufficient, even by the men of Torvaldsland, to drive one of the beasts out of their own district. They were especially pleased when they had managed to harry one into the district of an enemy.

"How will you know the one of the Kurii whom you seek?" asked Ivar.

"I think," I said, "he will know me."

"You are a brave, or foolish, man," said Ivar.

I drank more of the mead. I ate, too, of the roast tarsk.

"You are of the south," said Ivar. "I have a proposition, a scheme."

"What is that?" I asked.

The bond-maid, Olga, laughing and kicking, thrown helplessly over the shoulder of an oarsman, was carried past.

I saw several of the bond-maids in the arms of Ivar's men. Among them, too, some trying to resist, were the new girls. One, who had irritated an oarsman, her hands held, was beaten, crying out, with his belt. Released, she began to kiss him, weeping, trying to please him. Men laughed. Another of the new girls was thrown over one of the benches; she lay on her back; her head was down, her dark hair, long, wild, was in the dirt and reeds, strewn on the floor of the hall; her head twisted from side to side; her eyes were closed; her lips were parted; I saw her teeth. "Do not stop, my Jarl," she begged. "Your bond-maid begs you not to stop!"

"I am an outlaw," said Ivar. "In a duel I killed Finn Broadbelt."

"It was in a duel," I said.

"Finn Broadbelt was the cousin of Jarl Svein Blue Tooth."

"Ah," I said. Svein Blue Tooth was the high jarl of Torvaldsland, in the sense that he was generally regarded as the most powerful. In his hall, it was said he fed a thousand men. Beyond this his heralds could carry the war arrow, it was said, to ten thousand farms. Ten ships he had at his own wharves, and, it was said, he could summon a hundred more.

"He is your Jarl?" I asked.

"He was my Jarl," said Ivar Forkbeard.

"The wergild must be high," I speculated.

93

The Forkbeard looked at me, and grinned. "It was set so high," said he, "out of the reach of custom and law, against the protests of the rune-priests and his own men, that none, in his belief, could pay it."

"And thus," said I, "that your outlawry would remain in effect until you were apprehended or slain?"

"He hoped to drive me from Torvaldsland," said Ivar.

"He has not succeeded in doing so," I said.

Ivar grinned. "He does not know where I am," said he. "If he did, a hundred ships might enter the inlet."

"How much," asked I, "is the wergild?"

"A hundred stone of gold," said Ivar.

"You have taken that much, or more," said I, "in the sack of Kassau's temple."

"And the weight of a full-grown man in the sapphires of Schendi," said the Forkbeard.

I said nothing.

"Are you not surprised?" asked Ivar.

"It seems a preposterous demand," I admitted, smiling.

"You know, however, what I did in the south?" asked Ivar.

"It is well known," I said, "that you freed Chenbar, the Sea Sleen, Ubar of Tyros, from the chains of a dungeon of Port Kar, your fee being his weight in the sapphires of Schendi."

I did not mention to the Forkbeard that it had been I, as Bosk of Port Kar, admiral of the city, who had been responsible for the incarceration of Chenbar.

Yet I admired the audacity of the man of Torvaldsland, though his act, in freeing Chenbar to act against me, had almost cost me my life last year in the northern forests. Sarus of Tyros, acting under his orders, had struck to capture both Marlenus of Ar and myself. He had failed to capture me, and I had, eventually, managed to free Marlenus, his men and mine, and defeat Sarus.

"Now," laughed Ivar Forkbeard, "I expect that these nights Svein Blue Tooth rests less well in his furs."

"You have already," I said, "accumulated one hundred stone of gold and the weight of Chenbar of Tyros, the Sea Sleen, in the sapphires of Schendi."

"But there is one thing more which the Blue Tooth demanded of me," said Ivar.

"The moons of Gor?" I asked.

"No," said he, "the moon of Scagnar."

"I do not understand," I said.

"The daughter," said he, "of Thorgard of Scagnar, Hilda the Haughty."

I laughed. "Thorgard of Scagnar," I said, "has power comparable to that of the Blue Tooth himself."

"You are of Port Kar," said Ivar.

"My house is in that city," said I.

"Is Thorgard of Scagnar not an enemy of those of Port Kar?" he asked.

"We of Port Kar," I said, "have little quarrel generally with those of Scagnar, but it is true that the ships of this Thorgard have preyed with devastation upon our shipping. Many men of Port Kar has he given to the bosom of Thassa."

"Would you say," asked Ivar, "that he is your enemy?"

"Yes," I said, "I would say that he is my enemy."

"You hunt one of the Kurii," said Ivar.

"Yes," I said.

"It may be dangerous and difficult," he said.

"It is quite possible," I admitted.

"It might be good sport," said he, "to engage in such a hunt."

"You are welcome to accompany me," I said.

"Is it of concern to you whether or not the daughter of Thorgard of Scagnar wears a collar?"

"It does not matter to me," said I, "whether she wears a collar or not."

"I think, soon," said he, "his daughter might be fetched to the hall of Ivar Forkbeard."

"It will be difficult and dangerous," I said.

"It is quite possible," said he.

"Am I welcome to accompany you?" I asked.

He grinned. "Gunnhild," said he, "run for a horn of mead."

"Yes, my Jarl," said she, and sped from his side.

In a moment, through the dark, smoky hall, returned Gunnhild, bearing a great horn of mead.

"My Jarls," said she.

The Forkbeard took from her the horn of mead and, together, we drained it.

We then clasped hands.

"You are welcome to accompany me," said he. Then he rose to his feet behind the table. "Drink!" called he to his men. "Drink mead to Hilda the Haughty, daughter of Thorgard of Scagnar!"

His men roared with laughter. Bond-maids, collared and naked, fled about, filling horns with mead.

"Feast!" called Ivar Forkbeard. "Feast!"

Much meat was eaten; many horns were drained.

Though the hall of Ivar Forkbeard was built only of turf and stone, and though he himself was outlaw, he had met me at its door, after I had been bidden wait outside, in his finest garments of scarlet and gold, and carrying a bowl of water and a towel. "Welcome to the hall of Ivar Forkbeard," he had said. I had washed my hands and face in the bowl, held by the master of the house himself, and dried myself on the towel. Then invited within I had been seated across from him in the place of honor. Then from his chests, within the hall, he had given me a long, swirling cloak of the fur of sea sleen; a bronze-headed spear; a shield of painted wood, reinforced with bosses of iron; the shield was red in color, the bosses enameled yellow; a helmet, conical, of iron, with hanging chain, and a steel nosepiece, that might be raised and lowered in its bands; and, too, a shirt and trousers of skin; and, too, a broad ax, formed in the fashion of Torvaldsland, large, curved, single-bladed; and four rings of gold, that might be worn on the arm.

"My gratitude," said I.

"You play excellent Kaissa," had said he.

I surmised to myself that the help of the Forkbeard might, in the bleak realities of Torvaldsland, be of incalculable value. He might know the haunts of Kurii; he might know dialects of the north, some of which are quite divergent from standard Gorean, as it is spoken, say, in Ar or Ko-ro-ba, or even in distant Turia; the habits and customs of the northern halls and villages might be familiar to him; I had no wish to be thrown bound beneath the hoes of thralls because I had inadvertently insulted a free man-at-arms or breached a custom, perhaps as simple as using the butter before someone who sat closer to the high-seat pillars than myself. Most importantly, the Forkbeard was a mighty fighter, a brave man, a cunning mind; in my work in the north I was grateful that I might have so formidable an ally.

To put a collar on the throat of the daughter of Thorgard of Scagnar seemed small enough price to pay for the assistance of so mighty a comrade.

Thorgard of Scagnar, vicious and cruel, one of the most powerful of the northern Jarls, was my enemy.

Too, he had, in his ship, Black Sleen, hunted us at sea. I smiled.

Let his daughter, Hilda the Haughty, beware.

I looked to the Forkbeard. He had one arm about the full, naked waist of the daughter of the administrator of Kassau, Pudding, and the other about the waist of marvelously breasted, collared Gunnhild. "Taste your Pudding, my Jarl," begged Pudding. He kissed her. "Gunnhild! Gunnhild!" protested Gunnhild. Her hand was inside his furred shirt. He turned and thrust his mouth upon hers. "Let Pudding please you," wept Pudding. "Let Gunnhild please you!" cried Gunnhild. "I will please you better," said Pudding. "I will please you better!" cried Gunnhild. Ivar Forkbeard stood up; both bond-maids looked up at him, touching him; "Run to the furs," said Ivar Forkbeard, "both of you!"

Both girls quickly fled to his furs.

He stepped over the bench, and followed them. At the foot of the ground level, which is the sleeping level, which lies about a foot above the dug-out floor, the long center of the hall, on the floor, against the raised dirt, here and there, were rounded logs, laid lengthwise. Each log is ten to fifteen feet long, and commonly about eight inches to a foot thick. If one thinks of the sleeping level, on each side, as constituting, in effect, a couch, almost the length of the hall, except for the cooking area, the logs lie at the foot of these two couches, and parallel to their foot. About each log, fitting snugly into deep, wide, circular grooves in the wood, were several iron bands. These each contained a welded ring, to which was attached a length of chain, terminating in a black-iron fetter.

Gunnhild thrust out her left ankle; the Forkbeard fettered her; a moment later Pudding, too, had thrust forth her ankle, and her ankle, too, was locked in a fetter of the north. The Forkbeard threw off his jacket. There was a rustle of chain as the two bond-maids turned, Pudding on her left side, Gunnhild on her right, waiting for the Forkbeard to lie between them.

I heard men, down the table laughing. One of the new girls, from Kassau, had been thrown on her back, on the table. She lay in meat, and spilled mead. She was kicking and laughing, trying to push back from her body the pressing jackets of fur of the men of Torvaldsland. Another girl, I saw, was seized and thrown to the darkness of the sleeping platform. I saw her white body, briefly, trying to crawl away, but he who had thrown her upon the furs, seized her ankle and drew her to him. She was thrown mercilessly under him, her shoulders pressed back, her beauty his prize. I saw her head lift, thrusting her lips to his, but it was then thrust back, and she whimpered, her body squirming, held helpless, loot, his to be done with as he pleased. When he lifted his mouth from hers, she put her arms about his neck, and thrust up her head again, lips parted. "My Jarl!" she wept, "my Jarl!" Then he again thrust her back to the furs, with such force that she cried out, and then he, with rudeness and incredible force, used her for his pleasure. I saw her body struck again and again, she clinging to him, helplessly. He gave her no quarter. Bond-maids are treated without mercy. "I love you, my Jarl!" she screamed.

Men at the tables, mead spilling, chewing on meat, laughed at her.

She wept, and cried out with pleasure.

When the oarsman had finished with her and would return to the table, she tried to hold him. He struck her back on the furs. Weeping she held out her arms to him. He returned to his mead.

I saw another oarsman then crawl to her and, by the hair, pull her into his arms. In a moment I saw her collared body, desperately pressing and rubbing against him, he in her small, white arms, her belly thrust against the great buckle of the master belt. Then he, too, threw her to her back. "I love you, my Jarls," she wept. "I love you, my Jarls!"

There was much laughter.

I looked to one side; there, at a bench, lethargic, somnolent, like a great stone, or a sleeping larl, sat Rollo, he of such great stature, with grayish skin. He was bare-chested. About his neck, looped, was a cord of woven, golden wire, with a golden pendant, in the shape of an ax. He was shaggy haired. He seemed not to be aware of the wildness of the feast; he seemed not to hear the laughter, the screams of the yielding bond-maids; he sat with his hands on his knees; his eyes were closed. A bond-maid, passing him, carrying mead, brushed him. Frightened, she hurried past him. His eyes did not open.

Rollo rested.

"Oh, no!" I heard Pudding say.

I turned to look to the Forkbeard's couch. From about his neck he had taken the silver chain which had been the symbol of office of Gurt, Administrator of Kassau. He had forcibly drawn Pudding's hands behind her, and, cunningly twisting the chain, had fastened her wrists behind her with it. She sat on the furs, her left ankle clasped in the iron fetter, which chained her to the log at the foot of the Forkbeard's

98

couch, her wrists fastened behind her with her father's chain of office.

She looked at the Forkbeard with fear. He then threw her to her back. "Do not forget Gunnhild," whined Gunnhild, pressing her lips to the Forkbeard's shoulder. I heard the movement of her own chain on the log.

Male thralls are chained for the night in the bosk sheds; bond-maids are kept in the hall, for the pleasure of the free men. They are often handed from one to the other. It is the responsibility of he who last sports with them to secure them.

I heard screams of pleasure.

I looked down at Thyri, kneeling beside my bench. She looked up at me, frightened. She was a beautiful girl, with a beautiful face. She was delicate, sensitive. Her eyes were highly intelligent, beautiful and deep. A collar of black iron was riveted on her throat.

"Run to the furs, Bond-maid," I said, harshly.

Thyri leaped to her feet and fled to my furs, weeping. I finished a horn of mead, rose to my feet, and went to my sleeping area.

She lay there, her legs drawn up.

"Ankle," I said to her.

I looked upon her. Her eyes were on mine, frightened. Her body, small, white, curved, luscious, contrasted with the shadowed redness and blackness of the soft, deep furs on which she lay. She trembled.

"Ankle," I told her.

She extended her shapely limb.

I took her ankle and, about it, closed the fetter of black iron.

I then joined her upon the furs.

7

THE KUR

The next five days were pleasant ones for me.

In the mornings, under the eye of Ottar, keeper of Fork-beard's farm, I learned the ax.

The blade bit deep into the post.

"More back," laughed Ottar. "Put more back into it!"

The men cried out with pleasure as the blade then, with a single stroke, split through the post.

Thyri, and other bond-maids, leaped and clapped their hands.

How alive and vital they seemed! Their hair was loose, in the fashion of bond-maids. Their eyes shone; their cheeks were flushed; each inch of them, each marvelous imbonded inch of them, was incredibly alive and beautiful. How incredibly feminine they were, so living and uninhibited and delightful, so utterly fresh, so free, so spontaneous, so open in their emotions and the movements of their bodies; they now moved and laughed and walked, and stood, as women; pride was not permitted them; joy was. Only a kirtle of thin, white wool, split to the belly, stood between their beauty and the leather of their masters.

"Again! Again! Please, my Jarl!" cried Thyri.

Once more the great ax struck the post. It jerked in the earth, and another foot of it, splintering, flew from the ax.

"Well done!" said Ottar.

Then suddenly he struck at me with his own ax. I caught the blow on its handle, with the handle of my ax, and, lifting my left fist, not releasing my ax, hurled him from his feet to his left. He sprawled on the turf and I leaped over him, my ax raised.

"Splendid!" he cried.

The bond-maids cried out with pleasure, Gunnhild, Pouting Lips, Olga, Thyri and others.

100

Ottar leaped up, laughing, and raised his ax against the delighted girls.

They fled back from him, squealing and laughing.

"Olga," he said, "there is butter to be churning in the churning shed."

"Yes, my Jarl," said she, holding her skirt up, running from the place of our exercises.

"Gunnhild, Pouting Lips," said he, "to the looms."

"Yes, Jarl," said they, turning, and hurrying toward the hall. Their looms lay against its west wall.

"You, little wench," said Ottar to Thyri.

She stepped back. "Yes, Jarl," she said.

"You," he said, "gather verr dung in your kirtle and carry it to the sul patch!"

"Yes, Jarl," she laughed, and turned away. I watched her, as she ran, barefoot, to do his bidding. She was exquisite.

"You other lazy girls," cried Ottar, addressing the remaining bond-maids, "is it your wish to be cut into strips and fed to parsit fish?"

"No, my Jarl!" they cried.

"To your labors!" cried he.

Shrieking they turned about and fled away.

"Now, twice more," said Ottar to me, his hand on his broad black belt inlaid with gold. "Then we will find another post!"

There are many tricks in the use of the ax; feints are often used, and short strokes; and the handle, jabbing and punching; a full swing, of course, should it miss, exposes the warrior; certain elementary stratagems might be mentioned; the following are typical; it is pretended to have taken a full swing, even to the cry of the kill, but the swing is held short and not followed through; the antagonist then, if unwary, may rush forward, and be taken, the ax turned, off guard, by the back cut, from the left to right; sometimes it is possible, too, if the opponent carries his shield too high, to step to the left, and, with a looping stroke, cut off the shield arm; a low stroke, too, can be dangerous, for the human foot, as swift as a sapling, may be struck away; defensively, of course, if one can lure the full stroke and yet escape it, one has an instant to press the advantage; this is sometimes done by seeming to expose more of the body than one wary to the ax might, that to tempt the antagonist, he thinking he is dealing with an unskilled foe, to prematurely commit the weight of his body to a full blow. The ax of Torvaldsland is one of the most fearful of the weapons on Gor. If one can get behind the ax, of course, one can meet it; but it is not easy to get behind the ax of one who knows its use; he need only strike one blow; he is not likely to launch it until it is assured of its target.

An Ahn later the Forkbeard, accompanied by Ottar, keeper of his farm, and Tarl Red Hair, now of Forkbeard's Landfall, inspected his fields.

The northern Sa-Tarna, in its rows, yellow and sprouting, was about ten inches high. The growing season at this latitude, mitigated by the Torvaldstream, was about one hundred and twenty days. This crop had actually been sown the preceding fall, a month following the harvest festival. It is sown early enough, however, that, before the deep frosts temporarily stop growth, a good root system can develop. Then, in the warmth of the spring, in the softening soil, the plants, hardy and rugged, again assert themselves. The yield of the fall-sown Sa-Tarna is, statistically, larger than that of the spring-sown varieties.

"Good," said the Forkbeard. He climbed to his feet. He knocked the dirt from the knees of his leather trousers. "Good," he said.

Sa-Tarna is the major crop of the Forkbeard's lands, but, too, there are many gardens, and, as I have noted, bosk and verr, too, are raised. Ottar dug for the Forkbeard and myself two radishes and we, wiping the dirt from them, ate them. The tospits, in the Forkbeard's orchard, which can grow at this latitude, as the larma cannot, were too green to eat. I smiled, recalling that tospits almost invariably have an odd number of seeds, saving the rarer, long-stemmed variety. I do not care too much for tospits, as they are quite bitter. Some men like them. They are commonly used, sliced and sweetened with honey, and in syrups, and to flavor, with their juices, a variety of dishes. They are also excellent in the prevention of nutritional deficiencies at sea, in long voyages, containing, I expect, a great deal of vitamin C. They are sometimes called the seaman's larma. They are a fairly hard-fleshed fruit, and are not difficult to dry and store. On the serpents they are carried in small barrels, usually kept, with vegetables, under the overturned keel of the longboat. We stopped by the churning shed, where Olga, sweating, had finished making a keg of butter. We dipped our fingers into the keg. It was quite good. "Take it to the kitchen," said the Forkbeard. "Yes, my Jarl," she said. "Hurry, lazy girl," said he. "Yes, my Jarl," she said, seizing the rope handle of the keg and, leaning to the right to balance it, hurried from the churning shed. Earlier, before he had begun his tour of inspection, Pudding had come to him, and knelt before him, holding a plate of Sa-Tarna loaves. The daughter of Gurt, the Administrator of Kassau, was being taught to bake. She watched fearfully as the Forkbeard bit into one. "It needs more salt," he had said to her. She shuddered. "Do you think you are a bond-maid of the south?" he asked. "No, my Jarl," she had said. "Do you think it is enough for you to be pleasant in the furs?" he asked. "Oh, no, my Jarl!" she cried. "Bond-maids of the north must know how to do useful things," he told her. "Yes, my Jarl!" she cried. "Take these," said he, "to the stink pen and, with them, swill the tarsks!" "Yes, my Jarl," she wept, leaping to her feet, and fleeing away. "Bond-maid!" called he. She stopped, and turned. "Do you wish to go to the whipping post?" he asked. This is a stout post, outside the hall, of peeled wood, with an iron ring near the top, to which the wrists of a bond-maid, crossed, are lashed over her head. Near the bosk shed there is a similar post, with a higher ring, used for thralls. "No, my Jarl!" cried Pudding. "See then," said he, "that your baking improves!" "Yes, my Jarl," she said, and fled away. "It is not bad bread," said Ivar Forkbeard to me, when she had disappeared from sight. He broke me a piece. We finished it. It was really quite good, but, as the Forkbeard had said, it could have used a dash more salt. When we left the side of the hall we had stopped, briefly, to watch Gunnhild and Pouting Lips at the standing looms. They worked well, and stood beautifully, under the eyes of the Forkbeard. Ottar had then joined us and we had begun our inspection. Shortly before concluding our inspection, we had stopped at the shed of the smith, whose name was Gautrek. We had then continued on our way. On the way back to the hall, cutting through the tospit trees, we had passed by the sul patch. In it, his back to us, hoeing, was the young broad-shouldered thrall, in his white tunic, with cropped hair. He did not see us. Approaching him, her kirtle held high in two hands, it filled with verr dung, was blond, collared Thyri.

"She has good legs," said Ottar.

We were quite close to them; neither of them saw us.

Thyri, in the afternoon, had made many trips to the sul patch. This, however, was the first time she had encountered the young man. Earlier he had been working with other thralls at the shore, with parsit nets.

"Ah," said he, "greetings, my fine young lady of Kassau." She looked at him, her eyes flashing.

"Did you think in Kassau," he asked, "that you would one day be dunging the fields of one of Torvaldsland?"

She said nothing to him.

"I did not know in Kassau," said he, "that you had such fine legs." He laughed. "Why did you not, in Kassau," he asked, "show us what fine legs you have?"

She was furious.

She, holding her kirtle with her left hand, angrily scattered the dung about the sul plants. It would be left to a thrall to hoe it in about the plants.

"Oh, do not lower your kirtle, Thyri," said he. "Your brand is quite lovely. Will you not show it, again, to Wulfstan of Kassau?"

Angrily she drew her kirtle up, revealing her thigh. Then, furiously, she thrust it down.

"How do you like it, Thyri," asked he, "to find that you are now a girl whose belly lies beneath the sword?"

"It lies not beneath your sword," she snapped. "I belong to free men!"

Then, with the brazeness of a bond-maid, she, Thyri, who had been the fine young lady of Kassau, threw her kirtle up over her hips and, leaning forward, spit furiously at the thrall.

He leaped toward her but Ottar was even quicker. He struck Wulfstan, the thrall, Tarsk, behind the back of his neck with the handle of his ax. Wulfstan fell stunned. In an instant Ottar had bound the young man's hands before his body. He then jerked him to his knees by the iron collar.

"You have seen what your ax can do to posts," said he to me, "now let us see what it can do to the body of a man." He then threw the young thrall to his feet, holding him by the collar, his back to me. The spine, of course, would be immediately severed; moreover, part of the ax will, if the blow be powerful, emerge from the abdomen. It takes, however, more than one blow to cut a body, that of a man, in two. To strike more than twice, however, is regarded as clumsiness. The young man stood, numbly, caught. Thyri, her kirtle down, shrank back, her hand before her mouth.

"You have seen," said Ottar, to the Forkbeard, "that he has been bold with a bond-maid, the property of free men."

"Thralls and bond-maids, sometimes," said I, "banter."

"He would have put his hands upon her," said Ottar. That seemed true, and was surely more serious. Bond-maids were, after all, the property of free men. It was not permitted for a thrall to touch them.

"Would you have touched her?" asked the Forkbeard.

"Yes, my Jarl," whispered the young man.

"You see!" cried Ottar. "Let Red Hair strike!"

I smiled. "Let him be whipped instead," I said.

"No!" cried Ottar.

"Let it be as Red Hair suggests," said the Forkbeard, He then looked at the thrall. "Run to the whipping post," he said. "Beg the first free man who passes to beat you."

"Yes, my Jarl," he said.

He would be stripped and bound, wrists over his head, to the post at the bosk shed.

"Fifty strokes," said the Forkbeard.

"Yes, my Jarl," said the young man.

"The lash," said the Forkbeard, "will be the snake."

His punishment would be heavy indeed. The snake is a single-bladed whip, weighted, of braided leather, eight feet long and about a half an inch to an inch thick. It is capable of lifting the flesh from a man's back. Sometimes it is set with tiny particles of metal. It was not impossible that he would die under its blows. The snake is to be distinguished from the much more common Gorean slave whip, with its five broad striking surfaces. The latter whip, commonly used on females, punishes terribly; it has, however, the advantage of not marking the victim. No one is much concerned, of course, with whether or not a thrall is marked. A girl with an unmarked back, commonly, will bring a much higher price than a comparable wench, if her back be much-ly scarred. Men commonly relish a smooth female, except for the brand scar. In Turia and Ar, it might be mentioned, it is not uncommon for a female slave to be depilated.

The young thrall looked at me. It was to me that he owed his life.

"Thank you, my Jarl," he said. Then he turned and, wrists still bound before his body, as Ottar had fastened them, ran toward the bosk shed.

"Go, Ottar, to the forge shed," said the Forkbeard, grinning. "Tell Gautrek to pass by the bosk shed."

Ottar grinned. "Good," he said. Gautrek was the smith. I did not envy the young man.

"And Ottar," said the Forkbeard, "see that the thrall returns to his work in the morning."

"I shall," said Ottar, and turned toward the forge shed.

"I hear, Red Hair," said Ivar Forkbeard, "that your lessons with the ax proceed well."

"I am pleased if Ottar should think so." I said.

"I, too, am pleased that he should think so," said Ivar Forkbeard, "for that is indication that it is true." Then he turned away. "I shall see you tonight at the feast," he said.

"Is there to be another feast?" I asked. "What is the occasion?"

There had been feasts the past four nights.

"That we are pleased to feast," said Ivar Forkbeard. "That is occasion enough."

He then turned away.

I turned to the girl, Thyri. I stood over her. "Part of what occurred here," I told her, "is your fault, Bond-maid."

She put her head down. "I hate him," she said, "but I would not have wanted him to be killed." She looked up. "Am I to be punished, my Jarl?" she asked.

"Yes," I told her.

Fear entered her eyes. How beautiful she was.

"But with the whip of the furs," I laughed.

"I look forward eagerly, my Jarl," laughed she, "to my punishment."

"Run," said I.

She turned and ran toward the hall, but, after a few steps turned, and faced me. "I await your discipline, my Jarl," she cried, and then turned again, and fled, that fine young lady of Kassau, barefoot and collared, now only a bond-maid, to the hall, to the furs, to await her discipline.

"Is it only a bond-maid, my Jarl," asked Thyri, "who can know these pleasures?"

"It is said," I said, "that only a bond-maid can know them."

She lay on her back, her head turned toward me. I lay at her side, on one elbow. Her left knee was drawn up; about her left ankle, locked, was the black-iron fetter, with its chain. On her throat was the collar of iron.

"Then, my Jarl," said she, "I am happy that I am a bond-maid."

I took her again in my arms.

"Red Hair!" called Ivar Forkbeard. "Come with me!"

Rudely I thrust Thyri from me, leaving her on the furs, chained.

In moments, ax in its sheath on my back, I joined the Forkbeard.

Outside were gathered several men, both of Ivar's ship and of the farm. Among them, eyes terrified, crooked-backed, was a cringing, lame thrall.

"Lead us to what you have found," demanded the Fork-beard.

We followed the man more than four pasangs, up the slopes, leading to the summer pastures.

Then, on a height, from which we could see, far below, the farm and ship of Ivar Forkbeard, we stopped. Behind a large rock, the cringing thrall, frightened, indicated what he had found. Then he did not wish to look upon it.

I was startled.

"Are there larls in these mountains?" I asked.

The men looked at me as though I might have been insane.

"No sleen did this," said I.

We looked down at the remains of a bosk, torn apart, eaten through. Even large bones had been broken, snapped apparently in mighty jaws, the marrow sucked from them. The brains, too, had been scooped, with a piece of wood, from the skull.

"Do you not know," asked Ivar Forkbeard, "of what animal this is the work?"

"No," I said.

"This has been killed by one of the Kurii," he said.

For four days we hunted the animal, but we did not find it. Though the kill was recent, we found no trace of the predator.

"We must find it," had said the Forkbeard. "It must learn it cannot with impunity hunt on the lands of Forkbeard."

But we did not find it.

We did not have a feast, as we had intended, on the night on which the bosk had been found eaten, nor on the next nights. In vain we hunted. The men grew angry, sullen, apprehensive. Even the bond-maids no longer laughed and sported. There might, for all we knew, be somewhere in the lands of Ivar Forkbeard one of the Kurii.

"It must have left the district," said Ottar, on the fourth night.

"There have been no further kills," pointed out Gautrek, the smith, who had hunted with us.

"Do you think it is the one who killed the verr last month," I asked Ottar, "and similarly disappeared?"

"I do not know," said Ottar. "It could be, for those of the Kurii are quite rare this far to the south."

"It may have been driven from its own kind," said the

107

Forkbeard, "one too vicious even to be tolerated in its own caves."

"It might, too," said Ottar, "be insane or ignorant."

"Perhaps," suggested Gorm, "it is diseased or injured, and can no longer hunt the swift deer of the north?"

In these cases, too, I supposed one of the Kurii might be driven, by teeth and claws, from its own caves. Kurii, I suspected, those of Gor as well as those of the ships, did not tolerate weakness.

"At any rate," I said, "it seems now to be gone."

"We are safe now," said Gautrek.

"Shall we have a feast?" asked Gorm.

"No," said the Forkbeard. "This night my heart is not in feasting."

"At least the beast is gone," said Gautrek.

"We are safe now," said Gorm.

I awakened in the darkness. Thyri's body was snuggled against mine; she was asleep; I had not used her this night. She was fettered, of course.

I lay very still.

For some reason I was uneasy.

I heard the heavy breathing of the men in the hall. At my side, I heard Thyri's breathing, too, deep and soft, that of the smaller lungs of a girl.

I did not move.

I felt, or thought I felt, a breath of fresh air.

I lay in the darkness. I did not move.

Then I smelled it.

With a cry of rage I leaped to my feet on the couch, hurling away the furs.

In the same instant I felt myself seized in great, clawed paws and lifted high into the air of the hall. I could not see my assailant. Then I was hurled over the couch against the curved wall of turf and stone.

"What is going on!" I heard cry.

Thyri, awakened, screamed.

I lay, stunned, at the foot of the wall, on the couch.

"Torches!" cried the Forkbeard. "Torches!"

Men cried out; bond-maids screamed.

I heard the sound of feeding.

Then in the light of a torch, lifted by the Forkbeard, lit from being thrust beneath the ashes of the fire pit, we saw it.

It was not more than ten feet from me. It lifted its face from the half-eaten body of a man. Its eyes, large, round,

108

blazed in the light of the torch. I heard the screaming of bond-maids, the movements of their chains. Their ankles were held by their fetters. "Weapons!" cried the Forkbeard. "Kur! Kur!" I heard men cry. The beast stood there, blinking, bent over the body. It was unwilling to surrender it. Its fur was sable, mottled with white. Its ears, large, pointed and wide, were laid back flat against its head. It was perhaps seven feet tall and weighed four or five hundred pounds. Its snout was wide, leathery. There were two nostrils, slitlike. Its tongue was dark. It had two rows of fangs, four of which were particularly prominent, those in the first row of fangs, above and below, in the position of canines; of these, the upper two were particularly long, and curved. Its arms were longer and larger than its legs; it held the body it was devouring in clawed, pawlike hands, yet six-digited, extra-jointed, almost like tentacles.

It hissed, and howled and, eyes blazing, fangs bared, threatened us.

No one could seem to move. It stood there in the torch-light, threatening us, unwilling to surrender its body. Then, behind it I saw an uplifted ax, and the ax struck down, cutting its backbone a foot beneath its neck. It slumped forward, over the couch half falling across the body of a hysterical bond-maid. Behind it I saw Rollo. He did not seem in a frenzy; nor did he seem human; he had struck, when others, Gautrek, Gorm, I, even the Forkbeard, had been unable to do other than look upon it with horror. Rollo again lifted the ax. "No!" cried Ivar Forkbeard. "The battle is done!"

The giant lowered his ax and, slowly, returned to his couch, to sleep.

One of the men touched its snout with the butt of his spear, and then thrust it into the beast's mouth; the butt of the spear was torn away; the bond-maids screamed. "It is still alive!" cried Gorm.

"Get it out of here," said Ivar Forkbeard. "Beware of the jaws."

With chains and poles the body of the Kur was dragged and thrust from the hall. We took it outside the palisade, on the rocks. It was getting light.

I knelt beside it.

It opened its eyes.

"Do you know me?" I asked.

"No," it said.

"This is a small Kur," said the Forkbeard. "They are

109

generally larger. Note the mottling of white. Those are disease marks."

"I hope," I said, "that it was not because of me that it came to the hall."

"No," said the Forkbeard. "In the dark they have excellent vision. If it had been you it sought, it would have been you it killed."

"Why did it enter the hall?" I asked.

"Kurii," said Ivar Forkbeard, "are fond of human flesh."

Humans, like other animals, I knew, are regarded by those of the Kurii as a form of food.

"Why did it not run or fight?" I asked.

The Forkbeard shrugged. "It was feeding," he said. Then he bent to the beast. "Have you hunted here before?" he asked. "Have you killed a verr here, and a bosk?"

"And, in the hall," it said, its lips drawing back from its jaws, "last night a man."

"Kill it," said Ivar Forkbeard.

Four spears were raised, but they did not strike.

"No," said Ivar Forkbeard. "It is dead."

8

HILDA OF SCAGNAR

"So is this the perfume that the high-born women of Ar wear to the song-dramas in En'Kara?" asked the blond girl, amused.

"Yes, Lady," I assured her, bowing before her, lisping in the accents of Ar.

"It is gross," said she. "Meaningless."

"It is a happy scent," I whined.

"For the low-born," said she.

"Lalámus!" said I.

My assistant, a large fellow, but obviously stupid, smooth-shaven as are the perfumers, in white and yellow silk, and golden sandals, bent over, hurried forward. He carried a tray of vials.

"I had not realized, Lady," said I, "that perception such as yours existed in the north."

My accent might not have fooled one of Ar, but it was not bad, and to those not often accustomed to the swift, subtle liquidity of the speech of Ar, melodius yet expressive, it was more than adequate. My assistant, unfortunately, did not speak.

The eyes of Hilda the Haughty, daughter of Thorgard of Scagnar, flashed. "You of the south think we of the north are barbarians!" she snapped.

"Such fools we were," I admitted, putting my head to the floor.

"I might have you fried in the grease of tarsk," she said, "boiled in the oil of tharlarion!"

"Will you not take pity, great Lady," I whined, "on those who did not suspect the civilization, the refinements, of the north?"

"Perhaps," said she. "Have you other perfumes?"

My assistant, hopefully, lifted a vial.

"No," I hissed to him. "In an instant such a woman will see through such a scent."

"Let me smell it," said she.

"It is nothing, lady," I whined, "though among the highest born and most beautiful of the women of the Physicians it is much favored."

"Let me smell it," she said.

I removed the cork, and turned away my head, as though shamed.

She held it to her nose. "It stinks," she said.

Hastily I corked the vial and, angrily, thrust it back into the hand of my embarrassed assistant, who returned it to its place.

Hilda sat in a great curule chair, carved with the sign of Scagnar, a serpent-ship, seen frontally. On each post of the chair, carved, was the head of a snarling sleen. She smiled, coldly.

I reached for another vial.

She wore rich green velvet, closed high about her neck, trimmed with gold.

She took the next vial, which I had opened for her. "No," she said, handing it back to me.

Her hair, long, was braided. It was tied with golden string .

"I had no understanding," said she, "that the wares of Ar were so inferior."

Ar, populous and wealthy, the greatest city of known Gor, was regarded as a symbol of quality in merchandise. The stamp of Ar, a single letter, that which appears on its Home Stone, the Gorean spelling of the city's name, was often forged by unscrupulous tradesmen and placed on their own goods. It is not a difficult sign to forge. It has, however, in spite of that, never been changed or embellished; the stamp of Ar is a part of its tradition. In my opinion the goods of Ko-ro-ba were as good, or better, than those of Ar but, it is true, she did not have the reputation of the great city to the southeast, across the Vosk. Ar is often looked to, by those interested in such matters, as the setter of the pace in dress and manners. Fashions in Ar are eagerly inquired into; a garment "cut in the fashion of Ar" may sell for more than one of better cloth but less "stylish"; "as it is done in Ar" is a phrase often heard. Sometimes I had little objection to the spreadings of such fashions. After the restoration of Marlenus of Ar, in 10,119 Contasta Ar, from the founding of Ar, he had at his victory feast decreed a two-hort, about two and one half inches, shortening of the already briefly skirted garment of the female state slave. This was adopted immediately in Ar, and, city by city, became rather general. Proving that I myself am not above fashion I had had this scandalous alteration implemented in my own house; surely I would not have wanted my girls to be embarrassed by the excessive length of their livery; and, in fact, I did the Ubar of Ar one better, by ordering their hemlines lifted by an additional quarter inch; most Gorean slave girls have lovely legs; the more I see of them the better; I wondered how many girls, even as far away as Turia, knew that more of their legs were exposed to free men because, long ago, drunkenly, Marlenus of Ar, at his victory feast, had altered the length of the livery of the female state slaves of Ar. Another custom, long practiced in the far south, below the Gorean equator, in Turia, for example, is the piercing of the ears of the female slave; this custom, though of long standing in the far south, did not begin to spread with rapidity in the north until, again, it was introduced in Ar. At a feast Marlenus, as a special treat for his high officers, presented before them a dancer, a female slave, whose ears had been pierced. She had worn, in her degradation, golden loops in her ears; she had not been able, even, to finish her dance; at a sign from Marlenus she had been seized, thrown to the tiles on which she had danced, and raped by more than a hundred men. Ear piercing, from this time, had begun to spread rapidly through the north, masters, and slavers, often inflicting it on their girls. Interestingly, the piercing of the septum, for the insertion of a nose ring, is regarded, generally, a great deal more lightly by female slaves than the piercing of the ears. Perhaps this is partly because, in the far south, the free women of the Wagon Peoples wear nose rings; perhaps it is because the piercing does not show; I do not know. The piercing of the ears, however, is regarded as being the epitome of a slave girl's degradation. Any woman, it is said, with pierced ears, is a slave girl.

"You insult me," said Hilda the Haughty, "to present me with such miserable merchandise! Is this the best that great Ar can offer?"

Had I been of Ar I might have been angry. As it was I was somewhat irritated. The perfumes I was displaying to her had been taken, more than six months ago, by the Forkbeard from a vessel of Cos. They were truly perfumes of Ar, and of the finest varieties. "Who," I asked myself, "is Hilda, the daughter of a barbarian, of a rude, uncouth northern pirate, living in a high wooden fortress, overlooking the sea, to so demean the perfumes of Ar?" One might have thought she was a great lady, and not the insolent, though curvacious, brat of a boorish sea rover.

I put my head to the floor. I groveled in the white and yellow silk of the perfumers. "Oh, great lady," I whined, "the finest of Ar's, perfumes may be too thin, too frail, too gross, for one of your discernment and taste."

Her hands wore many rings. About her neck she wore, looped, four chains of gold, with pendants. On her wrists were bracelets of silver and gold.

"Show me others, men of the south," said she, contemptuously.

Again and again we tried to please the daughter of Thorgard of Scagnar. We had little success. Sometimes she would wince, or make a face, or indicate disgust with a tiny motion of her hand, or a movement of her head.

We were almost finished with the vials in the flat, leather case.

"We have here," said I, "a scent that might be worthy of a Ubara of Ar."

I uncorked it and she held it, delicately, to her nostrils.

"Barely adequate," she said.

I restrained my fury. That scent, I knew, a distillation of a hundred flowers, nurtured like a priceless wine, was a secret guarded by the perfumers of Ar. It contained as well the separated oil of the Thentis needle tree; an extract from the glands of the Cartius river urt; and a preparation formed from a disease calculus scraped from the intestines of the rare Hunjer Long Whale, the result of the inadequate digestion of cuttlefish. Fortunately, too, this calculus is sometimes found free in the sea, expelled with feces. It took more than a year to distill, age, blend and bond the ingredients.

"Barely adequate," she said. But I could tell she was pleased.

"It is only eight stone of gold," said I, obsequiously, "for the vial."

"I shall accept it," said she, coldly, "as a gift."

"A gift!" I cried.

"Yes," said she. "You have annoyed me. I have been patient with you. I am now no longer patient!"

"Have pity, great lady!" I wept.

"Leave me now," said she. "Go below. Ask there to be stripped and beaten. Then swiftly take your leave of the

114

house of Thorgard of Scagnar. Be grateful that I permit you your lives."

I hastily, as though frightened, made as though to close the flat, leather case of vials.

"Leave that," she said. She laughed. "I shall give it to my bond-maids."

I smiled, though secretly. The haughty wench would rob us of our entire stores! None of that richness, I knew, would grace the neck or breasts of a mere bond-maid. She, Hilda the Haughty, daughter of Thorgard of Scagnar, would keep it for herself.

I attempted to conceal one vial, which we had not permitted her to sample. But her eye was too quick for me.

"What is that?" she asked, sharply.

"It is nothing," I said.

"Let me smell it," she said.

"Please, no, great lady!" I begged.

"You thought to keep it from me, did you?" she laughed.

"Oh, no, great lady," I wept.

"Give it to me," she said.

"Must I, lady?" asked I.

"I see," said she, "beating is not enough for you. It seems you must be boiled in the oil of tharlarion as well!"

I lifted it to her, piteously.

She laughed.

My assistant and I knelt before her, at her feet. She wore, beneath her green velvet, golden shoes.

"Uncork it for me, you sleen," said she. I wondered if I had, in my life, seen ever so scornful, so proud, so cold a woman.

I uncorked the vial.

"Hold it beneath my nostrils," she said. She bent forward. I held the vial beneath her delicate nostrils.

She closed her eyes, and breathed in, deeply, expectantly.

She opened her eyes, and shook her head. "What is this?" she said.

"Capture scent," I said.

I held her forearms. Ivar Forkbeard quickly pulled the bracelets and rings from her wrists and fingers. He then threw from her neck the golden chains. I pulled her to her feet, holding her wrists. Ivar tore the golden string from her hair, loosening it. It fell behind her, blond, below the small of her back. He tore the collar of her gown back from her throat, opening it at her neck.

"Who are you?" she whispered.

He snapped fetters of black iron on her wrists. They, by the fetters and their single link, were held about three inches apart.

"Who are you?" she whispered.

"A friend of your father," said he. He tore away from his body, swiftly, the gown of the perfumers, that of white and yellow silk. I, too, cast aside the perfumer's gown.

She saw that we wore the leather and fur of Torvaldsland.

"No!" she cried.

My hand was over her mouth. Ivar's dagger was at her throat.

"While Thorgard roves at sea," said the Forkbeard, "we rove in Scagnar."

"Shall I hold again the vial beneath her nose?" I asked. Soaked in a rag and scarf and held over the nose and mouth of a female it can render her unconscious in five Ihn. She squirms wildly for an Ihn or two, and then sluggishly, and then falls limp. It is sometimes used by tarnsmen; it is often used by slavers. Anesthetic darts, too, are sometimes used in the taking of females; these may be flung, or entered into her body by hand; they take effect in about forty Ihn; she awakens often, stripped, in a slave kennel.

"No," said Ivar. "It is important for my plan that she be conscious."

I felt the mouth of the daughter of Thorgard of Scagnar move beneath my hand.

The Forkbeard's dagger's point thrust slightly into her throat.

She winced.

"If you speak now above a whisper," said he, "you die. Is that understood?"

She nodded her head, miserably. At a gesture from the Forkbeard, I released her mouth. I continued to hold her arm.

"You will never get me past the guards," she hissed.

The Forkbeard was looking about the room. From a small chest, he took a thick, covering cloth, orange. From the chest he took a scarf.

"There are guards," she hissed. "You are fools! You will never get me past the guards!"

"I have no intention of getting you past the guards," said Ivar Forkbeard.

She looked at him, puzzled. He went to the high window

116

of her room, high in the wooden fortress, on its cliff, overlooking the dark bay below. We could hear waves crashing
on rocks.

Ivar went to the window. He looked down. Then he came
back into the room and took a clay lamp, lit, and went
again to the window. He moved the lamp up and down,
once. I went to the window, holding the girl. Together we
looked down into the wave-crashing blackness. Then we
saw, briefly, uncovered and then covered again, a ship's
lantern. Below, at the nineteenth hour, in the longboat of
Ivar's ship, was Gorm, with four oarsmen.

"You have no ropes to lower me to your boat," she said.
She lifted her wrists. "Remove, and swiftly," said she, "these
disgusting fetters!"

Ivar Forkbeard went to the door of her room and, silently,
slipped the two beams into place, in their iron brackets.

She looked to the floor; on it, scattered, lay her bracelets,
her rings, the golden chains she had worn about her neck.
Her throat, where Ivar had torn away the collar of the green
gown, was now bared.

"Do you not want my rings," she asked, "my golden chains,
my bracelets?"

"It is only for you that I have come to this place," he said.
He grinned.

I, too, grinned. It was mighty insult to Thorgard of Scagnar. The golden chains, the rings, the bracelets, stripped
from her, would be left behind. How could it be made more
clear that her captor scorned these as baubles, that he had
no need of them, and that it had been the girl herself, and
only she, her body and her person, that had been sought
and boldly taken.

Ivar Forkbeard then bent to the girl's feet and pulled
away her golden shoes, and, his hands at her legs, she, her
eyes closed, removed from her, too, her scarlet, silken hose,
of the style of Ar.

She stood, her arm held by my hand, in the fetters, in the
dress of green velvet, it torn open at the collar to reveal
her throat; she had been stripped of her rings, the bracelets,
the chains; her hair was loose; her hose and shoes had been
removed.

"Are you going to tie my ankles?" she asked.

"No," he said.

"You have no rope to lower me," she said.

"No," he said.

She looked at him, puzzled.

117

"I will bring high ransom," she said. She looked down at her jewelry on the floor. "I will bring higher ransom," she said, "if I am adorned."

"Your adornments," said he, "will be simple, a kirtle of white wool, a brand, a collar of iron."

"You are insane!" she hissed. "I am the daughter of Thorgard of Scagnar!"

"Wench," said he, "I did not take you for ransom."

"For what reason then," begged she, "have I been taken?"

"Are you so cold, Hilda the Haughty," asked he, "that you cannot guess?"

"Oh, no!" she hissed. "No! No!"

"You will be well taught to heel and obey," said he.

"No!" she hissed.

He lifted the orange coverlet, to throw it over her head.

"I ask only one thing," she begged, "should you be successful in this mad scheme."

"What is that?" asked Ivar Forkbeard.

"Never, never," she said, "let me fall into the hands of Ivar Forkbeard!"

"I am Ivar Forkbeard," said Forkbeard.

Her eyes widened with horror.

He threw the mantle over her head and, with the scarf, turned twice about her neck, and knotted tightly, tied it under her chin.

He had not rendered her unconscious, or gagged her, or tied her ankles. He wanted her to be able to cry out; her cries, of course, would be muffled; they would not be discernible on the height of the fortress; they might, however, be heard by Gorm and those in the boat; too, he wanted her to be able to thrash about; this, too, would help Gorm to locate her in the darkness.

The Forkbeard then lifted her from her feet, lightly. Her dress slid back, over her knees. We heard her muffled voice. "No!" she wept. "I cannot swim!"

The Forkbeard then hurled her from the window and she fell, twisting and crying out, some hundred feet to the black waters below. With the waves, striking on rocks about, we did not hear the splash.

We gave Gorm time to find her and fish her out, throwing her in the boat and binding her ankles. Then the Forkbeard stood on the sill of the tall window, poised, and then he dived into the darkness; after about an Ehn, giving him time to surface and swim to the boat, I followed him.

In less than another Ehn, soaked and cold, teeth chat-

118

tering, I had crawled over the bulwark of the longboat and joined the Forkbeard. He had already stripped and was rubbing himself with a fur cloak. I followed his example, and soon both of us were warmed and in dry clothes. The Forkbeard then bent to the soaked, shuddering captive. He removed one of the fetters and jerked the girl's hands behind her back. He then fettered her hands behind her. Her ankles had already been crossed and bound by Gorm. The Forkbeard then threw Hilda the Haughty face down in the longboat, and, from Gorm, took the tiller. She lay lengthwise, head toward the stem, between his booted feet.

"Shhh!" said the Forkbeard.

The men rested on the oars. We carried no lights.

We were much surprised. To one of the wharves of the holding of Thorgard of Scagnar, silently, like the serpent of the sea it was, carrying two lanterns at its prow, came Black Sleen. We had thought Thorgard's roving, his gathering of the harvests of the sea, would have taken him much longer. We saw men running down the boards of the wharf, carrying lanterns. Words were exchanged. I looked up. I could see the window of the quarters of Hilda the Haughty, daughter of Thorgard of Scagnar. There was a lamp lit still in the room. Apparently she stayed up late. Outside the door of the compartment of her five bond-maids, curled sleeping on the floor, on their straw-filled mats, chained by their ankles, which area led into her own apartment, somnolent and bored, were four guards. Hilda whimpered. The Forkbeard kicked her with his boot. "Be silent," he said to her. I saw her hands twist futilely in the manacles. She, on her belly, soaked, miserable, lay silent.

"Go closer," said the Forkbeard. Almost noiselessly oars dipped, bringing us closer to the hull of Black Sleen.

We saw mooring ropes tossed and caught.

The oars were brought inboard. The men were weary. We saw shields, one by one, being tied over the bulwarks.

A gangplank was slid over the gunwale to the wharf. Then we saw Thorgard of Scagnar, cloak swirling, in his horned helmet, descend the gangplank. He was met by his men, and, high among them, by his holding's keeper, and the keeper of his farms.

He spoke to them shortly and then, in the light of the lanterns, strode down the wharf.

The men did not follow him, nor did his men on the ship yet leave it.

I gasped.

119

I heard, too, the intake of breath of the Forkbeard, and of Gorm, and the oarsmen.

Another shape emerged from the darkness of the ship.

It moved swiftly, with an agility startling in so huge a bulk. I heard the scrape of claws on the gangplank. It was humped, shaggy.

It followed Thorgard of Scagnar.

After it, then, came his men, timidly, those who had met Thorgard and those, too, from the ship. A wharf crew then busied themselves about the ship.

The Forkbeard looked at me. He was puzzled. "One of the Kurii," he said.

It was true. But the beast we had seen was not an isolated, degenerate, diseased beast, of the sort we had encountered at Forkbeard's Landfall. It had seemed in its full health, swift and powerful.

"What has such a beast to do with Thorgard of Scagnar?" I asked.

"What has Thorgard of Scagnar to do with such a beast?" smiled Ivar Forkbeard.

"I do not understand this," I said.

"Doubtless it means nothing," said Ivar Forkbeard. "And at least it is of no concern to us."

"I shall hope not," I said.

"I have an appointment with Svein Blue Tooth," said Ivar Forkbeard. He kicked the captive with the side of his boot. She uttered a small noise, but made no other sound. "The Thing will soon be held," he said.

I nodded. What he had said was true. "But surely," I said, "you will not dare, an outlaw, attend the Thing?"

"Perhaps," said Ivar. "Who knows?" He grinned. "Then," said he, "if I should survive, we will hunt Kurii."

"I hunt only one," I said.

"Perhaps the one you hunt," said Ivar, "is even now within the holding of Thorgard of Scagnar."

"It is possible," I said. "I do not know." It seemed to me not unlikely that the Forkbeard's speculation might be true. But I had no wish to pursue Kurii at random.

"How will you know the one of the Kurii whom you seek?" Ivar had asked me, in his hall.

"I think," I had said, "he will know me."

Of this I had little doubt.

I was certain that the Kur which I sought would know me, and well.

I did not know it, but I did not think that would make much difference.

It was my intention to hunt openly, and, I expected, this understood, my quarry, hunting, too, would find me, and, together, we would do war.

It had doubtless been its plan to lure me to the north. I smiled. Surely its plan had been successful.

I looked at the holding of Thorgard of Scagnar. If the Kur within it were he whom I sought, I had little doubt but what we should later meet. If it were not it which I sought, I had, as far as I knew, no quarrel with it.

But I wondered what it might be doing in the holding of Thorgard of Scagnar. The Kurii and men, as far as I knew, met only in feeding and killing.

"Let us go," said I to Ivar Forkbeard.

"Oars," said he, softly, to his oarsmen.

The oars, gently, noiselessly, entered the water, and the boat moved away, into the darkness.

There was a small sound, from the fetters on the prone girl's wrists.

9

THE FORKBEARD WILL ATTEND THE THING

"My Jarl!" cried Thyri, running into my arms. I lifted her and swung her about. She wore the kirtle of white wool, the riveted collar of black iron.

I drank long at the lips of the bond-maid.

About me I heard the joyous cries of the men of Ivar's farm, the excited cries of bond-maids.

Ivar Forkbeard crushed to his leather Pudding and Gunnhild, kissing first one and then the other, as each eagerly sought his lips, their hands, too, those of bond-maids, eager upon his body.

Other bond-maids pressed past me to greet favorites among the oarsmen of Forkbeard's serpent.

Behind Forkbeard, and to his left, her head high, disdainful, stood Hilda the Haughty, daughter of Thorgard of Scagnar.

The men, and the bond-maids, many in one another's arms, fell back to regard her.

She stood behind the Forkbeard, and to his left. Her back was quite straight; her head was in the air. She was not fettered. Her dress of green velvet, trimmed in gold, she still wore; it was torn back from the collar, as the Forkbeard had done in Scagnar, revealing the whiteness of her throat, hinting at the delights of her bosom; the gown, however, now, was discolored, stained and torn; much of the trip she had been fettered, her belly to the mast; also, on the right side, it was torn to the hip, revealing her thigh, calf and ankle; this had happened when, on the voyage, she had been put on the oar; her hose and shoes had been removed in Scagnar. She stood proudly. She was what the Forkbeard had sought; she was his prize.

"So that," said Ottar, his hands on his heavy belt, inlaid with gold, "is Hilda the Haughty, daughter of Thorgard of Scagnar!"

"Gunnhild is better!" said Pouting Lips.

"Who is Gunnhild?" asked Hilda, coldly.

"I am Gunnhild," said Gunnhild. She stood proudly on the arm of the Forkbeard, the white kirtle split to her belly, the black iron at her throat.

"A bond-maid!" laughed Hilda, contemptuously.

Gunnhild stared at her, in fury.

"Gunnhild is better!" said Pouting Lips.

"Strip them and see," said Ottar.

Hilda turned white.

The Forkbeard turned about and, one arm about Pudding, the other about Gunnhild, started from the dock.

Hilda followed him, to his left.

"She heels nicely," said Ottar. The men and bond-maids laughed. The Forkbeard stopped. Hilda's face burned red with fury, but she kept her head high.

Pet sleen are taught to heel; so, too, sometimes, are bond-maids; I was familiar with this sort of thing, of course; in the south it was quite common for slave girls, in various fashions in various cities, to heel their masters.

Hilda, of course, was a free woman. For her to heel was an incredible humiliation.

The Forkbeard started off again, and then again stopped. Again, Hilda followed him as before.

"She is heeling!" laughed Ottar.

There were tears of rage in Hilda's eyes. What he said, of course, was true. She was heeling. On his ship the Forkbeard had taught her, though a free woman, to heel.

It had not been a pleasant voyage for the daughter of Thorgard of Scagnar. She had been, from the beginning, fettered with her belly to the mast. For a full day, too, the coverlet had been left tied over her head, fastened by the twice-turned, knotted scarf about her neck. On the second day, it had been thrust up only that the spike of a water bag could be thrust between her teeth, and then replaced; on her third day the coverlet was torn away and, with the scarf, thrown overboard; Ivar Forkbeard, on that day, watered her and, with a spoon, fed her a bit of bond-maid gruel.

Starving, she had snatched at it greedily.

"How eagerly you eat the gruel of bond-maids," he had commented.

Then she had refused to eat more. But, the next day, **to**

123

his amusement, she reached forth her mouth eagerly for the nourishment.

On the fifth day, and thereafter, for her feedings, he would tie her ankles and release her from the mast, her wrists then fettered before her, that she might feed herself.

After the fifth day he fed her broths and some meats, that she might have good color.

With the improvement in her diet, as was his expectation, something of her haughtiness and temper returned.

On the eighth day he released her from the mast, that she might walk about the ship.

After she had walked about, he had said to her, "Are you ready to heel?"

"I am not a pet sleen!" she had cried.

"Put her to the oar," had said the Forkbeard.

Hilda, clothed, had been roped, hand and foot, and body, on her back, head down, to one of the nineteen-foot oars.

"You cannot do this to me," she cried.

Then, to her misery, she felt the oar move. "I am a free woman!" she cried.

Then, like any bond-maid, she found herself plunged beneath the cold green surface of Thassa.

The oar lifted.

"I am the daughter of Thorgard of Scagnar!" she cried, spitting water, half blinded.

Then the oar dipped again. When it pulled her next from the water, she was clearly terrified. She had swallowed water. She had learned what any bond-maid swiftly learns, that one must apply oneself, and be rational, if one will survive on the oar. One must follow its rhythm, and, as soon as the surface is broken, expel air and take a deep breath. In this fashion a girl may live on the oar.

For a time the Forkbeard watched her, leaning on his elbows, on the rail, but then he left the rail.

He did, however, have Gorm watch her, with a spear. Twice in the afternoon Gorm struck away sea sleen from the girl's body. Once he thrust away one of the white sharks of the northern waters. The second of the sea sleen it had been which, with its sharp teeth, making a strike, but falling short, had torn away her green velvet gown on the right side from the hip to the hemline; a long strip of it, like a ribbon, was in its teeth as it darted away.

She had not been on the oar for half an Ahn when she had begun to beg her release; a few Ehn later, she had begun to beg to heel the Forkbeard.

But it was not until evening that the oar lifted, and she was released. She was fed hot broths and fettered again to the mast.

The Forkbeard said nothing to her, but, the next day, when the sun was hot on the deck, and he released her for her exercise, and he walked about the deck, she, though a free woman, heeled him perfectly. The crew had roared with laughter. I, too, had smiled. Hilda the Haughty, daughter of Thorgard of Scagnar, had been taught to heel.

Ivar Forkbeard left the dock, his arms about Pudding and Gunnhild, who leaned against him.

Hilda, head high, followed him.

Pouting Lips ran beside her. "Gunnhild is better!" she cried.

Hilda paid her no attention.

"Thick ankles!" said Pretty Ankles.

"She has a rowing bench inside her gown," said Olga.

"Broad in the beam!" laughed another girl.

Suddenly, in fury, Hilda struck at them. The Forkbeard turned about. "What is going on here?" he asked.

"We were telling her how ugly she is," said Pouting Lips.

"I am not ugly!" cried Hilda.

"Remove your clothing," said the Forkbeard.

Her eyes widened with horror. "Never!" she cried. "Never!"

The men and bond-maids about laughed.

"You have taught me to heel," she said, "Ivar Forkbeard, but you have not taught me to obey!"

"Strip her," said the Forkbeard to the bond-maids. They leaped eagerly upon Hilda the Haughty.

In moments the proud girl, naked, was held before the Forkbeard. Olga held one arm, Pretty Ankles the other.

"Gunnhild is better," said Pouting Lips.

It was true. But Hilda the Haughty was a superb piece of female flesh. In almost any market she would surely have drawn a high price.

She struggled, held. She had a fair throat, good shoulders; she was marvelously breasted; her waist was such that one could get his hands on it well; she might have been a bit broad in the beam but I had no objection to this; in the north it is called the love cradle; it was well adapted to cushion the shocks of an oarsman's pleasure; in the south she would have been said to be sweetly hipped; if the Forkbeard wished to breed her she would bear healthy, strong young to his thralls, enriching his farm; her thighs, too, were

125

lovely, and her calves; her ankles, while not thick, as Pretty Ankles had asserted, were heavier than those of Thyri, or Pretty Ankles herself; Hilda was, of course, a somewhat larger girl; she was probably some five years older than Pretty Ankles, and a year or so older than Thyri; Gunnhild was larger than Hilda; she was also, I expected, about a year or two older. I had no objection to Hilda's ankles; I found them quite lovely; they would take a common girl-fetter nicely, with about a quarter inch tolerance.

Then Hilda stopped struggling and, held, head high, regarded the Forkbeard.

He examined her with great care, as he had his Sa-Tarna, and his animals, when he had inspected his farm.

He got up from his knees, where he had been feeling the firmness of her left calf and ankle.

Then he said to the bond-maids. "Take her to the whipping post."

The bond-maids, laughing, dragged Hilda to the post, stout, of peeled wood, which stood outside the hall. Ottar then, with a scrap of binding fiber, crossed and rudely bound, before her body, the wrists of the daughter of Thorgard of Scagnar; he then, reaching up, fastened her wrists to the heavy iron ring over her head. Her breasts were against the post; she could not place her heels on the ground.

"How dare you place me in this position, Ivar Forkbeard!" she demanded. "I am a free woman!"

"Bring the five-strap slave slash," said Ivar Forkbeard to Gunnhild.

"Yes, my Jarl," she said, smiling. She ran to fetch it.

"I am the daughter of Thorgard of Scagnar," said Hilda. "Release me immediately."

The lash was placed by Gunnhild in the hand of Ivar Forkbeard.

Ottar threw the girl's hair forward, so that it fell before her shoulders.

"No!" cried Hilda.

The Forkbeard touched her back with the whip; his fist held the handle and, too, beneath his fist, folded back, were the five straps. He tapped her twice.

"No!" she cried. "Please, no!"

We fell back to give the Forkbeard room, and he shook loose the straps and drew back his arm.

The first stroke threw her against the post; I saw the astonishment in her eyes, then the pain; the daughter of Thorgard seemed stunned; then she howled in misery; it

was only then that she realized what the whip might do to a
girl. "I will obey you!" she screamed. "I will obey you!" Ivar
Forkbeard, experienced in the disciplining of women, did not
deliver the second stroke for a full Ehn. In this time, she
screamed, over and over, "I will obey you!" Then he struck
again. Her body, again, was struck against the post; her
hands twisted in the binding fiber; her entire body rubbed on
the post, in agony, pressing against it; tears burst from her
eyes; she was on her tiptoes, pressing against the post; her
thighs were on either side of the post; but the post did not
yield; she was fastened to it. Then he struck again. She
writhed, twisting and howling. "I ask only to obey you!" she
cried. "I beg to obey you!" When he next struck she could

127

only close her eyes in pain. She could then scarcely breathe. She gasped. No longer could she howl or scream. She tensed, teeth gritted, her body itself a silent scream of agony. But the blow did not then fall. Was the beating done? Then she was struck again. The last five blows were delivered with her hanging in the binding fiber, her body against the post, her face to one side of it. She was then released from the post and fell to her hands and knees. The beating had been quite light, only twenty strokes. Yet I did not think it would be soon that the daughter of Thorgard of Scagnar would wish to find herself again at the post. The beating had been, though light, quite adequate to its purpose, which was to teach her, a captive, the whip.

No female forgets it.

She looked up at the Forkbeard in misery.

"Bring her clothing," said the Forkbeard.

It was brought.

"Garb yourself," said the Forkbeard.

Painfully, almost unable to stand, tears in her eyes, inch by inch, the girl drew on her garments.

She then stood there among us, bent over, tears staining her cheeks. She wore the dress of green velvet trimmed with gold, it torn from the collar, it ripped at the right side.

She looked at him.

"Remove your clothing," he said.

She stripped herself.

"Gather the clothing," said the Forkbeard.

She did so.

"Go now to the kitchen of the hall," said he. "In the fire there, burn your clothing, completely."

"Yes, Ivar Forkbeard," she said.

"Gunnhild will accompany you," he said. "When you have burned your garments, every bit of them, then beg Gunnhild to set you about your duties."

"What duties, my Jarl," asked Gunnhild.

"Tonight we feast," said Ivar Forkbeard. "The feast must be prepared."

"She is to help prepare the feast?" asked Gunnhild.

"And serve it," said the Forkbeard.

"I see, then, the nature of her duties," said Gunnhild, smiling.

"Yes," said Ivar Forkbeard. He regarded Hilda. "You will beg Gunnhild to set you about the duties of a bond-maid."

"Yes," said she, "Ivar Forkbeard."

"Hurry now," laughed he.

Weeping, clutching her clothing, she ran to the hall. The men and bond-maids laughed muchly. I, too, roared with laughter. Hilda the Haughty, daughter of Thorgard of Scagnar, had been taught to obey.

The shrieking of Pouting Lips, as she yielded to Gorm, supine, kicking in the furs, rang through the low, smoking hall.

I thrust Thyri from my lap, and seized Olga by the wrist, as she hurried past, throwing her across my knees. She, laughing, was fleeing Ottar who, drunkenly, was stumbling after her. I pulled Olga's face to mine and our lips met, I forcing my kiss to her teeth. Her naked body, collared, suddenly responded to mine, and she reached for me with her hands. "My Jarl!" she whispered. But I thrust her up, holding her by the arms, into the hands of Ottar, who, laughing, threw her lightly over his shoulder and turned about. I saw her head and shoulders, and her body, to the waist, over his shoulder, her small fists pounding meaninglessly on his back. He carried her into the darkness and threw her to the furs. "My Jarl," whimpered Thyri, crouching beside me, touching me. With a laugh, she crying out with pleasure, I took again the young lady of Kassau, the bond-maid, Thyri, in my arms.

Pretty Ankles hurried past, carrying a great trencher of roast meat on her small shoulder.

"Mead!" called Ivar Forkbeard, from across from me. "Mead!" He held out the great, curved horn, with its rim of filigreed gold.

Pudding and Gunnhild knelt on the bench, snuggling against him, one on either side. But they did not run to fetch his mead. That duty, this night, befell another.

Hilda the Haughty, daughter of Thorgard of Scagnar, as stripped as any bond-maid, from a large bronze vessel, poured mead for the Forkbeard.

The men laughed.

She, though free, poured mead as a bond-maid. The hall roared with pleasure. Mighty insult had thus been wrought upon Thorgard of Scagnar, enemy of Ivar Forkbeard. His daughter, stripped, poured mead in the hall of his enemies.

Too, they had taught her to heel and obey. Rich was the pleasure of Ivar Forkbeard.

He reached out his hand, to touch the daughter of Thorgard of Scagnar.

She shrank back, terrified.

The Forkbeard looked upon her, amused. "Would you not care to play in the furs?" he asked her.

"No," she said, shuddering.

"Let me play," whimpered Pudding. "Let me play," whispered Gunnhild.

"Do not misunderstand me, Ivar Forkbeard," whispered Hilda. "If you order me to the furs I shall obey you, and swiftly. I will comply with your slightest wish, exactly and promptly. I will do whatever I am told."

Pudding and Gunnhild laughed.

Ottar stumbled up, putting his hand on one of the posts. By a length of ship's rope, he had tied Olga to his belt. She looked at me; her eyes shone; her lips were parted; she put out her hand; I paid her no attention; she looked down, fists clenched, and whimpered. I smiled. I would use her before the night was done.

"It is said," intoned Ottar, "that Hilda the Haughty, daughter of Thorgard of Scagnar, is the coldest of women."

"Do you find men of interest?" asked the Forkbeard of Hilda.

"No," she said. "I do not."

Ottar laughed.

"Are you not curious," asked Ivar of the daughter of Thorgard of Scagnar, "what it would be to feel on your body their hands, their mouths?"

"Men are beasts!" she cried.

"Their teeth?" he asked.

"Men are hateful," she wept. "They are terrible beasts, using girls as their prey!" She looked about at the bond-maids. "Resist them!" she cried. "Resist them!"

Pudding threw back her head and laughed. "Resistance is not permitted," she laughed.

"Throw her in the furs," cried Pretty Ankles. "Then she will learn whether she knows what she is talking about or not."

"Throw her in the furs," cried another bond-maid. "Throw her in the furs," called yet another.

"Throw her in the furs," cried the bond-maids.

Hilda shuddered, terrified.

"Silence!" called out Ivar Forkbeard.

There was silence.

"What," asked Ivar Forkbeard of Hilda, "if I should order you to the furs?"

"I would obey you immediately," she said. "I have felt the whip," she explained.

"But of your own free will you would be unlikely to enter upon the furs?" asked Ivar.

130

"Of course not," she said.

Gorm, who had now disentangled himself from Pouting Lips, joined the circle about the table, where we sat, others standing. She was behind him, combing her hair with a comb of horn.

"She is Hilda the Haughty," laughed Ottar. "She is the coldest of women!"

Hilda stood straight, her head high.

"Ottar, Gorm," said the Forkbeard. "Take her to the ice shed. Leave her there, bound hand and foot."

The bond-maids shrieked with pleasure. Men pounded their left shoulders with the palms of their right hands. Some pounded their plates on the heavy boards of the wooden table.

Ottar delayed only long enough to untie Olga from his belt. He had tied her there by ship's rope, knotted about her stomach. He left the rope about her stomach, but, with its free end, pulling her arms about one of the roof posts, tied her hands together.

He then left, following Gorm, who had dragged Hilda from the hall.

She tried futilely to free herself. She looked at me, agonized. "Untie me," she begged.

I looked at her.

"My body wants you, Tarl Red Hair," she wept. "My body needs you!"

I looked away from her, paying her no more attention. I heard her moan, and rub her body on the post. "I need you, Tarl Red Hair," she whimpered.

I would let her smolder for another Ahn or two. By that time her body would be ready. To my slightest touch it would leap, helpless, squirming, in my arms. I would use her twice, the second time in the lengthy use of the Gorean master, that use in which, over an Ahn, the female slave or bond-maid is shown no mercy.

"Mead!" I called. Pretty Ankles rushed to serve me. I again bent to the kiss the lips of Thyri.

Late and fully were we feasting when the thrall-boy, tugging on the sleeve of Ivar Forkbeard, said to him, "My Jarl, the wench in the ice shed begs to be freed."

"How long has she begged?" asked the Forkbeard.

"For more than two Ahn," said the boy, grinning. He was male.

"Good boy," said the Forkbeard, and tore him a piece of meat.

"Thank you, my Jarl," said the boy. The boy, unlike the adult male thralls, was not chained at night in the bosk shed. Ivar was fond of him. He slept, chained, in the kitchen.

"Red Hair, Gorm," said the Forkbeard. "Fetch the little Ubara of Scagnar."

We smiled.

"Gorm," said the Forkbeard. "Before she is freed, see that her thirst is assuaged."

"Yes, Captain," said Gorm.

We carried a torch to the ice shed. We opened the heavy door, lined with leather, and lifted the torch, closing the door behind us.

In the light of the torch we saw Hilda. We approached more closely.

She lay on her side, in misery, across great blocks of ice; she could lift her head and shoulders no more than six inches from the ice; she could draw her ankles toward her body no more than six inches; small chips of wood, in which the ice is packed, clung about her body; she was bound, hand and foot, her wrists behind her, her ankles crossed and tied. Two ropes prohibited her from struggling to either a sitting or kneeling position, one running from her right ankle across the ice to a ring in the side of the shed, the other running from her throat across the ice to a similar ring on the other side of the shed.

"Please," she wept.

Her teeth chattered; her lips were blue.

She lay before us, on her back.

"Please," she wept, piteously, "I beg to be permitted to run to the furs of Ivar Forkbeard."

We looked down on her. "I beg!" she cried. "I beg to be permitted to run to his furs!"

Gorm unbound the rope from her ankle, that which had held her legs straight, and that on her throat, which had prevented her from lifting her shoulders and head.

He did not unbind her wrists and ankles. He lifted her to a sitting position. She trembled with cold, whimpering. "I have brought you a drink," he said. "Drink it eagerly, Hilda the Haughty."

"Yes, yes!" she whispered, her teeth chattering.

Then, holding her head back, and lifting the cup to her mouth, he gave her of the drink he had brought with him.

And eagerly, whimpering, shuddering with cold, did Hilda the Haughty drink down the slave wine.

Gorm unbound her and threw her over his shoulder; so

132

stiff and trembling with cold, and stiff from the ropes, was she that she could not stand.

I put my hand on her body; it was like ice. She was whimpering with cold, her head hanging down, over Gorm's back; her long hair fell to the back of his knees.

I lit the way with the torch, and we took her to the hall of the Forkbeard.

We carried her through the darkness and smoke of the hall, between the posts.

The Forkbeard was sitting on the end of his couch, his boots on the floor.

Gorm threw her, on her knees, at the feet of the Forkbeard. Her head was down; her hair was over his boots. She trembled with cold.

Men and bond-maids gathered about.

The left side of her body was illuminated dully, redly, from the coals of the fire pit. The right side of her body was in darkness.

"Who are you?" demanded the Forkbeard.

"Hilda," she wept, "daughter of Thorgard of Scagnar."

"Hilda the Haughty?" he asked.

"Yes," she wept, head down, "Hilda the Haughty."

"What do you want?" he asked.

"To share your furs," she wept.

"Are you not a free woman?" he asked.

"I beg to share your furs, Ivar Forkbeard," she wept.

He rose to his feet and shoved back a long table, and a bench, on the other side of the fire pit. With his heel he drew in the dirt of the floor a bond-maid circle.

She looked at him.

Then he gestured that she might enter his couch. Gratefully, she crawled upon the couch, his section of that fur-covered, dirt sleeping level, and, trembling, shuddering with cold, drawing her body up, drew the furs about her. She lay huddled in the furs. Her body shook beneath them. We heard her moan.

"Mead!" called Ivar Forkbeard, returning to the table. Pudding was first to reach him, with a horn of mead.

"Please come to my side, Ivar Forkbeard!" wept Hilda. "I freeze! Hold me! Please hold me!"

"Let that be a lesson in passion to you other bond-maids," laughed Ottar.

There was much laughter, and most from the beautiful, nude slaves of the men of Torvaldsland, hot, collared, and eager in their brawny arms.

The Forkbeard, laughing, drained the horn. "Mead!" he cried. Gunnhild served him.

After this second horn of mead the Forkbeard, wiping his mouth with his arm, turned about and went to his furs.

He howled with misery.

"She is the coldest of women!" laughed Ottar.

"Hold me, Forkbeard!" she wept. "Hold me please!"

"Will you serve me well?" asked the Forkbeard.

"Yes," she cried. "Yes! Yes! Yes! Yes!"

But the Forkbeard did not make her serve him then but, firmly, held her body, locked in his arms, that of his prisoner, to his, warming her. After half of an Ahn I saw her, delicately, eyes frightened, lift her head and put her lips to his shoulder; softly, timidly, she kissed him; and then looked into his eyes. Suddenly she was flung on her back and his huge hand, roughened from the hilt of the sword, the handle of the ax, was at her body. "Oh, no!" she cried. "No!"

Bets were made at the table. I bet on Ivar Forkbeard. Within an Ahn, Hilda the Haughty, to the jeers of men, the taunts of bond-maids, on her hands and knees, head down, hair falling forward, crept to the circle of the bond-maid, which Ivar Forkbeard had drawn in the dirt of the hall floor, between the posts. The coals of the fire pit illuminated the left side of her body. She crawled before the bond-maids, the oarsmen. She entered the circle, and then, within the circle, stood up. She stood very straight, and her head was up. "I am yours, Ivar Forkbeard," she said. "I am yours!"

He gestured to her, and she fled from the circle, to join him, to throw herself at his side, to beg his touch, his bond-maid.

I collected nine tarn disks and two pieces of broken plate, plundered two years ago from a house on the eastern edge of Skjern.

Gunnhild had been given by the Forkbeard to Gorm for the night. I saw him holding her by the arm and pushing her ahead of him to his furs. This night her ankle would be held by his fetter, not that of the Forkbeard. The Forkbeard had offered me Pudding, but, generously, thinking to have Thyri, I had, after using her once, given her for the night to Ottar. Even now she was, kneeling on his furs, being fettered by the keeper of Ivar Forkbeard's farm. You can imagine my irritation when I saw Thyri led past me, her left wrist in the grip of an oarsman. She looked over her shoulder at me, agonized. I blew her a kiss in the Gorean fashion, kissing and gesturing, my fingers at the right side of my mouth, almost vertical, then, with the kiss, brushing gently toward her. I had no special claim on the pretty little bond-maid, no more than any other among the Forkbeard's men. The delicious little thing, like the other goods of the hall, was, for most practical purposes, for the use of us all. I heard the movements of chain, the moans of the bond-maids in the arms of their masters, men of Torvaldsland.

I thought I would sleep alone this night.

"Tarl Red Hair," I heard.

I followed the sound of the voice and, to my delight, as Ottar had left her, she slipping his mind apparently, as she had mine, her hands still tied before her, about the post, kneeling in the dirt, was Olga.

"I hate you, Tarl Red Hair," she said.

I knelt beside her. I had intended to permit her to smolder for a time, she much aroused, and then later, when she had been much heated with need and desire, when, cruelly deprived, she had been aching to break into flame, throw her to my furs, but, unfortunately, I had forgotten about her.

"I forgot about you," I told her.

"I hate you, Tarl Red Hair," she said.

I reached out to touch her. She shrank back in fury.

"Would you please untie me?" she asked.

I did not wish to sleep alone. I wondered if the fires in Olga which, earlier, had burned so deeply, so hotly, could be truly out. I wondered if they might be rekindled.

I slipped, kneeling, behind her. I heard her body move against the post.

I pushed her collar up, under her chin, and, with two fingers of my right hand and two fingers of my left, rubbed the sides of her throat.

"Please untie me," she whispered.

Her hands writhed in the bonds; her body pressed against the post; her left cheek was at the right side of the post.

My hands lowered themselves on her body. And then, her hands tied about the post, we both kneeling, I caressed her. She tried to resist, in fury, but I was patient. At last I heard her sob. "You are master," she said, "Tarl Red Hair." I kissed her on the back of the right shoulder. She put back her head. "Take me to your furs," she begged. I untied her hands from the post, taking, too, the rope from her belly, by which Ottar had fastened her to his belt, but left the rope on her right wrist, its free end in my hand, to lead her. But I needed not lead her. She followed eagerly, trying to press her lips to my left shoulder.

135

Before my sleeping area, my rude couch, my furs, I stopped. I stood behind her.

She stood very still, facing the couch, at its foot. She was a bond-maid. She was property. She was owned. "Force me," she whispered. Bond-maids know they are chattel, and relish being treated as such. Deep in the belly, too, of every female is a desire, more ancient than the caves, to be forced to yield to the ruthless domination of a magnificent, uncompromising male, a master; deep within them they all wish to submit, vulnerably and completely, nude, to such a beast. This is completely clear in their fantasies; Earth culture, of course, gives little scope to these blood needs of the beauties of our race; accordingly, these needs, frustrated, tend to express themselves in neurosis, hysteria and hostility. Technology and social structures, following their own dynamics, integral to their development and expansion, have left behind the pitiful, rational animals who are their builders and their victims. We have built our own cage, and defend it against those who would shatter its locks.

My left hand held her left arm; with my right hand I forced her right wrist behind her back; I thrust it up; she cried out, suddenly, with misery; I threw her to the furs; scarcely had she struck them, crying out, belly down, than I had clasped the fetter of black iron about her ankle; chained, she turned to face me, sitting on the furs, tears in her eyes, her hands back, her legs flexed. I discarded the leather and fur of Torvaldsland. With a movement of the chain she knelt on the furs, her head down. I entered upon the furs. "To your belly," I said, "ankles a foot apart." "Yes, my Jarl," she said. I then began to caress her, beneath the shins, on the inside, of her feet, behind the backs of her knees, at the sides of her breasts, high between her thighs. By the tensility of her muscles, the movements of her body, sometimes her tiny cries, her breathing, she instructed me in her weaknesses, which I, as a warrior, might then exploit. When I was satisfied, I threw her to her back.

"I am told," I told her, "that Olga is one of the best of the bond-maids."

She lifted her body to me, begging for my touch. I fondled the extent of her, kissing and licking.

"What have you done to my body?" she whispered. "I have never felt this way, this deeply, this fully, before."

"What does your body tell you?" I asked.

"That I will be a marvel to you, Tarl Red Hair," she whispered. "A marvel!"

"Please me," I told her.

"Yes, my Jarl," she wept. "Yes!"

And when she had much pleased me, I finished with her, in the first taking.

"Hold me," she wept.

"I shall hold you," I told her, "and then, in a time, Bond-maid, you will be again used."

She looked at me, startled.

"This," I told her, "is the first taking. It's purpose is only to warm you for the second."

She clutched me, not speaking.

I held her, tightly.

"Can I endure such pleasure?" she asked, frightened.

"You are bond," I told her. "You will have no choice."

"My Jarl," she asked, frightened, "is it the second taking of the Gorean master, to which you intend to subject me?"

"Yes," I told her.

"I have heard of it," she wept. "In it," she gasped, "the girl is permitted no quarter, no mercy!"

"That is true," I told her.

We lay together, silently, I holding her, she against me, chained, for something like half of an Ahn. Then I touched her.

"She lifted her head. "Is it beginning?" she asked.

"Yes," I told her.

"May a bond-maid beg one favor of her Jarl?" she asked.

"Perhaps," I said.

She leaned over me. I felt her hair brush my body. "Be merciless," she whispered. "Be merciless," she begged.

"That is my intention," I told her, and threw her to her back.

"Never have I yielded as I yielded now," she wept. "I would not exchange my collar for all the jewels on Gor!"

I held her. In time, she slept. I, too, then, slept. It was two Ahn before dawn. In one Ahn Ottar and the Fork-beard would be up, arousing the men. The serpent, the afternoon before, had been readied. This morning, at dawn, the serpent would leave the small wharf, dipping oars, gliding through fog on the inlet, the result of the cooler land winds moving over the somewhat warmer water of the encroaching Torvaldstream. Ivar Forkbeard, not wisely perhaps, was determined to attend the Thing. He had there, in his opinion, an appointment to keep, with Svein Blue Tooth, a great Jarl of Torvaldsland, who had outlawed him.

10

A KUR WILL
ADDRESS THE THING

Roped together by the waist, on the turf of the thing-fair, we grappled.

His body slipped in my hand. I felt my right wrist drawn back, at the side of my head, his two hands closed on it. He grunted. He was strong. He was Ketil, of Blue Tooth's high farm, champion of Torvaldsland.

My back began to bend backward; I braced myself as I could, right leg back, bent, left leg forward, bent.

The men about cried out. I heard bets taken, speculations exchanged.

Then my right wrist, to cries of wonder, began to lift and straighten; my arm was then straight, before my body; I began, inch by inch, to lower it, toward the ground; if he did retain his grip he would, at my feet, be forced to his knees. He released my wrist, with a cry of fury. The rope between us, a yard in length, pulled taut. He regarded me, astonished, wary, enraged.

I heard hands striking the left shoulders; weapons struck on shields.

Suddenly the champion's fist struck toward me, beneath the rope. I caught the blow, turning, on the side of my left thigh.

There were cries of fury from the watchers.

I took then the right arm of the champion, his wrist in my right hand, my left hand on his upper arm, and extended the arm and turned it, so that the palm of his hand was up. Then, at the elbow, I broke it across my right knee. I had had enough of him.

I untied the rope from my waist and threw it down. He knelt on the turf, whimpering, tears streaming down his face.

The hands of men pounded on my back. I heard their cries of pleasure.

I turned about and saw the Forkbeard. His hair was wet; he was drying his body in a cloak. He was grinning. "Greetings, Thorgeir of Ax Glacier," said I. "Greetings, Red Hair," said he. Ax Glacier was far to the north, a glacier spilling between two mountains of stone, taking in its path to the sea, spreading, the form of an ax. The men of the country of Ax Glacier fish for whales and hunt snow sleen. They cannot farm that far to the north. Thorgeir, it so happened, of course, was the only man of the Ax Glacier country, which is usually taken as the northern border of Torvaldsland, before the ice belts of Gor's arctic north, who was at the thing-fair. "How went the swimming?" I asked him. "The talmit of skin of sea sleen is mine!" he laughed. The talmit is a headband. It is not unusual for the men of Torvaldsland to wear them, though none of Forkbeard's men did. They followed an outlaw. Some talmits have special significance. Special talmits sometime distinguish officers, and Jarls; or a district's lawmen, in the pay of the Jarl; different districts, too, sometimes have different styles of talmit, varying in their material and design; talmits, too, can be awarded as prizes. That Thorgeir of Ax Glacier had won the swimming must have seemed strange indeed to those of the thing-fair. Immersion in the waters of the Ax Glacier country, unprotected, will commonly bring about death by shock, within a matter of Ihn. Sometimes I wondered if the Forkbeard might be mad. His sense of humor, I thought, might cost us all our lives. There was probably not one man at the thing-fair who took him truly to be of Ax Glacier; most obviously he did not have the epicanthic fold, which helps to protect the eyes of the men of Ax Glacier against extreme cold; further, he was much too large to be taken easily as a man of Ax Glacier; their diet does not produce, on the whole, large bodies; further, their climate tends to select for short, fat bodies, for such, physiologically, are easiest to maintain in thermostatic equilibrium in great cold; long, thin bodies, of course, are easiest to maintain in thermostatic equilibrium in great heat, providing more exposure for cooling. Lastly, his coloring, though his hair was dark, was surely not that of the far north, but, though swarthy, more akin to that of Torvaldsland, particularly western Torvaldsland. Only a madman, or a fool, might have taken seriously his claim to be of the Ax Glacier country. Much speculation had coursed among the contest fields as to the true identity of the smooth-shaven Thorgeir.

Prior to his winning the swimming he had won talmits for climbing the "mast," a tall pole of needle wood, some fifty feet high, smoothed and peeled: for jumping the "crevice," actually a broad jump, on level land, where marks are made with strings, to the point at which the back heel strikes the earth; walking the "oar," actually, a long pole; and throwing the spear, a real spear I am pleased to say, both for distance and accuracy; counting the distance and the accuracy of the spear events as two events, which they are, he had thus, prior to the swimming, won five talmits.

He had done less well in the singing contest, though he much prided himself on his singing voice; he thought, in that one, the judges had been against him; he did not score highly either in the composition of poetry contest nor in the rhyming games; "I am not a skald," he explained to me later; he did much better, I might mention, in the riddle guessing; but not well enough to win; he missed the following riddle; "What is black, has eighty legs and eats gold?"; the answer, though it might not seem obvious, was Black Sleen, the ship of Thorgard of Scagnar; the Forkbeard's answer had been Black Shark, the legendary ship of Torvald, reputed discoverer and first Jarl of Torvaldsland; he acknowledged his defeat in this contest, however, gracefully; "I was a fool," he grumbled to me. "I should have known!" Though I attempted to console him, he remained much put out with himself, and for more than an Ahn afterward.

In spite of his various losses, he had, even in his own modest opinion, done quite well in the contests. He was in excellent humor.

Perhaps the most serious incident of the contests had occurred in one of the games of bat and ball; in this contest there are two men on each side, and the object is to keep the ball out of the hands of the other team; no one man may hold the ball for more than the referee's count of twenty; he may, however, throw it into the air, provided it is thrown over his head, and catch it again himself; the ball may be thrown to the partner, or struck to him with the bat; the bat, of course, drives the ball with incredible force; the bats are of heavy wood, rather broad, and the ball, about two inches in diameter, is also of wood, and extremely hard; this is something like a game of "keep away" with two men in the middle. I was pleased that I was not involved in the play. Shortly after the first "knock off," in

which the ball is served to the enemy, Gorm, who was
Ivar's partner, was struck cold with the ball, it driven
from an opponent's bat; this, I gathered, is a common trick;
it is very difficult to intercept or protect oneself from a ball
struck at one with great speed from a short distance; it
looked quite bad for Ivar at this point, until one of his
opponents, fortunately, broke his leg, it coming into violent
contact with Ivar's bat. This contest was called a draw. Ivar
then asked me to be his partner. I declined. "It is all
right," said Ivar, "even the bravest of men may decline a
contest of bat-and-ball." I acceded to his judgment. There
are various forms of ball game enjoyed by the men of Torvaldsland; some use bats, or paddles; in the winter, one such
game, quite popular, is played, men running and slipping
about, on ice; whether there is any remote connection between this game and ice hockey, I do not know; it is, however, ancient in Torvaldsland; Torvald himself, in the sagas,
is said to have been skilled at it.

Ivar Forkbeard, or Thorgeir of Ax Glacier, as we might
call him, had won, all told, counting the swimming talmit,
six talmits.

He was much pleased.

In the morning talmits would be awarded personally by
the hand of Svein Blue Tooth.

"Let us, this afternoon," said Ivar Forkbeard, "give ourselves to strolling."

That seemed to me not a bad idea, unless a better might
have been to flee for our lives.

In the morning we might find ourselves chained at the
foot of cauldrons of boiling tharlarion oil.

But soon I, following the Forkbeard, together with some
of his men, pressed in among the throngs of the thing.

I carried my short sword. I carried, too, the great bow,
unstrung, with quiver of arrows.

The Forkbeard, too, and his men, were armed. Blows are
not to be struck at the thing, but not even the law of the
thing, with all its might, would have the temerity to advise
the man of Torvaldsland to arrive or move about unarmed.
The man of Torvaldsland never leaves his house unless he is
armed; and, within his house, his weapons are always near at
hand, usually hung on the wall behind his couch, at least a
foot beyond the reach of a bond-maid whose ankle is
chained. Should she, lying on her back, look back and up,
she sees, on the wall, the shield, the helmet, the spear and
ax, the sword, in its sheath, of her master. They are visible

symbols of the force by which she is kept in bondage, by which she is kept only a girl, whose belly is beneath his sword.

Most of the men at the thing were free farmers, blond-haired, blue-eyed and proud, men with strong limbs and work-roughened hands; many wore braided hair; many wore talmits of their district; for the thing their holiday best had been donned; many wore heavy woolen jackets, scrubbed with water and bosk urine, which contains ammonia as its cleaning agent; all were armed, usually with ax or sword; some wore their helmets; others had them, with their shields, slung at their back. At the thing, to which each free man must come, unless he work his farm alone and cannot leave it, each man must present, for the inspection of his Jarl's officer, a helmet, shield and either sword or ax or spear, in good condition. Each man, generally, save he in the direct hire of the Jarl, is responsible for the existence and condition of his own equipment and weapons. A man in direct fee with the Jarl is, in effect, a mercenary; the Jarl himself, from his gold, and stores, where necessary or desirable, arms the man; this expense, of course, is seldom necessary in Torvaldsland; sometimes, however, a man may break a sword or lose an ax in battle, perhaps in the body of a foe, falling from a ship; in such a case the Jarl would make good the loss; he is not responsible for similar losses, however, among the free farmers. Those farmers who do not attend the thing, being the sole workers on their farms, must, nonetheless, maintain the regulation armament; once annually it is to be presented before a Jarl's officer, who, for this purpose, visits various districts. When the war arrow is carried, of course, all free men are to respond; in such a case the farm may suffer, and his companion and children know great hardship; in leaving his family, the farmer, weapons upon his shoulder, speaks simply to them. "The war arrow has been carried to my house," he tells them.

We saw, too, many chieftains, and captains, and minor Jarls, in the crowd, each with his retinue. These high men were sumptuously garbed, richly cloaked and helmeted, often with great axes, inlaid with gold. Their cloaks were usually scarlet or purple, long and swirling, and held with golden clasps. They wore them, always, as is common in Torvaldsland, in such a way that the right arm, the sword arm, is free.

Their men, too, often wore cloaks, and, about their

142

arms, spiral rings of gold and silver, and, on their wrists, jewel-studded bands.

In the crowd, too, much in evidence, were brazen bondmaids; they had been brought to the thing, generally, by captains and Jarls; it is not unusual for men to bring such slaves with them, though they are not permitted near the law courts or the assemblies of deliberation; the voyages to the thing were not, after all, ventures of raiding; they were not enterprises of warfare; there were three reasons for bringing such girls; they were for the pleasure of the men; they served, as display objects, to indicate the wealth of their masters; and they could be bought and sold.

The Forkbeard had brought with him, too, some bondmaids. They followed us. Their eyes were bright; their steps were eager; they had been long isolated on the farm; rural slave girls, the Forkbeard's wenches, they were fantastically stimulated to see the crowds; they looked upon the thingfields with pleasure and excitement; even had they been permitted, some of them, to look upon certain of the contests. It is said that such pleasures improve a female slave. Sometimes, in the south, female slaves are dressed in the robes of free women, even veiled, and taken by their masters to see tarn races, or games, or song-dramas; many assume that she, sitting regally by his side, is a companion, or being courted for the companionship; only he and she know that their true relation is that of master and slave girl; but when they return home, and the door to his compartment closes, their charade done, she immediately strips to brand and collar, and kneels, head to his feet, once again only an article of his property; how scandalized would have been the free woman, had they known that, next to them perhaps, had been sitting a girl who was only slave; but there were no disguises in Torvaldsland; there was no mistaking that the girls who followed the Forkbeard, or "Thorgeir of Ax Glacier," were bond; to better display his pets, and excite the envy of others, the Forkbeard had had his girls drop their kirtles low upon their hips, and hitch them high, that their beauty might be well exhibited, from their collars to some inches below their navels, and, too, that the turns of their calves and ankles might be similarly displayed; I would have thought that they might have groaned with humiliation and attempted to hide themselves among us, but, instead, even Pudding and Thyri, they walked as proud, shameless bondmaids; the exposure of the female's navel, on Gor, is known as the "slave belly"; only female slaves expose their navels;

143

from a vendor, the Forkbeard bought his girls honey cake; with their fingers they ate it eagerly, crumbs at the side of their mouths.

"Look!" cried Pudding. "A silk girl!" The expression 'silk girl' is used, often, among bond-maids of the north, to refer to their counterparts in the south. The expression reflects their belief that such girls are spoiled, excessively pampered, indulged and coddled, sleek pets, who have little to do but adorn themselves with cosmetics and await their masters, cuddled cutely, on plush, scarlet coverlets, fringed with gold. There is some envy in this charge, I think. More literally, the expression tends to be based on the fact that the brief slave tunic of the south, the single garment permitted the female slave, is often of silk. Southern girls, incidentally, in my opinion, though scarcely as worked as their northern sisters in bondage, a function of the economic distinction between the farm and city, are often worked, and worked hard, particularly if they have not pleased their masters. Yet, I think their labors less than those often performed by the wife of Earth. This is a consequence of Gor's simpler culture, in which there is literally less to do, less to clean, less to care for, and so on, and also of the fact that the Gorean master, if pleased with the wench, takes care that she is fresh and ready for the couch. An overworked, weary woman, despondent and tired, is less responsive to her master's touch; she does not squirm as well. The Gorean master, treating her as the animal she is, works and handles her in such a way that the responses of his passionate, exciting, hot-eyed, slim-legged pet are kept honed to perfection. Some men are better at this, of course, than others. There are scrolls, books, on Gor, which may be purchased inexpensively, on the feeding, care and training of female slaves. There are others who claim, as would be expected, that the handling of a slave girl, in order to get the most out of her, is an inborn gift. Incidentally, for what it is worth, though the southern girl is, I expect, worked less hard than the northern girl, who is commonly kept on an isolated farm, she is more often than her northern sister put to the switch or whip; I think she lives under a harsher discipline; southern masters are harder with their girls, expecting more from them and seeing that they get it; northern girls, for example, are seldom trained in the detailed, intricate sensuous arts of the female slave; the southern girl, to her misery, must often learn these to perfection; moreover, upon command, she must perform, joyfully and skillfully.

The silk girl was heeling her master, a captain of Torvaldsland. She wore, indeed, a brief tunic of the south, of golden silk. She wore a collar of gold, and, hanging in her ears, were loops of gold.

"High-farm girls!" she whispered, as she passed the bond-maids of Ivar Forkbeard. In the south the southern slave girl commonly regards her northern counterparts as bump-kins, dolts from the high farms on the slopes of the moun-tains of Torvaldsland; she thinks of them as doing little but swilling tarsk and dunging fields; she regards them as, essentially, nothing more than a form of bosk cow, used to work, to give simple pleasure to rude men, and to breed thralls.

"Cold fish!" cried out Pudding. "Stick!" cried out Pout-ing Lips.

The silk girl, passing them, did not appear to hear them. "Pierced-ear girl!" screamed Pouting Lips.

The silk girl turned, stricken. She put her hands to her ears. There were sudden tears in her eyes. Then, weeping, she turned away, her head in her hands, and fled after her master.

The bond-maids of Ivar Forkbeard laughed delightedly. The Forkbeard reached out and seized Pudding by the back of the neck. He looked at her. He also looked at Pouting Lips, who shrank back. He turned Pudding's head. "You wenches," he said, "might look well with pierced ears." "Oh, no, my Jarl," wept Pudding. "No!" "No," wept Pouting Lips. "Please, no, my Jarl!"

"Perhaps," mused the Forkbeard, "I shall have it done to the batch of you upon my return. Gautrek can perform this small task, I expect."

"No," whimpered the girls, huddled together. The Fork-beard turned then, and we continued on our way. The Fork-beard whistled. He was in an excellent mood. In moments the girls, too, were again laughing and sporting, and point-ing out sights to one another. There was only one of the Forkbeard's wenches who did not sport and laugh. Her name was Dagmar. There was a strap of binding fiber knotted about her collar. She was led by Thyri. Her hands were tied together, behind her back. She had been brought to the thing to be sold off.

"Let us watch duels," said the Forkbeard. The duel is a device by which many disputes, legal and personal, are set-tled in Torvaldsland. There are two general sorts, the formal duel and the free duel. The free duel permits all weapons;

there are no restrictions on tactics or field. At the thing, of course, adjoining squares were lined out for these duels. If the combatants wished, however, they might choose another field. Such duels, commonly, are held on wave-struck skerries in Thassa. Two men are left alone; later, at nightfall, a skiff returns, to pick up the survivor. The formal duel is quite complex, and I shall not describe it in detail. Two men meet, but each is permitted a shield bearer; the combatants strike at one another, and the blows, hopefully, are fended by each's shield bearer; three shields are permitted to each combatant; when these are hacked to pieces or otherwise rendered useless, his shield bearer retires, and he must defend himself with his own weapon alone; swords not over a given length, too, are prescribed. The duel takes place, substantially, on a large, square cloak, ten feet on each side, which is pegged down on the turf; outside this cloak there are two squares, each a foot from the cloak, drawn in the turf. The outer corners of the second of the two drawn squares are marked with hazel wands; there is thus a twelve-foot-square fighting area; no ropes are stretched between the hazel wands. When the first blood touches the cloak the match may, at the agreement of the combatants, or in the discretion of one of the two referees, be terminated; a price of three silver tarn disks is then paid to the victor by the loser; the winner commonly then performs a sacrifice; if the winner is rich, and the match of great importance, he may slay a bosk; if he is poor, or the match is not considered a great victory, his sacrifice may be less. These duels, particularly of the formal variety, are sometimes used disreputably for gain by unscrupulous swordsmen. A man, incredibly enough, may be challenged by such a fellow for his farm, or his companion, or daughter; if the challenge is not accepted, the stake is forfeit; if the challenge is accepted, of course, he who is challenged risks his life among the hazel wands; he may be slain; then, too, of course, the stake, the farm, the companion, the daughter, is surrendered by law to the challenger. The motivation of this custom, I gather, is to enable strong, powerful men to obtain land and attractive women; and to encourage those who possess such to keep themselves in fighting condition. All in all I did not much approve of the custom. Commonly, of course, the formal duel is used for more reputable purposes, such as settling grievances over boundaries or permitting an opportunity where, in a case of insult, satisfaction might be obtained.

One case interested us in particular. A young man, not more than sixteen, was preparing to defend himself against a large, burly fellow, bearded and richly helmeted.

"He is a famous champion," said Ivar, whispering to me, nodding to the large, burly fellow. "He is Bjarni of Thorstein Camp." Thorstein Camp, well to the south, but yet north of Einar's Skerry, was a camp of fighting men, which controlled the countryside about it, for some fifty pasangs, taking tribute from the farms. Thorstein of Thorstein's Camp was their Jarl. The camp was of wood, surrounded by a palisade, built on an island in an inlet, called the inlet of Thorstein Camp, formerly known as the inlet of Parsit, because of the rich fishing there.

The stake in this challenge was the young man's sister, a comely, blond lass of fourteen, with braided hair. She was dressed in the full regalia of a free woman of the north. The clothes were not rich, but they were clean, and her best. She wore two brooches; and black shoes. The knife had been removed from the sheath at her belt; she stood straight, but her head was down, her eyes closed; about her neck, knotted, was a rope, it fastened to a stake in the ground near the dueling square. She was not otherwise secured.

"Forfeit the girl," said Bjarni of Thorstein Camp, addressing the boy, "and I will not kill you."

"I do not care much for the making of women of Torvaldsland bond," said Ivar. "It seems improper," he whispered to me. "They are of Torvaldsland!"

"Where is the boy's father?" I asked one who stood next to me.

"He was slain in an avalanche," said the man.

I gathered then that the boy was then owner of the farm. He had become, then, the head of his household. It was, accordingly, up to him to defend, as best he could, against such a challenge.

"Why do you not challenge a baby?" asked Ivar Forkbeard.

Bjarni looked upon him, not pleasantly. "I want the girl for Thorstein Camp," he said. "I have no quarrel with children."

"Will she be branded there, and collared?" asked Ivar.

"Thorstein Camp," said Bjarni, "needs no free women."

"She is of Torvaldsland," said Ivar.

"She can be taught to squirm and carry mead as well as any other wench," said Bjarni.

I had no doubt that this was true. Yet the girl was young.

I doubted that a girl should be put in a collar before she was fifteen.

Ivar looked at me. "Would you like to carry my shield?" he asked.

I smiled. I went to the young man, who was preparing to step into the area of hazel wands. He was quite a brave lad.

Another youngster, about his own age, probably from an adjoining farm, would carry his shield for him.

"What is your name, Lad?" I asked the young man preparing to enter the square marked off with the hazel wands.

"Hrolf," said he, "of the Inlet of Green Cliffs."

I then took both of the boys, by the scruff, and threw them, stumbling, more than twenty feet away to the grass.

I stepped on the leather of the cloak. "I'm the champion," said I, "of Hrolf of the Inlet of Green Cliffs." I unsheathed the sword I wore at my belt.

"He is mad," said Bjarni.

"Who is your shield bearer?" asked one of the two white-robed referees.

"I am!" called the Forkbeard, striding into the area of hazel wands.

"I appreciate the mad bravery," said I, "of the good fellow Thorgeir of Ax Glacier, but, as we all know, the men of Ax Glacier, being of a hospitable and peaceful sort, are unskilled in weapons." I looked at the Forkbeard. "We are not hunting whales now," I told him, "Thorgeir."

The Forkbeard sputtered.

I turned to the referee. "I cannot accept his aid," I told him. "It would too much handicap me," I explained, "being forced, doubtless, to constantly look out for, and protect, one of his presumed ineptness."

"Ineptness!" thundered the Forkbeard.

"You are of Ax Glacier, are you not?" I asked him, innocently. I smiled to myself. I had, I thought, hoisted the Forkbeard by his own petard.

He laughed, and turned about, taking his place on the side.

"Who will bear your shield?" asked one of the referees.

"My weapon is my shield," I told him, lifting the sword. "He will not strike me."

"What do you expect to do with that paring knife?" asked Bjarni of Thorstein Camp, looking at me, puzzled. He thought me mad.

"Your long sword," I told him, "is doubtless quite useful in thrusting over the bulwarks of ships, fastened together by

148

grappling irons, as mine would not be, but we are not now, my dear Bjarni, engaging in combat over the bulwarks of ships."

"I have reach on you!" he cried.

"But my blade will protect me," I said. "Moreover, the arc of your stroke is wider than mine, and your blade heavier. You shall shortly discover that I shall be behind your guard."

"Lying sleen!" cried out the man of Thorstein Camp.

The girl, the rope on her throat, looked wildly at me. The two boys, white-faced, stood behind the hazel wands. They understood no more of what was transpiring than most others of those present.

The chief referee looked at me. His office was indicated by a golden ring on his arm. To his credit, he had, obviously, not much approved of the former match.

"Approve me," I told him.

He grinned. "I approve you," said he, "as the champion of Hrolf of the Inlet of Green Cliffs." Then he said to me, "As you are the champion of the challenged, it is your right to strike the first blow.

I tapped the shield of Bjarni of Thorstein Camp, it held by another ruffian from his camp, with the point of my sword.

"It is struck," I said.

With a cry of rage the shield bearer of Bjarni of Thorstein Camp rushed at me, to thrust me back, stumbling, hopefully to put me off my balance, for the following stroke of his swordsman.

I stepped to one side. The shield bearer's charge carried him almost to the hazel wands. Bjarni, sword high, had followed him. I now stood beside Bjarni, the small sword at the side of his neck. He turned white. "Let us try again," I said. Quickly he fled back, and was joined by his shield bearer. In the second charge, though I do not know if it were elegant or not, given the proprieties of the formal duel, I tripped the shield bearer. One is not supposed to slay the shield bearer but, as far as I knew, tripping, though perhaps not in the best form, was acceptable. I had, at any rate, seen it done in an earlier match. And, as I expected, neither of the referees warned me of an infraction. I gathered, from the swift looks on their faces, that they had thought it rather neatly done, though they are supposed to be objective in such matters. The fellow went sprawling. Bjarni, quite wisely, he obviously brighter than his shield bearer, had not

149

followed him so closely this time, but had hung back. Our swords met twice, and then I was under his guard, the point of my sword under his chin. "Shall we try again?" I asked.

The shield bearer leaped to his feet. "Let us fight!" he cried.

Bjarni of Thorstein Camp looked at me. "No," he said. "Let us not try again." He took the point of his sword and made a cut in his own forearm, and held it out, over the leather. Drops fell to the leather. "My blood," said Bjarni of Thorstein Camp, "is on the leather." He sheathed his sword.

The girl and her brother, and his friend, and the others cried with pleasure.

Her brother ran to her and untied the rope from about her neck.

His friend, though she was but fourteen, took her in his arms.

Bjarni of Thorstein Camp went to the boy whom he had challenged. From his wallet he took forth three tarn disks of silver and placed them, one after the other, in the boy's hand. "I am sorry, Hrolf of the Inlet of Green Cliffs," he said, "for having bothered you."

Then Bjarni came to me and put out his hand. We shook hands. "There is fee for you in Thorstein Camp," said he, "should you care to share our kettles and our girls."

"My thanks," said I. "Bjarni of Thornstein Camp." Then he, with his shield bearer, left the leather of the square of hazel wands.

"These I give to you, Champion," said the boy, trying to push into my hands the three tarn disks of silver.

"Save them," said I, "for your sister's dowry in her companionship."

"With what then," asked he, "have you been paid?"

"With sport," I said.

"My thanks, Fighter," said the girl.

"My thanks, too, Champion," said the boy who held her.

I bowed my head.

"Boy!" cried the Forkbeard. The boy looked at him. The Forkbeard threw him a golden tarn disk. "Buy a bosk and sacrifice it," said the Forkbeard. "Let there be much feasting on the farms of the Inlet of Green Cliffs!"

"My thanks, Captain!" cried the boy. "My thanks!"

There was cheering from the men about, as I, the Forkbeard, some of his men, and some of his bond-maids, left the place of dueling.

We passed one fellow, whom we noted seized up two bars

of red-hot metal and ran for some twenty feet, and then threw them from him.

"What is he doing?" I asked.

"He is proving that he has told the truth," said the Forkbeard.

"Oh," I said.

I noted that the bond-maids of Ivar Forkbeard attracted more than their expected share of attention. They were quite beautiful, from collars to low bellies, and the turn of their legs.

"Your girls walk well," I told Ivar.

"They are bond-maids," said he, "under the eyes of strange men."

I smiled. The girls wore their kirtles as they did not simply that the riches owned by Ivar Forkbeard might be well displayed, the better to excite the envy of others and brighten his vanity, but for another reason as well; the female slave, knowing she is slave, finds it stimulating to be exposed to the inspection of unknown men; do they find her body pleasing; do they want it; is she desired; she sees their looks, their pleasure; these things, for example, do they wish they owned her, she finds gratifying; she is a female; she is proud of her allure, her beauty; further, she is stimulated by knowing that one of these strange men might buy her, might own her, and that then she would have to please him, and well; the eyes of a handsome free man and a slave girl meet; she sees he wonders how she would be in the furs; he sees that she, furtively, speculates on what it would be like to be owned by him; she smiles, and, in her collar, hurries on; both receive pleasure.

"When we return to Forkbeard's Landfall," said the Forkbeard, "they will be better, for having looked, and having been looked upon."

In the south, a girl is sometimes sent to the market clad only in her brand and collar; not infrequently, upon her return home, she begs her master for his touch. To be seen and desired is stimulating to the female slave.

A girl must be careful, of course; should she in any way irritate, or not please, her master she may be switched or whipped.

In some cities, once a day, a girl must kneel and kiss the whip which, if she is not sufficiently pleasing to her master, will be used to beat her.

A farmer, in the crowd, reached forth. His heavy hand, swiftly, from her left hip to her right breast, caressed Thyri,

151

lingering momentarily on her breast. She stopped, startled. Then she darted away. "Buy me, my Jarl!" she laughed. "Buy me!"

The Forkbeard grinned. His girls, he knew, were good. Few who looked upon them would not have liked to own them.

We saw thralls, too, in the crowd, and rune-priests, with long hair, in white robes, a spiral ring of gold on their left arms, about their waist a bag of omen chips, pieces of wood soaked in the blood of the sacrificial bosk, slain to open the thing; these chips are thrown like dice, sometimes several times, and are then read by the priests; the thing-temple, in which the ring of the temple is kept, is made of wood; nearby, in a grove, hung from poles, were the bodies of six bosk, one of them the ceremonial bosk, six tarsk, and six verr; in past days, it is my understanding, there might have hung there, in place of the six verr, six thralls; it had been decided, however, a generation ago, by one of the rare meetings of the high council of rune-priests, attended by the high rune-priests of each district, that thralls should no longer be sacrificed; this was not defended, however, on grounds of the advance of civilization, or such, but rather on the grounds that thralls, like urts and tiny, six-toed tharlarion, were not objects worthy of sacrifice; there had been a famine and many thralls had been sacrificed; in spite of this the famine had not abated for more than four growing seasons; this period, too, incidentally, was noted for the large number of raids to the south, often involving entire fleets from Torvaldsland; it had been further speculated that the gods had no need of thralls, or, if they did, they might supply this need themselves, or make this need known through suitable signs; no signs, however, luckily for thralls, were forthcoming; this was taken as a vindication of the judgment of the high council of rune-priests; after the council, the status of rune-priests had risen in Torvaldsland; this may also have had something to do with the fact that the famine, finally, after four seasons, abated; the status of the thrall, correspondingly, however, such as it was, declined; he was now regarded as much in the same category with the urts that one clubs in the Sa-Tarna sheds, or are pursued by small pet sleen, kept there for that purpose, or with the tiny, six-toed rock tharlarion of southern Torvaldsland, favored for their legs and tails, which are speared by children. If the thrall had been nothing in Torvaldsland before, he was now less than nothing; his status was now, in effect, that of the southern, male work slave, found often in the quarries and mines, and, chained, on the great farms. He, a despised animal, must obey instantly and perfectly, or be subject to immediate slaughter. The Forkbeard had brought one thrall with him, the young man, Tarsk, who, even now, followed in the retinue of the Forkbeard; it was thought that if the Forkbeard should purchase a crate of sleen fur or a chest of bog iron the young man, on his shoulders, might then bear it back to our tent, pitched among other tents, at the thing; bog iron, incidentally, is inferior to the iron of the south; the steel and iron of the weapons of the men of Torvaldsland, interestingly, is almost uniformly of southern origin; the iron extracted from bog ore is extensively used, however, for agricultural implements.

In the crowd, too, I saw some merchants, though few of them, in their white and gold. I saw, too, four slavers, perfumed, in their robes of blue and yellow silk, come north to buy women. I saw, by the cut of their robes, they were from distant Turia. Forkbeard's girls shrank away from them. They feared the perfumed, silken slavery of the south; in the south the yoke of slavery is much heavier on a girl's neck; her bondage is much more abject; she is often little more than the pleasure plaything of her master; it is common for a southern master to care more for his pet sleen than his girls. In the north, of course, it is common for a master to care more for his ship than his girls. I saw, too, in the crowd, a physician, in green robes, from Ar and a scribe from Cos. These cities are not on good terms but they, civilized men, both in the far north, conversed affably.

"Send that one to the platform!" cried out a farmer, indicating Gunnhild.

"To the platform!" roared Ivar Forkbeard.

He tore away her kirtle. Soon she, barefoot, was climbing the wooden steps to the platform.

This is a wooden walkway, about five feet wide and one hundred feet long. On the walkway, back and forth, smiling, looking one way and then the other, turning about, parade stripped bond-maids. They are not for sale, though many are sold from the platform. The platform is instituted for the pleasure of the free men. It is not unanalogous to the talmit competitions, though no talmit is awarded. There are judges, usually minor Jarls and slavers. No judge, incidentally, is female. No female is regarded as competent to judge a female's beauty; only a man, it is said, can do that.

"Smile, you she-sleen!" roared the Forkbeard.

Gunnhild smiled, and walked.

No free woman, of course, would even think of entering such a contest. All who walk on such a platform are slave girls.

At last only Gunnhild and the "silk girl," she who had worn the earrings, walked on the platform.

And it was Gunnhild who was thrown the pastry, to the delight of the crowds, shouting, pounding their spear blades on their wooden shields.

"Who owns her?" called the chief judge.

"I do!" called the Forkbeard.

He was given a silver tarn disk as prize.

Many were the bids on Gunnhild, shouted from the crowd, but the Forkbeard waved such offers aside. The man laughed. Clearly he wanted the wench for his own furs. Gunnhild was very proud.

"Kirtle yourself, wench," said the Forkbeard to Gunnhild, throwing her her kirtle. She fixed it as it had been before, low on her hips, hitched above her calves.

At the foot of the steps leading down from the platform, the Forkbeard stopped, and bowed low. I, too, bowed. The slave girls fell to their knees, heads down, Gunnhild with them.

"How shameful!" said the free woman, sternly.

The slave girls groveled at her feet. Slave girls fear free women muchly. It is almost as if there were some unspoken war between them, almost as if they might be mortal enemies. In such a war, or such an enmity, of course, the slave girl is completely at the mercy of the free person; she is only slave. One of the great fears of a slave girl is that she will be sold to a woman. Free women treat their female slaves with incredible hatred and cruelty. Why this is I do not know. Some say it is because they, the free women, envy the girls their collars and wish that they, too, were collared, and at the complete mercy of masters.

Free women view the platform with stern disapproval; on it, female beauty is displayed for the inspection of men; this, for some reason, outrages them; perhaps they are furious because they cannot display their own beauty, or that they are not themselves as beautiful as women found fit, by lusty men with discerning eyes, for slavery; it is difficult to know what the truth is in such matters; these matters are further complicated, particularly in the north, by the conviction among free women that free women are above such things as sex, and that only low and loose girls, and slaves, are interested

154

in such matters; free women of the north regard themselves as superior to sex; many are frigid, at least until carried off and collared; they often insist that, even when they have faces and figures that drive men wild, that it is their mind on which he must concentrate his attentions; some free men, to their misery, and the perhaps surprising irritation of the female, attempt to comply with this imperative; they are fools enough to believe what such women claim is the truth about themselves; they should listen instead to the dreams and fantasies of women, and recall, for their instruction, the responses of a free woman, once collared, squirming in the chains of a bond-maid. These teach us truths which many woman dare not speak and which, by others, are denied, interestingly, with a most psychologically revealing hysteria and vehemence. "No woman," it is said, "knows truly what she is until she has worn the collar." Some free women apparently fear sex because they feel it lowers the woman. This is quite correct. In few, if any, human relationships is there perfect equality. The subtle tensions of dominance and submission, universal in the animal world, remain ineradicably in our blood; they may be thwarted and frustrated but, thwarted and frustrated, they will remain. It is the nature of the male, among the mammals, to dominate, that of the female to submit. The fact that humans have minds does not cancel the truths of the blood, but permits their enrichment and enhancement, their expression in physical and psychological ecstasies far beyond the reach of simpler organisms; the female slave submits to her master in a thousand dimensions, in each of which she is his slave, in each of which he dominates her.

"Shameful!" cried the free woman.

In the lowering of the woman, of course, a common consequence of her helplessness in the arms of a powerful male, her surrendering, her being forced to submit, she finds, incredibly to some perhaps, her freedom, her ecstasy, her fulfillment, her exaltation, her joy; in the Gorean mind this matter is simple; it is the nature of the female to submit; accordingly, it is natural that, when she is forced to acknowledge, accept, express and reveal this nature, that she should be almost deliriously joyful, and thankful, to her master; she has been taught her womanhood; no longer is she a sexless, competitive pseudoman; she is then, as she was not before, female; she then finds herself, perhaps for the first time, clearly differentiated from the male, and vulnerably, joyfully, complementary to him; she has, of course, no choice

155

in this matter; it is not permitted her; collared, she submits; I know of no group of women as joyful, as spontaneous, as loving and vital, as healthy and beautiful, as excited, as free in their delights and emotions, as Gorean slave girls; it is true they must live under the will of men, and must fear them, and the lash of their whips, but, in spite of these things, they walk with a sensuous beauty and pride; they know themselves owned; but they wear their collars with a shameless audacity, a joy, an insolent pride that would scandalize and frighten the bored, depressed, frustrated women of Earth.

"I do not approve of the platform," said the free woman, coldly.

Forkbeard did not respond to her, but regarded her with great deference.

"These females," she said, indicating the Forkbeard's girls, who knelt at her feet, their heads to the turf, "could be better employed on your farm, dunging fields and making butter."

The free woman was a tall woman, large. She wore a great cape of fur, of white sea-sleen, thrown back to reveal the whiteness of her arms. Her kirtle was of the finest wool of Ar, dyed scarlet, with black trimmings. She wore two brooches, both carved of the horn of kailiauk, mounted in gold. At her waist she wore a jeweled scabbard, protruding from which I saw the ornamented, twisted blade of a Turian dagger; free women in Torvaldsland commonly carry a knife; at her belt, too, hung her scissors, and a ring of many keys, indicating that her hall contained many chests or doors; her hair was worn high, wrapped about a comb, matching the brooches, of the horn of kailiauk; the fact that her hair was worn dressed indicated that she stood in companionship; the number of her keys, together with the scissors, indicated that she was mistress of a great house. She had gray eyes; her hair was dark; her face was cold, and harsh.

"But I am of Ax Glacier," said the Forkbeard. In the Ax Glacier country, of course, there were no farms, and there were no verr or bosk, there being insufficient grazing. Accordingly there would be little field dunging to be done, there being no fields in the first place and no dung in the second; too, due to the absence of verr or bosk, butter would be in scarce supply.

The free woman, I could see, was not much pleased with the Forkbeard's response.

"Thorgeir, is it not?" she asked.

"Thorgeir of Ax Glacier," said the Forkbeard, bowing.

"And what," asked she, "would one of Ax Glacier need with all these miserable slaves?" She indicated the kneeling girls of Forkbeard.

"In Ax Glacier country," said the Forkbeard, with great seriousness, "the night is six months long."

"I see," smiled the woman. Then she said, "You have won talmits, have you not, Thorgeir of Ax Glacier?"

"Six," said he, "Lady."

"Before you claim them," she said, "I recommend that you recall your true name."

He bowed.

Her recommendation did not much please me.

She lifted the hem of her kirtle of scarlet wool about the ankles of her black shoes and turned away. She looked back, briefly, once. She indicated the kneeling slaves. "Kirtle their shame," she said. Then she strode away, followed by several men-at-arms.

"Kirtle your shame!" cried the Forkbeard.

His girls, quickly, frightened, tears in their eyes, drew about them as well as they could their kirtles. They covered, as well as they could, their bodies, having been shamed by the free woman. It is a common practice of free women, for some reason, to attempt to make the female slave ashamed of her body.

"Who was that?" I asked.

"Bera," said he, "the companion of Svein Blue Tooth."

My heart sank.

"He should put her in a collar," said the Forkbeard. I was scandalized at the very thought.

"She needs the whip," he said. Then he looked at his girls. "What have you done?" he asked. "Drop your kirtles, and hitch them up!"

Laughing, once more proud of their bodies, the girls of the Forkbeard insolently slung their kirtles low on their hips, and hitched them high over their calves, even half way up their delightful thighs.

Then, we again continued on our way, leaving the place of the platform, the place of Gunnhild's triumph, where she had received a pastry, and where her master, the Forkbeard, had made a silver tarn disk on her beauty. She gave the other girls crumbs of the pastry and permitted Dagmar, who was to be sold off, to lick frosting from her fingers.

In the bond-maid shed there was a rustle of chain, as the girls looked up.

Light filtered into the shed from windows cut high in the wall on our right. The girls sat, or knelt or laid on straw along the wall at our left. The shed is some two hundred feet long, about ten feet wide, and eight feet in height.

An officer of Svein Blue Tooth, assisted by two thralls, quickly assessed Dagmar, stripping her, feeling her body, the firmness of her breasts, looking in her mouth.

"A tarn disk of silver," he said.

Dagmar had, two months ago, stolen a piece of cheese from Pretty Ankles; she had been beaten for that, at the post, fastened there by Ottar and switched by Pretty Ankles, until Pretty Ankles had tired of switching her; too, she had not been found sufficiently pleasing by several of the Forkbeard's oarsmen; she was, accordingly, to be sold off, as an inferior girl.

"Done," said the Forkbeard.

Dagmar was sold.

There were some one hundred bond-maids for sale in the shed. They all wore the collars of the north, with the projecting iron ring. They were fastened by a single chain, but it was not itself run through the projecting loop on their collars; rather, a heavy padlock, passing through a link of the chain and the projecting loop, secured them; in this way the chain, when a girl is taken from the chain, or added to it, need not be drawn through any of the loops; the girls may thus, with convenience, be spaced on the chain, removed from it, and added to it.

The Forkbeard was given the tarn disk, which he placed in his wallet. It had been taken from a sack slung about the shoulder of Blue Tooth's officer.

The officer then, pulling Dagmar by the arm, went to the right wall. There, from one of several small wooden boxes projecting at intervals from the wall, he took an opened padlock. He then walked across the shed, still holding Dagmar by the arm, and threw her to her knees. He then lifted the chain and, by means of the padlock, passing it through the loop on her collar and a link in the chain, secured her.

The Forkbeard, meanwhile, was looking at the bond-maids.

They were, of course, stripped for the view of buyers.

Behind the Forkbeard were myself, his men, those bond-maids who had accompanied us, and the thrall, Tarsk, who had been brought along, should the Forkbeard have made any heavy purchases.

"My Jarl," said Thyri.

"Yes," said the Forkbeard.

"Should this thrall," she asked, indicating Tarsk, once Wulfstan of Kassau, "be permitted to look upon the beauty of bond-maids?"

"What do you mean?" asked Ivar Forkbeard.

"He is, after all," said Thyri, "only a thrall."

I wondered that she would deny the young man this pleasure. I recalled that she had said she hated him. I, personally, had no objection to his presence in the shed. Thralls, I expected, had few pleasures. It might have been more than a year since he had been permitted a female.

The young man looked upon proud Thyri with great bitterness.

She lifted her head, and laughed.

"I think," said Ivar Forkbeard, "that I will send him back to the tent."

"Excellent," she said. She smiled at the thrall.

"Chain!" said the Forkbeard. One of his men took from over his shoulder a looped chain. At each end it terminated in a manacle. It had been held, looped, by these manacles being locked into one another. He removed it from his shoulder and opened the manacles. The chain itself was about a yard long. He handed it to the Forkbeard.

The young man would go chained to the tent.

"Wrist," said the Forkbeard.

The young man extended his wrists. Thyri watched, delighted.

The Forkbeard closed the manacle about the young man's left wrist.

Thyri laughed.

Then the Forkbeard took Thyri's right wrist and closed it in the other fetter.

"My Jarl!" she cried.

"She is yours until morning," the Forkbeard told the young thrall. "Use her behind the tent."

"My thanks, my Jarl!" he cried.

"My Jarl!" wept Thyri.

Tarsk seized the length of chain in his right fist, about a foot from her fetter. He jerked it. The fetter was large on her wrist, but she could not slip it. She was held. She looked at him with horror. "Hurry, Bond-maid!" he cried. He turned about, dragging her by the right wrist, his left hand on the chain about a foot from her wrist, and, almost running, pulled her, stumbling, crying out, after him.

The Forkbeard, and I, and his men, laughed. We had not

been much pleased at the insolence of the bond-maid with respect to the young thrall; once, we recalled, her taunting of him had almost cost him his life; I had intervened, and he had only been whipped instead; I had little doubt that Wulfstan of Kassau, the thrall, Tarsk, had many scores to settle with the pretty little she-sleen, once a fine young lady of Kassau; too, I recalled, she had once refused his suit, he supposedly not being good enough for her. I wished him much pleasure with her. "I hope," said the Forkbeard, "he will not make her scream all night behind the tent. I wish to obtain a good night's rest."

"It would seem a shame," said I, "to interfere with his pleasure."

"If necessary," said the Forkbeard, "I will simply have him gag her with her own kirtle."

"Excellent," I said.

The Forkbeard then turned his attention to the chained female slaves in the shed.

Some extended their bodies to him; some turned, to display themselves, provocatively; for he was obviously a desirable master; but others affected not to notice him; though I noticed that their bodies were held beautifully as he passed, particularly should he pause to regard them; other girls, perhaps newer to their collars, shrank back against the boards, trying to cover themselves; some regarded him with tears in their eyes; some with fear; some with open hostility; others with sullen resentment; all knew that he might, like any man, own them, completely.

To my surprise, he stopped before a dark-haired girl who sat with her legs drawn up, her arms about them, her ankles crossed; her cheek was laid across her knees; she seemed startled that the Forkbeard stopped before her; she looked up at him, frightened, and then put her face again down, across her knees, but now her eyes were frightened, and every inch of her seemed tense.

She looked up at him, but then could not meet his eyes. She seemed a shy, introverted girl, one who might, before her capture, have been much alone.

Then she had been caught by slavers.

"I would make a poor slave, my Jarl," she whispered.

"What do you know of this girl?" asked the Forkbeard of the officer of Svein Blue Tooth, who was accompanying him.

"She speaks little and, as she can, when not chained, as in the exercise pen, she keeps to herself."

The Forkbeard reached his hand toward her knee, but,

she watching, terrified, did not touch it, and then withdrew it.

She took a deep breath, closed her eyes, then opened them. She had feared to be touched.

Whereas fear inhibits sexual performance in a male, rendering it impossible, because neutralizing aggression, essential to male power, fear in a woman, some fear, not terror, can, interestingly, improve her responsiveness, perhaps by facilitating her abject submission, which can then lead to multiple orgasms. This is another reason, incidentally, why Goreans favor the enslavement of desirable women; the slave girl knows that she must please her master, and that she will be punished, and perhaps harshly, if she does not; this makes her not only desperate to please the brute who fondles her, but also produces in her a genuine fear of him; this fear on her part enhances her receptivity and responsiveness; also, of course, since fear stimulates aggression, which is intimately connected with male sexuality, her fear, which she is unable to help, to her master's amusement, deepens and augments the very predation in which she finds herself as quarry; and if she should not be afraid, it is no great matter; any woman, if the master wishes, can be taught fear.

After the Forkbeard had withdrawn his hand he studied her eyes, intently. I, too, detected that for which he had sought, the object of his experiment. Though she had feared his touch, yet, when he had withdrawn his hand, there was, momentarily, disappointment in her eyes. She both feared to be touched, and desperately yearned for the touch.

"Is she healthy?" asked the Forkbeard.

"Yes," said the officer of Svein Blue Tooth.

I had seen such women, sometimes on Earth. They were often studious, quiet girls, keeping much to themselves, lonely girls, yet with brilliant minds, marvelous imaginations, and fantastic, suppressed latent sexuality. They were often among the greatest surprises, and bargains, in the Gorean slave markets. Virginia Kent, whom I had known in Ar, years ago, who had become the companion of the warrior Relius of Ar, had been such a girl. On Earth she had taught ancient history and classical languages at a small college on Earth; to many she might then have seemed a rather bluestocking, forbidding girl; Gorean slavers, however, with greater perception perhaps then her fellow Earthlings, had seen her potential; she had been, one of several such items of cargo, abducted to Gor; on Gor, given no choice, suitably trained, she had become one of the most exquisite and delicious female slaves it had ever been my pleasure to see in a collar. Relius, given her, had freed her; his friend, Ho-Sorl, given another Earth girl, Phyllis Robertson, had kept the latter in a collar; Relius was younger than Ho-Sorl, and a romantic. Ho-Sorl, doubtless, was more experienced in the handling of females; I wondered if Virginia, to her astonishment, perhaps after a quarrel or after a night of depriving Relius in order to obtain some whim of hers had awakened one morning recollared, again the slave of a master.

"Kneel," said the Forkbeard to the girl, "legs apart, palms of your hands on your thighs.

With a movement of chain, she did so.

He crouched before her.

"I may wish to use you to breed thralls," he said. "You must be healthy for the farm. Put your head back, close your eyes and open your mouth."

She did as she was told, that the Forkbeard might examine her teeth. Much may be told of the age and condition of a female slave, as of a kaiila or bosk, from her teeth.

But the Forkbeard did not look into her mouth. His left hand slipped to the small of her back, holding her, and his right hand went suddenly to her body. She cried out, trying to pull back, but could not, and then, her eyes closed, whimpering, she thrust forward, writhing and then, sobbing, held herself immobile, teeth gritted, eyes screwed shut, trying not to feel. When his hands left her body she tried, sobbing, to strike him, but he caught both her small wrists, holding them. She struggled futilely, held kneeling.

"Put your head back," he said. "Open your mouth."

She shook her head, wildly.

"I am holding your hands," he pointed out.

Warily, eyes open, she opened her mouth. He looked at her teeth.

"I may wish to use you to breed thralls," he said. "You must be healthy for the farm."

He stood up.

"What do you want for her?" he asked the officer of Svein Blue Tooth.

"I had her for a broken coin," he said, "half a silver tarn disk of Tharna. I will let you have her for a whole coin."

The Forkbeard returned to the man the tarn disk of silver which he had received for Dagmar.

The officer of Svein Blue Tooth, with a key at his belt, unlocked the padlock which held the girl's collar to the common chain. He tossed the padlock, open, into one of the wooden boxes projecting from the right wall.

The girl, kneeling, looked up at the Forkbeard. "Why did my Jarl buy me?" she asked.

"You have excellent teeth," said the Forkbeard.

"For what will my Jarl use me?" she asked.

"Doubtless you can learn to swill tarsks," he said.

"Yes, my Jarl," she said. Then she put her cheek, to our surprise, to the side of his leg, and, lowering her head, holding his boot, kissed it.

It was very delicately, and lovingly, done.

"What is your name?" he asked.

"Peggie Stevens," she said. I smiled. It was an Earth name.

"You are an Earth female," I told her.

"Once," she said. "Now I am only a female."

"American?" I asked.

"Prior to my enslavement," she said.

"From what state?" I asked.

"Connecticut," she said.

Since the Nest War the probes of aliens had grown more bold, even on Gor; they had little difficulty in taking female slaves on Earth; gold, exchangeable for materials essential to their enterprises, was well guarded on Earth; it could seldom be obtained in quantities without attracting the attention of the agents of Priest-Kings; on the other hand, the women of Earth, dispersed, abundant, many of them beautiful, superb slave stock, the sort a Gorean master enjoys training to the collar, were, generally, unguarded; Earth took greater care to guard her gold than her females; accordingly, the women of Earth, unprotected, vulnerable, like luscious fruit on wild trees, were free for the pickings of Gorean slavers; a network, I gathered, existed for their selection and acquisition; Earth was helpless to prevent the taking of their most beautiful women; they were eventually sold naked from blocks in Gorean markets. I supposed that the governments of Earth, or some of them, were aware of the slaving; perhaps merchants of Middle Eastern countries were suspected; there were, however, delicate negotiations concerning oil to be respected; it would not be well to be too bold in pressing accusations; what were a few beautiful women, taken as slave girls into the harems of Middle Eastern businessmen and potentates, to the commodity which supported civilization and turned the wheels of industry; but the evidence would not point to the Middle East; further, the small amount of slaving, if any, which might be done commercially in Western Europe or on the Eastern Seaboard of the United States would not account for the numbers of missing beauties; hundreds a year, I surmised, turned up in Gorean markets. I speculated that Earth governments, or some of them, were reasonably well aware that their planet must now be the locus of frequent alien slave raids; but why would the alien power not make itself known and openly demand their jewels among the female resources of the planet; the governments would not know of the power of the Priest-Kings, which the agents of the Kurii profoundly and wisely feared; what could these governments of Earth do; they could do nothing; could they, wisely, inform their populations that their planet lay under the attacks of technologically advanced aliens, with which their own primitive technologies were incapable of coping; that they, and all of Earth, seemed to lie at the mercies of invaders from outer space; such an announcement could only bring about the loss of confidence in governments, panic, hoarding, crime, perhaps a breakdown in communication, perhaps anarchy, perhaps a shattering of trust and civilizations themselves. No. It was better to say nothing. Accordingly, I supposed, this very night, on Earth, there were completely unsuspecting beautiful girls, thinking it a night like any other, who would undress themselves and snap off the light, and retire, not knowing that they had been, perhaps for weeks, scouted by slavers; I wondered if they would awaken in terror, the slaver's rope on their throat, his needle, with its drug, thrusting into their side; or if, days later, perhaps weeks, they would awaken sluggishly, then suddenly alert to the change of gravity, and find themselves in a barred, cemented slave kennel, on their left ankles, locked, the steel identification device of the agents of the Kurii, that their manifests be correct, their records precise.

"How did you come to the north?" I asked the slave girl, Miss Stevens.

"I was sold in Ar," she said, "to a merchant from Cos. I was chained in a slave ship, with many other girls, on tiers in the hold. The ship fell to four raiding vessels of Torvaldsland. I have been, by my reckoning, eight months in the north."

"What did your last Jarl call you?" asked the Forkbeard.

"Butter Pan," she said.

The Forkbeard looked to Gunnhild. "What shall we call this pretty little slave?" he asked.

"Honey Cake," suggested Gunnhild.

"You are Honey Cake," said the Forkbeard.

"Yes, my Jarl," said Miss Stevens.

The Forkbeard then left the bond-maid shed. We all followed him. He did not restrain Honey Cake in any way. She, nude, in her collar, back straight, accompanied him. Her head was high. She was a bought girl. The other girls, still on the chain, regarded her with envy, with resentment, hostility. She paid them no attention. She had been purchased. They remained unbought girls, wenches left on the chain; they had not yet been found desirable enough to be purchased.

Few suspected, on this day, in the thing, that something unprecedented would occur.

After we had left the bond-maid shed I had let the Forkbeard and his retinue return to their tent. Honey Cake, when last I saw her, dared to cling to his arm, her head to his shoulder. He, with a laugh, thrust her back with the other girls that she, as they, might heel him. Happily, she did so.

I watched them disappear among the crowds.

Ivar Forkbeard had won six talmits. He had done quite well.

Honey Cake, too, I thought, would make him a delicious little slave.

We would all enjoy her.

I was at the archery range when the announcement was made.

I had not intended to participate in the competition. Rather, it had been my plan to buy some small gift for the Forkbeard. Long had I enjoyed his hospitality, and he had given me many things. I did not wish, incidentally, even if I could, to give him a gift commensurate with what he had, in his hospitality, bestowed upon me; the host, in Torvaldsland, should make the greatest gifts; it is, after all, his house or hall; if his guest should make him greater gifts than he makes the guest this is regarded as something in the nature of an insult, a betrayal of hospitality; after all, the host is not running an inn, extending hospitality like a merchant, for profit; and the host must not appear more stingy than the guest who, theoretically, is the one being welcomed and sheltered; in Torvaldsland, thus, the greater generosity is the host's prerogative; should the Forkbeard, however, have come to Port Kar then, of course, it would have been my prerogative to make him greater gifts than he did me. This is, it seems to me, an intelligent custom; the host, giving first, and knowing what he can afford to give, sets the limit to the giving; the guest then makes certain that his gifts are less than those of the host; the host, in giving more, wins honor as a host; the guest, in giving less, does the host honor. Accordingly, I was concerned to find a gift for the Forkbeard; it must not be too valuable, but yet, of course, I wanted it to be something that he would appreciate.

I was on my way to the shopping booths, those near the wharves, where the best merchandise is found, when I stopped to observe the shooting.

"Win Leah! Win Leah, Master!" I heard.

I looked upon her, and she looked upon me.

She stood on the thick, rounded block; it was about a yard high, and five feet in diameter; she was dark-haired, long-haired; she had a short, luscious body, thick ankles; her hands were on her hips. "Win Leah, Master!" she challenged. She was naked, except for the Torvaldsland collar of black iron on her neck, with its projecting ring, and the heavy chain padlocked about her right ankle; the chain was about a yard long; it secured her, by means of a heavy ring, to the block. She laughed. "Win Leah, Master!" she challenged. She, with the archery talmit, was the prize in the shooting.

I noted her brand. It was a southern brand, the first letter, in cursive script, of Kajira, the most common expression for a Gorean female slave. It was entered deeply in her left thigh. Further, I noted she had addressed me as "Master," rather than "my Jarl." I took it, from these indications, she had learned her collar in the south; probably originally it had been a lock collar, snugly fitting, of steel; now, of course, it had been replaced with the riveted collar of black iron, with the projecting ring, so useful for running a chain through, or for padlocking, or linking on an anvil, with a chain. The southern collar, commonly, lacks such a ring; the southern ankle ring, however, has one, and sometimes two, one in the front and one in the back.

"Will you not try to win Leah, Master?" she taunted.

"Are you trained?" I asked.

She seemed startled. "In Ar," she whispered. "But surely you would not make me use my training in the north."

I looked upon her. She seemed the perfect solution to my problem. The gift of a female is sufficiently trivial that the honor of the Forkbeard as my host would not be in the least threatened; further, this was a desirable wench, whose cuddly slave body would be much relished by the Forkbeard and his crew; further, being trained, she would be a rare and exquisite treat for the rude giants of Torvaldsland; beyond this, of course, commanded, she would impart her skills to the best of her abilities to his other girls.

"You will do," I told her.

"I do not understand," she said, stepping back. The chain slid on the wood.

"Your name, and accent," I said, "bespeak an Earth origin."

"Yes," she whispered.

"Where are you from?" I asked.

"Canada," she whispered.

"You were once a woman of Earth," I said.

"Yes," she said.

"But now you are only a Gorean slave girl," I told her.

"I am well aware of that, Master," she said.

I turned away from her. The target in the shooting was about six inches in width, at a range of about one hundred yards. With the great bow, the peasant bow, this is not difficult work. Many marksmen, warriors, peasants, rencers, could have matched my shooting. It was, of course, quite unusual in Torvaldsland. I put twenty sheaf arrows into the target, until it bristled with wood and the feathers of the Vosk gull.

When I retrieved my arrows, to the shouting of the men, the pounding of their bows on their shields, the girl had been already unchained from the block.

I gave my name to the presiding official. Talmits would be officially awarded tomorrow. I accepted his congratulations.

My girl prize knelt at my feet. I looked down upon her. "What are you?" I asked.

"Only a Gorean slave girl, Master," she said.

"Do not forget it," I told her.

"I shall not, Master," she whispered.

"Stand," I told her.

She stood and I lashed her wrists tightly together behind her back.

It was then that the announcement was heard. It swept like oil, aflame in the wind, through the crowds of the thing. Men looked at one another. Many grasped their weapons more tightly.

"A Kur," it was said, "One of the Kurii, would address the assembly of the thing!"

The girl looked at me, pulling against the fiber that bound her wrists. "Have her delivered to the tent of Thorgeir of Ax

Glacier," I told the presiding official. "Tell him that she is a gift to him from Tarl Red Hair."

"It will be done," said the official. He signaled two burly thralls, each of whom seized her by one arm.

"Deliver her to the tent of Thorgeir of Ax Glacier," he told them. "Tell him that she is a gift to him from Tarl Red Hair."

The girl was turned about, each of the thralls holding one of her arms. She looked once over her shoulder. Then, between the thralls, moaning, crying out, stumbling, a gift being delivered, she was thrust toward the tent of he who was known at the thing as Thorgeir of Ax Glacier.

My eyes and those of the official who had presided at the archery contest met.

"Let us hasten to the place of the assembly," he said. Together we hurried from the field where I had won the talmit in archery, and a girl, to the place of the assembly.

11

THE TORVALDSBERG

It lifted its head.

It stood on the small hill, sloping above the assembly field. This hill was set with stones, rather in the manner of terraces. On these stones, set in semicircular lines, like terraces, stood high men and minor jarls, and rune-priests, and the guard of Svein Blue Tooth. Just below the top of the small hill, cut into the hill, there was a level, stone-paved platform, some twelve feet by twelve feet in dimension.

On this platform stood Svein Blue Tooth, with two high men, officers, lieutenants, to the jarl.

The thing, its head lifted, surveyed the assembly of free men. The pupils of its eyes, in the sunlight, were extremely small and black. They were like points in the yellowish green cornea. I knew that, in darkness, they could swell, like dark moons, to fill almost the entire optic orifice, some three or four inches in width. Evolution, on some distant, perhaps vanished world, had adapted this life form for both diurnial and nocturnal hunting. Doubtless, like the cat, it hunted when hungry, and its efficient visual capacities, like those of the cats, meant that there was no time of the day or night when it might not be feared. Its head was approximately the width of the chest of a large man. It had a flat snout, with wide nostrils. Its ears were large, and pointed. They lifted from the side of its head, listening, and then lay back against the furred sides of the head. Kurii, I had been told, usually, in meeting men, laid the ears back against the sides of their heads, to increase their resemblance to humans. The ears are often laid back, also, incidentally, in hostility or anger, and, always, in its attacks. It is apparently physiologically impossible for a Kur to attack without its shoulders hunching, its claws emerging, and its ears lying back against the head. The nostrils of the beast drank in what information it wished, as they, like its eyes, surveyed the throng. The trailing capacities of the Kurii are not as superb as those of the sleen, but they were reputed to be the equal of those of larls. The hearing, similarly, is acute. Again it is equated with that of the larl, and not the sharply-sensed sleen. There was little doubt that the day vision of the Kurii was equivalent to that of men, if not superior, and the night vision, of course, was infinitely superior; their sense of smell, too, of course, was incomparably superior to that of men, and their sense of hearing as well. Moreover, they, like men, were rational. Like men, they were a single-brained organism, limited by a spinal column. Their intelligence, by Priest-Kings, though the brain was much larger, was rated as equivalent to that of men, and showed similar random distributions throughout gene pools. What made them such dreaded foes was not so much their intelligence or, on the steel worlds, their technological capacities, as their aggressiveness, their persistence, their emotional commitments, their need to populate and expand, their innate savagery. The beast was approximately nine feet in height; I conjectured its weight in the neighborhood of eight or nine hundred pounds. Interestingly, Priest-Kings, who are not visually oriented organisms, find little difference between Kurii and men. To me this seems preposterous, for ones so wise as Priest-Kings, but, in spite of its obvious falsity, Priest-Kings regard the Kurii and men as rather similar, almost equivalent species. One difference they do remark between the human and the Kur, and that is that the human, commonly, has an inhibition against killing. This inhibition the Kur lacks.

"Fellow rational creatures!" called the Kur. It was difficult at first to understand it. It was horrifying, too. Suppose that, at some zoo, the tiger, in its cage, should look at you, and, in its rumbles, its snarls, its growls, its half roars, you should be able, to your horror, to detect crude approximations of the phonemes of your native tongue, and you should hear it speaking to you, looking at you, uttering intelligible sentences. I shuddered.

"Fellow rational creatures!" called the Kur.

The Kur has two rows of fangs. Its mouth is large enough to take into it the head of a full-grown man. Its canines, in the front row of fangs, top and bottom, are long. When it closes its mouth the upper two canines project over the lower lip and jaw. Its tongue is long and dark, the interior of its mouth reddish.

"Men of Torvaldsland," it called, "I speak to you."

Behind the Kur, to one side, stood two other Kurii. They, like the first, were fearsome creatures. Each carried a wide, round shield, of iron, some four feet in diameter. Each, too, carried a great, double-bladed iron ax, which, from blade tip to blade tip, was some two feet in width. The handle of the ax was of carved, green needle wood, round, some four inches in diameter. The axes were some seven or eight feet in height. The speaker was not armed, save by the natural ferocity of his species. As he spoke, his claws were retracted. About his left arm, which was some seven feet in length, was a spiral golden armlet. It was his only adornment. The two Kurii behind him, each, had a golden pendant hanging from the bottom of each ear. The prehensile paws, or hands, of the Kurii are six-digited and multiple jointed. The legs are thick and short. In spite of the shortness of the legs the Kur can, when it wishes, by utilizing its upper appendages, in the manner of a prairie simian, like the baboon, move with great rapidity. It becomes, in running, what is, in effect, a four-footed animal. It has the erect posture, permitting brain development and facilitating acute binocular vision, of a biped. This posture, too, of course, greatly increases the scanning range of the visual sensors. But, too, its anatomy permits it to function, in flight and attack, much as a four-legged beast. For short distances it can outrun a full-grown tarsk. It is also said to possess great stamina, but of this I am much less certain. Few animals, which have not been trained, have, or need, stamina. An exception would be pack hunters, like the wolves or hunting dogs of Earth.

"We come in peace," said the Kur.

The men of Torvaldsland, in the assembly field, looked to one another.

"Let us kill them," I heard one whisper to another.

"In the north, in the snows," said the Kur, "there is a gathering of my kind."

The men stirred uneasily. I listened intently.

I knew that Kurii did not, for the most part, inhabit areas frequented by men. On the other hand, the Kurii on the platform, and other Kurii I had encountered, had been dark-furred, either brownish, or brownish red or black. I wondered if it were only the darker furred Kurii that roamed southward. But if these Kurii on the platform were snow-adapted, their fur did not suggest this. I wondered if they might be from the steel ships, either recently, or within too few generations for a snow-adaption pattern to have been developed. If the Kurii were sufficiently successful, of course,

171

there would be no particular likelihood of evolution selecting for snow adaption. Too, it could be that, in summer, the Kurii shed white fur and developed, in effect, a summer coat. Still I regarded it unlikely that these Kurii were from as far north as his words might suggest.

"How many gather?" asked Svein Blue Tooth, who was on the platform with the Kurii.

Blue Tooth was a large man, bearded, with a broad, heavy face. He had blue eyes, and was blond haired. His hair came to his shoulders. There was a knife scar under his left eye. He seemed a shrewd, highly intelligent, competent, avaricious man. I thought him probably an effective jarl. He wore a collar of fur, dyed scarlet, and a long cloak, over the left shoulder, of purple-dyed fur of the sea sleen. He wore beneath his cloak yellow wool, and a great belt of glistening black, with a gold buckle, to which was attached a scabbard of oiled, black leather; in this scabbard was a sword, a sword of Torvaldsland, a long sword, with a jeweled pommel, with double guard.

"We come in peace," said the Kur.

"How many gather?" pressed Blue Tooth.

About his neck, from a fine, golden chain, pierced, hung the tooth of a Hunjer whale, dyed blue.

"As many as the stones of the beaches," said the Kur, "as many as the needles on the needle trees."

"What do you want?" called one of the men from the field.

"We come in peace," said the Kur.

"They do not have white fur," said I to Ivar Forkbeard, standing now beside me. "It is not likely that they come from the country of snows."

"Of course not," said the Forkbeard.

"Should this information not be brought to the attention of Svein Blue Tooth?" I asked.

"Blue Tooth is no fool," said the Forkbeard. "There is not a man here who believes Kurii to gather in the country of snows. There is not enough game to support many in such a place."

"Then how far would they be away?" I asked.

"It is not known," said the Forkbeard.

"You know us, unfortunately," said the Kur, to the assembly, "only by our outcasts, wretches driven from our caves, unfit for the gentilities of civilization, by our diseased and our misfits and our insane, by those who, in spite of our

172

efforts and our kindness, did not manage to learn our ways of peace and harmony."

The men of Torvaldsland seemed stunned.

I looked at the great axes in the hands of the two Kurii who accompanied the speaker.

"Too often have we met in war and killing," said the speaker. "But, in this, you, too, are much to blame. You have, cruelly, and without compunction, hunted us and, when we sought comradeship with you as brothers, as fellow rational creatures, you have sought to slay us."

"Kill them," muttered more than one man. "They are Kurii."

"Even now," said the Kur, the skin drawing back from its fangs, "there are those among you who wish our death, who urge our destruction."

The men were silent. The Kur had heard and understood their speech, though he stood far from us, and above us, on the platform of the assembly, that platform cut into the small, sloping hill over the assembly field. I admired the acuteness of its hearing.

Again the skin drew back from its fangs. I wondered if this were an attempt to simulate a human smile. "It is in friendship that we come." It looked about. "We are a simple, peaceful folk," it said, "interested in the pursuit of agriculture."

Svein Blue Tooth threw back his head and roared with laughter. I regarded him then as a brave man. Beside me, Ivar Forkbeard, too, laughed, and then others.

I wondered if the stomach or stomachs of the Kurii could digest vegetable food.

The assembly broke into laughter. It filled the field.

The Kur did not seem angry at the laughter. I wondered if it understood laughter. To the Kur it might be only a human noise, as meaningless to him as the cries of whales to us.

"You are amused," it said.

The Kurii, then, had some understanding of laughter. Its own lips then drew back, revealing the fangs. I then understood this clearly as a smile.

That the Kurii possessed a sense of humor did not much reassure me as to their nature. I wondered rather at what sort of situations it would take as its object. The cat, if rational, might find amusement in the twitching and trembling of the mouse which it is destroying, particle by particle. That a species laughs bespeaks its intelligence, its capacity

173

to reason, not its goodness, not its harmlessness. Like a knife, reason is innocent; like a knife, its application is a function of the hand that grasps it, the energies and will which drive it.

"We were not always simple farmers," said the Kur. It opened its mouth, that horrid orifice, lined with its double rows of white, heavy, curved fangs. "No," it said, "once we were hunters, and our bodies still bear, as reminders, the stains of our cruel past." It dropped its head. "We are by these," it said, and then it lifted its right paw, suddenly exposing the claws, "and these, reminded that we must be resolute in our attempts to overcome a sometimes recalcitrant nature." Then it regarded the assembly. "But you must not hold our past against us. What is important is the present. What is important is not what we were, but what we are, what we are striving to become. We now wish only to be simple farmers, tilling the soil and leading lives of rustic tranquillity."

The men of Torvaldsland looked at one another.

"How many of you have gathered?" asked Svein Blue Tooth again.

"As many," said the Kur, "as the stones on the beaches, as many as the needles on the needle trees."

"What do you want?" he asked.

The Kur turned to the assembly. "It our wish to traverse your country in a march southward."

"It would be madness," said the Forkbeard to me, "to permit large numbers of Kurri into our lands."

"We seek empty lands to the south, to farm," said the Kur. "We will take only as much of your land as the width of our march, and for only as long as it takes to pass."

"Your request seems reasonable," said Svein Blue Tooth. "We shall deliberate."

The Kur stepped back with the other Kurii. They spoke together in one of the languages of the Kurii, for there are, I understood, in the steel worlds, nations and races of such beasts. I could hear little of what they said. I could detect, however, that it more resembled the snarls and growling of larls than the converse of rational creatures.

"What crop," asked Ivar Forkbeard, who wore a hood, of the platform, "do the Kurii most favor in their agricultural pursuits?"

I saw the ears of the Kur lie swiftly back against its head. Then it relaxed. Its lips drew back from its fangs. "Sa-Tarna," it said.

The men in the field grunted their understanding. This was the staple crop in Torvaldsland. It was a likely answer.

Ivar then spoke swiftly to one of his men.

"What will you pay us to cross our land?" asked one of the free men of Torvaldsland.

"Let us negotiate such fees," said the beast, "when such negotiations are apt."

It then stepped back.

Various free men then rose to address the assembly. Some spoke for granting the permission to the Kurii for their march, many against it.

Finally, it was decided that it was indeed germane to the decision to understand what the Kurii would offer to obtain this permission.

I, in this time, had come to understand that Torvaldsland stood, in effect, as a wall between the Kurii and the more southern regions of Gor. The Kur, moveover, tends to be an inveterate land animal. They neither swim well nor enjoy the water. They are uneasy on ships. Moreover, they knew little of the craftsmanship of building a seaworthy ship. That now, suddenly, large numbers of Kurii were conjoined, and intent upon a march southward could not be a coincidence in the wars of such beasts with Priest-Kings. I supposed it quite probable this was, in effect, a probe, and yet one within the laws of the Priest-Kings. It was Gorean Kurii that were clearly, substantially, involved. They carried primitive weapons. They did not even use a translator. In the laws of Priest-Kings it was up to such species, those of Kurii and men, to resolve their differences in their own way. I had little doubt but what the Kurii, perhaps organized by Kurii from the steel worlds, were to begin a march in Torvaldsland, which might extend, in a generation to the southern pole of Gor. The Kurii were now ready to reveal themselves. At last they were ready to march. If they were successful, I had little doubt that the invasion from space, in its full power, would follow. In their mercy or disinterest, Priest-Kings had spared many Kurii who had been shipwrecked, or shot down, or marooned on Gor. These beasts, over the centuries grown numerous and strong, might now be directed by the Kurii of the steel worlds. Doubtless they had been in contact with them. I expected the speaker himself was of the steel ships, painfully taught Gorean. The Kurii native to Gor, or which had been permitted to survive and settle on Gor, would surely not be likely to have this facility. They and men seldom met, save to kill one another.

175

The Kurii, I gathered, did not wish to fight their way to more fertile lands south, but to reach them easily, thus conserving their numbers and, in effect, cutting Torvaldsland from the south. There was little to be gained by fighting an action the length of Torvaldsland, and little to be lost by not doing so, which could not be later recouped when power in the south had been consolidated. I had strong doubts, of course, as to whether a Kur invasion of the south was practical, unless abetted by the strikes of Kur ships from the steel worlds. The point of the probe, indeed, might be to push Kur power as far south as possible, and, perhaps, too, for the first time, result in the engagement of the forces of Priest-Kings to turn them back. This would permit an assessment of the power of Priest-Kings, the extent and nature of which was largely unknown to the Kurii, and, perhaps, to lure them into exposing themselves in such a way that a space raid might be successfully launched. All in all, I expected the invasion of the south was, at this point, primarily a probe. If it was successful, the Priest-Kings, to preserve men on the planet might be forced to intervene, thus breaking their own laws. If the Priest-Kings did not do this, perhaps for reasons of pride, their laws having been given, then, in effect, Gor might become a Kur world, in which, given local allies, the Priest-Kings might finally be isolated and destroyed. This was, to my knowledge, the boldest and most dangerous move of the Others, the Kurii, to this date. It utilized large forces on Gor itself, largely native Kurii in its schemes. Kurii from the ships, of course, as organizers, as officers, might be among them. And doubtless there would be communication with the ships, somehow. This march might be the first step in an invasion, to culminate with the beaching of silver ships, in their thousands, raiders from the stars, on the shores of Gor.

It was possible, of course, that the Kurii would attack Torvaldsland when well within it, without large forces marshaled against them. Once within the country, before an army could be massed against them, they might cut it to pieces, farm by farm.

It was possible, too, of course, that the Kurii had become gentle beasts, fond of farming, renouncing their warlike ways, and turning humbly to the soil, and the labors of the earth, setting perhaps therein an excellent example for the still half-savage human animals of Gor, so predatory, so savage, so much concerned with wars, and their codes and honor. Perhaps we could learn much from the Kurii. Perhaps we could learn from them not to be men, but a more benign animal, more content, more bovine; perhaps they could teach us, having overcome their proud, restless natures, to become, too, a gentler, sweeter form of being, a more pleasant, a softer, a happier animal. Perhaps, together with them, tilling the soil, we could construct a more placid world, a world in which discipline and courage, and curiosity and adventure, and doing what pleases one, would become no more than the neglected, scorned, half-forgotten anachronisms of remote barbarians. We would then have overcome our manhood, and become one with the snails, the Kurii and the flowers.

"What will you pay," asked Svein Blue Tooth, "for permission to traverse our land, should that permission be granted?"

"We will take little or nothing," said the Kur, "and so must be asked to pay nothing."

There was an angry murmur from the men in the field.

"But," said the Kur, "as there are many of us, we will need provisions, which we will expect you to furnish us."

"That we will furnish you?" asked Svein Blue Tooth. I saw spear points lifted among the crowd.

"We will require," said the Kur, "for each day of the march, as provisions, a hundred verr, a hundred tarsk, a hundred bosk, one hundred healthy property-females, of the sort you refer to as bond-maids."

"As provisions?" asked the Blue Tooth, puzzled.

Among the Kurii, in their various languages, were words referring to edible meat, food. These general terms, in their scope, included human beings. These terms were sometimes best translated as "meat animal" and sometimes "cattle" or, sometimes, simply "food." The human being was regarded, by Kurii, as falling within the scope of application of such terms. The term translated "cattle" was sometimes qualified to discriminate between four-legged cattle and two-legged cattle, of which the Kurii were familiar with two varieties, the bounding Hurt and the human.

"Yes," said the Kur.

Svein Blue Tooth laughed.

The Kur, this time, did not seem amused. "We do not ask for any of your precious free females," it said.

The soft flesh of the human female, I knew, was regarded as a delicacy among the Kurii.

"We have better uses for our bond-maids," said Svein Blue Tooth, "than to feed them to Kurii."

There was great laughter in the field.

I knew, however, that if such a levy was agreed upon, the girls would be simply chained and, like the cattle they would be, be driven to the Kurii march camps. Female slaves are at the mercy of their masters, completely.

But I did not expect men of Torvaldsland to give up female slaves. They were too desirable. They would elect to keep them for themselves.

"We will require, too," said the Kur, "one thousand male slaves, as porters, to be used, too, in their turn, as provisions."

"And if all this be granted to you," asked Svein Blue Tooth, "what will you grant us in return?"

"Your lives," said the Kur.

There was much angry shouting. The blood of the men of Torvaldsland began to rage. They were free men, and free men of Gor.

Weapons were brandished.

"Consider carefully your answer, my friends," said the Kur. "In all, our requests are reasonable."

He seemed puzzled at the hostility of the men. He had apparently regarded his terms as generous.

And I supposed that to one of the Kurii, they had indeed been generous. Would we have offered as much to a herd of cattle that might stand between us and a desired destination?

I saw then the man of Ivar Forkbeard, whom he had earlier sent from his side, climbing to the platform. He carried a wooden bucket, and another object, wrapped in leather. He conferred with Svein Blue Tooth, and the Blue Tooth smiled.

"I have here," called Svein Blue Tooth, "a bucket of Sa-Tarna grain. This, in token of hospitality, I offer to our guest."

The Kur looked into the bucket, at the yellow grain. I saw the claws on the right paw briefly expose themselves, then, swiftly, draw within the softness of the furred, multiple digited appendage.

"I thank the great Jarl," said the beast, "and fine grain it is. It will be our hope to have such good fortune with our own crops in the south. But I must decline to taste your gift, for we, like men, and unlike bosk, do not feed on raw grain."

The Jarl, then, took, from the hands of Ivar Forkbeard's man, the leather-wrapped object.

It was a round, flat, six-sectioned loaf of Sa-Tarna bread.

The Kur looked at it. I could not read his expression.

"Feed," invited Svein Blue Tooth.

The Kur reached out and took the loaf. "I shall take this to my camp," it said, "as a token of the good will of the men of Torvaldsland."

"Feed," invited Svein Blue Tooth.

The two Kurii behind the speaker growled, soft, like irritated larls.

It made the hair on my neck rise to hear them, for I knew they had spoken to one another.

The Kur looked upon the loaf, as we might have looked on grass, or wood, or the shell of a turtle.

Then, slowly, he put it in his mouth. Scarcely had he swallowed it than he howled with nausea, and cast it up.

I knew then that this Kur, if not all, was carnivorous.

It then stood on the platform, its shoulders hunched; I saw the claws expose themselves; the ears were back flat against its head; its eyes blazed.

A spear came too close to it. It seized it, ripping it from the man, and, with a single snap of its teeth, bit the shaft in two, snapping it like I might have broken a dried twig. Then it lifted its head and, fangs wild, like a maddened larl, roared in fury. I think there was not a man in the field who was not, for that instant, frozen in terror. The roar of the beast must have carried even to the ships.

"Do we, free men of Torvaldsland," called out Svein Blue Tooth, "grant permission to the Kurii to traverse our land?"

"No!" cried one man.

"No," cried others.

Then the entire field was aflame with the shouts of angry men.

"A thousand of you can die beneath the claws of a single Kur!" cried the Kur.

There was more angry shouting, brandishing of weapons. The speaker, the Kur, with the golden spiral bracelet, turned angrily away. He was followed by the two others.

"Fall back!" cried out Svein Blue Tooth. "The peace of the thing is upon them!"

Men fell back, and, between them, shambling, swiftly moved the three Kurs.

"We are done with them," said Ivar Forkbeard.

"Tomorrow," called Svein Blue Tooth, "we will award the talmits for excellence in the contests." He laughed. "And tomorrow night we shall feast!"

There was much cheering, much brandishing of weapons.

"I have won six talmits," Ivar Forkbeard reminded me.

"Will you dare to claim them?" I asked.

He looked at me, as though I might be mad. "Of course," said he, "I have won them."

In leaving the thing field I saw, in the distance, a high, snow-capped mountain, steep, sharp, almost like the blade of a bent spear.

I had seen it at various times, but never so clearly as from the thing field. I suppose the thing field might, partly, have been selected for the aspect of this mountain. It was a remarkable peak.

"What mountain is that?" I asked.

"It is the Torvaldsberg," said Ivan Forkbeard.

"The Torvaldsberg?" I asked.

"In the legends, it is said that Torvald sleeps in the mountain," smiled Ivar Forkbeard, "to awaken when, once more, he is needed in Torvaldsland."

Then he put his arm about my shoulder. "Come to my camp," said he. "You must still learn to break the Jarl's Ax's gambit."

I smiled. Not yet had I mastered a defense against this powerful gambit of the north.

12

IVAR FORKBEARD INTRODUCES HIMSELF TO SVEIN BLUE TOOTH

About my forehead were bound two talmits, one which I had won in wrestling, the other in archery.

The men of the Forkbeard, and many others, clapped me on the back. I was much pleased. On the other hand I was not certain that I had much longer to live. Soon it would come the time to award the talmits to the mysterious Thorgeir of Ax Glacier.

Two men of Svein Blue Tooth rose to their feet and silenced the crowd with two blasts on curved, bronze signal horns, of a sort often used for communication between ships. The men of Torvaldsland have in common a code of sound signals, given by the horns, consisting of some forty messages. Messages such as 'Attack,' 'Heave to,' 'Regroup,' and 'Communication desired' have each their special combination of sounds. This sort of thing is done more effectively, in my opinion, in the south by means of flags, run commonly from the prow cleats to the height of the stem castle. Flags, of course, are useless at night. At night ship's lanterns may be used, but there is no standardization in their use, even among the ships of a given port. There are shield signals, too, however, it might be mentioned, in Torvaldsland, though these are quite limited. Two that are universal in Torvaldsland are the red shield for war, the white for peace. The men of Torvaldsland, hearing the blasts on the bronze horns, were silent. The blasts had been the signal for attention.

On the wooden dais, draped in purple, set on the contest fields, in heavy, carved chairs, sat Svein Blue Tooth and his woman, Bera. Both wore their finery. About them, some on the dais, and some below it, stood his high officers, and his men of law, his counselors, his captains, and the chief men from his scattered farms and holdings; too, much in evidence, were more than four hundred of his men-at-arms. In the crowd, too, in their white robes, were rune-priests.

Svein Blue Tooth rose to his feet, standing before the heavy, carved wooden chair. Bera remained sitting. About his neck, on its golden chain, hung the tooth of the Hunjer whale, dyed blue.

"Never in the history of the thing," called Svein, "has there been so high a winner in the contests as he whom we now proceed to honor."

I was not surprised that this was true.

Ivar Forkbeard had won six talmits.

He had won a talmit for climbing the "mast," a tall pole of needle wood; it was some fifty feet high, and was peeled and smoothed; he had won one for "leaping the crevice," which was actually a broad jump, performed on level ground; one for walking the "oar," which was actually a long pole; two in contests of the spear, one for distance and one for accuracy; and one in swimming. He had done less well in singing, poetry composition, rhyming and riddle guessing. He had come in, however, in second place in riddle guessing.

"This man," called out Svein Blue Tooth, obviously impressed, "has earned in these contests six talmits. Never in the history of the thing has there been so high a winner." Svein Blue Tooth was of Torvaldsland himself. He well understood the mightiness of the winner's exploits. It was rare for one man to win even two talmits. Thousands entered the contests. Only one, in each contest, could achieve the winner's talmit. "I distinguish myself, and enter into the history of our land," said the Blue Tooth, "in being the high Jarl to award these talmits in the games. As we honor this man we, in doing this, similarly do honor onto ourselves." This was cultural in Torvaldsland. One is regarded as being honored when one rightly bestows honor. It is not like one man taking something from another, so much as it is like an exchanging of gifts. To a somewhat lesser extent, it might be mentioned, this is also cultural in the south.

Svein Blue Tooth was obviously pleased that it had been in his Jarlship that six talmits had been won at the thing by a single, redoubtable champion.

Ivar Forkbeard, large, robed in gray, hooded in gray, stood beside me.

His features could not be well seen.

From a leather box, proffered to him by a high officer, who, too, had been the presiding official at the contests, Svein Blue Tooth lifted a fistful of talmits.

There was much cheering, much shouting, much lifting of weapons. Spear blades struck the surfaces of the round, painted, wooden shields.

There were steps leading to the dais.

"He who calls himself Thorgeir of Ax Glacier," proclaimed Svein Blue Tooth, "let him approach!"

Ivar Forkbeard eagerly bounded up the stairs toward the dais. There was not one of his men who did not tense, and reach to his weapons, reassuring himself as to their readiness. I looked about, considering the most opportune paths of flight.

If one is immersed in boiling tharlarion oil one dies quickly. On the other hand, if it is heated slowly, over a tiny fire, this same process consumes several hours. I studied the face of Svein Blue Tooth. I had little doubt that he was a patient man.

I shuddered.

Ivar Forkbeard, Thorgeir of Ax Glacier, now stood, hooded, on the top stair of the dais, before his enemy.

I hoped that Svein Blue Tooth would simply hand him the talmits and he might rapidly back down, and we might run for the ship.

My heart sank.

It was obviously the intent of Svein Blue Tooth, himself, to honor this great winner, to bind on his forehead, with his own hands, the talmits.

The Blue Tooth reached to brush back the hood. Ivar drew back his head.

Svein Blue Tooth laughed. "Do not fear, Champion," said he. "There is none here who believes your name, truly, to be Thorgeir of Ax Glacier."

Ivar Forkbeard shrugged and spread his hands, as though he had been found out, as though his ruse had failed.

I felt like beating his head in with the handle of an ax.

"What is your name, Champion?" asked Bera, the woman of Jarl Svein Blue Tooth.

Ivar was silent.

"That you have disguised yourself tells us," said the Blue Tooth, "that you are outlaw."

Ivar looked at him, as though startled at his perception.

"But the peace of the thing is upon you," said Svein Blue

183

Tooth. "You are safe among us. Do not fear, great Champion. We meet here not to threaten you, but to do you honor. Be not afraid, for the peace of the thing is upon you, as on all men here."

"Great Jarl," said Ivar Forkbeard, "will you swear upon me the oath of peace, for the time of the thing, your personal oath, sworn upon the ring of the temple of Thor?"

"It is not necessary," said the Blue Tooth, "but, if you wish, this oath I will swear."

The Forkbeard bowed his head in humble petition.

The great ring of the temple of Thor, stained in the blood of the sacrificial ox, was brought. It was held in the hands of the high rune-priest of the thing. Svein Blue Tooth grasped it in both hands. "I swear upon you the peace of the thing," said he, "and I make this oath of peace, for the time of the thing, mine own as well."

I breathed more easily. I saw the Forkbeard's men about me visibly relax.

Only the Forkbeard did not seem satisfied.

"Swear, too," he suggested, "by the side of the ship, by the shield's rim, by the sword's edge."

Svein Blue Tooth looked at him, puzzled. "I so swear," he said.

"And, too," begged the Forkbeard, "by the fires of your hearth, by the timbers of the hall and the pillars of your high seat."

"Come now!" said Svein Blue Tooth.

"My Jarl—" begged the Forkbeard.

"Very well," said the Blue Tooth, "I swear by the ship's side, the shield's rim, the sword's edge, the fires of my hearth, the timbers of my hall and the pillars of the high seat in my house."

He then made ready to brush back the hood, but the Forkbeard drew back once more.

"Will you swear, too," he asked, "by the grains of your fields, the boundary stones of your holdings, the locks on your chests and the salt on your table?"

"Yes, yes!" said Svein Blue Tooth, irritatedly. "I so swear."

The Forkbeard seemed lost in thought. I assumed he was trying to think of ways to strengthen the Blue Tooth's oath. It seemed to me a mighty oath already. I thought it quite sufficient.

"And, too, I swear," said Svein Blue Tooth, "by the bronze of my ladles and the bottoms of my butter pans!"

"That will not be necessary," said the Forkbeard, generously.

"What is your name, Champion?" asked Svein Blue Tooth.

Ivar Forkbeard threw back his hood. "My name is Ivar Forkbeard," he said.

13

VISITORS IN THE HALL
OF SVEIN BLUE TOOTH

The hall of Svein Blue Tooth was of wood, and magnificent.

The interior hall, not counting rooms leading from it on various sides, or the balcony which lined it, leading to other rooms, was some forty feet high, and forty feet in width, some two hundred feet in length. It, on the western side, was lined with a great, long table. Behind this table, its back to the western wall, facing the length of the hall, facing east, was the high seat, or the rightful seat, the seat of the master of the house. It was wide enough for three or four men to sit together on it, and, as a great honor, sometimes others were invited to share the high seat. On each side of this high seat were two pillars, about eight inches in diameter, and some eight feet high, the high-seat pillars, or rightful-seat pillars. They marked the seat, or bench, which might be placed between them as the high seat, or rightful seat. These pillars had been carved by craftsmen in the time of Svein Blue Tooth's great grandfather, and bore the luck signs of his house. On each side of the high seat were long benches. Opposite, on the other side of the table, too, were long benches. A seat of honor, incidentally, was that opposite the high seat, where one might converse with the host. The high seat, though spoken of as "high," was the same height as the other benches. The men of Torvaldsland, thus, look across the table at one another, not one down upon the other. The seat is "high" in the sense of being a seat of great honor. There was, extending almost the length of the hall, a pit for a "long fire" over which food was prepared for retainers. On the long sides of the hall, on the north and south, there were long tables, with benches. Salt, in its bowls on

186

the tables, divided men into rankings. Those sitting above the salt were accorded greater prestige than those sitting below it. If one sat between the salt and the high seat, one sat "above" the salt; if one sat between the salt and the entrance to the hall, one sat "below" the salt. At the high-seat table, that at which the high seat sat, all counted as being "above the salt." Similarly, at the tables parallel to the high-seat table, smaller tables flanking the long fire on both sides, the tables nearest the high seat counted as being above the salt, those farthest away being below the salt. The division was made approximately at the third of the hall closest to the high seat, but could shift, depending on the numbers of those in attendance worthy to be above the salt. The line, so to speak, imaginary to be sure, but definitely felt as a social reality, dividing those above from those below the salt, was uniformly "drawn" across the width of the hall. Thus, it was not the case that one at a long side table, who was above the salt, would be farther away from the high seat than one at one of the center tables, who was "below" the salt. In Ivar Forkbeard's hall, incidentally, the salt distinctions were not drawn; in his hall, all being comrades in arms, all were "above the salt." Svein Blue Tooth's holdings, on the other hand, were quite large and complexly organized. It would not have seemed proper, at least in the eyes of Svein Blue Tooth and others, for a high officer to sit at the same table with a fellow whose main occupation was supervising thralls in the tending of verr. Salt, incidentally, is obtained by the men of Torvaldsland, most commonly, from sea water or from the burning of seaweed. It is also, however, a trade commodity, and is sometimes taken in raids. The red and yellow salts of the south, some of which I saw on the tables, are not domestic to Torvaldsland. The arrangements of tables, incidentally, varies in different halls. I describe those appointments characterizing the hall of Blue Tooth. It is common, however, for the entrance of the hall to be oriented toward the morning sun, and for the high seat to face the entrance. None may enter without being seen from the high seat. Similarly, none are allowed to sit behind the high seat. In a rude country, these defensive measures are doubtless a sensible precaution.

About the edges of the hall hung the shields of warriors, with their weapons. Even those who sat commonly at the center tables, and were warriors, kept their shields and spears at the wall. At night, each man would sleep in his furs behind the tables, under his weapons. High officers, of course, and the Blue Tooth, and members of his family, would retire to private rooms.

The hall was ornately carved, and, above the shields, decorated with cunningly sewn tapestries and hangings. On these were, usually, warlike scenes, or those dealing with ships and hunting. There was a lovely scene of the hunting of tabuk in a forest. Another tapestry, showing numerous ships, in a war fleet, dated from the time of the famine in Torvaldsland, a generation ago. That had been a time of great raids to the south.

Svein Blue Tooth had not been much pleased on the fields of the contests, on his purple-draped dais, when Ivar Forkbeard had announced his identity.

"Seize him and heat oil!" had been the first cry of the Blue Tooth.

"Your oath! Your oath!" had cried the horrified, startled rune-priests.

"Seize him!" screamed the Blue Tooth, but his men had, forcibly, restrained him, they glaring at Ivar Forkbeard with ill-disguised disapproval.

"You tricked me!" cried out the Blue Tooth.

"Yes," admitted the Forkbeard. "It is true."

Svein Blue Tooth, held in the arms of his men, struggled to unsheath his great sword of blued steel.

The high rune-priest of the thing interposed himself between the violent Blue Tooth and the Forkbeard, who was, innocently, regarding cloud formations.

The rune-priest held up the heavy, golden ring of Thor, the temple ring itself, stained in the blood of the sacrificial ox. "On this ring you have sworn!" he cried.

"And by many other things as well," added the Forkbeard, unnecessarily to my mind.

The veins stood out on the forehead and neck of Svein Blue Tooth.

He was a powerful man. It was not easy for his officers to restrain him.

At last, eyes blazing, he subsided. "We will hold parley," he said.

He, with his high officers, retired to the back of the dais. Many heated words were passed between them. More than one cast a rather dark look in the direction of the Forkbeard, who, then, his disguise cast off, was cheerily waving to various acquaintances in the crowd.

"Long live the Forkbeard!" cried a man in the throng. The men-at-arms of Svein Blue Tooth stirred uneasily. They

188

edged more closely about the dais. I ascended the steps of the dais and stood at the back of the Forkbeard, hand on the hilt of the sword, to protect him if necessary. "You are insane," I informed him. "Look," he said, "there is Hafnir of the Inlet of Iron Walls. I have not seen him since I was outlawed." "Good," I said. He waved to the man. "Ho, there, Hafnir!" he cried. "Yes, it is I, Ivar Forkbeard!" The men-at-arms of Svein Blue Tooth were now uncomfortably close. I pushed away spear points with my left hand.

Meanwhile the debate at the back of the dais went on. The issues seemed reasonably clear, though I could catch only snatches of what was said; they concerned the pleasures of boiling the Forkbeard and his retinue alive as opposed to the dangerous precedent which might be set if the peace of the thing was sundered, and the loss of credit which might accrue to Svein Blue Tooth if he reneged on his pledged oaths, deep oaths publicly and voluntarily given. There were also considerations to the effect that the rune-priests would be distressed if the oaths were broken, and that the gods, too, might not look lightly upon such a violation of faith, and might, too, more seriously, evidence their displeasure by such tokens as blights, plagues, hurricanes and famines. Against these considerations it was argued that not even the gods themselves could blame Svein Blue Tooth, under these circumstances, for not honoring a piddling oath, extracted under false pretenses; one bold fellow even went so far as to insist that, under these special circumstances, it was a solemn obligation incumbent on the Blue Tooth to renounce his oath and commit the Forkbeard and his followers, with the exception of slaves, who would be confiscated, to the oil pots. Fortunately, in the midst of his eloquence, this fellow sneezed, which omen at once, decisively, wiped away the weightiness of his point.

At last the Blue Tooth turned to face the Forkbeard. Svein's face was red with rage.

The high rune-priest lifted the sacred temple ring.

"The peace of the thing," said the Blue Tooth, "and the peace of my house, for the time of the thing, is upon you. This I have sworn. This I uphold."

There was much cheering. The Forkbeard beamed. "I knew it would be so, my Jarl," he said. The high rune-priest lowered the temple ring.

I rather admired Svein Blue Tooth. He was a man of his word. By his word he would stand, even though, as in the present case, any objective observer would have been forced to admit that his provocation to betray it, his temptation to betray it, must have been unusual in the extreme. In honor such a high jarl must set an example to the men of Torvaldsland. He had, nobly, if not cheerfully, set the example.

"By tomorrow night," said he, "when the thing is done, be free of this place. My oath is for the time of the thing, and for no longer."

"You have six talmits of mine, I believe," said the Forkbeard.

Svein Blue Tooth looked at him in rage.

"There is one for swimming," said the Forkbeard, "one for climbing the mast, one for leaping the crevice, one for walking the oar, and two for prowess with the spear."

Blue Tooth was speechless.

"That is six," said the Forkbeard. "Never before in the history of the thing has a champion done this well."

The Blue Tooth thrust the talmits toward the Forkbeard. But the Forkbeard, humbly, inclined his head.

Then Svein Blue Tooth, as high jarl in Torvaldsland, one by one, tied about the forehead of Ivar Forkbeard the six talmits.

There was much cheering. I, too, cheered. Svein Blue Tooth was, in his way, not a bad fellow.

"By tomorrow night," repeated Svein Blue Tooth to the Forkbeard, "when the thing is done, be free of this place. My oath is for the time of the thing, and for no longer."

"You frown upon me, and would put me below the salt," said Ivar Forkbeard, "because I am outlaw."

"I frown upon you, and would not let you within the doors of my hall," said Svein Blue Tooth, "because you are the greatest scoundrel and rogue in Torvaldsland!"

I could see that this compliment much pleased the Forkbeard, who, a vain fellow, was jealous of his reputation.

"But I have," said the Forkbeard, "the means wherewith to buy myself free of the outlawry you yourself pronounced upon me."

"That is preposterous!" snorted the Blue Tooth. Several of his men laughed.

"No man," said the Blue Tooth, looking suddenly at Ivar Forkbeard, "could pay such wergild as I set for you."

"You have heard," inquired Ivar Forkbeard, "of the freeing of Chenbar, the Sea Sleen, from the dungeons of Port Kar?" He smiled. "You have heard," he inquired, "of the sack of the temple of Kassau?"

"You!" cried the Blue Tooth.

I saw the eyes of the Blue Tooth suddenly gleam with avarice. I knew then, surely, that he was of Torvaldsland. There is a streak of the raider in them all.

"The wergild I set you," said he slowly, "was such that no man, by my intent, could pay it. It was one hundred stone of gold, the weight of a grown man in the sapphires of Schendi, and the only daughter of my enemy, Thorgard of Scagnar."

"May I pay my respects to you this night in your hall?" asked the Forkbeard.

Svein Blue Tooth looked at him, startled. He fingered the heavy tooth, on its chain, which hung about his neck, that tooth of a Hunjer whale, dyed blue.

Bera, his woman, rose to her feet. I could see that her mind was moving with rapidity.

"Come tonight to our hall, Champion," said she.

The Blue Tooth did not gainsay her. The woman of the Jarl had spoken. Free women in the north have much power. The Jarl's Woman, in the Kaissa of the north, is a more powerful piece than the Ubara in the Kaissa of the south. This is not to deny that the Ubara in the south, in fact, exercises as much or more power than her northern counterpart. It is only to recognize that her power in the south is less explicitly acknowledged.

The Forkbeard looked to Svein Blue Tooth. Svein fingered the tooth on its chain.

"Yes," said he, "come tonight to my hall—Champion."

There had then been again much cheering. Svein Blue Tooth, high jarl of Torvaldsland, followed by his woman, and high officers and counselors, and other followers, then took his way from the dais.

We had fed well in the hall of Svein Blue Tooth.

Many were the roast tarsk and roast bosk that had roasted over the long fire, on the iron spits. Splendid was the quality of the ale at the tables of the Blue Tooth. Sweet and strong was the mead.

The smoke from the fire found its way high into the rafters, and, eventually, out of the holes cut in the peaked roof. Some of these were eighteen inches square. Light was furnished from the cooking fire but, too, from torches set in rings on the wall, backed with metal plating; too, here and there, on chains from the beams, high above, there hung large tharlarion oil lamps, which could be raised and lowered from the sides. At places, too, there were bowls, with

191

oil and wicks, with spikes on their bottoms, set in the dirt floor, some six inches from the floor, others as high as five feet; this mode of lamp, incidentally, is more common in the private chambers. It was not unusual, incidentally, that the floor of the great hall, rich as it was, was of dirt, strewn with rushes. This is common in the halls of Torvaldsland. When the Forkbeard, and I, and other followers, many of them bearing riches, entered the hall we had been given a room to one side, in which we might wash and dry ourselves before the feast. In this room, unusual in halls, was a window. I had put my finger against it, and pressed outward. It was not paned with glass, but with some sort of membrane, but the membrane was almost as clear as glass. "What is this?" I had asked the Forkbeard. "It is the dried afterbirth membrane of a bosk fetus," he said. "It will last many months, even against rain." Looking out through the window I could see the palisade about the hall and its associated buildings. The palisade inclosed some two acres; within it were many shops and storage houses, even an ice house; in the center, of course, reared the great hall itself, that rude, high-roofed palace of the north, the house of Svein Blue Tooth. Through the membrane, hardly distorted, I saw the palisade, the catwalk about it, the guards, and, over it, the moons of Gor. In the far distance, the moonlight reflected from its snowy heights I saw, too, the Torvaldsberg, in which the legendary Torvald was reputed to sleep, supposedly to waken again if needed once more in Torvaldsland.

I smiled.

I turned to Ivar Forkbeard. I saw that treasures, borne by his men, had been placed in this side room.

He grinned.

The Forkbeard was in a good mood. The last night had been quite a pleasant one for him. He had handed off Pudding and Gunnhild to his men, for the night, and had ordered to his furs Honey Cake, the former Miss Stevens of Earth, and the wench, Leah, the Canadian girl, whom I had won at archery and given to him as a gift. Honey Cake, like many shy, introverted, timid girls, fearing her own sexuality and fearing that of men, sensing them in terror as her natural masters, was the mistress of secret, incredible depths of repressed sexual emotion and feeling; the Forkbeard, of course, a rude barbarian, was not in the least concerned with the walls which she had, carefully, over years, built to conceal her own needs and desires from herself; he simply shattered them; he had forced her, unable to resist, as

192

only a bond-maid, without choice, to look deeply and openly on her own naked needs and desires; then he had used her as a slave; she had yielded to him helplessly, wondrously, laughing, weeping, crying out with joy; the wench, Leah, whom I had won at archery, had tried to resist the Forkbeard; he had her beaten and thrown back to his furs; soon she, too, in her turn, was moaning with pleasure; helplessly; she was responding beautifully to him; by morning both girls, on and about him, fighting one another, jealous of one another, were begging for his touch; at dawn he had ordered one of his men, that he might get some sleep, to chain them prone head to foot, the right ankle of each chained to the projecting ring on the collar of the other; the Forkbeard did not rise until afternoon; he was then much refreshed; I had, in my turn, with several of the other of the Forkbeard's men, enjoyed Pudding and Gunnhild; both were superb; toward morning, too, I had felt Olga's small fingers at my ankle; she was, like several of the other bond-maids, chained by the right ankle, the chain some eight feet in length, to a stake driven into the earth near the center of the Forkbeard's tent; she had crawled to the extent of her chain, her right leg extended behind her, and had stretched her right hand toward me; I took the furs to her side, wrapped her within them with me, and had much pleasure with her; we fell asleep two Ahn afterward, she still held in my arms, her head on my shoulder. When the Forkbeard himself rose, of course, the camp became quite active, and the slaves were put about many menial labors; the thrall, Tarsk, was unchained from Thyri, and set about the sawing of wood; Thyri herself, her kirtle thrown to her, was ordered to pound grain to make flour; she could not even look Tarsk in the face, I noted; she looked down, shyly; from her cries the night before I knew that she had, behind the tent, yielded to him; the other girls much teased her for yielding to a thrall; "I would have been beaten had I not yielded," she said in defense; then she looked down once more, and smiled; she did not seem discontent.

I saw her, late in the afternoon, unbidden, secretly bringing him water at his work.

"Thank you, Bond-maid," said he.

She put down her head.

"You are pretty, Bond-maid," he said.

"Thank you, my Jarl," she said.

He looked after her, as she sped away. He grinned. He then, whistling, worked with gusto.

He did not then seem to me unlike a free man.

"If you are washed and readied," said a young thrall, collared, in a kirtle of white wool, "it is permissible to present yourselves before the high seat of the house, before my master, Svein Blue Tooth, Jarl of Torvaldsland."

"We are honored," had said the Forkbeard. He designated four of his men to guard the treasures.

We looked at one another.

"I feel," I said, "as though I were walking into the jaws of a larl."

"Do not fear," said Ivar. "I, Forkbeard, am at your side."

"Were you not at my side," I said, "I doubt that I should feel as I do."

"I see," said the Forkbeard.

"Could we not," I suggested, "simply leap naked into a pit of venomous osts, or, perhaps, race madly across the plains of the Wagon Peoples during a lightning storm, our swords raised over our heads?"

"The trick," said the Forkbeard, "is not simply to walk into the jaws of a larl. Any fool can do that."

"I am well aware of that," I said.

"The trick," said the Forkbeard, winking, but not thereby much reassuring me, "is to walk back out again!"

"You have some intention, then," I asked, "of emerging from this escapade alive?"

"That is a portion of my plan," acknowledged the Forkbeard. "And, failing that, we will die nobly, against heavy odds. Thus, my plan is foolproof."

"You have reasoned it out well," I admitted. "Lead on."

The Forkbeard lifted his head boldly and, smiling, emerged from the side room, at the entrance to which he stopped and raised his hands, saluting the tables. He was greeted with warmth from the many warriors there. He had won six talmits. "The Forkbeard greets you!" shouted Ivar. I blinked. The hall was light. I had not understood it to be so large. At the tables, lifting ale and knives to the Forkbeard were more than a thousand men. Then he took his way to the bench opposite the high seat, stopping here and there to exchange pleasantries with the men of Svein Blue Tooth. I, and his men, followed him. The Blue Tooth, I noted, did not look too pleased at the Forkbeard's popularity with his men. Near him, beside the high seat, sat his woman, Bera, her hair worn high on her head, in a kirtle of yellow wool with scarlet cape of the fur of the red sea sleen, and, about her neck, necklaces of gold.

We had fed well in the hall of Svein Blue Tooth. During the meal, for Svein was a rich man, there had been acrobats, and jugglers and minstrels. There had been much laughter when one of the acrobats had fallen into the long fire, to leap scrambling from it, rolling in the dirt. Two other men, to settle a grievance, had had a tug of war, a bosk hide stretched between them, across the long fire. When one had been pulled into the fire the other had thrown the hide over him and stomped upon him. Before the fellow in the fire could free himself he had been much burned. This elicited much laughter from the tables. The jugglers had a difficult time, too, for their eyes on the cups and plates they were juggling, they were not infrequently tripped, to the hilarity of the crowd. More than one minstrel, too, was driven from the hall, the target of barrages of bones and plates.

The Forkbeard was, at one point, so furious at the ineptness of the musicians, that he informed me of his own intention to regale the tables with song. He was extremely proud of his singing voice. I prevailed upon him to desist. "You are a guest," I told him, "it would not be seemly for you, by your talents, to shame the entertainers, and thereby perhaps reflect upon the honor of your host, who doubtless has provided the best he can." "True," admitted the Forkbeard. I breathed more easily. Had Ivar Forkbeard broken into song I would have given little for our chances.

Male thralls turned the spits over the long fire; female thralls, bond-maids, served the tables. The girls, though collared in the manner of Torvaldsland, and serving men, were fully clothed. Their kirtles of white wool, smudged and stained with grease, fell to their ankles; they hurried about; they were barefoot; their arms, too, were bare; their hair was tied with strings behind their heads, to keep it free from sparks; their faces were, on the whole, dirty, smudged with dirt and grease; they were worked hard; Bera, I noted, kept much of an eye upon them; one girl, seized by a warrior, her waist held, his other hand sliding upward from her ankle beneath the single garment permitted her, the long, stained woolen kirtle, making her cry out with pleasure, dared to thrust her lips eagerly, furtively, to his; but she was seen by Bera; orders were given; by male thralls she was bound and, weeping, thrust to the kitchen, there to be stripped and beaten; I presumed that if Bera were not present the feast might have taken a different turn; her frigid, cold presence was, doubtless, not much welcomed by the men. But she was the woman of Svein Blue Tooth. I supposed, in time,

195

normally, she would retire, doubtless taking Svein Blue Tooth with her. It would be then that the men might thrust back the tables and hand the bond-maids about. No Jarl I knew can hold men in his hall unless there are ample women for them. I felt sorry for Svein Blue Tooth. This night, however, it seemed Bera had no intention of retiring early. I suspected this might have accounted somewhat for the ugliness of the men with the entertainers, not that the men of Torvaldsland, under any circumstances, constitute an easily pleased audience. Generally only Kaissa and the songs of skalds can hold their attention for long hours, that and stories told at the tables.

After the entertainers had been driven from the hall and much food had been eaten, Svein Blue Tooth, who had showed much patience, said to Ivar Forkbeard, "It is my understanding that you believe yourself to have that wherewith your deed's wergild might be met."

"Perhaps," admitted the Forkbeard.

Svein Blue Tooth's eyes gleamed. He fingered the tooth of the Hunjer whale, on its golden chain, slung about his neck.

"The wergild was high," said the Blue Tooth.

The Forkbeard stood up. "Bring gold and sapphires," said he, "and bring scales."

To the astonishment of all those in the hall, from the side room, boxes and sacks of gold were brought forth by the Forkbeard's men, and, too, a large, heavy sack of leather, filled with tiny objects.

Men left the back tables; men crowded about; even the thralls and the bond-maids, astonished, disbelieving, crowded near.

"Room! Make room here!" called the Forkbeard.

For more than two Ahn gold was weighed, on two pairs of scales, one furnished by the Forkbeard, the other by the house of Svein Blue Tooth. To my relief the scales, almost perfectly, agreed.

The gold accumulated.

The eyes of Svein Blue Tooth and Bera, narrow, shining, were filled with pleasure.

"There is forty weight of gold here," said Svein Blue Tooth's man, almost as though he could not believe it, "four hundred stone of gold."

There was a gasp from the throng.

The Forkbeard then went to the heavy leather sack and, ripping the leather away at its throat, poured onto the dirt, lustrous, scintillating, a shower of jewels, mostly a deep blue, but some were purple, and others white and yellow, the carved sapphires of Schendi, each in the shape of a tiny panther.

"Aiii!" cried the throng. Svein Blue Tooth leaned forward, his fists clenched. Bera, her eyes blazing, could not speak.

The Forkbeard shook the sack further. More jewels fell forth, some among them more unusual varieties of sapphire, pale pink, orange, violet, brown and even green.

"Ah," cried the throng. "How beautiful!" cried a bond-maid, who did not, herself, own even her collar of iron.

"Weigh them," said the Forkbeard.

I had not, myself, realized there were so many varieties of sapphires. Until this time I had been familiar only with the bluish stones.

I had little doubt, however, that the stones were genuine. Chenbar, the Sea Sleen, would have insisted on the fee for his rescue being paid in genuine stones, as a matter of pride. Too, the Forkbeard, in dealing with his Jarl, Svein Blue Tooth, would not use false stones. He would be above that. It is one thing to cheat one not of Torvaldsland, quite another to attempt to defraud one of one's own country, particularly one's Jarl. I had no doubt that the spilled glory heaped gleaming in the dirt of the hall of Svein Blue Tooth was what it seemed, true stones, and an incredible treasure.

The jewels, like the gold, were patiently weighed.

There were many exclamations from the warriors present, and others in the throng. The weight of the stones was more than that of a full-grown man.

Ivar Forkbeard stood behind these riches, and grinned, and spread his hands.

"I did not think there were such riches in all of Torvaldsland," whispered Bera.

Svein Blue Tooth was much impressed. He could scarcely speak. With such riches there would be no Jarl in Torvaldsland who could even remotely compare to him. His power would be the equal of that of a Ubar of the south.

But the men of Torvaldsland are not easily pleased. The Blue Tooth leaned back. "There was, Forkbeard," said he, smiling, "a third condition to the wergild."

"Oh, my Jarl?" asked Ivar.

"It seems I must keep this treasure," said he, "and you remain outlaw. It may, however, count as the first two installments of a completed transaction. I shall revoke your outlawry when, and only when, too, you deliver to me the daughter of my enemy, Thorgard of Scagnar."

The Blue Tooth's men, not pleased, murmured angrily. "The Forkbeard, surely, has more than paid wergild," cried one. "What man has been set such a price and has paid it?" cried another.

"Silence!" cried Svein Blue Tooth, standing behind the table. He scowled at his men.

"No one, not an army or a fleet," cried another, "could take the daughter of so powerful a Jarl as Thorgard of Scagnar!"

"You seem to ask the impossible, my Jarl," observed Ivar Forkbeard.

"I do ask the impossible," said Svein Blue Tooth. "Of you, my friend, Ivar Forkbeard, I choose to ask the impossible."

The Forkbeard's men muttered angrily. Weapons were grasped.

Even the men of Svein Blue Tooth, perhaps a thousand in the hall, were angry. Yet the Blue Tooth, boldly, their Jarl, matched his will to theirs. Which one of them would dare to challenge the will of their Jarl?

I admired the Blue Tooth in his way. He was courageous. In the final analysis, I had little doubt that his men would abide by his decision.

The Blue Tooth sat down again in the high seat. "Yes, friend Forkbeard," said he, "of you, as is my right, I ask what cannot be done, the impossible."

The Forkbeard turned and, facing the entrance of the hall, called out, "Bring forth the female."

There was no sound in the great hall, save the crackle of the fires and torches.

The men, and the thralls and bond-maids, parted. From the doors to the hall, swung wide, now approaching, came four figures, Ottar, who had accompanied the Forkbeard to the thing, two of the Forkbeard's men, with spears, and, between them, clad in rich robes of concealment, such as are worn in the south, even to the veils, the figure of a girl.

These four stopped before the table, opposite the high seat of Svein Blue Tooth. The girl stood among the gold, and the heaped sapphires. Her robes were marvously wrought, subtle, soft, seeming almost in their sheens, like the jewels, to shift their colors in the light of the lamps and the flickering torches. The robes were hooded; she was twice veiled, once in white silk and, under it, in purple silk.

"What mockery is this?" demanded the Blue Tooth, sternly.

"No mockery, my Jarl," said the Forkbeard. He extended his hand toward the girl. "May I present to my Jarl," he asked, "Hilda, daughter of Thorgard of Scagnar?"

The girl reached to her hoods and brushed them back, freeing her hair, and then, pin by pin, she unfastened the two veils, one after the other, and dropped them.

"It is she," whispered a man at the table of Svein Blue Tooth. "I was once in the hall of Thorgard. It is she!"

"Are you—are you," asked Svein Blue Tooth, "the daughter of Thorgard, Thorgard of Scagnar?"

"Yes, my Jarl," she said.

"Before Thorgard of Scagnar had the ship Black Sleen," said Svein, slowly, "he had another ship. What was its name?"

"Horned Tharlarion," she said. "He still has this ship, too," she added, "but it does not now serve as his flagship."

"How many oars has it?" he asked.

"Eighty," said she.

"Who keeps the fisheries of Thorgard?" asked a man.

"Grim, once of Hunjer," she said.

"Once in battle," said Svein Blue Tooth, "I wounded Thorgard of Scagnar."

"The scar," she said, "is on his left wrist, concealed under a studded wristlet."

Svein leaned back.

"In this same engagement," she said, "he wounded you, and more grievously. You will bear the scar in your left shoulder."

Bera flushed.

"It is true," said Svein Blue Tooth.

"I tell you," cried the man at the table, "it is Hilda, daughter of Thorgard of Scagnar. I have been in his hall. It is she!"

The women of the north, commonly, do not veil themselves.

"How were you taken?" asked Svein Blue Tooth.

"By trickery, my Jarl," said she. "In my own compartments was I taken, braceleted and hooded."

"How were you conveyed past guards?" asked the Blue Tooth.

"From the window of my compartments, braceleted and hooded, late at night, helpless, in darkness, I was hurled into the sea, more than a hundred feet below. A boat was waiting.

199

Like a fish I was retrieved and made prisoner, forced to lie on my belly in the boat, like a common maid. My captors followed."

There was a great cheer from the men in the hall, both those of Ivar Forkbeard and those of Svein Blue Tooth.

"You poor, miserable girl," cried Bera.

"It could happen to any female," said Hilda, "even you, great lady."

"Men are beasts," Bera cried. She regarded Ivar, and me, and his men, with fury. "Shame be upon you, you beasts!" she cried.

"Svein Blue Tooth, Jarl of Torvaldsland, meet Hilda, daughter of Thorgard of Scagnar," said Ivar. "Hilda, daughter of Thorgard of Scagnar, meet Svein Blue Tooth, Jarl of Torvaldsland."

Hilda inclined her head in deference to the Jarl.

There was another great cheer in the hall.

"Poor girl," cried Bera, "how you must have suffered!"

Hilda lowered her head. She did not respond to Bera. I thought she smiled.

"Never had I thought to have Hilda, daughter of Thorgard of Scagnar, stand prisoner before me, before the high seat of my house," said Svein Blue Tooth.

"Before you I stand more than prisoner, my Jarl," said she.

"I do not understand," said Svein Blue Tooth.

She did not raise her head.

"You need not address me as your Jarl, my dear," said Svein Blue Tooth. "I am not your Jarl."

"But every free man is my Jarl," she said. "You see, my Jarl," said she, lifting her head proudly and pulling her rich, glistening robes some inches down upon her shoulders, "I wear the collar of Ivar Forkbeard."

The collar of black iron, with its heavy hinge, its riveted closure, its projecting ring of iron, for a chain or padlock, showed black, heavy, against the whiteness of her lovely throat.

"You have dared to collar the daughter of Thorgard of Scagnar!" cried Bera to Ivar Forkbeard.

"My master does what he pleases, Lady," said Hilda.

I wondered what Bera would say if she knew that Hilda had been put at the oar, and taught to heel; that she had been whipped, and taught to obey; that she had been caressed, and taught to respond.

"Silence, Bond-maid!" cried Bera.

Hilda put down her head.

"To think," cried Bera, "that I expressed solicitude for a collar-girl!"

Hilda dared not speak. For a bond-maid to speak in such a situation might be to invite a sentence of death. She shuddered.

In fury, Bera, lifting her skirt from about her ankles, took her way from the long table, retiring to her own quarters.

"You collared her!" laughed Svein Blue Tooth.

"Of course," said the Forkbeard.

"Superb!" laughed Svein Blue Tooth, rubbing his hands together.

"Lift your head, Wench," he said. His attitude toward Hilda had changed, completely.

She did so.

She had a beautiful face, blue eyes, long, loose blond hair.

"Is she pretty?" asked Svein Blue Tooth.

"Remove your slippers," said the Forkbeard.

The girl did so. She stepped from them. She did not wear stockings.

Roughly the Forkbeard, then, his hands at her shoulders, tore away the robes of concealment.

The men, and the bond-maids, cried out with pleasure, with admiration.

Hilda stood proudly, her head high, amidst the heaped gold, jewels, sapphires, in the dirt about her feet.

She had been branded. It had been done by the hand of Ivar Forkbeard himself, before dawn, some days ago, shortly before his ship had left for the thing. She had been carried weeping, over his shoulder, her brand fresh, aboard his ship. The collar, too, before the brand, that very morning, had been closed about her neck, and riveted shut.

I observed the brand. She was now only another girl whose belly lay beneath the sword, a property-girl, a collar-girl, a slave, a bond-maid.

The eyes of Svein Blue Tooth, and those of his men, glistened as they feasted upon her bared beauty.

"It seems," said Svein Blue Tooth, "that the wergild has been well met."

"Yes," said the Forkbeard, "it might seem so."

"In the morning I shall proclaim the lifting of your outlawry," said the Blue Tooth.

I relaxed. It seemed we would come alive, after all, out of the hall of the Blue Tooth. I had only feared some treachery, or trickery, upon his part, some northern trick. Yet he had now, before his men, spoken. And I knew him, by this time, to be one who stood with his word, and stood well with it, and proudly. His word was to him as his land, and his sword, as his honor and his ship; it would be kept; it would be neither demeaned nor broken.

"I think there is some mistake," said Ivar Forkbeard.

Inwardly I groaned.

"How is that?" asked the Blue Tooth.

"How is it that the wergild is met?" asked Ivar Forkbeard.

The Blue Tooth looked puzzled. He pointed to the jewels, the gold, the girl. "You have that here wherewith to meet the wergild," said he.

"That is true," said the Forkbeard. Then he drew himself up to a not inconsiderable full height. "But who has told you that I choose to meet it?"

Suddenly the men in the hall, both those of the Forkbeard and of Svein Blue Tooth, began to cheer. I, too, was on my feet among them. None of us had suspected it, and yet it was what one should have expected of such a man as the Forkbeard. Never in the north had there been such a coup of honor! Though it might mean the death of us all, those who followed the Forkbeard, and that of perhaps hundreds of the men of Svein Blue Tooth, we cheered. My heart bounded, my blood raced. I struck, again and again, my left shoulder with the palm of my right hand. I heard swords clashing against the sides of plates, spear blades clattering on shields, and ringing, one against the other.

Slowly Svein Blue Tooth rose to his feet. He was livid with rage.

There was not a man in the hall but knew that his kinsman, a distant cousin, Finn Broadbelt, whom the Forkbeard had slain, had fallen in fair duel, and that wergild should not have been levied; and there was not a man in that hall but knew that the Blue Tooth had decreed, even were such justified, a wergild to the deed of the Forkbeard whose conditions were outrageous, deliberately formulated to preclude their satisfaction, a wergild contrived to make impossible the meeing of its own terms, a wergild the intent of which was, in its spitefulness, to condemn the Forkbeard to perpetual outlawry. Then, to the astonishment of all Torvaldsland, and most to that of Svein Blue Tooth, the Forkbeard, redoubtable, after earning six talmits in the contests, delivered to his hall the very wergild no man had supposed it possible to pay, and had then, arrogantly, before the high seat of the Blue Tooth itself, refused to pay!

"In this land," said Ivar Forkbeard, "rather than accept pardon at the hands of such a Jarl, one such as you, Svein Blue Tooth, I make what choice a free man must. I choose the sleen, the forest and the sea!"

Svein Blue Tooth regarded him.

"I do not pay the wergild," said the Forkbeard. "I choose to remain outlaw."

Once again there was much cheering. I clapped the Forkbeard about the shoulders. Gorm, and Ottar, too, stood with him, and his other men. Hilda knelt at his feet, among the gold, the jewels, her lips pressed to his furred boots. "My Jarl! My Jarl!" she wept.

Then there was silence in that high-roofed hall.

All eyes turned to Svein Blue Tooth.

He stood before the high seat of his house, standing before the long table; behind him, on each side, were the high-seat pillars of his house.

He prepared to speak. Suddenly he lifted his head. I, too, and several of the others, at the same time, detected it. It was smoke. "The hall is afire!" cried one man. Flames, above and behind us, crept at the southeast corner of the interior roof, above and, as we faced it, to the right of the doors. Smoke, too, began to drift in from one of the side rooms. We saw something move within it.

"What is going on?" cried a man at one of the tables.

The doors behind us, both of them, great, carved doors, suddenly thrust open.

In the doorway, silhouetted against flames behind them, we saw great, black, shaggy figures.

Then one leapt within the hall. In one hand it carried a gigantic ax, whose handle was perhaps eight feet long, whose blade, from tip to tip, might have been better than two feet in length; on its other arm it carried a great, round, iron shield, double strapped; it lifted it, and the ax; its arms were incredibly long, perhaps some seven feet in length; about its left arm was a spiral band of gold; it was the Kur which had addressed the assembly.

It threw back its head and opened its jaws, eyes blazing, and uttered the blood roar of the aroused Kur; then it bent over, regarding us, shoulders hunched, its claws leaping from its soft, furred sheaths; it then laid its ears back flat against the sides of its great head.

No one could move.

Then, other Kurii behind it, crowding about it, past it, it shrieked, lips drawn back, with a hideous sound, which, somehow, from its lips and mien, and mostly from its eyes, I took to be a sign of pleasure, of anticipation; I would learn later that this sound is instinctively uttered by Kurii when they are preparing to take blood. This cry, like a stimulus, acted upon the others, as well; almost instantly, with the velocity that the stranger signal can course through a pack of urts, this shriek was picked up by those with it; then, the hall filled with their horrid howling, eyes blazing, led by the Kur with the golden band, frenzied by the blood shriek, they leaped forward, great axes flailing.

14

THE FORKBEARD AND I DEPART FROM THE HALL OF SVEIN BLUE TOOTH

I saw half of the body of a man spinning crazily past.

Kurii leapt down the long sides of the hall, slashing, cutting men down as they fled to their weapons. The wooden shields of Torvaldsland no more stopped the great axes than dried skins of larma fruit, stretched on sewing frames, might have resisted the four-bladed dagger cestus of Anango or the hatchet gauntlet of eastern Skjern.

More than once the blades of the Kurii axes bit through the spines of men, reaching for their weapons, and splintered, gouging, in the beams of the hall.

I choked in the smoke. My eyes stung. Near me a man screamed. I was knocked from my feet, buffeted in the crowd. For an instant I was conscious only of the dirt floor, the reeds strewn upon it, the mad forest of running feet. My left hand slipped in the dirt, in blood. I was knocked again, but then managed to force my way to my feet. I was carried in the panic-stricken throng a dozen yards in one direction, then, meaninglessly, carried back in the other. I could not even draw my weapon.

The Kur axes fell again and again. The hall rang with their howling. I saw a man-at-arms lifted, back broken, in the black, furred, tentacled hand of one of the marauders. The thing roared, head back. The white fangs seemed scarlet in the light of the fires from the roof. Then it threw the man more than a hundred feet against the back of the hall. I saw another man-at-arms hanging from the jaws of a Kur. He was still alive. His eyes betrayed shock, staring blindly outward. I do not think he saw. I suspect he was not in pain. He was alive, but I did not think he any longer felt. He doubtless understood what was occurring but, to him, somehow, it did not seem of concern. It was as though it were happening to someone else. Then the Kur's jaws closed. For the least instant there was a terrifying recognition in the eyes. Then he was bitten through.

I briefly saw Ivar Forkbeard. He was trying to thrust Hilda, held by the arm, toward one of the side rooms, between killing Kurii. He was shouting orders to his men, who clustered about him. Svein Blue Tooth stood on the long table, behind which was his high seat. I could not hear him in the shouting, the screams, the howling of the frenzied Kurii.

A great Kur ax swept near me. Four men, trying to back away, but held as though against a wall by the throng, were cut down.

Those nearest the Kurii tried to crawl back within the throng.

The Kurii axes, in their sweeps, at the edges of the throng, kept us helpless, crowded together.

Few men could as much as draw their weapons.

Some men, behind Kurii, fled away, out of the great, opened, double doors of the hall. I saw them fleeing, outlined briefly against the fires outside. But outside, too, I saw, silhouetted against the flames, waiting Kurii. Many fled into the axes of the Kurii in the yard of the hall. Then Kurii stood before the threshold, snarling, axes lifted.

Men came before them and threw themselves to their knees, that they might be spared, even were it but for the Ahn, but these, like others, no differences drawn between them, were cut down, destroyed by strokes of the swift axes. Kurii take prisoners only when it pleases them.

I saw several of the Forkbeard's men manage to slip into one of the side rooms. Gorm, and Ottar, were among them.

I hoped they might make good their escape. Perhaps they could tear out the membrane in one of the windows and crawl through and, in the confusion outside, make away.

The Forkbeard, to my surprise, momentarily reappeared from within the room, looking about. His face looked red in the fires. He carried his sword.

I did not see Hilda. I assumed she had, with the men, entered the small room. It was my hope that she, and the others, could manage to slip away somehow, perhaps climbing to the catwalk, and dropping over the side of the palisade to the ground below.

I saw then the Forkbeard, one hand on the arm of the strange giant, Rollo, leading him to the door of the small room. Rollo, though the room about him was frenzied with Kurii and their killing, did not seem disturbed. His eyes were vacant. He was led like a child to the small room. I noted that his ax, which he always carried, was bloodied. The blood of Kurii, like that of men, is red, and of similar chemical composition. It is another similarity adduced by Priest-Kings when they wish to argue the equivalence of the warring species. The major difference between the blood content of the Kur and of men is that the plasma of the Kur contains a greater percentage of salt, this acting in water primarily as a protein solvent. The Kur can eat and digest quantities of meat which would kill a man.

Rollo disappeared within the small room.

From my right I heard the scream of a bond-maid. I saw a Kur leash her. He pulled her, struggling, by the neck, choking, to a place to the left of the door. There there waited another Kur, who held in his tentacled hand the leashes of more than twenty bond-maids, who knelt, terrified, about its legs. The Kur who had leashed his catch then handed the leash to the other Kur, who accepted it, adding it to the others. The girl knelt swiftly among the others. I knew human females were regarded as delicacies by Kurii. The Kur who had taken the girl then took another leash from the interior of his shield, where there were several wrapped about the shield straps, and surveyed the hall. A girl, kneeling in the dirt, near the long fire, saw him, and ran screaming away. Methodically, moving her toward a corner of the hall, leash swinging, he followed her.

Behind me I heard the blows of axes.

I fought to free myself of the throng.

The axes behind me were the axes of men, and striking on wood. Turning I saw Svein Blue Tooth and four others, trying to splinter their way from the hall. They had difficulty, though, for many men pressed against them.

I saw Ivar Forkbeard nearby. He had not chosen to escape.

His sword was drawn, but it would prove of little efficacy against the great metal shields, the sweeping axes of the Kurii. They could cut a man down before he could approach them, even with the long blade of the North.

The Forkbeard looked about.

There had been more than a thousand men in the hall. Surely at least two or three hundred lay dead, most at the walls, at the foot of the walls, under the weapons which, for the most part, they had been unable to touch.

I saw the Kur who had pursued the bond-maid now again going toward that holding area near the door. On her back, then on her side, then on her stomach, rolling and squirming, eyes wild, her fingers hooked inside the collar, trying to keep it from choking her, was dragged the bond-maid. Then her leash was surrendered into the keeping of the Kur who held the others, and then the first Kur, leaving his prize in the care of the other, turned about, to hunt yet another delicacy from the herd within the hall.

The Kurii now, on both sides, stood between us and the weapons. The side doors, leading from the hall, were now also closed to us. Kurii, too, stood before the entrance to the hall, axes ready, eyes flaming. We were, some six or seven hundred men, crowded together, effectively surrounded. At our backs was the western wall of the hall. "Clear room!" cried Svein Blue Tooth. "Let us use our axes!"

Trying to draw back from the Kurii, approaching slowly, great, bloody axes ready, terrified men pushed back, further and further.

I managed to free myself from the crowd, and take a position on its fringe, between men and Kurii. If I were cut down I would prefer it to be in a situation where I might move freely. I unsheathed my sword.

I saw the lips of one of the Kurii drawing back.

"Your blade is useless," said Ivar Forkbeard, now standing at my side.

The Kurii crept closer.

I heard a scream from a height, and, looking up, saw a human thrown from the balcony which ringed the hall, some thirty feet above the dirt floor, some ten feet below the roof beams. I saw then that Kurii held the balcony.

I did not think they would long delay finishing us. The smoke was thick in the hall. Men choked. Men coughed. I saw, too, the nostrils of the Kurii closing to narrow slits. Sparks fell in their fur.

I brushed aside one of the hanging vessels of bronze, a tharlarion-oil lamp which, on its chain, hung from the ceiling, some forty feet above. It is such that it can be raised and lowered by a side chain.

"Spears!" cried Ivar. "We need spears!"

But there were few spears in the fear-maddened, terrified crowd of men cringing back from the beasts. What spears there were could not be thrown because of the press.

To one side I saw the Kur with the golden band on its arm. At the side of its mouth were saliva and blood, the fur matted.

It looked at me.

I knew then it was my enemy.

We had found one another.

An ax struck toward me. It had been wielded by the Kur whose lips had drawn back. I darted to one side, the ax buried itself in the dirt, I found myself within the beast's guard, I thrust the blade, to its hilt, into the chest of the beast. It gave a puzzled snarl which I heard, jerking the blade free, only as I leaped back. The other Kurii looked at it, puzzled; then it fell into the dirt.

There was silence, save for the crackling of flames.

The horror of what I had done then was understood by the leader of the Kurii.

A Kur had been killed.

"Attack!" cried Ivar Forkbeard. "Attack! Are you docile tarsk that you dare not attack? Men of Torvaldsland, attack!"

But no man moved.

Mere humans, they dared not set themselves against Kurii. They would rather, helpless, await their slaughter.

They could not move, so struck with terror they were.

The body of the dead Kur, inert, lay heavy, crooked, in the dirt. The bloodied ax was to one side. The shield arm was twisted in one of the straps. The other strap was broken.

The eyes of the leader of the Kurii, whom I knew to be my enemy, blazed upon me. His horror, seeing his fallen brother of the killing blood, had now become rage, outrage.

I, one of the herd, of the cattle, had dared to strike one of the master species, a superior form of life.

A Kur had been killed.

I set myself.

Again in the hall of Svein Blue Tooth rang the blood shriek of the Kurii. On each side of the leader, plunging toward us, howling, swept Kurii. Too, they pressed in from the sides, axes falling.

I do not choose to speak in detail of what followed. Kurii themselves, axes like sheets of iron rain, shattered that fearful throng, splitting it into hundreds of screaming fragments of terror. A man not more than a yard from me was cut half in two, from the head to the belt, in one stroke. I

209

managed, as the Kur was twisting his ax, trying to free it, of the body, to drive my blade through its neck, under the left ear. I saw Ivar Forkbeard, his sword gone, lost in the body of a nearby Kur, his knife in his hand, one hand thrusting away and upward the jaws of a Kur, repeatedly plunge his knife into the huge chest of the beast. There was uneven footing in the hall. We slipped in the blood. It filled the pit of the long fire. It was splashed about our trousers and tunics. Near one wall I yanked a spear free from the hands of a fallen man-at-arms. Momentarily I sickened at the sight of the exposed lungs, sucking air, the hand scratching at the wall beside him. I hurled the spear. It had a shaft of seven foot Gorean, a head of tapered bronze, some eighteen inches in length. At close range it can pierce a southern shield, shatter its point through a seven-inch beam. It passed half through the body of a Kur. Its ax fell. My act had saved a man. But, in the next instant, he had fallen beneath the ax of another. I pressed my back against the wall. A beam fell, burning, from the roof at the southeastern corner of the hall. I heard bond-maids screaming. Kurii looked upward. Their nostrils were shut against the smoke. The eyes of many of them, commonly black-pupiled, yellowish in the cornea, seemed red, swollen, veined. I saw one, suffering in the smoke and sparks, look up from feeding, and then again thrust his head down to the meat, clothes torn away from the chest, on which it was feeding. I saw Ivar Forkbeard, with a spear, set himself against the charge of an unarmed Kur. He set the butt of the spear deep in the earth behind him. The spear's shaft gouged a trench six inches deep behind him, and then stopped, and the Kur, biting in the air, eyes like fire, backed away, and fell backward; Ivar leaped away as another ax sought him.

I saw, across the room, the leader of the Kurii, it with the golden band on its arm.

I recalled its words on the platform of the assembly, in the field of the thing. In rage it had cried, "A thousand of you can die beneath the claws of a single Kur!"

There were perhaps now no more than a hundred or a hundred and fifty men left alive in the hall.

"Follow me!" cried Svein Blue Tooth. His ax, and those of his men, had shattered through the rear of the hall. Like panic-stricken urts thirty-five or forty men thrust through the hole, sometimes jamming themselves momentarily within it, some tearing the flesh from their bodies and the sides of their faces on the splintered wood. "Hurry! Hurry!" cried the

Blue Tooth. His garments were half torn from him but, still, about his neck, on its chain, was the tooth of the Hunjer whale, dyed blue, by which men in Torvaldsland knew him. Svein thrust two more of his men through the aperture. Kurii were between me and the opening. Ivar Forkbeard, and others, too, were similarly cut off. Another beam fell, flaming and smoking from the roof, striking into the dirt floor, and leaning against the wall. The hangings which had decorated the hall were now gone, burned away, the walls scorched behind them. The only portion of the wall that was clearly afire, however, and threatening to cave in, was the eastern edge of the southern wall.

I saw ten Kurii leap to the back of the hall, to where Svein Blue Tooth and his men had made their opening, to prevent the escape of others.

They stood before the opening, axes lifted, snarling. One man who approached too closely was slashed to the spine with a sweep of the bluish ax.

One who begged mercy in the center of the hall was cut in twain, the blade of the ax driving into the very dirt itself, emerging covered with dirt and blood, streaked with ash.

"The lamps!" cried the Forkbeard to me. "Red Hair," he cried, "the lamps!"

Another beam from the roof, burning, dropped heavily to the floor of the hall.

I saw the Kur who held the leashes of the caught bondmaids dragging the girls from the hall. He held the leashes, several in each hand, of more than forty catches. The collars were of thick leather, with metal insert locks, flat metal bolts slipping, locking, into spring catches; when closed, two rectangular metal plates adjoined; sewn into each collar was a light, welded metal ring; about this was closed the leash snap; the action of the leash snap was mechanical but, apparently, it was beyond the strength of a woman to open it. The leashes were some fifteen feet in length, allowing in this radius one Kur to hold several captives at once. The Kur left the hall. Screaming, stumbling, helplessly, the caught women followed their beast master.

I saw Kurii, methodically, blow after blow, striking the fallen, lest any might have sought to hide among the dead. Some men, tangled in the bodies, screamed, the axes falling upon them. The wounded, too, were methodically dispatched. I observed the patterns; they were regular, linear, of narrow width; no body was missed. The Kurii, I realized,

211

were efficient; they were, of course, intelligent; they were, of course, like men, rational animals. One man leaped screaming to his feet and ran. He was cut down immediately, running almost headlong into a Kur, one of the Kurii set before the killing line, to intercept such fugitives. Men, it seemed to me, could be no match for such animals.

Kurii now encircled the group of men near the western wall of the hall.

Most of them moaned, crying out with misery; many fell to their knees.

I saw two Kurii turn in my direction.

I saw Ivar Forkbeard standing among the huddled men near the western wall of the hall. He was easily visible, being one of the few standing. He looked red and terrible in the reflection of the flames; the veins on his forehead looked like red cables; his eyes, almost like those of the Kurii themselves, blazed. His long sword, now again in his hand, which he had recovered from the body of the Kur in which he had left it, was again bloodied, and freshly so; his left sleeve was torn away; there were claw marks on his neck. "On your feet!" he cried to the men. "On your feet! Do battle!" But even those who stood seemed numb with terror. "Are you of Torvaldsland?" he asked. "Do battle! Do battle!" But no man dared to move. In the presence of Kurii they seemed only cattle.

I saw the lips of Kurii draw back. I saw axes lift.

Then again the Forkbeard's voice, through the smoke, the sparks, suddenly half choking, drifted across the hall to me.

"The lamps!" he cried again, as he had before. "Red Hair," he cried, "the lamps!"

Then I understood him, as I had not before. The tharlarion-oil lamps, on their chains, hanging from rings on the roof beams! The apertures in the ceiling of the hall, through which smoke might pass! He had intended that I would escape.

But I had played Kaissa with him.

"First," I called, "the Forkbeard!" I would not leave without him. We had played Kaissa.

"You are a fool!" he cried.

"I have not yet learned to break the Jarl's Ax's gambit," I rejoined.

I sheathed my sword. I leaned back, casually against the wall. My arms were folded.

"Fool!" he cried.

He looked about, at the men who could not fight, who could not move, who could not stir.

He slammed his sword into its sheath and leaped up, seizing one of the lamps on its chain.

The two Kurii who had turned toward me now lifted their axes.

I turned over the table, behind which I stood. The two axes hit the heavy beams simultaneously, exploding wood in great chunks between the walls, shattering it as high as the ceiling itself.

I vaulted the table.

I heard the startled snarls of the Kurii.

Then I had my hands on one of the large, swinging, bronze lamps. Oil spilled, flamed from the wick. I swung, wildly. My right sleeve caught afire.

I heard a Kur below me scream with pain; I looked down, and hauled myself up to avoid the stroke of an ax; one Kur reeled about; the left side of its furred head, wet, drenched in oil, was aflame; it screamed hideously; it clawed at its left eye. Hand over hand I crawled up the chain; then the chain shook, wildly; I struggled to hold it; the fire at my right sleeve snapped back and forth: I lost my breath; I feared my neck would break; blood was on the chain; I held it; Kurii howled beneath me; I moved further up the chain; then the chain stretched down, taut; an ax flew wheeling past, half cutting into one of the crossbeams in the roof; I climbed higher; then, suddenly, I realized why the chain had been pulled taut; the beam, above me, creaked; the chain was now tight, like a cable; the links strained, grating on one another; it now bore, besides mine, the weight of a Kur, rapidly climbing; the ring above me, through which the chain passed, pulled part way from the wood; I scrambled up the last few feet of the chain; I threw my arm over the beam; I felt claws seize at my leg, then close about it; I released the beam, screaming the war cry of Ko-ro-ba, falling tearing and ripping with fingers and teeth about the neck and head of the startled Kur; stiffened fingers, like daggers, drove at its eyes; my teeth tore at the veins in its wrist, in the arm that held the chain; in that instant the Kur realized, and, I realized, too, for the first time, that there were on the surface of Gor animals as savage as its kind, slighter animals, smaller, weaker, but no less vicious, in their way no less terrible; fending me away, screaming, biting, it released me, but I clung about its shoulders and neck; I bit through half of its ear; I pulled myself up to the beam;

213

an orifice, red, projecting fangs like white nails, stretched below me; I drew the sword and, as it climbed, eyes bleeding, ear torn, after me, I cut away its hand; it fell back, growing smaller, until it struck heavily on the reeded earth, stained with its churned, reddish mud, forty feet below; it broke its neck; I tore away the flaming sleeve of my garment and thrust it, on the sword point, into the face of the next Kur; the hand of the first still clung to the chain, with its six multiple jointed fingers; the Kur, with a shake of its head, dislodged the burning cloth and pulled its pierced face from the sword; it bit at the sword, cutting its mouth; it reached to the beam; I cut at the fingers; it lost its balance; it, too, fell backward. "Come!" I heard. I saw the Forkbeard on a nearby beam. "Hurry!" he cried. I choked in the smoke. I thrust at the next Kur, driving the blade through its ear into the brain. Part of the roof fell away, tumbling burning to the ground below. "Hurry!" I heard, as though from far away. I cut down at the next Kur. It snarled, grasping for me. The ring, through which the chain passed, unable to bear longer the weight of Kurii, splintered free of the wood. I saw the ring and chain dart downward. Four Kurii, climbing, two leaping free, two clinging to the chain, fell to the earth below. Another portion of the roof fell, not more than twenty feet from me. Below, covered with sparks, scarcely visible in the smoke, I saw Kurii looking up, cheated of their prey. A beam fell, not more than a dozen feet from them. Their leader uttered some sound to them. His eyes, blazing, looked up at me. About his left arm was the spiral golden band. Then he, with the others, turned about and, swiftly shambling, some looking back, fled the hall. I sheathed my sword. "Hurry!" cried the Forkbeard. I leaped from beam to beam to join him. After him, I squeezed through one of the smoke holes in the roof of the burning hall. Then we were standing on the wooden-shingled blazing roof of the hall of Svein Blue Tooth. I looked up and saw the stars and moons of Gor. "Follow me," cried Ivar. In the distance I saw the Torvaldsberg. There was moonlight reflecting from its snows. He sped to the northwest corner of the hall. He disappeared over the edge of the roof. I looked over and saw him, in the moonlight, making his way downward, hand by hand, foot by foot, using the clefts, projections and niches in the ornate carvings of the exterior corner beams of the Blue Tooth's hall. Swiftly, my arm scorched from the fire which had torn at my sleeve, heart pounding, breathing heavily, I followed him.

15

ON THE HEIGHT OF
THE TORVALDSBERG

It was noon, on the snowy slopes of the Torvaldsberg.

Ivar and I looked behind us. We could see them following, four of them, like black dots.

"Let us rest," said Ivar.

I shut my eyes against the glare of the sun on the snow. He sat down, with his back against a rock. I, too, sat down, crosslegged, as a warrior sits.

We had climbed down from the roof of the Blue Tooth's burning hall, using the projections and relief of the ornately carved corner beams. Climbing down, I had seen Kurii moving about, but near the front of the hall. In the light of the burning hall, here and there, scattered in the dirt of the courtyard, we saw sprawled, scattered bodies, and parts of bodies. Some Kurii, squatting among them, fed. In one corner of the stockade, huddled together, their white bodies, now stripped, red in the light of the flames, were the bond-maids, in their leather collars, leashed, the straps in the furred fists of their master. Several Kurii, not feeding, carrying shields, axes, moved to and fro. We dropped to the courtyard, unseen. We slipped behind the hall, keeping, where possible, buildings between us and the yard. We reached the palisade, climbed to its catwalk and, unnoticed, leaped over.

I opened my eyes, and looked down into the valley. The four dots were larger now.

The Forkbeard, after our escape from the stockade of Svein Blue Tooth, had been intent upon reaching his camp. It had been dangerous, furtive work. To our astonishment the countryside was swarming with Kurii. I could not conjecture their numbers. There might have been hundreds; there might have been thousands. They seemed everywhere.

Twice we were pursued, but, in the midst of the scents, and distracted by fresh blood, our pursuers turned aside. We saw, at one point, two Kurii fighting over a body. Sometimes we threw ourselves to the ground, among the fallen. Once a Kur passed within a yard of my hand. It howled with pleasure at the moons, and then was gone. As many as four or five times we crept within yards of feeding Kurii, oblivious to our presence. The attack had been simultaneously launched, obviously, on the hall and the surrounding thing-camps. Even more to our astonishment than the Kurii, and their numbers, about, was the presence of men, wearing yellow scarves, among them, men whom they did not attack. My fists clenched in rage. Kurii, as is often the case, had enlisted human allies.

"Look," had said the Forkbeard, pointing from a height, on which we lay prone, to the beach. Offshore, some few yards, among the other ships, lay new ships, many of them, strange ships. They lay black, rocking, on the sparkling water. One ship was prominent among them. It was large. It had eighty oars. "Black Sleen," said Ivar, "the ship of Thorgard of Scagnar!"

There were hundreds of Kurii between us and the ships.

Ivar and I had looked at one another.

We now understood the meaning of the Kur we had seen on Black Sleen, long ago, who had accompanied Thorgard of Scagnar into his holding. We had seen the beast from the darkness, from our longboat, when we were escaping Scagnar, Thorgard's daughter hooded and secured, bound hand and foot, lying between our feet.

Kurii are land animals, not fond of water. In their march south, the fleet of Thorgard of Scagnar would cover their western flank. More importantly, it would give them the means of communication with the Gorean islands, and, if desirable, a means whereby their invasion might be accomplished. The fleet, further, could, if necessary, provision the advancing horde and, if necessary, if danger should threaten, evacuate large portions of it. The Kurii march would have its sea arm, its naval support. Kurii, as I have indicated, are rational animals. The strategies seemed elementary, but sound. The full extent of the strategy, however, I suspected, was known only on the steel wolves, the steel worlds in space, on which it had doubtless been constructed and from which, perhaps, it might be conducted. If Kurii native to Gor could, within the laws of Priest-Kings, not violating technology restrictions, much advance the Kurii

216

cause on the planet, those on the ships had little to lose and much to gain. It was even possible that Priest-Kings, a usually consistent form of life, might permit the Kurii conquest of Gor rather than surrender their accustomed neutrality. I could imagine the words on Misk's translator, one after the other, ticked off mechanically, "We have given our word." But if Priest-Kings, eventually, should halt the invasion, that, too, might be of interest to the Kurii of the steel ships, remote, prowling outside the fifth ring, that of the planet on Earth called Jupiter, that on Gor called Hersius, after one of Ar's legendary heroes. Not only would the decision to halt the invasion be in violation of the practices and commitments of Priest-Kings, which would doubtless create dissension in the Nest, producing a leverage the Kurii might be able to exploit, but, if the invasion were halted, it being a large movement, complex, its termination might provide useful data on the nature and disposition of the powers of the Priest-Kings. It might provide the equivalent of drawing a sniper's fire, using a dupe or fool to do so, in order to ascertain his position. In the Nest War, when the Priest-Kings had been locked in internecine warfare, their powers had been severely reduced and disrupted. The Nest itself had been severely damaged. I knew that ships of Priest-Kings flew, but I knew little of their numbers, or power, or of the retained power in general of the delicate, tall, golden masters of Gor. I thought it quite likely that they would be unable to resist a full-scale invasion. Probes, I had learned from Misk, had become increasingly frequent. Slave raids on Earth, I recalled, had become a matter of course, routine. These were small matters in the scope of planetary politics, but were indicative. In just the past few days we had encountered, even in far Trovaldsland, two Earth females, suitably collared, Peggy Stevens of Connecticut, Honey Cake, and the girl, Leah, of Canada. The movements of Kurii and their allies were becoming bolder. Their boldest move had begun most recently, the gathering of the Gorean Kurii, the initiation of the march to the south, the incursion into lands of human habitation, the beginning of the invasion from the north. This was the boldest and most fearful probe of the Kurii of the ships, directed toward humans but doubtless, in fact, a testing of the will and nature of Priest-Kings, their true foes. If Priest-Kings permitted the conquest of Gor, perhaps over a generation or two, by Kurii, they would have lost the security of their own base; they would become an island in the midst of a hostile sea; it would then be a matter of time until the end, until adequate weaponry could be smuggled to Gor, or built upon it, to destroy them. This would now be no simple matter of policing primitive weapons, crude attempts at the art of gunnery or explosives, but of protecting themselves against perfected weapons of great technological power. Sooner or later, if Gor fell to native Kurii, those of the ships would destroy the denizens of the Sardar. Earth, too, then, would inevitably fall. Earth was so proud. It had managed to put a handful of men, for a few hours, on the surface of its moon. The Kurii, for more than twenty thousand years at least, had possessed deep-space capability.

Ivar had motioned me to silence.

We lay still. Within yards of us, strung out, approaching, was a column of pairs of men, each wearing a yellow scarf. Some carried torches. Kurii were not among them. They were led by a large man in swirling cape, and horned helmet, a bearded man. It was Thorgard of Scagnar. He, too, tied at his shoulder, wore a yellow scarf.

They passed.

"Would we not move about more freely," inquired Ivar Forkbeard, "if we, too, sported scarves of yellow?"

"It is not impossible," I said.

"Let us borrow some then," suggested he.

"Very well," I agreed.

Two shadows enveloped the last two men in the column of pairs led by Thorgard of Scagnar.

Ivar had thrust the yellow scarf into his belt; I looped mine over the right shoulder, fastening it loosely at the left hip; we left Thorgard's two men for the Kurii.

In the journey to Ivar's tent a Kur loomed before us, snarling.

"Foolish beast, stupid animal," said Ivar, brandishing his scarf, "can you not see the yellow scarf?"

He then brushed past the Kur. I felt its fur as I moved by it. It was smooth, not unpleasant to the touch, some two inches or so in depth. Its body, beneath the fur, was hot, large.

The Kur, doubtless, could not understand Gorean. If it had it might have slain us both. It could see the scarf, however. Reluctantly, snarling, it let us past it.

Shortly thereafter Ivar, fists clenched, stood on the site of his camp. The tent had been half burned, and poles were down. It was deserted. There was no sign of life. Boxes lay about. An overturned pan lay in ashes. We saw spilled coins. A piece of rope, cut, lay to one side. The stake, to which the chains of the bond-maids had been fixed, had been torn from the ground.

"Look," I said to him, throwing back a part of the tent. Ivar joined me. We looked down on the carcass of a dead Kur, its jaws opened, its eyes staring at the moons. Its head was half cut from its body.

"Some man of mine did well," said the Forkbeard. Then he looked about.

"In the morning," I said, "we will be recognized as not being of Thorgard's forces. In the morning, we will be hunted."

"It is quite possible," said Ivar, looking at me, "that we are being hunted now, by those from the hall."

"Our scent is known," I said. "Yellow scarves will not protect us from those from the hall."

"What do you propose?" asked Ivar.

"We must flee," I told him.

"No," said Ivar. "We must go to the Torvaldsberg."

"I do not understand," I said.

"It is time," he said. He looked about himself, at the ruins of his camp. In the distance we could see burning tents. Too, in the distance, there was a great redness in the sky. Beneath this redness burned the hall of Svein Blue Tooth. Far off, we could hear the howls of Kurii. "It is time," said Ivar Forkbeard, turning away from me, "to go to the Torvaldsberg."

He strode from his camp. I followed him.

It was shortly past noon, on the snowy slopes of the Torvaldsberg.

I looked down into the valley. We could not make out clearly the lineaments of the Kurii pursuing us. They moved rapidly.

They were perhaps a pasang and a half away. They carried shields, axes.

"Let us continue our journey," said Ivar.

"Shall we meet them here?" I asked.

"No," said Ivar, "let us continue our journey."

I looked up at the looming crags of the Torvaldsberg. "It is madness to attempt to climb," I said. "We do not have ropes, equipment. Neither of us are of the mountain people of the Voltai."

I looked back. The Kurii were now a pasang away, on the rocky, lower slopes, scrambling upward. They had slung their shields and axes on their backs. When they came to a sheet of steep ice they did not go around it but, extending their claws, climbed it rapidly. The Forkbeard and I had lost several Ehn in circling such obstacles. In snow the Kurii, spreading their large, six-digited appendages, dropped to all fours. For their weight, they did not sink deeply. It had taken the Forkbeard and I an Ahn, wading through crusts of snow, to reach our present position. Kurii, it was evident, would accomplish the same distance in a much shorter time.

When snow gave way to patches of rock they would pause, momentarily, nostrils lowered, reading sign that would have been undetectable to a human. Then they would lift their heads, scan the rocks above them, and proceed swiftly.

Ivar Forkbeard stood up. There was no cover now for us between our present position and the beginning of the steeper heights.

Below us we heard Kurii, seeing him, howl with pleasure. One pointed us out to a fourth who had not yet seen us. Then all of them stood below, leaping, lifting their arms.

"They are pleased," I said.

The Kurii then, with redoubled speed, began to move toward us.

"Let us continue our journey," suggested the Forkbeard.

My foot slipped, and I hung by the hands, from the rocky ledge. Then I had my footing again.

The sun struck the cliff. My fingers ached. My feet were cold from the ice, the snow. But the upper part of my body sweated.

"Move only one hand or a foot at a time," said Ivar. "Follow me."

It was now the twelfth hour, two Ahn past the Gorean noon. I would not look down.

A rock struck near me, shattering into the granite of the mountain, scarring it. It must have been the size of a tarsk. Startled I almost lost my grip. I tried to remain calm. I heard a Kur climbing below me.

The Torvaldsberg is, all things considered, an extremely dangerous mountain. Yet it is clearly not unscalable, as I learned, without equipment. It has the shape of a spear blade, broad, which has been bent near the tip. It is something over four and a half pasangs in height, or something over seventeen thousand Earth feet. It is not the highest mountain on Gor but it is one of the most dramatic, and most impressive. It is also, in its fearful way, beautiful.

I followed, as closely as I could, the Forkbeard. It did not take me long to understand that he knew well what he was doing. He seemed to have an uncanny sense for locating tiny ledges and cuts in the stone which were almost invisible from even two or three feet below.

Kurii are excellent climbers, well fitted for this activity with their multiple jointed hands and feet, their long fingers, their suddenly extendable claws, but they followed us, nonetheless, with difficulty.

I suspected why this was.

It must have been about the fourteenth Ahn when Ivar reached down and helped me to a ledge.

I was breathing heavily.

"Kurii," he said, "cannot reach this ledge by the same route."

"Why?" I asked.

"The hand holds," said he, "are too shallow, their weight too great."

"Hand holds?" I asked.

"Yes," said he. "Surely you have noticed their convenience."

I looked at him. More than once I had almost slipped down the escarpment.

"And you have noticed how they have become shallower?"

"I noticed the climbing was more difficult," I admitted. "You seem to know the mountain well," I told him.

Ivar smiled.

It had been no accident that he had seemed to have an uncanny knack for locating an ascent path, where none seemed to promise.

"You have been here before," I told him.

"Yes," he said. "As a boy I climbed the Torvaldsberg."

"You spoke of hand holds," I said.

"I cut them," he said.

It then seemed to me no wonder that he had moved with such confidence on the escarpment. I had suspected earlier that he knew the mountain, this facilitating our ascent, and that this explained why the pursuing Kurii, natively better climbers than men, could do little better than keep our pace, if that. I had not suspected, however, that the Forkbeard was taking advantage of a previously wrought path, and one which, in part at least, he had made for himself in years past.

The Forkbeard leaned back, grinning. He rubbed his hands. His fingers were cold. We heard, some sixty feet below us, a Kur scraping with its claws on the mountain below us, feeling for crevices or chinks.

"This ledge," said the Forkbeard, "is a Kur trap. In my youth I was hunted by a Kur in this vicinity. It had trailed me for two days. I took to the mountain. It was sufficiently unwise to follow me. I chose, and cut, a path which it might follow, to the last twenty feet; for the last twenty feet I cut shallow holds in the surface, adequate for a man, climbing carefully, but too shallow for the fingers of a Kur."

Below us I heard a snarl of frustration.

"As a boy, thus," said Ivar, "I slew my first Kur." He rose to his feet. He went to a corner of the ledge where, heaped, there were several large stones. "The stones I then gathered are still here," he said. "I found several on the ledge, some I found higher."

I did not envy the Kur below.

I looked over the edge. "It is still climbing," I whispered. I drew my sword. It would not be difficult to prevent the animal from reaching the ledge by any direct route.

"It is stupid," said the Forkbeard.

Behind the first Kur, some feet below, was a second. Two others were far down the slope, where it was less sheer. The two closest to us had left their weapons below, with the others.

The first Kur was some eight or ten feet below us when, suddenly, it slipped on the rock and, with a wild shriek, scratching at the stone, slid some four feet downward and then plunged backward, turning in the air, howling, and, some five Ihn later, struck the rocks far below.

"The hand holds," said Ivar, "were not cut to be deep enough to support the weight of a Kur."

The second Kur was some twenty-five feet below. It looked up, snarling.

The rock hurled by Ivar struck it from the almost vertical wall of stone.

It, like its confrere, fell to the rocks below.

The trap, laid for an enemy by a boy of Torvaldsland many years ago, was still effective. I admired Ivar Forkbeard. Even in his youth he had been resourceful, cunning. Even as a boy he had been a dangerous foe, in guile and wit the match even for an adult Kur.

The other two Kurii crouched below on the slopes, looking up. They carried their shields, their axes, on their back.

They made no attempt to approach us.

Our position was not, now, a desirable one. We were isolated on a ledge. Here there was not food or water. We could, with some climbing, obtain ice or snow, but there was no food. In time we would weaken, be unable to climb well. As hunters Kurii were patient beasts. If these had fed well before taking up our pursuit, they would not need food for days. I had little doubt they had fed well. There had been much available meat. There was little possibility of leaving the ledge undetected. Kurii have supurb night vision. Furthermore, it would be extremely dangerous to attempt to move on the Torvaldsberg in the night; it was extremely dangerous even in full daylight.

I rubbed my hands together, and blew on them. My feet, too, were cold. The sweat in my shirt, now that I was not climbing, was frozen. The shirt was stiff, cold. In the night, on the Torvaldsberg, even in the middle of the summer, without warm garments, a man might freeze. The wind then began to rise, sweeping the ledge. From where we stood we could see the black ruins of Svein Blue Tooth's hall and holdings, the desolated thing fields, the sea, Thassa, with the ships at the beach.

I looked at the Forkbeard.

"Let us continue our journey," he said.

"Let us descend and meet the Kurii, while we still have strength," I said.

"Let us continue our journey," he said.

Moving carefully, he began to climb. I followed him. After perhaps half an Ahn, I looked back. The two Kurii, by a parallel route, were following.

That night on the Torvaldsberg we did not freeze.

We huddled on a ledge, between rocks, sheltered from the wind, shivering with cold, miserable, listening for Kurii.

But they did not approach.

We had chosen our ledge well.

Twice rocks rained down to the ledge, but we were protected by an overhang.

"Would you like to hear me sing?" asked Ivar.

"Yes," I said, "it might drive the Kurii away."

Undeterred by my sarcasm, brilliant though it was, Ivar broke into song. He knew, it seemed, a great many songs.

No more rocks rained down to the ledge.

"Song, you see," said Ivar, "soothes even Kurii."

"More likely," I said, "they have withdrawn from earshot."

"You jest delightfully," acknowledged the Forkbeard, "I had not thought it in you."

"Yes," I admitted.

"I will teach you a song," he said, "and we shall sing it together." The song dealt with the problems of a man attempting to content one hundred bond-maids, one after the other; it is rather repetitious, and the number of bond-maids decreases by one in each round. Needless to say, it is a song which is not swiftly dispatched. I have, incidentally, a very fine singing voice.

In singing, we little noticed the cold. Yet, toward dawn, we took turns napping. "We will need our strength," said the Forkbeard.

How marvelous in the morning seemed the sun.

"If the Kurii are above us," I said, recalling the rain of stones, "is this not our opportunity to descend?"

"Kurii corner their prey," said the Forkbeard. "In the light, they will be below us. They will wish to keep between us and escape. Further, we would have little opportunity to escape, even if they were above us. The descent is difficult." I recalled the two Kurii, precariously clinging to the wall of rock, one of which had fallen attempting to reach us, the other of which Ivar had struck from the wall with a heavy stone. I shuddered.

"There they are," said Ivar, looking over the brink. He waved to them. Then he turned, cheerily, to me. "Let us continue our journey," he said.

"You speak," I said, "as though you had some objective."

"I do," said the Forkbeard.

Again we began climbing. Not long after we had again taken to the rocks, we heard and saw the Kurii, some two hundred feet below and to one side, following us.

It was shortly after the tenth hour, the Gorean noon, that we reached the peak of the Torvaldsberg.

Although there is much snow on the heights of the Torvaldsberg, there were also, on the peak, many areas of bare rock, swept by the wind which, on the peak, seems almost constant. I crossed a patch of snow, ankle deep, crusted, to ascend a snow-free, rounded rock.

I cannot express the beauty of the view from the Torvaldsberg. I have climbed it, I thought. And I am here.

There had been danger, there had been the struggle, the challenge, and then, here, suddenly, torturously purchased, humbling me, exalting me, was a victory which I felt was not mine so much as that of a world, that of vision, that of beauty. I had not conquered a mountain; the mountain, when I had paid its price, that I might understand the value of the gift, had lifted me to where I might see how insignificant I was and how beautiful and precious was reality and life, and the sun on a bleak, cold land. Ivar stood beside me, not speaking.

"You were here once," I said, "as a boy."

"Yes," said Ivar. "I have never forgotten it."

"Did you come here to die?" I asked.

"No," he said. "But I have been unable to find it."

I looked at him, puzzled.

"I could not find it before," he said. "I cannot find it now."

"What?" I asked.

"It does not matter now," he said.

He turned about.

Approaching were the two Kurii. We watched them. They, too, interestingly, stopped. They stood together, in the snow, looking out, over the world.

Then they regarded us. We loosened our weapons. The Kurii unslung their shields, their axes. We drew our swords. The Kurii fixed on their left arms the heavy, rounded iron shields, took the great axes, seven feet in length, grasped some two feet from the bottom of the handle, in their massive right fists. I had never thought much of it before, but Kurii, like men, were dominantly right handed. I conjectured then, that like men, the left hemispheres of their brains were dominant.

Ivar and I leaped from the rock; the two Kurii, one to each of us, approached. Their ears were laid back; they were cautious; they leaned slightly forward, shambling, crouching.

Priest-Kings, I recalled, regarded Kurii and men as rather equivalent species, similiar products of similar processes of evolution, similar products of similarly cruel selections, though on worlds remote from one another.

"Kur," I wondered, "are you my brother?"

The great ax swept toward me. I rolled over it, hitting the snow, slipping. I tried to drive in to thrust with my blade. I slipped again. The ax fell where I had been. A piece of granite, shattered from the rock, stung me. I stumbled backward. The Kur, not hurrying, ax ready, stalked me. I saw its eyes over the shield, the ax light in its great fist. "Hah!" I cried, feinting as though to charge. The ax tensed, but did not swing. Then it snarled and drew back the ax, to the full length of its long arm. I knew the blade could not reach me in time. I charged. It was what the Kur desired. I had been outwitted. The heavy shield, with fantastic force, with a sidelong motion, a sweep, struck me, fending me away, hurtling me for forty feet through the air. I struck snow, rolling, half-blinded. The ax fell again, shattering granite. I was on my feet. Again the shield struck me, like a hammer, the striking surface of which is more than a yard across. Again I was hurled to one side. I stumbled to my feet. I could not move my left arm. I thought it broken. The shoulder was like wood. The ax swung again. I stumbled back. Crying out I lost my balance, turning, and plunged from the peak. I fell to a ledge twenty feet below. The ax, like a pendulum, swept down. I hugged the surface of the ledge. The ax swept past me. I saw, to my right, a small, dark opening, irregular, jagged, about a foot in width and height. I leaped to my feet and ran to the brink of the edge. There was no descent. The lips of the Kur drew back, revealing the fangs. I saw Ivar, on the flat above, wild-eyed. "Ivar!" I cried. "Ivar!" I heard the blood shriek of an unseen Kur. Ivar turned and leaped to the ledge below, joining me. The two Kurii stood on the flat above, snarling. "Look!" I cried to him, indicating the opening. His eyes saw the opening. They glinted. I moved the fingers of my left hand. There was feeling. I did not know if the arm were broken or not. I thrust the sword into its scabbard. Ivar nodded. One of the Kurii, snarling, leaped to the ledge with us. I hurled a rock at it. The rock struck the shield, bounding with a clang away, down into the abyss. I thrust the Forkbeard toward the hole. He leaped to it, and squirmed through. The second Kur dropped to the ledge. I threw another rock, weightier than the first. It, too, with a sound of granite on metal, was fended away, this time by the shield of the second Kur. I leaped to the hole and forced my body through the opening. The Forkbeard caught my hand and dragged me inside. One of the long arms of a Kur thrust inside, reaching for us. The Forkbeard thrust at it with his sword but the blade was diverted, his arm striking against stone. The Kur withdrew its arm. We crawled back further in the tiny opening. Outside, we could see the heads of the two Kurii, peering within. Their tentacled paws felt the width of the opening. One of them thrust his head within and half a shoulder. The Forkbeard, sword poised, crawled to thrust at it. The Kur withdrew. Then, both of them squatted down, some feet out on the ledge. Kurii are patient hunters. They would wait. I rubbed my left arm and shoulder. I lifted the arm, and moved it. It was not broken. I had learned that the Kur shield could be as devastating a weapon as the war hammer of Hunjer. I wondered how many who had learned that had lived.

I looked outside. The Kurii were waiting.

"Come with me," said Ivar. His voice was excited. I turned to face him. I wondered how deep might be this little cave. I expected not more than twenty or thirty feet at most. On my hands and knees I crawled to join him.

"Here," said Ivar. "On the wall!"

He took my fingers and pressed them to the wall. I felt marks, rather vertical, with angular extensions.

"You have found it!" he cried. "You have found it, Tarl Red Hair!"

"I do not understand," I said.

"Follow me!" whispered Ivar Forkbeard. "Follow me!"

16

THE WAR ARROW

Following the Forkbeard, on hands and knees, I crawled down the narrow passage, at one point turning to my left side to slide through a narrow aperture. Within this aperture, I extended my hands and then, carefully, hands held up, feeling, I stood up. To one side I heard the Forkbeard fumbling about in the darkness. I heard the strike of two small pieces of iron pyrite on one another, taken from the Forkbeard's belt wallet, and saw a scattering of sparks. Then it was dark again. "There is cut moss against the edge," said the Forkbeard. There was another scattering of sparks. This time the sparks fell into a heap, one of several, each about five inches high and four inches wide, of miniscule, lacelike moss twigs. This tinder flared immediately into flame. In that instant I saw we were in a large, squared passage. I saw a torch in a ring, one of others. There was carving in the passage, rune letterings and pictographs, in linear borders. Before the bit of flaring moss turned to a million red pinpoints the Forkbeard took one of the torches and thrust it to the moss. I saw that, near some of the patches of moss, were pieces of flint and steel, near others tiny piles of iron pyrites. I shivered.

The Forkbeard lifted the torch. I, too, took a torch.

Neither of us spoke.

The passage extended beyond us, disappearing in the darkness beyond the light of our torches. It was about eight feet in height and width. It was carved from the living rock. Along its edges, spaced some twelve feet from one another, on both sides, were torch rings, with unlit torches, which might be lit. The piles of tinder and flint and steel, or iron pyrites, lay now behind us, or to one side. I lifted the torch to the borders, running linearly down the chamber, disappearing into the darkness before us. The lettering was in the high, angular script of the north; the pictographs seemed primitive.

"These are old runes," said Ivar.

"Can you read them?" I asked.

"No," said Ivar.

My hair rose on the back of my neck. I looked at one of the pictographs. It was a man astride a quadruped.

"Look," said I to the Forkbeard.

"Interesting," said the Forkbeard. "It is a representation of a man riding a mythological beast, doubtless an illustration based upon some saga with which I am unfamiliar."

He continued on.

I lingered by the pictograph. I had seen nothing like it on Gor.

"Follow me," said the Forkbeard.

I left the pictograph to follow him. I wondered on the man who had carved it. It was indeed old, perhaps ancient. It was drawn by one who had been familiar with a world unknown to Ivar Forkbeard. There was no mistaking the quadruped on which the rider was mounted. It was a horse.

The passage now enlarged. We felt lost in it. It was still squarish, some twenty feet in height and width. It was now much more decorated and carved than it had been, and, in the light of the torches, we could see that much color had been used in its decoration. Pictographs were much more numerous now, and, instead of being linearly bordered the walls were now decorated in columns of runes and designs, and pictographs. Torches, unlit, in wall rings, were still illuminated as we passed near them. Many of the columns carved, with painted surfaces, on the walls, reminded me of rune stones. These stones, incidentally, are normally quite colorful, and can often be seen at great distances. Each year their paint is freshened, commonly on the vigil of the vernal equinox, which, in the north, as commonly in the south, marks the new year. Religious rune stones are repainted by rune-priests on the vigil of the fest-season of Odin, which, on Gor, takes place in the fall. If the stones were not tended, either by farmers on whose lands they lie, or by villagers in whose locales they lie, or by rune-priests, in a few years, the paint would be gone, leaving only the plain stone. The most famous rune stone in the north is that on Einar's Skerry, which marks the northland's southern border.

"Can you not read these runes?" I asked Ivar, again.

"I am not a rune-priest," he said.

Ivar's reply was not a little belligerent. I knew him able

to read some rune markings. I gathered that these, perhaps because of antiquity or dialect, were beyond him. Ivar's attitude toward reading was not unlike that of many of the north. He had been taught some rune signs as a boy, that he could understand important stones, for in these stones were the names of mighty men and songs of their deeds, but it had not been expected of him that he would be in any sense a fluent reader. Ivar, like many of those in the north, was a passable reader, but took care to conceal this fact. He belonged to the class of men who could hire their reading done for them, much as he could buy thralls to do his farming. It was not regarded as dignified for a warrior to be too expert with letters, such being a task beneath warriors. To have a scribe's skills would tend to embarrass a man of arms, and tend to lower his prestige among his peers. Many of the north, then, were rather proud of their illiteracy, or semi-illiteracy. It was expected of them. It honored them. His tools were not the pen and parchment, but the sword, the bow, the ax and spear. Besides simple runes, the boy in the north is also taught tallying, counting, addition and subtraction, for such may be of use in trading or on the farm. He is also taught weighing. Much of his education, of course, consists in being taken into a house, and taught arms, hunting and the sea. He profits, too, from the sagas, which the skalds sing, journeying from hall to hall. In the fest-season of Odin a fine skald is difficult to bring to one's hall. One must bid high. Sometimes they are kidnapped, and, after the season's singing, given much gold and freed. I had not, of course, intended to insult the Forkbeard.

"There is one sign here, of course," said the Forkbeard, "which any fool might read."

He pointed to the sign.

I had seen it frequently in the writings. Naturally, I could not read it.

"What does it say?" I asked.

"Do you truly not know?" he asked.

"No," I said, "I do not know."

He turned away, and, again, I followed him.

We lit new torches from the wall rings and discarded our old ones. We then continued on our journey.

Now, to one side and the other, we passed opened chests, in which we could see treasures, the spillings and tangles of coins and jewelries, rings, bracelets.

We came then to a great arch, which marked the entrance

to a vast room, lost in darkness beyond the flickering spheres of our uplifted torches.

We stopped.

Over the arch, deeply incised in the stone was the single, mighty sign, that which the Forkbeard had not explained to me.

We stood in silence, in that dark, lofty threshold.

The Forkbeard was trembling. I had never seen him so. The hair on the back of my neck lifted, short, stiff. I felt cold. I knew, of course, the legends.

He lifted his torch, to the sign over the door. "Do you not know that sign?" he asked.

"I know what sign it must be," I said.

"What sign?" asked he.

"The sign, the name-sign, of Torvald."

"Yes," said he.

I shuddered.

"Torvald," I said to the Forkbeard, "is only a figure of legend. Each country has its legendary heroes, its founders, its discoverers, its mythic giants."

"This," said the Forkbeard, looking up at the sign, "is the chamber of Torvald." He looked at me. "We have found it," he said.

"There is no Torvald," I said. "Torvald does not exist."

"This," said the Forkbeard, "is his chamber." His voice shook. "Torvald," said he, "sleeps in the Torvaldsberg, and has done so for a thousand years. He waits to be wakened. When his land needs him, he shall awake. He shall then lead us in battle. Again he will lead the men of the north."

"There is no Torvald," I said.

The Forkbeard looked within. "For a thousand years," he whispered, "has he slept."

"Torvald does not exist," I said.

"We must waken him," said the Forkbeard.

Ivar Forkbeard, lifting his torch, entered the great chamber.

I felt grief. It seemed to me not impossible that, at the root of the legends, the sagas, of Torvald, there might be some particles of truth. I did not think it impossible that there had once been a Torvald, one who had come to this land, with followers perhaps, more than a thousand years ago. He might have been a great leader, a mighty warrior, the first of the jarls of the north, but that had been, if it had ever been, more than a thousand years ago. There was now no Torvald. I felt grief at what misery, what disappoint-

232

ment, what disillusionment must now fall to my friend, the Forkbeard.

In his hope to find one strong enough to stand against Kurii, one who could rally the men of the north, he was bound to be disillusioned.

The myth, that dream of succor, of final recourse, would be shown barren, fraudulent.

This chamber, I knew, had been built by men, and the passages carved from the very stone of the mountain itself. That must be accounted for. But it was not difficult to do so. Perhaps there had once been a Torvald, hundreds of years ago. If so, it was not impossible that it had been his wish to be interred in the great mountain. We stood, perhaps, within, or at the brink, of the tomb of Torvald, lost for long ages until now, until we two, fleeing from Kurii, from beasts, had stumbled upon it. Perhaps it was true that Torvald had been buried in the Torvaldsberg, and that the tomb, the funeral chamber, had been concealed, to protect it from the curious or from robbers. And, in such a case, legends might well have arisen, legends in which the mystery of the lost tomb might figure. These would have spread from village to village, from remote farm to remote farm, from hall to hall. One such legend, quite naturally, might have been that Torvald, the great Torvald, was not truly dead, but only asleep, and would waken when once again his land had need of him.

"Wait!" I called to the Forkbeard.

But he had entered the chamber, torch high, moving quickly. I followed him, swiftly, tears in my eyes.

When he looked down, torch lifted, upon the bones and fragile cloths of what had once been a hero, when the myth had been shattered, the crystal of its dream beneath the iron of reality, I wanted to stand near him. I would not speak to him. But I would stand behind him, and near him.

The Forkbeard stood at the side of the great stone couch, which was covered with black fur.

At the foot of the couch were weapons; at its head, hanging on the wall, under a great shield, were two spears, crossed under it, and, to one side, a mighty sword in its scabbard. Near the head of the couch, on our left, as we looked upon the couch, was, on a stone platform, a large helmet, horned.

The Forkbeard looked at me.

The couch was empty.

He did not speak. He sat down on the edge of the couch, on the black fur, and put his head in his hands. His torch

233

lay on the floor, and, after some time, burned itself out. The Forkbeard did not move. The men of Torvaldsland, unlike most Gorean men, do not permit themselves tears. It is not cultural for them to weep. But I heard him sob once. I did not, of course, let him know that I had heard this sound. I would not shame him.

"We have lost," he said, finally, "Red Hair. We have lost."

I had lit another torch, and was examining the chamber. The body of Torvald, I conjectured, had not been buried in this place. It did not seem likely that robbers would have taken the body, and left the various treasures about. Nothing, it seemed, had been disturbed.

Torvald, I conjectured, doubtless as cunning and wise as the legends had made him out, had not elected to have himself interred in his own tomb.

It was empty.

The wiliness, the cunning, of a man who had lived more than a thousand years ago made itself felt in its effects a millennium later, in this strange place, deep within the living stone of a great mountain in a bleak country.

"Where is Torvald?" cried out Ivar Forkbeard.

I shrugged.

"There is no Torvald," said the Forkbeard. "Torvald does not exist."

I made no attempt to answer the Forkbeard.

"The bones of Torvald," said the Forkbeard, "even the bones of Torvald are not here."

"Torvald was a great captain," I said. "Perhaps he was burned in his ship, which you have told me was called Black Shark." I looked about. "It is strange though," I said, "if that were the case, why this tomb would have been built."

"This is not a tomb," said Ivar Forkbeard.

I regarded him.

"This is a sleeping chamber," he said. "There are no bones of animals here, or of thralls, or urns, or the remains of foodstuffs, offerings." He looked about. "Why," he asked me, "would Torvald have had carved in the Torvaldsberg a sleeping chamber?"

"That men might come to the Torvaldsberg to waken him," I said.

Ivar Forkbeard looked at me.

From among the weapons at the foot of the couch, from one of the cylindrical quivers, still of the sort carried in Torvaldsland, I drew forth a long, dark arrow. It was more than a yard long. Its shaft was almost an inch thick. It was plied

234

with iron, barbed. Its feathers were five inches long, set in the shaft on three sides, feathers of the black-tipped coasting gull, a broad-winged bird, with black tips on its wings and tail feathers, similar to the Vosk gull.

I lifted the arrow. "What is this?" I asked the Forkbeard.

"It is a war arrow," he said.

"And what sign is this, carved on its side?" I asked.

"The sign of Torvald," he whispered.

"Why do you think this arrow is in this place?" I asked.

"That men might find it?" he asked.

"I think so," I said.

He reached out and put his hand on the arrow. He took it from me.

"Send the war arrow," I said.

The Forkbeard looked down on the arrow.

"I think," I said, "I begin to understand the meaning of a man who lived more than a thousand winters ago. This man, call him Torvald, built within a mountain a chamber for sleep, in which he would not sleep, but to which men would come to waken him. Here they would find not Torvald, but themselves, themselves, Ivar, alone, and an arrow of war."

"I do not understand," said Ivar.

"I think," I said, "that Torvald was a great and a wise man."

Ivar looked at me.

"In building this chamber," I said, "it was not the intention of Torvald that it should be he who was awakened within it, but rather those who came to seek him."

"The chamber is empty," said Ivar.

"No," I said, "we are within it." I put my hand to his shoulder. "It is not Torvald who must awaken in this chamber. Rather it is we. Here, hoping for others to do our work, we find only ourselves, and an arrow of war. Is this not Torvald's way of telling us, from a thousand years ago, that it is we on whom we must depend, and not on any other. If the land is to be saved, it is by us, and others like us, that it must be saved. There are no spells, no gods, no heroes to save us. In this chamber, it is not Torvald who must awaken. It is you and I." I regarded the Forkbeard evenly. "Lift," said I, "the arrow of war."

I stood back from the couch, my torch raised. Slowly, his visage terrible, the Forkbeard lifted his arm, the arrow in his fist.

I am not even of Torvaldsland, but it was I who was

present when the arrow of war was lifted, at the side of the couch of Torvald, deep within the living stone of the Torvaldsberg.

Then the Forkbeard thrust the arrow in his belt. He crouched down, at the foot of the couch of Torvald. He sorted through the weapons there. He selected two spears, handing me one. "We have two Kurii to kill," he said.

17

TORVALDSLANDERS
VISIT THE CAMP
OF KURII

It was very quiet.

The men did not speak.

Below us, in the valley, spread out for more than ten pasangs we saw the encampment of Kurii.

At the feet of Ivar Forkbeard, head to the ground, nude, waiting to be commanded, knelt Hilda the Haughty, daughter of Thorgard of Scagnar.

"Go," said Ivar to her.

She lifted her head to him. "May I not have one last kiss, my Jarl?" she whispered.

"Go," said he. "If you live, you will be more than kissed."

"Yes, my Jarl," she said, and, obediently, slipped away into the darkness.

The ax I carried was bloodied. It had tasted the blood of a Kur guard.

We stood downwind of the encampment.

Not far from me was Svein Blue Tooth. He stood, not moving. It was cold. I could see the outline of his helmet, the rim of the shield, the spear, dark against darkness.

Near us, behind us, stood Gorm, Ottar and Rollo, and others of Forkbeard's Landfall. It was some Ehn before the Gorean dawn. On a distant world, lit by the same star, at a comparable time, men turned in their beds, mercury vapor lamps burned, lonely, heavy lorries rumbled down streets, keeping their delivery schedules, parts of yesterday's newspapers fluttered down lonely sidewalks. With us stood Bjarni of Thorstein Camp, and with him he who had in the formal duel carried his shield. At Bjarni's shoulder, too, stood the young man, scarcely more than a boy, whom he had in that duel intended to fight. With the boy, too, was his friend, who would have carried the shield for him. The war arrow had been carried. It had been carried to the Inlet of Green Cliffs, to Thorstein Camp, from Ax Glacier to Einar's Skerry; it had been carried to the high farms, to the lakes, to the coast; it had been carried on foot and by swift ship; a thousand arrows, each touched to the arrow of Torvald, had been carried, and where the arrow had been carried, men had touched it, saying "I will come." They came. Captains and rovers, farmers, fishermen, hunters, weavers of nets, smiths, carvers of wood, tradesmen and traders, men with little more than leather and an ax to their name, and jarls in purple cloaks, with golden pommels on their swords. And among them stood, too, thralls. Their heads were not lower than those with whom they stood. Among them was the lad called Tarsk, formerly Wulfstan of Kassau, to whom Thyri had once been given for the night. In the night of the attack he, at the Forkbeard's encampment near the thing field, with an ax, had slain a Kur. I remembered finding the carcass of the animal beneath the fallen, half-burned canvas of the Forkbeard's tent. Thralls are not permitted to touch the war arrow, but they are permitted to kneel to those who have. Wulfstan had handed the Forkbeard the ax, disarming himself, and had then knelt before him, putting his head to his feet. Thralls may be slain for so much as touching a weapon. He had taken dirt from beneath the feet of the Forkbeard and, kneeling, had poured it on his head. "Rise, Thrall," had said the Forkbeard. The young man had then stood, and straightly, head high, before the Forkbeard. The Forkbeard threw him back the ax. "Carry it," said the Forkbeard. On another world, lit by the same star, in another place, dawn, too, drew near. The distant light in the great cities, unknowing, soon to be occupied with the concerns of their days, piercing the haze of daily, customary poisons, first struck the heights of the lofty buildings, reflecting from the rectangular windows, like sheets of burnished copper reflecting the fire of the sun. Men would soon be up and about their duties, hurrying from one nothing to another, to compromises, to banal degradations, anxious lest they fail to be on time. They would not care for the blackened grass growing between the bricks; they would take no note of the spider's architecture, nor marvel at the flight of a wren darting to its nest among the smoke-blackened, carved stones. There would be no time. There would be no time for them, no time for seeing, or feeling, or touching, or loving or finding out what it might be to be alive. Clouds would be strangers to them; rain an inconvenience; snow a nuisance; a tree an anachronism; a flower an oddity, cut and frozen in a florist's refrigerator. These were the men without meaning, so full and so empty, so crowded, so desolate, so busy, so needlessly occupied. These were the gray men, the hurrying men, the efficient, smug, tragic insects, noiseless on soft feet, in the billion iron hills of technology. How few of them gazed ever on the stars. Is grandeur so fearful that men must shield themselves with pettiness from its glory; do they not understand that in themselves, and in perhaps a thousand other intelligences, reality has opened its eyes upon its own immensity; do they shut their eyes lest they see gods? We could see now a glimmer of light on the peak of the Torvaldsberg.

I wondered how many men would die. I wondered if I myself, this morning, in Torvaldsland, in bleak light, would die. I gripped the ax. It had good weight. The balance was apt.

Across the valley, there were others, men, waiting, too. The signal would be a shield signal, taking the morning sun, a flash, and then the attack. Hundreds of war cries would be mingled as men poured down the slopes. There were men here, too, even from Hunjer, Skjern, Helmutsport and Scagnar itself, on whose cliffs Thorgard's fortress ruled.

Never before, to my knowledge, had men attacked Kurii.

I gazed at the giant, Rollo, His eyes seemed vacant. He stood as a child, with his great ax. About his neck was a golden medallion. His chest was bare, beneath a leather vest.

Svein Blue Tooth fingered the tooth of the Hunjer whale, dyed blue, on its chain about his neck. He was a good jarl. He had been the third, after Ivar Forkbeard and Tarl Cabot, a warrior of Ko-ro-ba, to lift the arrow of Torvald. Not far away from him was even Ketil, of his high farm, the wrestler whose arm I had broken. It was splinted with a third of a spear shaft. In his left hand he carried a sword. Among the men, too, was a large fellow, as large as, or larger than, Rollo, whom I did not know. He was fiercely bearded, and carried a spear. He had told us he was Hrolf, and from the East. None had questioned him.

Below us, in the valley, we could see the coals of thousands of fires in the camp of the Kurii. They slept, curled, several in each shelter. The field shelters of the Kurii are made of skins and furs, arched over bent saplings. Each is little more than four or five feet high, with a comparable width, but is fifty or sixty feet in length, some being as long as a hundred feet in length. These shelters, too, are often curved and irregular in outline; sometimes they adjoin one another, with entrances giving mutual access. They resemble caves, sometimes networks of caves, constructed in the open. Kurii drop to all fours to enter and leave them. No Kur enjoys sleeping exposed. If in a field they will sometimes even burrow into the ground, almost like a sleen, and cover the opening with grass and sticks from the bottom. It always sleeps with its head toward the opening.

The Kurii herds were quiet. There was little stirring in them. I could see the white herd of verr, hundreds of the animals, penned in the northwest quadrant of the camp; in the northeast quadrant were the tarsk pens. I could smell them in the early morning air. I could smell, too, the odors of Kurii, and the trampled dung of bosk. The bosk were at the south of the camp. They would, effectively, prevent the Kurii from slipping free on the south. The herd numbered some several thousand. The northern pole of the camp would be left free, as a seeming avenue of escape, to lure embattled Kurii, should the tide of the war turn against them, into flight northward. It would be, in the language of Gorean strategists, the bridge of jewels, beckoning, alluring, promising safety, prophetic of escape.

Near the center of the camp, but somewhat to the south and east of the center, like the verr, the tarsk, the bosk, was another herd of Kurii animals; it, too, resided in its pen, a wide pen, more than a quarter of a pasang in diameter, formed of poles and crossbars, lashed together; this pen, however, was patrolled by prowling, domesticated sleen; the animals huddled together, within the pen, hundreds of them, terrified of the sleen; these were herd sleen, trained to group and control animals.

To the north and west of the camp's center I could see the tents of Thorgard of Scagnar and his men.

I smiled.

The Kurii had been in no hurry to initiate their march to the south. They had failed, several days ago, in the Thing Assembly, to intimidate the men of Torvaldsland into furnishing them provisions for their march. After their devastating victory of the night of Svein Blue Tooth's feast, in which his hall was burned, and the thing encampments laid waste, they had formed their own camp, and set methodically about gathering supplies for their southern march. Hundreds of sorties had penetrated the hills and valleys, burning farms, and gathering goods, generally tools and weapons, and live-stock. There were collection points to which such materials were brought, from which, by short marches, they were conveyed to the camp. During this time, a hundred pasangs to the south, Svein Blue Tooth had set the rallying point of the men of Torvaldsland.

In these days I had much spied on Kurii, living on the land, returning more than once to the Blue Tooth's war camp. It is nothing for a warrior to cover ninety pasangs on foot in a day. This is usually done by alternating the war-rior's pace with the warrior's stride, and allowing for pe-riods of rest. Few who have been invested in the scarlet of the warriors cannot match this accomplishment. I, and many others, can considerably improve upon it.

A typical Kurii foraging squad consists of six animals, called a "hand," with its "eye," or leader. Two such "hands," with their "eyes," constitutes a "Kur," or "Beast." The mili-tary Kur, in this sense a unit, is commanded by a "Blood." This seems peculiar perhaps but is explained by ancient Kurii belief, that thought is a function of the blood. One "thinks" thus with one's entire body, not just the brain. Contempo-rary Kurii understand, naturally, that cognitive processes are brain-centered, or largely brain-centered, but the ancient terminology, in their songs, poetry, and even military lexi-con, remains. Analogously, humans continue to speak of af-fairs of the heart, a man of good heart, that someone has a big heart, etc., which terminology perhaps lingers from times when the heart was regarded not as a chemomechanical pump but as the throne and home of the emotions. The commander of a military Kur, thus, might better be thought of as the "brain" or "mind," but continues, in their lan-guages, to be spoken of as the "blood." A "blood" thus com-mands the two eyes and the two hands. Twelve "Kurs," in the sense of military units, constitutes one "Band." This has one hundred and eighty animals, including subalterns and leaders, and is itself commanded by a "Blood," whose rank is indicated by two rings on the left arm. Twelve of these Bands constitutes a March. A March thus consists of 2,160 animals, or, counting the commanders of each Band, too, 2,172 animals. A March is commanded by a Blood, whose rank is indicated by one ring on the left arm. The rings of rank are quite plain, being of some reddish alloy, and are to be distinguished from decorative rings, of which many Kurii are fond. Kurii, generally, like men, seem vain beasts, but there appears to be an inverse correlation between height of rank and intricacy and variety of ornamentation. The higher the rank the simpler is likely to be the ornamentation. The commander, or Blood, of a March wears only a single, simple reddish ring. Whether or not this simplicity is honored off duty, so to speak, or in their privacy, I do not know. I further do not know the full significance of the rings. I do not understand how they are earned, or what is involved in moving from the "second ring" to the first ring. I do know that the rings are welded on the wrists of the beasts. The iron files of the Goreans, incidentally, will not cut the alloy. They may be obtained, of course, by the severing of the arm. Why the conjunction of bands is spoken of as a "March" is also unclear. This may refer to a military march, of course, but, I suspect, the term being apparently ancient, that it may also refer to migrations in the remote history of the Kurii, on their own world, putatively no longer existent or viable. There is some indirect evidence that this may be the case, because twelve "Marches" is referred to not as a Division or Army, or some such unit, but rather as a "People." A People would be commanded by a "Blood" of the People. Such a commander is said to stand "outside the rings." I do not fully understand the meaning of this expression. The Kurii, as I may have mentioned, consist of several "Peoples." Not all of these "Peoples" speak the same language, and, I gather, there are differences among them, and within, each People, for example, differences in marking, in texture of fur, in temperament, in tooth arrangement, in ear shape, and so on. These differences, negligible from the point of view of humans, are apparently of considerable importance among the Kurii themselves. The human, pursued by such an animal, is not likely to be concerned about the width of its ears or the mottling of its fur. Kurii, in their past, at least, were apparently torn by internecine strife, disrupted by "racial" and "civil" wars among themselves. It is not impossible that the defertilization or destruction of their former home was a consequence of such altercations. No Kur, however, I am told, of whatever race or type, will eat the meat of another. This is interesting, considering the ferocity of their carnivorous dispositions. They hold the human, unfortunately, in no such regard. It will be noted that the military arrangements of the Kurii are based on the number twelve or divisors and multiples of twelve. Kurii use, I understand, a base-twelve mathematics. The prehensible, appendage of the normal Kur is six digited.

Sometimes the foraging squads of the Kurii had been accompanied by trained sleen, often four of them. Twice, in my reconnoitering, I had had to kill such beasts. The sleen have various uses; some are merely used as watch animals or guard animals; others are used as points in the advance of squads, some trained to attack putative enemies, others to return to the squad, thus alerting it to the presence of a possible enemy; others are even more highly trained, and are used to hunt humans; of the human-hunting sleen, some are trained merely to kill, and others to hurry the quarry to a Kurii holding area; one type of sleen is trained to destroy males and herd females, distinguishing between the sexes by scent. A sleen may bring a girl in, stumbling and weeping, from pasangs away, driving her, as Kurii take little notice, through their very camp, until she is entered into a herd. Four days ago I had seen a girl drive in which several sleen, fanning out over a large area of territory, had scented out scattered, hiding slave girls and, from various points, driven them into a blind canyon, where a waiting Kur had swung shut a wooden gate on them, fastening them inside. Sleen are also used to patrol the large return marches of groups of foraging expeditions, those marches between the temporary holding areas and the main camp. The order of such a march is typically as follows: Captured humans, in single file, form its center. These humans are usually thralls and bond-maids, but not always. The spoils are carried by the captured male humans, unless there are too many, and then the residue is divided among the bond-maids. Kurii burden the males heavily; they can think of little more than the weight they carry, and the next step; furthermore, their wrists are usually tied to the straps of their improvised backpacks. Kurii, unlike Goreans, do not subject bond-maids to heavy labor; it toughens their meat; the bond-maids are separated from the males, that they be deprived of leadership; furthermore, the technique of keeping prisoners in single file, separating them by some feet, and preventing speech between them, tends to make conjoint action between them unlikely. Prowling the long single-file of prisoners, male and female, in alternate groups, bond-maids thus used to separate files of men from one another, will be sleen. Should any individual, either male or female, depart by so much as a yard from the line of march, or attempt to close the gap between himself and a fellow prisoner, the sleen prevent this. Once I saw a girl stumble and two sleen, immediately, snarling and hissing, sprang toward her. She leaped, weeping, to her feet and darted to her precise place in the line, keeping it perfectly, casting terrified glances at the vicious predators. The line of prisoners and sleen is, on both sides, flanked by the Kurii foragers. There are thus five lines, the center line of prisoners and spoils, its flanking lines of sleen, and, on either side, the flanking lines of the Kur foragers. Human prisoners of Kurii, incidentally, are usually stripped; Kurii see no reason to give animals clothing.

I glanced to the Torvaldsberg.

The sun now glinted more fully on its height.

Below us, in the broad valley, the camp of the Kurii lay still in darkness. We heard, below, the howling of a sleen, lonely. I wondered if Kurii dreamed. I supposed they did.

"It is almost time," said Ivar Forkheard to me.

I nodded.

Then, from below, we heard the hunting cry of a sleen, and then of two others, then others.

I did not envy Hilda, Ivar's slave. The Kurii would take little note of the sleen. Their cries were neither of alarm nor of fury. They were only gathering in another animal, perhaps a new one, wandered too close to the camp, or a stray, to be expeditiously returned to its herd. The first light then began to touch the valley. From the noises of the sleen we could detect the progress of their hunt, and the location of the imbonded daughter of Thorgard of Scagnar.

"There," said Ivar, pointing.

They caught her north of the bosk herd. We could see her white body, and the dark, sinuous, furred shapes converging upon it. Then she was surrounded, and she stopped. Then the spleen opened a passage for her, indicating to her which direction she was to go. Where else she turned she was met with the fangs and hisses of the accompanying animals. When she tried to move in any direction other than that of the opened passage they snapped at her, viciously. A single snap could tear off a hand or foot. Then two of the sleen fell in behind her and, snarling and snapping at her heels, drove her before them. We saw her fleeing before them, trying to escape the swift, terrible jaws. We feared, more than once, that they would kill her. A female who cannot be herded is destroyed by the herding sleen.

In the northwest quadrant of the camp was the herd of verr; in the northeast quadrant were the tarsk pens. The bosk were penned at the southern end of the camp. Near the center of the camp but somewhat to the south and east of the center, behind its poles and crossbars, lashed together, was a different herd of Kurii livestock. It was to this pen that the daughter of Thorgard of Scagnar, running before the snapping, snarling sleen, was driven. She darted between the crossbars and, in a moment, no longer harried by sleen, found herself on the trampled turf within, another member of the herd. It was as we had planned. The sleen now resumed their rounds, patrolling the perimeter of the pen. The new animal had been added to the herd. They were no longer interested in it, unless it should attempt to leave the pen. We saw Hilda, a speck in the grayish light, hurrying to the herd within, it huddled on the damp, soiled, trampled turf.

"I wish," said Ivar Forkbeard, "that I had such a herd."

The herd, indeed, consisted of sleek, beautiful animals, fair and two-legged. There must have been three or four thousand chattels confined in the great pen.

"Some of the girls are yours," I reminded him.

"And I intend to have them back," he said. In that herd, I surmised, were several of our women, Thyri, Aelgifu or Pudding, Gunnhild, Olga, Pouting Lips, Pretty Ankles, the former Miss Stevens of Connecticut, now Honey Cake, the girl named Leah, from Canada, whose last name was of no interest, and others. Too, among them now, prisoner, was Hilda, perhaps Ivar's preferred slave.

Hilda, even now, would be conveying our instructions to the frightened girls, for the most part, bond-maids. We would soon see if such feared sleen and Kurii more, or Gorean males, their masters. If they did not obey, they would be slain. As slaves, they were commanded; as slaves, did they fail to comply, they would be put to death. They had no choice. They would obey.

The sun was now sharp and beautiful on the heights of the Torvaldsberg.

"Tie on the scarves," said Svein Blue Tooth. The word slipped from man to man. On the other side of the valley, too, men would be performing the same action. Each of us tied about our left shoulder a yellow scarf. It was by such a device that the Kurii had recognized their confederates in the men of Thorgard of Scagnar. We would, too, wear such scarves. This was our vengeance on those who had betrayed their kind.

"Loosen your weapons," said Svein Blue Tooth. The men shifted. Swords were withdrawn from scabbards; arrows were fitted to the string, spears more firmly gripped.

It seemed strange to me that men, only men, would dare to pit themselves against Kurii.

I did not know then, of course, about the fury.

Svein Blue Tooth had his head down.

I sensed it first in the giant, Rollo. It was not a human noise. It was a snarl, a growl, like the sound of a larl, awakening from its sleep. The hair on my neck stood on end. I turned. The giant head was slowly lifting itself, and turning. Its eyes were closed. I could see blood beginning to move through the veins of its forehead. Then the eyes opened, and no longer were they vacant, but deep within them, as though beginning from far away, there seemed the glint of some terrible light. I saw his fists close and open. His shoulders were hunched down. He half crouched, as though waiting, tense, while the thing, the frenzy, the madness, began to burn within him.

"It is beginning," said Ivar Forkbeard to me.

"I do not understand," I said.

"Be quiet," said he. "It is beginning."

I saw then Svein Blue Tooth, the mighty jarl of Torvaldsland, lift his own head, but it did not seem, then, to be him. It seemed rather a face I had not seen before. The eyes did not seem those of the noble Blue Tooth, but of something else, unaccountable, not understood. I saw him suddenly thrust his left forearm against the broad blade of his spear. To my horror I saw him sucking at his own blood.

I saw a man, fighting the frenzy, tear handfuls of his own hair from his head. But it was coming upon him, and he could not subdue it.

Other men were restless. Some dug at the earth with their boots. Others looked about themselves, frightened.

The eyes of one man began to roll in his head; his body seemed shaken, trembling; he muttered incoherently.

Another man threw aside his shield and jerked open the shirt at his chest, looking into the valley.

I heard others moan, and then the moans give way to the sounds of beasts, utterances of incontinent rage.

Those who had not yet been touched stood terrified among their comrades in arms. They stood among monsters.

"Kurii," I heard someone say.

"Kill Kurii," I heard. "Kill Kurii."

"What is it?" I asked Ivar Forkbeard.

I saw a man, with his fingernails, blind himself, and feel no pain. With his one remaining eye he stared into the valley. I could see foam at the side of his mouth. His breathing was deep and terrible.

"Look upon Rollo," said the Forkbeard.

The veins in the neck, and on the forehead, of the giant

246

bulged, swollen with pounding blood. His head was bent to one side. I could not look upon his eyes. He bit at the rim of his shield, tearing the wood, splintering it with his teeth.

"It is the frenzy of Odin," said the Forkbeard. "It is the frenzy of Odin."

Man by man, heart by heart, the fury gripped the host of Svein Blue Tooth.

It coursed through the thronged warriors; it seemed a tangible thing, communicating itself from one to another; it was almost as though one could see it, but one could not see it, only its effects. I could trace its passage. It seemed first a ghastly infection, a plague; then it seemed like a fire, invisible and consuming; then it seemed like the touching of these men by the hands of gods, but no gods I knew, none to whom a woman or child might dare pray, but the gods of men, and of the men of Torvaldsland, the dread, harsh divinities of the cruel north, the gods of Torvaldsland. And the touch of these gods, like their will, was terrible.

Ivar Forkbeard suddenly threw back his head and, silently, screamed at the sky.

The thing had touched him.

The breathing of the men, their energy, their rage, the fury, was all about me.

A bowstring was being drawn taut.

I heard the grinding of teeth on steel, the sound of men biting at their own flesh.

I could no longer look on Ivar Forkbeard. He was not the man I had known. In his stead there stood a beast.

I looked down into the valley. There were the lodges of the Kurii. I recalled them. Well did I remember their treachery, well did I remember the massacre, hideous, merciless, in the hall of Svein Blue Tooth.

"Kill Kurii," I heard.

Within me then, irrational, like lava, I felt the beginning of a strange sensation.

"I must consider the beauty of the Torvaldsberg," I told myself. But I could not look again at the cold, bleak beauty of the mountain. I could look only into the valley, where, unsuspecting, lay the enemy.

"It is madness," I told myself. "Madness!" In the lodges below slept Kurii, who had killed, who had massacred in the night. In my pouch, even now, there lay the golden armlet, which once had been worn by the woman, Telima.

Below, unsuspecting, they lay, the enemy, the Kurii.

"No," I said. "I must resist this thing."

I drew forth the golden armlet which had been worn by Telima.

On a bit of fiber I tied it about my neck. I held it. Below lay the enemy.

I closed my eyes. Then I sucked in the air between my teeth.

Somewhere, far off, on another world, lit by the same star, men hurried to work.

I fought the feelings which were rearing within me. As well might I have fought the eruption of the volcano, the shifting of the strata of the earth.

I heard the growling, the fury, of those about me.

Below us lay the Kurii.

I opened my eyes.

The valley seemed to me red with rage, the sky red, the faces of those about me. I felt a surge of frenzy building within me. I wanted to tear, to cut, to strike, to destroy.

It had touched me, and I stood then within its grip, in that red, burning world of rage.

The bowstring was taut.

There was foam at the mouth of Svein Blue Tooth. His eyes were those of a madman.

I lifted my ax.

The thousands of the men of Torvaldsland, on either side of the valley, made ready. One could sense their seething, the unbearable power, the tenseness.

The signal spear, in the hand of the frenzied Blue Tooth, its scarlet talmit wrapped at the base of its blade, was lifted.

The breathing of thousands of men, waiting to be unleashed, to plunge to the valley, for an instant was held.

The sun flashed on the shield. The signal spear thrust to the valley.

With one frenzied cry the host, in its fury, from either side of the valley, plunged downward.

"The men of Torvaldsland," they cried, "are upon you!"

18

WHAT THEN OCCURRED IN THE CAMP OF THE KURII

The Kur dropped back from the blade. Howling I leapt upon another, striking it before it could rise, and then another.

Simultaneously with the attack from the slopes the girls in the cattle pen, following the orders of masters, conveyed to them by Hilda, crying out, fled in their hundreds from the pen, streaming throughout the camp. The herd sleen rushed among them but, confused in the numbers, found it difficult to single out women for returning to the pen. Similarly the marine predator attacking a school of shimmering, flashing bodies makes fewer successful strikes than he would if he were able, undistracted, to single out individual quarries. A sleen would no sooner mark out a girl for return to the pen than three or four others would constantly enter and disappear from his ken, often luring him into their pursuit, while the first slips free, in her turn later perhaps to save another similarly. Furthermore, when a sleen would fasten on a given girl she would permit herself, rapidly, to be returned to the pen. Thus the sleen, obedient to its training, would not harm her. As soon as she was back in the pen, of course, she would leave it again, escaping from a different sector. Any girl found remaining in the pen by a man of Torvaldsland, seeking her own safety, unless she had been ordered there by a free attacker, was to be summarily slain. I was pleased to note that the women feared more the men of Torvaldsland than even sleen and Kurii. Danger to them was of no interest to us. Their lives were unimportant. They were slaves. Accordingly, we used them to create a diversion.

Many Kurii, springing from their tents, emerging from the leather and fur shelter tunnels, confused, first saw only the sleek, two-legged cattle streaming past, until perhaps axes fell upon them. The nature of the attack, and its extent, would not be clear to them.

A Kur lifted its great ax. I charged him, my ax swift before he could strike.

I wrenched free the blade of the ax, as it slumped down, breaking it free from its jawbone and shoulder.

"Tarl Red Hair!" I heard cry. It was the voice of a girl, wild, slender. I turned. I realize now it was Thyri, but I did not recognize her at the time. I stood mighty and terrible, the ax ready, my clothes drenched with blood, the Kur rolling and jerking at my feet. She put her hand before her mouth, her eyes terrified, and fled away.

I saw a Kur seize a man of Thorgard of Scagnar's camp and tear his head from his body.

The attackers, as well as the men of Thorgard of Scagnar, wore yellow scarves at their shoulders. Many Kurii, confused in the beginning, had fallen to the axes of scarved men, putatively their allies. Now, however, indiscriminately, they sought to destroy all armed male humans. Many were the men of Thorgard who fell beneath the teeth and steel of Kurii, and several were the Kurii who fell to the weapons of Thorgard's men, as they fought madly to defend themselves.

Once I saw Thorgard of Scagnar and Ivar Forkbeard trying to reach him. But Ivar was blocked by Kurii and warriors, and joined in their combat.

I heard the screaming of slave girls.

I saw two Kurii converging on Gorm. Twice, from behind, the ax swept laterally, once to the left, the second time to the right, chopping through the spines.

A sleen, more than eleven feet in length, six-legged, slid past, its fur wiping against my thigh.

Gorm, in his madness, was cutting at the bodies of the Kurii fallen now before him, shrieking.

Shoulder to shoulder, fighting, I saw Bjarni of Thorstein Camp and the young man, whom I had championed on the dueling ground in the thing.

I smelled fire. There was the howling of Kurii.

I saw a Kur, barred with brown, turning, backing away, snarling, limping, from Ottar, who kept the Forkbeard's farm. Ottar pursued it, heedless of his safety, his eyes wild, killing it, cutting its body then in two with repeated blows of his ax.

I saw the huge, little-known man of Torvaldsland, who had joined the host late, calling himself Hrolf, from the East, who had come from the direction of the Torvaldsberg. With a cry he thrust his spear through the chest of a Kur.

He fought magnificently.

A Kur charged. I side-stepped, catching it in the belly with the ax.

I saw another Kur, undecided, startled. I slipped in gut. It charged. I reared the handle of the ax, catching it in the stomach, turning it to one side. It grunted. I leapt up, catching it in the side of the neck before it could rise. Its head half to one side it rose to its feet and ran for a dozen yards before it slipped, falling sideways, rolling into the fur and burning leather of one of their lodges.

"Protect me!" I heard. A female threw herself to my feet, putting her head to my ankle. "Protect me!" she wept. I looked down. She lifted her face, terrified, tear-stained. She had dark hair, dark eyes. I saw the iron collar, dark, on her white throat. It was Leah, the Canadian girl. With my foot I thrust her, weeping, to one side. There was men's work to do.

I met the attack of the Kur squarely. The handle of its ax smote down across the handle of mine, forcing me to one knee. Slowly I reared up, forcing the handle, now held in the two paws of the Kur, upward and backward. It again thrust down, with its full weight and strength, certain that it could crush the puny strength of a human. I held it only long enough to satisfy myself that I could, then I withdrew the handle swiftly, twisting to one side and lifting the ax. It fell forward, startled. I stepped on the handle of the ax. It tried to dislodge it. My ax was raised. It rolled wildly to one side. My blow fell against its left shoulder blade, dividing it. Howling, it leapt to its feet, backing away from me, baring its fangs. I followed it. It turned suddenly and leapt away. I caught it before the opening of a pavilion tent, one of those of Thorgard of Scagnar, perhaps his own. The tent was striped. The Kur, turning, now facing me, moved backward; it stumbled against a tent rope, jerking loose its peg. I leaped forward, striking it again, at the left hip. The side of its furred leg was drenched with blood. Hunched over, snarling, it backed into the tent, where I followed it. There was screaming from within the tent, the screaming of Thorgard's silken girls, many of them short, plump, lusciously bodied. Some were chained by the left ankle. The silks they wore, clinging and diaphanous, were designed not to conceal their beauty but to reveal it, to enhance and accentuate it, to expose it sensuously to the survey of a master. They, collared, shrank back, cowering on the cushions, drawing back to the side of the tent. I scarcely glanced at them. They would belong to the victors.

The Kur, backing away, with its right arm, reaching across its body, tore up one of the tent poles, wrenching it free of the earth, the tent. The tent sagged near him. He snarled, He thrust out with the tent pole, using the spike at its top like a spear. Then he swung the pole, striking at me. I waited. It was weak from the loss of blood. It turned about again and fled to the opposite wall of the tent. It tried to tear the silk, and it was at the wall of the tent that I caught it. I lifted my ax from the body, and turned to face the women. I strode to them. They knelt, huddled together, holding one another, at the side of the tent. They put down their eyes, trembling. I left the tent.

"Where is Thorgard of Scagnar?" asked Ivar Forkbeard. His shirt was half torn away. There was Kur blood on his chest and against the side of his face.

"I do not know," I told him.

Behind Ivar Forkbeard, naked, wearing his collar, I saw Hilda, Thorgard's daughter.

"There is a rallying of Kurii by the verr pens!" cried a man.

Quickly Ivar and myself hurried to the verr pens.

The rally was ill fated. Spears fell among the determined Kurii. Several fell in the mud and filth of the verr pens themselves, the bleating animals, frightened, darting about, leaping over the bodies.

Near the verr pens we found chained male slaves, picked up by Kurii on foraging expeditions, and used as porters. There were more than three hundred such wretches.

Svein Blue Tooth was at the pens, leading the attack that had broken the rally. The rally had been led by the Kur who had been foremost in the attack on his hall. This Kur, it seemed, had disappeared, scattering with the others. The Blue Tooth stepped over the body of a fallen Kur. He gestured to the chained male slaves. "Free them," he said, "and give them weapons. There is yet work to do." Eagerly the slaves, when their manacles had been struck away, picked up weapons and sought Kurii.

"Do not permit Kurii to escape to the south," said Svein

Blue Tooth to Ketil, keeper of his high farm, who had been famed as a wrestler.

"The bosk herd blocks their escape in numbers," said Ketil. "Some have even been trampled."

"We have been tricked!" cried a man. "Across the camp is the true rally, hundreds of Kurii! All falls before them! This was a ruse to draw men here, permitting Kurii to regroup in numbers elsewhere!"

My heart leaped.

No wonder the commander of the Kurii had left his forces here, disappearing. I wondered if they knew his real intent had been elsewhere. I admired him. He was a true general, a most dangerous and lethal foe, unscrupulous, brilliant.

"It seems," grinned Ivar Forkbeard, "we have a worthy adversary."

"The battle turns against us!" cried a man.

"They must be held!" said Ivar Forkbeard. We heard the howling of Kurii, from almost a pasang away, on the other side of the camp. Drifting to us, too, were the cries of men. "Let us join the fray, Tarl Red Hair," invited the Forkbeard.

Fleeing men rushed past us. The Forkbeard struck one, felling him.

"To the battle," said he. The man turned, and, taking his weapon, fled back to the fighting. "To the battle!" cried the Forkbeard. "To the battle!"

"They cannot be held!" cried a man. "They will sweep the camp!"

"To the battle!" cried the Forkbeard.

We ran madly toward the fighting.

There, already lifted, we saw the signal spear of Svein Blue Tooth. About it swept Kurii. It was like a flag on an island. At its foot stood the mighty Rollo, striking to the left and right with his ax. No Kur who approached the signal spear did not die. Hundreds of men, in ragged, scattered lines, strung out laterally, accompanied us. Kurii, overextended, meeting this new resistance, to piercing howls, fell back, to regroup for another charge.

"Form lines!" cried Svein Blue Tooth. "Form lines!" The Blue Tooth, their Jarl, was with them! Men fought to take their place, under his eyes, in the first line.

The Blue Tooth himself now stood with Rollo, his own hand on the signal spear.

We saw the overlapping shields of the Kurii line, the axes. There must have been better than two thousand Kurii formed.

Then, to our surprise, from within the Kurii lines we saw two or three hundred slave girls whipped forth. They were bound together in fours and fives. Some were bound together by the wrists, others by the ankles, some by the waist, many by the throat. They were cattle, caught and tethered in the camp, in the confusion, by Kurii. They were to be used to break our lines. I saw Aelgifu, Pudding, among them. Her wrists were pulled out from the side of her body, bound to the wrist of a girl on either side, as they themselves were fastened. We heard the cracking of whips, and the cries of pain. Faster and faster ran the girls toward us, fleeing the whips. Behind them, rapidly, the Kurii advanced.

"Charge!" cried Svein Blue Tooth. The lines of men, too, hurtled forward.

Not ten yards before the clash took place, Svein Blue Tooth and his lieutenants before the running line, as the girls, under the whips of Kurii, fled, terrified, seeing the axes, the leveled weapons, toward them, made a sign no bond-maid of the north mistakes, the belly sign. Almost as one the girls, crying out, flung themselves to their bellies among the bodies and the charge of the men of Torvaldsland, missing not a step, took its way over them, striking the startled Kurii with an unimpeded impact. I cut down one of the Kurii with its whip. "When the whip is put to the back of slaves," I told it, "it is we who shall do so." There was, instantly, fierce fighting, in and among, and over, the bodies of the tethered bond-maids. Those who could covered their heads with their hands. Bodies, human and Kur, fell bloodied to the grass. Bond-maids, half crushed, some with broken bones, screamed. They struggled, some to rise, but, tethered, few could do so. Most lay prone, trembling, as the feet shifted about them, weapons clashing over their heads. The Kurii, some seventeen or eighteen hundred of them, fell back.

"Cut the wenches free," ordered Svein Blue Tooth. Blades swiftly freed the prone, hysterical bond-maids. Many were covered with blood. Svein Blue Tooth, and others, by the hair, hurled bond-wenches to their feet. "Get to the pen!" he cried. They stumbled away, hurrying to the pen. "Help her!" ordered the Blue Tooth to two frightened girls. They bent to lift and support one of their sisters in bondage, whose leg was broken, binding fiber still knotted about the ankle. "Tarl Red Hair!" wept Gunnhild. My blade flashed at her throat, cutting the tether that bound her, on either side, to two other girls. "Get to the pen," I told her. "Yes, my

Jarl!" she cried, running toward the pen. The girls, those who could, fled the field, to return to the pen in which the Kurii had originally confined them. Those who could not walk were, under the orders of men, by other bond-maids, carried or aided to the pen. I saw Pretty Ankles put out her hand to Ivar Forkbeard. Severed binding fiber was knotted tight about her belly. "To the pen," commanded the Forkbeard. Weeping, she hurried to the pen.

"They charge!" cried a man.

With a great howling, again Kurii ran toward us. Our lines buckled but, again, after minutes of terrible fighting, they fell back.

On one side of me fought the mighty Rollo, his lips foaming, his eyes wild, on the other side he who called himself Hrolf, from the East, the bearded giant with bloodied spear. Well did he acquit himself. Then others stood with me. Rollo went to the signal spear. He who spoke of himself as Hrolf disappeared.

Twice more were there charges, once by Kurii, once by men. We were thrown back from the shield wall with devastating losses. Had it not been for the force of Svein Blue Tooth, the power of his voice, the mightiness of his presence, Kurii might then have taken the initiative. "Form lines!" he cried. "Regroup! Spears to the second line!" A hedge of spears, projecting from the lines of men, men with axes between them, waited for Kurii, should they try to press their advantage.

Then the spear line faced the shield wall. A hundred yards of bloodied grass, of bodies, of men and Kurii, separated two species of warring animal.

Kurii from within the camp, where they could, streamed to join their comrades. Men, too, where they could break away from small battles, individual combats, found their way to our lines.

It seemed startling to me that we had stood against Kurii, but we had.

The Kurii showed no signs of emerging from the shield wall. It consists of two lines, one on the ground, the other at chest level, of overlapping shields. The shields turn only for the blows of axes. We could see the two front lines, one kneeling, one standing, of Kurii. Similar lines, fierce, obdurate, protective, extended about the formation, on all sides, forming the edges of the Kurii war square. Within the square, formed into ragged "Hands," "Kurii," and "Bands," with their appropriate leaders, were massed a considerable

255

number of Kurii, ready to charge forth should the shield wall open, or to support it if it seemed in danger of weakening. It was my supposition that their square contained, now, better than twenty-three hundred beasts.

"Let us again attack the square!" cried a man.

"No," said Svein Blue Tooth. "We cannot break the square."

"They will wait for night," said Ivar Forkbeard.

Men shuddered. The Kur has excellent night vision. Men would, for practical purposes, be blind.

"They will slaughter us with the fall of night," said a man.

"Let us withdraw now," said another.

"Do you not think they will hunt us in the darkness?" asked Svein Blue Tooth. He looked up. "It is past noon," he said. Then he said, "I am hungry." He looked to some of his men. "Go to Kurii fallen. Cut meat. Roast it before our lines."

"Good," said Ivar Forkbeard. "Perhaps they will break the square for us."

But the square did not break. Not a beast moved. Svein Blue Tooth threw Kur meat into the dirt, in disgust.

"Your plan has failed," said Ivar Forkbeard.

"Yes," said Svein Blue Tooth grimly, "they are waiting for night."

I saw the general within their square, the huge Kur whom I had seen before, in the hall of Svein Blue Tooth, it with the golden ring on the left arm. The ring of gold, as far as I knew, had no military signifiance. Many Kurii wear such rings, and necklaces and earrings. That no ring of reddish alloy was worn, which would distinguish the leader of a Band or March was of interest. The leader of a Band wears two welded, reddish rings, the leader of the March, which contains twelve bands, only one. The general in the formation against which we stood wore not even one reddish ring. Surely he was not a "Blood" of a "People." Yet there was little doubt of his authority, or his right to such authority. I expected he stood as a commander from one of the steel worlds themselves, sent to unite and command native Kurii.

"Sometimes," said I. "Kurii react to blood, reflexively."

"They have had their fill of blood," said Ivar Forkbeard. "The air is heavy with it." Even I could smell blood, mixing with the smoke of fires, where Kurii lodges burned.

But the Kurii square held. It did not move.

"They are patient," said Svein Blue Tooth. "They wait for night."

At the same time Ivar Forkbeard and myself looked to one another. I smiled. He grinned.

"We shall break the square," I told Svein Blue Tooth. "We shall do so in one Ahn. Find what food and water you can. Feed the men. Give them drink. Be ready."

He looked at us, as though we might be mad. "I shall," he said, fingering the stained tooth of the Hunjer whale which hung about his neck.

Kurii lifted their heads, apprehensive. They heard the bellowing, before it came to the ears of men.

The earth began to tremble.

Dust, like smoke, like the earth was burning, rolled into the air.

They looked to one another.

Then the air was filled with the thunder of hoofs, the bellowing of the bosk.

The bosk, in their charging hundreds, heads down, hoofs pounding, maddened, relentless, driven, struck the square. We heard, even from behind the herd, Ivar, and I, and a hundred men, screaming and shouting, the howling, the startled shrieks of Kurii, the enraged roars of Kurii. We heard the scraping of horns on metal, the screams of gored Kurii, the howls of Kurii fallen beneath the hoofs. Nothing on Gor withstands the charge of the maddened bosk. Larls themselves will flee before it. The herd thrust through the square and, half milling, half still running, emerged from its other side, making for the slopes of the valley. Dazed, injured Kurii, their formations disrupted, reeled, only to find, among them, screaming men, the launched horde of Svein Blue Tooth. His charge was unleashed while the last of the bosk were still striking the western edge of the square, and other animals were streaming, bellowing, goring, through it. Screaming men, axes raised, emerged from the dust, running, falling upon the devastated Kurii. Not an instant had they been given to regroup themselves. Kurii, howling, fled, knots of men following individuals.

"Press them! Press them!" screamed the Blue Tooth. "No quarter. No quarter!"

Once again the camp became a melee of small combats, only now the Kurii, where they could, fled. If they fled north, they were permitted to do so, for north lay the "bridge of jewels." Since morning this "bridge" had lain in wait, more than four hundred archers surmounting the pass. That there is an apparent avenue of escape serves to make the enemy think in terms of escape; a cornered foe, desperate, is doubly dangerous; a foe who thinks he may, by swift decision, save himself, is less likely to fight with ferocity; he is quicker to abandon his lines, quicker to give up the combat.

Ivar and I strode through the burning camp, axes in our hand. Men followed us.

Where we came on them we killed Kurii.

We passed the poles of the vast pen. Within it, looking through the bars, not daring to leave it, were hundreds of bond-maids. We saw Pouting Lips within. Behind her was Leah, the Canadian girl. Ivar blew Pouting Lips a kiss, in the Gorean fashion, brushing the kiss with his fingertips toward her. She extended her hands through the poles but we turned away, leaving her, and the Canadian girl, behind them.

We saw a sleen herding a girl back to the pen. She was turning about, crying, scolding it, but it, snarling, relentless, snapped at her, cutting at her heels with its fangs. She fled before it, weeping, running to the pen.

Ivar and I laughed. "They are useful beasts in herding women," he observed.

"My Jarl," said a voice. We turned about. Hilda knelt to Ivar Forkbeard, her hair to his feet. "May I not follow my Jarl?" she begged. "A lowly bond-maid begs to heel her Jarl."

"Then, heel," said Ivar, good-naturedly, turning away.

"Thank you, my Jarl!" she wept, leaping to her feet, and falling into step on his left, two steps behind him.

We heard, behind a tent, the snarl of a Kur. Ivar and I, swiftly, circled the tent.

It was a large Kur, brownish, with blazing eyes, rings in its ears. In its right hand it dragged a human female. It was Thyri. Ivar motioned me back. Blocking the path of the Kur was a man, in a kirtle of white wool, a collar of black iron at his throat. He held his ax lifted. The Kur snarled, but the man, Tarsk, Thrall of the Forkbeard, once Wulfstan of Kassau, did not move. More than once today had I seen this fellow Tarsk at work in the fighting. In the lines of Svein Blue Tooth, once he had fought not more than six men from my right. His ax, and his kirtle, were much bloodied. Many times had his ax in the ferocities of combat drunk of the blood of Kurii.

The Kur threw the girl to one side. In her collar she fell whimpering, her eyes filled with terror.

The Kur cast about and suddenly darted its great hand down and clutched an ax, a Kur ax.

Wulfstan did not strike. He waited. The lips of the Kur drew back. He now had the ax firmly in his two heavy fists. He snarled.

Thyri lay on her side, the palms of her hands on the ground, her right leg under her. She watched the two beasts, contesting her, the Kur and the human beast, terrible with the bloodied ax, Wulfstan of Kassau. The fight was swift, sharp. Ivar was pleased. "You did well," he told the young man. "You did well earlier today, and now. You are free." At his feet lay the bloodied Kur. He stood over it, a free man. "Wulfstan," cried Thyri. She sprang to her feet and ran to him, burying her head, weeping, in her hair against his chest. "I love you," she wept. "I love you!"

"The wench is yours," laughed Ivar Forkbeard.

"I love you," wept Thyri.

"Kneel," said Wulfstan. Startled, Thyri did so. "You are mine now," said Wulfstan.

"But surely you will free me, Wulfstan!" she cried.

Wulfstan lifted his head and uttered a long, shrill whistle, of the sort with which Kurii summon herd sleen. One of the animals must have been within a hundred yards for it came immediately. Wulfstan lifted Thyri by one arm and threw her before the beast. "Take her to the pen," said Wulfstan to the animal. "Wulfstan!" cried Thyri. Then the beast, snarling, half-charged her, stopping short, hissing, eyes blazing. "Wulfstan!" cried Thyri, backing away from the beast, shaking her head. "No, Wulfstan!" "If I still wish you later," he said, "I will retrieve you from the pen, with others which I might claim as my share of the booty." "Wulfstan!" she cried, protesting. The sleen snapped at her, and, weeping, she turned and fled to the pen, the beast hissing and biting at her, driving her before it.

The three of us laughed. Ivar and I had little doubt that Wulfstan, upon reflection, would indeed retrieve his pretty Thyri, vital and slim, from the pen, and, indeed, perhaps others as well. Once the proud young lady of Kassau had spurned his suit, regarding herself as being too good for him. Now he would see that she served him completely, deliciously, helplessly, as a bond-maid, an article of his property, his to do with as he wished, and perhaps serve him as only one of several such lowly wenches. We laughed. Thyri would wear her collar well for a master such as Wulfstan, once of Kassau, now of Torvaldsland. We looked after her. We saw her, furious, running helplessly for the pen, the sleen at her heels.

Ivar Forkbeard, followed by Tarl Red Hair and Wulfstan of Torvaldsland, heeled by the bond-maid, Hilda, picked his way toward the burned, looted tents of Thorgard of Scagnar. In the valley there burned, still, a thousand fires. Here and there, mounted on stakes, were the heads of Kurii. We stepped over broken axes, shattered poles, torn leather, from the lodges of the Kurii. We passed a dozen men emptying a keg of ale. It had become cloudy. We heard a ship's song from two hundred yards to our right. We passed a group of men who had captured a Kur. A heavy block of wood had been thrust into its jaws and, with leather, bound there. It was bleeding at the left side of its face. Its paws had been tied together at its belly and its legs tied in leather ankle shackles. They were beating it back and forth between them with the butts of spears. "Down! Roll over!" commanded one of the men. It was beaten to its knees and then belly. Prodded by spears it rolled over. A girl fled past us, a sleen, brown and black, padding at her heels. I slipped once. The dirt, in many places, was soft, from the blood. We picked our way among bodies, mostly those of Kurii, for the surprise, the fury, had been ours. We passed five men, about a fire, roasting a haunch of Kur. The smell was heavy, and sweet, like blood. In the distance, visible, was the height of the Torvaldsberg. I saw Hrolf, from the East, the bearded giant who had joined our forces, asking only to fight with us, leaning on his spear, soberly, surveying the field. In another place we saw a framework of poles set on the field. From the crossbar, hung by their ankles, were the bodies of five Kurii. Two were being dressed for the spit; two, as yet, had been untouched; blood was being drained into a helmet from the neck of the fifth.

"Ivar Forkbeard!" cried the man holding the helmet. He lifted the helmet to Ivar. Over the helmet Ivar doubled and held his fist, making the sign of Thor. Then he drank, and handed to me the helmet. I poured a drop from the helmet, to the reddish, muddied earth. "Ta-Sardar-Gor," said I, "to the Priest-Kings of Gor." I looked into the blood. I saw nothing. Only the blood of a Kur. Then I drank. "May the ferocity of the Kur be in you!" cried the man. Then, taking the helmet back, and throwing his head back, he drained it, blood running at the side of his mouth, trickling to the fur at the collar of his jacket. Men about cheered. "Come," said Ivar to us. "Look," said a man nearby. He was cutting, with a ship's knife, a ring of reddish alloy from the arm of a fallen Kur. The knife could not cut the ring. He lifted it, obdurate and bloody. It was the only ornament the beast wore. "A high officer," said Ivar. "Yes," said the man. Behind him stood a blond slave girl, naked, her hair falling to her waist. I gathered she belonged to him. "We are victorious!" said the man to her, brandishing the ring. Over her iron collar she wore a heavy leather Kur collar, high, heavily sewn, with its large ring. He thrust her two wrists, before her body, into the ring he had cut from the Kur. He then tied them inside, and to, the ring. He then, from his belt, took a long length of binding fiber and, doubling it, looped it, securing it, at its center to the ring, leaving two long ends. He then threw her, on her back, over the body, head down, of the fallen Kur. He took the two loose ends of the binding fiber and, taking them under the body of the fallen Kur, dragged her wrists, elbows bent, over and above her head; he then, bending her knees, tied one of the loose ends about her left ankle, and the other about her right. It was the Gorean love bow. He then, regarding her, cut the Kur collar from her throat with the ship's knife. He threw it aside. She now wore only one collar, his. She closed her eyes. She moved, lying across it, on the body of the Kur. It was still warm. "It is we who are victorious," said he. She opened her eyes. "It is you who are victorious, Master," she said. Already her hips were moving. "I am only a slave girl," she wept. With a roaring laugh he fell upon her.

"Ivar! Ivar!" cried a voice.

We heard the slave girl cry out with pleasure.

"Ivar!" cried a voice.

Ivar Forkbeard looked up, to see Ottar up the slope of the valley, waving to him.

We made our way toward Ottar, who stood near the burned, fallen tents of Thorgard of Scagnar.

"Here are prisoners and much loot," said Ottar. He gestured at some eleven men of Thorgard of Scagnar. They were stripped of their helmets, belts and weapons. They stood, chained by the neck, their wrists shackled before them.

"I see only loot," said the Forkbeard.

"Kneel!" ordered Ottar.

"Sell them as slaves in Lydius," said the Forkbeard. He turned away from the men.

"Heads down!" commanded Ottar.

They knelt, their heads to the muddied dirt.

The Forkbeard looked at many of the boxes and chests, and sacks, of wealth. I had seen this, or much of it, earlier in the morning, when I had pursued the Kur to the tents of Thorgard of Scagnar.

To one side knelt the silken girls I had seen in the tent. There were seventeen of them. Under the dark sky, kneeling in the mud, they looked much different than they had in the tent. Their silks were soiled, their legs and the bottoms of their feet stained with mire. Their hands were tied behind their backs. They were fastened to one another by binding fiber in throat coffle. Those that had been wearing chains had had the locks unfastened, the keys found in one of the chests in a nearby tent. Over them, proud and regal, a switch in her hand, stood Olga. She waved the switch at them. "I took them all for you, my Jarl!" she elated. "I simply ordered them, with confidence and authority, to kneel in a line, facing away from me, to be bound. They did so!" The Forkbeard laughed at the lovely chattels. "They are slaves," he said. None of the girls even dared to lift her eyes to him. We saw, too, to one side, the former Miss Peggy Stevens of Earth, now Honey Cake. Her eyes were joyous, seeing the Forkbeard, seeing that he lived. She ran to the Forkbeard, kneeling, putting her head to his feet. She, too, like Pretty Ankles had severed binding fiber knotted about her belly. By the ring of the Kur collar which she wore Ivar Forkbeard jerked her to her feet, so that she stood on her tiptoes, looking up at him. He grinned. "To the pen with you, Slave," he said. She looked at him, adoringly. "Yes, Master," she whispered.

"Wait," said Olga. "Do not permit her to go alone."

"How is this?" asked Ivar.

"Recollect you, my Jarl," asked Olga, "the golden girl, she with ringed ears, from the south, who lost in the assessments of beauty to Gunnhild?"

"Well do I do so," responded Ivar, licking his lips.

"Behold," laughed Olga. She went to a piece of tent canvas, which, casually, loosely, was thrown over some object. She threw it back. Lying in the dirt, her legs drawn up, her wrists tied behind her back, was the deliciously bodied little wench, dark-haired, in gold silk, now dirtied and torn, in golden collar, and gold earrings, who had exchanged words with Ivar's wool-kirtled wenches at the thing. She was

262

the trained girl, the southern silk girl. In fury, she squirmed to her feet.

"I am not a Kur girl," she cried. Indeed, she did not wear the heavy leather collar, with ring and lock, which Kurii fastened on their female cattle. She wore a collar of gold, and earrings, and, torn and muddied, a slip of golden silk, of the sort with which masters sometimes display their girl slaves. It was incredibly brief. "I have a human master," she said, angrily, "to whom I demand to be immediately returned."

"We took her, Honey Cake and I," said Olga.

"Your master," said Ivar, thinking, recollecting the captain behind whom he had seen her heeling at the thing, "is Rolf of Red Fjord." Rolf of Red Fjord, I knew, was a minor captain. He, and his men, had participated in the fighting.

"No!" laughed the girl. "After the contest of beauty, in which, through the cheating of the judges, I lost, I was sold to the agent of another, a much greater one than a mere Rolf of Red Fjord. My master is truly powerful! Release me this instant! Fear him!"

Olga, to the girl's outrage, tore away her golden silk, revealing her to the Forkbeard. "Oh!" she cried, in fury. Gunnhild had won the contest, and won it fairly. But I was forced to admit that the wench now before us, struggling to free her wrists, now revealed to us, luscious, sensuous, short, squirming, infuriated, was incredibly desirable; we considered her body, her face, her obvious intelligence; she would bring a high price; she would make a delicious armful in the furs.

"How is it that you have dared to strip me!" demanded the girl.

"Who is your master?" inquired Ivar Forkbeard.

She drew herself up proudly. She threw back her shoulders. In her eyes, hot with fury, was the arrogance of the high-owned slave. She smiled insolently, contemptuously. Then she said, "Thorgard of Scagnar."

"Thorgard of Scagnar!" called a voice, that of Gorm. We turned. Thorgard of Scagnar, raiment torn, bloodied, a broken spear shaft bound behind his back and before his arms, his wrists pulled forward, held at the sides of his rib cage, fastened by a rope across his belly, herded by men with spears, stumbled forward. A length of simple, coarse tent rope, some seven feet in length, had been knotted about his neck. By this tether Gorm dragged him before Ivar Forkbeard.

The golden girl regarded Thorgard of Scagnar with horror.

Then, eyes terrified, she regarded Ivar Forkbeard, of Fork-beard's Landfall. "You are mine now," said the Forkbeard. Then he said to Honey Cake, "Take my new slave to the pen."

"Yes, Master," she laughed. Then she took the golden girl, the southern girl, by the hair. "Come, Slave," she said. She dragged the bound silk girl, bent over, behind her. "I think," said Ivar Forkbeard, "I will give her for a month to Gunn-hild, and my other wenches. They will enjoy having their own slave. Then, when the month is done, I will turn her over to the crew, and she will be, then, as my other bond-maids, no more or less."

Ivar turned to regard Thorgard of Scagnar. He stood proudly, bound, feet spread.

Hilda, naked, in her collar, knelt to one side and behind the Forkbeard. She covered herself with her hands as best she could, her head down.

The Forkbeard gestured to the several captive slave girls, loot from Thorgard's tent, kneeling, wrists bound behind their backs, in their brief, mired silk, in throat coffle, those girls Olga, light-heartedly, had secured for him. "Take them to the pen," he said to Olga. Olga slapped her switch in the palm of her hand. "On your feet, Slaves," she said. The girls struggled to their feet. "To the pen, hurry!" she snapped. "You will be given to men!" The girls began to run. As each one passed Olga, she, below the small of the back, was expedited with a sharp stroke of the switch. Then Olga, much pleased, laughing, trotting beside them, herded the running, weeping, stumbling coffle toward the pen.

Now the Forkbeard returned his attention to Thorgard of Scagnar, who regarded him evenly.

"Some of his men escaped," said Gorm. Then Gorm said, "Shall we strip him?"

"No," said the Forkbeard.

"Kneel," said Gorm to Thorgard of Scagnar, roughly. He prodded him with the butt of a spear.

"No," said the Forkbeard.

The two men faced one another. Then the Forkbeard said, "Cut him loose."

It was done.

"Give him a sword," said the Forkbeard.

This, too, was done, and the men, and the girl, too, Hilda, stepped back, clearing a circle for the two men. Thorgard gripped the hilt of the sword. It was cloudy. "You were al-ways a fool," said Thorgard to the Forkbeard.

264

"No man is without his weakness," said Ivar.

Suddenly, crying with rage, his beard wild behind him, Thorgard of Scagnar, a mighty foe, now armed, rushed upon the Forkbeard, who fended away the blow. I could tell the weight of the stroke by the way it fell on the blade, and how the Forkbeard's blade responded to it. Thorgard was an immensely strong man. I had little doubt that he could beat the arm of a man to weakness, and then, when it was slowed, tired, no longer able to respond with sureness, with reflexive swiftness, in a great attack, he would hack through to the body. I had seen such men fight before. Once the sheer weight of the attacker's blows had turned and driven, interposed, his opponent's sword half through the man's own neck. But I did not think the Forkbeard would weary. On his own ship he, not unoften, drew oar. He accepted the driving blows, like iron thunderbolts, on his own blade, turning them aside. But he struck little. Hilda, her hand before her mouth, eyes frightened, watched this war of two so mighty combatants. Too, of course, the weight of such blows, particularly with the long, heavy swords of Torvaldsland, take their toll from the striking arm, as well as the fending arm.

Suddenly Thorgard stepped back. The Forkbeard grinned at him. The Forkbeard was not weakened. Thorgard stepped back another step, warily. The Forkbeard followed him. I saw stress in the eyes of Thorgard, and, for the first time, apprehension. He had spent much strength.

"It is I who am the fool," said Thorgard.

"You could not know," said the Forkbeard.

Then Ivar Forkbeard, as we followed, step by step, drove Thorgard back. For more than a hundred yards did he drive him back, blow following blow.

They stopped once, regarding one another. There seemed to be now little doubt as to the outcome of the battle.

Then we followed further, even up the slope of the valley, and to a high place, cliffed, which overlooked Thassa.

It puzzled me that the Forkbeard had not yet struck the final blow.

At last, his back to the cliff, Thorgard of Scagnar could retreat no further. He could no longer lift his arm.

Behind him, green and beautiful, stretched Thassa. The sky was cloudy. There was a slight wind, which moved his hair and beard.

"Strike," said Thorgard.

On Thassa, some hundreds of yards offshore, were ships.

One of these I noted was Black Sleen, the ship of Thorgard. Gorm had told us that some of his men had escaped. They had managed to flee to the ship, and make away.

Beside me, agonized, I saw the eyes of Hilda.

"Strike," said Thorgard.

It would have been a simple blow. The men of Ivar Forkbeard were stunned.

Ivar returned to us. "I slipped," he said.

Gorm and others ran to the cliff. Thorgard, seizing his opportunity, had turned and plunged to the waters below. We could see him swimming. From Black Sleen we saw a small boat being lowered, rowing toward him.

"It was careless of me," admitted the Forkbeard.

Hilda crept to him, and knelt before him. She put her head softly to his feet, and then lifted her head and, tears in her eyes, looked up at him. "A girl is grateful," she said, "—my Jarl."

"To the pen with you, Wench," said the Forkbeard.

"Yes," she said, "my Jarl! Yes!" She leapt up. When she turned about, the Forkbeard dealt her a mighty blow, swift and stinging, with the flat of his sword. She was, after all, only a common bond-maid. She cried out, startled, sobbing, and stumbled more than a dozen steps before she regained her balance. Then she turned and, sobbing, laughing, cried out joyfully, "I love you, my Jarl! I love you!" He raised the weapon again, flat side threatening her, and she turned and, laughing, sobbing, only one of his girls, fled to the pen.

The Forkbeard and I, and the others, returned to the tents of Thorgard of Scagnar.

Svein Blue Tooth was there. We saw, in a long line, shackled, fur matted, Kurii being herded with spear butts through the camp. "The bridge of jewels worked well," said Svein Blue Tooth to Ivar Forkbeard. "Hundreds, fleeing, were slain by our archers. Arrows of Torvaldsland found the slaughter pleasing."

"Did any escape?" inquired Ivar.

The Blue Tooth shrugged. "Several," he said, "but I think the men of Torvaldsland now need fear little the return of any Kur army."

I thought what he said doubtless true. Single, or scattered, Kurii might, as before, forage south, but I did not think they would again regroup in vast numbers. They had learned, and so, too, had the men of Torvaldsland, that men could stand against them. This fact, red with blood of both beasts and men, had been demonstrated in a remote valley of the north. I smiled to myself. The demonstration would not have been lost, either, on the advanced Kurii of the steel worlds. It was ironic. I, Tarl Cabot, who had abandoned the service of Priest-Kings, had yet, in this far place, been instrumental in their work. The Forkbeard and I, it had been, who had found the arrow of war in the Torvaldsberg, who had touched it to other arrows, which, in hundreds of villages and camps, over thousands of square pasangs of rugged, inlet-cleft terrain, had been carried to the free men of the north, that they might fetch their weapons, rally and, shoulder to shoulder, do battle. And, too, I had fought. It was strange, as it seemed to me, that it should be so. I thought of golden Misk, the Priest-King, of once, long ago, when his antennae had touched the palms of my uplifted hands, and Nest Trust had been pledged between us. Then I dismissed the thought.

I saw, to one side, large Hrolf, from the East, who had fought with us, he leaning on his spear.

We knew little of him. But he had fought well. What else need one know of a man?

"What is to be done with these captive Kurii?" I asked Svein Blue Tooth, indicating the line of imprisoned beasts, some wounded, being driven past us, survivors of the slaughter on the Bridge of Jewels.

"We shall break the teeth from their jaws," he said. "We shall tear the claws from their paws. They, suitably chained, will be used as beasts of burden."

The great plan of the Others, of the Kurii of the steel worlds, their most profound and brilliant probe of the defenses of Priest-Kings, had failed. Native Kurii, bred from ship's survivors over centuries, would not, it seemed, if limited to the primitive weapons permitted men, be capable of conquering Gor, isolating the Priest-Kings in the Sardar, until they could be destroyed, or, alternatively, be used to lure the Priest-Kings into a position where they would be forced to betray their own weapons laws, arming men, which would be dangerous, or utilizing their own significant technology, thereby, perhaps, revealing the nature, location and extent of their power, information that might then be exploited at a later date by the strategists of the steel worlds. The plan had been brilliant, though careless of the value, if any, placed on Kurii life. I supposed native Kurii did not command the respect of the educated, trained Kurii of the ships. They were regarded, perhaps, as a different, lesser, or inferior breed, expendable in the strategems of their betters.

The failure of the Kurii invasion, of course, moved the struggle to a new dimension. I wondered what plans now, alternate plans doubtless formed years or centuries ago, would now be implemented. Perhaps, already, such plans were afoot. I looked at the ragged line of defeated, shackled Kurii. They had failed. But already, I suspected, Kurii, fresh, brilliant, calculating, masters in the steel worlds, in their command rooms, their map rooms and strategy rooms, were, even before the ashes in this remote valley in the north had cooled, engaged in the issuance of orders. I looked about at the field of battle, under the cloudy sky. New coded instructions, doubtless, had already been exchanged among the distant steel worlds. The Kur is a tenacious beast. It seems well equipped by its remote, savage evolution to be a dominant life form. Ivar Forkbeard and Svein Blue Tooth might congratulate themselves on their victory. I, myself, more familiar with Kurii, with the secret wars of Priest-Kings, suspected that men had not yet heard the last of such beasts.

But these thoughts were for others, not for Bosk of Port Kar, not for Tarl Red Hair.

Let others fight for Priest-Kings. Let others do war. Let others concern themselves with such struggles. If I had had any duty in these matters, long ago I had discharged it.

Suddenly, for the first time since I had left Port Kar, my left arm, my left leg, the left side of my body, felt suddenly cold, and numb. For an instant I could not move them. I nearly fell. Then it passed. My forehead was covered with sweat. The poison of the blade of Tyros lurked yet in my system. I had come north to avenge the slaying of the wench Telima. This resolution, the hatred, had driven me. Yet it seemed I had failed. In my pouch now lay the armlet, which Ho-Hak had given me in Port Kar, that found where Telima had been attacked. I had failed.

"Are you all right?" asked Ivar.

"Yes," I said.

"I have found your bow, and your arrows," said Gorm. "They were among weapons in the loot.

"I am grateful," I said. I strung the bow and drew it, and unstrung it. I slipped the quiver, with its arrows, flight and sheaf, over my left shoulder.

"In four days, when supplies can be gathered," said Svein Blue Tooth, "we shall have a great feast, for this has been a great victory."

"Yes," I said, "let us have a great feast, for this has been a great victory."

19

THE NOTE

The Kur came that night, the night of the battle, in the light of torches, ringed by men with spears. It held, in sign of truce, over its head, the two parts of a broken ax.

Many men stood about, armed, several with torches. Down a hall of men, standing in the field, came the Kur.

He stopped before Svein Blue Tooth and Ivar Forkbeard, who, on seats of rock, awaited it. Ivar, chewing on a vulo wing, motioned Hilda, and Gunnhild, Pudding and Honey Cake, who, naked and collared, his girls, knelt about him, to withdraw. They crept back, bond-maids, behind him. Their flesh was in the shadows. They knelt.

At the feet of the two leaders the Kur laid the pieces of the broken ax.

Then it surveyed the grouping.

To the astonishment of all the beast did not address itself to the two leaders.

It came and stood before me.

With one hand I thrust Leah to one side. I stood.

The lips of the beast drew back from its teeth. It towered over me.

It did not speak. It reached into a pouch, slung over its shoulder, and handed me a paper, rolled, bound, incongruously, with a ribbon.

Then the beast went to Svein Blue Tooth and Ivar Forkbeard, and there, from the ground at their feet, lifted again the two parts of the ax.

There were angry cries from the men. Spears were lowered.

But Svein Blue Tooth, regal, stood. "The peace of the camp is on him," he said.

Again the lips of the Kur drew back from its teeth. Then, holding the pieces of the ax over his head, he departed, escorted by armed men from the fire, to the edge of the camp, past the guards.

The eyes of those of the camp, in the torchlight, were upon me. I stood, holding the piece of paper, rolled, bound with its ribbon.

I looked at Leah, standing back, the light of the torches felicitous and provocative on her flesh. Her eyes were terrified. She trembled. Her breasts, in her agitation, rose and fell, her hand at them. I smiled. Women fear Kurii, terribly. I was pleased that I had not given her clothing. She looked at me. Her collar became her. "Kneel, Slave," I said. Swiftly, Leah, the slave girl, obeyed the word of a free man.

I opened the note, and unrolled it.

"Where is the Skerry of Vars?" I asked.

"It is five pasangs to the north," said Ivar Forkbeard, "and two pasangs offshore."

"Take me there," I said.

"Very well," he said.

I crumpled the note. I threw it away. But inside the note, curled within it, was a length of hair, long and blond. It was the hair of Telima. I put it in my pouch.

20

WHAT OCCURRED ON THE SKERRY OF VARS

The girl approached me.

She wore a long gown, white. She threw back the hood. She shook loose the long, blond hair.

"I have been a fool," I said. "I have come to the north, thinking you slain. I had come north, in fury, tricked, to avenge you."

It was near dusk. She faced me. "It was necessary," she said.

"Speak," I told her.

The Skerry of Vars is roughly a hundred foot, Gorean, square. It is rough, but, on the whole, flat. It rises some fifteen to twenty feet from the water. It is grayish rock, bleak, upthrust, igneous, forbidding.

We stood alone, facing one another.

"Are you unarmed?" she asked.

"Yes," I told her.

"I have arranged this meeting," she said.

"Speak," I told her.

"It is not I," she smiled, "who wish to speak to you."

"I had supposed as much," I said. "Does Samos know of this?" I asked.

"He knows nothing," she said.

"You are acting, then, independently?" I asked.

"Yes," she said, drawing herself up, beautifully. I wondered if she were wise, to stand so beautifully before a Gorean warrior.

"You fled my house," I said. "You returned to the marshes."

She tossed her head. "You sought Talena," she said.

"Talena, once," I said, "was my companion."

Telima shrugged. She looked at me, irritably. I had forgotten how beautiful she was.

"When I, in the hall of Samos, before leaving for the northern forests to seek Talena, learned of your flight, I wept."

"Always," she said, "you were weak." Then she said, "We have more important things to discuss."

I regarded her.

"In the marshes," she said, "I was contacted by Kurii." She looked at me. "They desire peace," she said.

I smiled.

"It is true," she said, angrily. "Doubtless," she said, "you find it difficult to believe. But they are sincere. There has been war for centuries. They weary of strife. They need an envoy, one known to Priest-Kings, yet one independent of them, one whom they respect, a man of valiance and judgment, with whom to negotiate, one to carry their proposals to Priest-Kings."

"I thought you knew little of these matters," I said.

"What little I know," said Telima, "is more than enough. In the marshes was I contacted by a mighty Kur, but one courteous, one strong and gentle. It would be difficult to speak directly with you. It would be difficult to begin this work if Priest-Kings understood our enterprise."

"And so," I said, "you pretended to be slain in the marshes. A Kur was seen. Your screams were heard. A bloodied armlet, bloodied hair, was found on the rence. The Kur departed north. I, as expected, informed of this deed, took pursuit."

"And now," she smiled, "you are here. It is the first act in the drama wherewith peace will be purchased between warring peoples."

"Your plan," said I, "was brilliant."

In the gown, long and white, flowing, Telima straightened, glowing.

"Your raiment," said I, "is of high quality. There is little like that in the rence."

"The Kurii, misunderstood," she said, "are a gentle people. They have treated me as a Ubara."

I looked now beyond Telima. I saw now, head first, then shoulders, then body, a Kur, climbing to the surface of the skerry. He was large, even for a Kur, some nine feet in height. His weight, I conjectured, was some eight or nine hundred pounds. Its arms were some seven feet in length. About its left arm was a spiral band of gold. It carried, on

272

its shoulder, a large, long, flattish object, wrapped in purple cloth, dark in the dusk. I knew the Kur. It had been he who had addressed the assembly. It had been he who had been first in the hall of Svein Blue Tooth, the night of the attack. It had been he who had rallied the Kurii in the raid on their camp, in the ensuing battle. It had been he, doubtless a Kur from the steel worlds themselves, who had commanded the Kurii army, who had been the leader of their forces.

I inclined my head to him. "We have met before, have we not?" I asked.

The Kur rested back on its haunches, some twenty feet from me. It laid the large, flattish object, wrapped in dark cloth, on the stone before him.

"May I present," inquired Telima, "Rog, emissary of peace from the Kurii."

"Are you Tarl Cabot?" asked the beast.

"Yes," I said.

"Have you come unarmed?" it asked.

"Yes," I said.

"We have sought you before," it said, "once in Port Kar, by poison."

"Yes," I said.

"That attempt failed," it said.

"That is true," I said.

He unwrapped the object which lay before him. "The woman has told you my name is Rog. That is sufficient. Yet my true name could not be pronounced in your mouth. Yet, you shall hear it." He then, regarding me, uttered a sound, a modulated emanation from the cords in its throat, which I could not duplicate. It was not a human noise. "That," it said, "is whom you face. It is unfortunate that you do not know the ways of Kurii, or the dynasties of our clans. In my way, to use concepts you may grasp, I am a prince among my people, not only in blood, but by battle, for in such a way only does one become prince among the Kurii. I have been trained in leadership, and have, in assuming such a leadership, killed for the rings. I say this that you may understand that it is much honor that is done to you. The Kurii know you, and, though you are a human, an animal, this honor they do to you."

He now lifted the object from the cloth. It was a Kur ax, its handle some eight feet in length, the broad head better than two feet in sharpened width.

"You are a brilliant foe," said I. "I have admired your strategies, your efficiency and skills. The rally at the camp,

273

misdirecting our attention by a diversion, was masterful. That you should stand first among such beasts as Kurii says much for your worth, the terribleness of your power, your intellect. Though I am only human, neither Kur nor Priest-King, I give you salute."

"I wish," it said, "Tarl Cabot, I had known you better."

It stood there, then, the ax in its right fist. Telima, eyes wide with horror, screamed. With his left paw the beast brushed her, rolling and sprawling, twenty feet across the stone.

It lifted the ax, now over its right shoulder, gripping it in both hands.

"Had you known me better," said I, "you would not have come to the skerry."

The ax drew back to the termination of its arc, ready for the flashing, circular, flattish sweep that would cut me in two. Then the beast stopped, puzzled. Scarcely had it seen the flash of Tuchuk steel, the saddle knife, its blade balanced, nine inches in length, which had slipped from my sleeve, turned, and, hurled, struck him. It tottered, eyes wild, not understanding, then understanding, the hilt protruding from its chest, stopped only by the guard, the blade fixed in the vast eight-valved heart. It took two steps forward. Then it fell, the ax clattering on the stone. It rolled on its back. Long ago, at a banquet in Turia, Kamchak of the Tuchuks had taught me this trick. Where one may not go armed, there it is well to go armed.

The huge chest shook. I saw it rise and fall. Its eyes turned toward me.

"I thought," it said, "humans were honorable."

"You are mistaken," I said.

It reached out its paw toward me. "Foe," it said. "Yes," I said. The paw gripped me, and I it. Long ago, in the Sardar, Misk, the Priest-King, had told me that Priest-Kings see little difference between Kurii and men, that they regarded them as equivalent species.

The lips of the Kur drew back. I saw the fangs. It was, I suppose, a frightening expression, terrifying, but I did not see it that way.

It was a Kur smile.

Then it died.

I rose to my feet and regarded Telima. She stood some ten feet away, her hand before her mouth.

"I have something for you," I told her. From my pouch I withdrew the golden armlet which had been hers. It had been that which, presented to me in Port Kar, bloodied, had lured me to the north, seeking to avenge her.

She placed the golden armlet on her upper left arm. "I shall return to the rence," she said.

"I have something else for you," I told her. "Come here."

She approached me. From my pouch I drew forth a leather Kur collar, with its lock, and, sewn in leather, its large, rounded ring. "What is it?" she asked, apprehensively. I took it behind her neck, and then, closing it about her throat, thrust the large, flattish bolt, snapping it, into the locking breech. The two edges of metal, bordered by the leather, fitted closely together. The collar is some three inches in height. The girl must keep her chin up. "It is the collar of a Kur cow," I told her.

"No!" she cried. I turned her about and, taking a pair of the rude iron slave bracelets of the north, black and common, with which bond-maids are commonly secured, locked her wrists behind her back. I then, with the bloodied Quiva, the Tuchuk saddle knife, cut her clothes from her. Then, by a length of binding fiber, looped double in the ring of her collar, tied her on her knees to the foot of the Kur. Then, with the knife, I knelt at the Kur's throat.

"Tarl! Tarl Red Hair!" I heard call. It was Ivar Forkbeard. I could see the longboat, four torches uplifted in it, men at the oars, putting in to the skerry.

I stood on the surface of the skerry.

Then I went down to meet the boat, finding my way among the rocks.

On the tiny rock promontory, footing the skerry, some eight or nine feet in width, I met Ivar Forkbeard, and his men. With him were Gorm, Ottar and Wulfstan of Torvaldsland.

The torches were lifted.

The men gasped. I lifted the head of the Kur in my right hand over my head. In my belt was thrust the spiral ring of gold, taken from its arm. To my belt, too, looped twice about it, was the length of binding fiber which went to the ring on Telima's collar. She knelt to my left, a bit behind me, on the stone. "I have here three objects," I said, "acquired on the skerry, the head of a Kur, he who was commander of the Kur army, a spiral ring of gold, taken as loot from his carcass, and a slave girl." I threw the head into the longboat. I then threw the ring after it. Then, unlooping the binding fiber from my belt, but leaving it looped, double, in her collar ring, with its loose ends, I crossed Telima's ankles and tied them together. Her wrists were still confined behind her back in the rude, black bracelets of the north, with their one heavy link. I carried her, wading on the stones, to the side of the longboat. She looked at me. Then I threw her into the boat, between the feet of the oarsmen.

21

I DRINK TO THE
HONOR OF TYROS

"Permit me to kiss you, Master," begged Leah. She snuggled against me. She was naked on the rough bench of the north. My right arm was about her, holding her to me, in my right hand, held in its grip of golden wire, was a great horn of steaming mead. The girl, in her need, pressed herself against the coarse woolen tunic of Torvaldsland. I looked down into her uplifted eyes, pleading. It was the need of a slave girl. I turned from her and drank. She sobbed. I laughed, and turned toward her. I looked into the large dark eyes, moist. About her throat she wore the north's collar of black iron, riveted. Then our lips met.

Mead was replenished in the drinking horn by a dark-haired bond-maid, who filled it, head down, shyly, not looking at me. She was the only one in the hall who was not stripped, though, to be sure, her kirtle, by order of her master, was high on her hips, and, over the shoulders, was split to the belly. Like any other wench, on her neck, riveted, was a simple collar of black iron. She had worn a Kur collar before, and, with hundreds of others, had been rescued from the pens. The fixing of the Kur collar, it had been decided by Svein Blue Tooth, was equivalent to the fixing of the metal collar and, in itself, was sufficient to reduce the subject to slavery, which condition deprives the subject of legal status, and rights attached thereto, such as the right to stand in companionship. Accordingly, to her astonishment, Bera, who had been the companion of Svein Blue Tooth, discovered suddenly that she was only one wench among others. From a line, as part of his spoils, the Blue Tooth picked her out. She had displeased him mightily in recent years. Yet was the Blue Tooth fond of the arrogant

277

wench. It was not until he had switched her, like any other girl, that she understood that their relationship had undergone a transformation, and that she was, truly, precisely what she seemed to be, now his bond-maid. No longer would her dour presence deprive his feasts of joy. No longer would she, in her free woman's scorn, shower contempt on bond-maids, trying to make them ashamed of their beauty. She, too, now, was no more than they. She now had new tasks to which to address herself, cooking, and churning and carrying water; the improvement of her own carriage, and beauty and attractiveness; and the giving of inordinate pleasure in the furs to her master, Svein Blue Tooth, Jarl of Torvaldsland; if she did not do so, well she knew, as an imbonded wench, that others would; it was not, indeed, until her reduction to slavery that she realized, for the first time, how fine a male, how attractive and how powerful, was Svein Blue Tooth, whom she had for years taken for granted; seeing him objectively for the first time, from the perspective of a slave girl, who is nothing herself, and comparing him with other free men, she realized suddenly how mighty, how splendid and magnificent he truly was. She set herself diligently to please him, in service and in pleasure, and, if he would permit it, in love. Bera went to the next man, to fill his cup with mead, from the heavy, hot tankard, gripped with cloth, which she carried. She was sweating. She was barefoot. The bond-maid was happy.

I drank.

The wench Leah again pressed herself against me. I looked down upon her. "You are a wanton slave," I said. She looked up at me, laughing. "A girl in a collar is not permitted inhibitions," she said. It was true. Slave girls must reveal their sexual nature, totally. Do they not do so, they are beaten. On Earth, Leah had been a prim girl, reserved, even haughty and formal. I had forced these truths from her. But on Gor, as with others of her ilk, such lies and false dignities were not permitted her. On Gor, should the girl be so unfortunate as to fall into slavery, the total depth of her needs, her sensations, her deepest and most concealed sensualities, must expose themselves helplessly to the master, even though he may, if he choose, mock her cruelly, to her misery, for her vulnerabilities. An example will make this clear. Every woman, of glandular normality, has an occasional desire, often frightening her, to writhe lasciviously, naked, before a powerful male. Should she miserably fall to slavery the passion dance of a nude slave girl will surely be among the least of what is commanded of her. Consider then the plight of the girl. She is forced, to her shame, to do what she has, for years in the secret heart of her, yearned to do. But how helpless, how vulnerable, she is! The dance ended, she falls to the sand, or tiles. Has she pleased him? She can do no more. She looks up. Her pride is gone, like her clothing, save for brand and collar, stripped away. There are tears in her eyes. She is at his mercy. If he repudiates her, she is shamed; she has failed as a female. Probably she will be sold in disgust. But if she discovers, to her terror, that she has pleased him, and he gestures her to him, she knows that she, after such a performance, cannot be respected but can be only a slave in his arms. She has danced as a slave; she will be used as a slave. She is a slave. Leah looked up at me. I kissed her again, full on her rouged slave mouth. She kissed well, trembling. And earlier, too, she had danced well. And then, too, later, at first given no choice, then, excited, helplessly aroused, unrestrainable, abandoned, uncontrollable, had performed superbly, serving me well, in the furs. I looked down upon her. Eyes moist, she lifted her lips, eagerly, to mine. I kissed her again. I was pleased that the Forkbeard had given her to me.

"I would speak!" called Svein Blue Tooth, rising to his feet, lifting a horn of mead. "Outlawry," said he, "once proclaimed by the hall of Blue Tooth against the person of Ivar Forkbeard, he of Forkbeard's Landfall, is herewith, in this hall, in this place, in the name of Svein Blue Tooth, Jarl of Torvaldsland, lifted!"

There was a great cheer.

"Charges appertaining thereto," roared the Blue Tooth, spilling mead, "are revoked!"

There were more cheers among the ashes, the blackened, fallen timbers, of the Blue Tooth's razed hall, amidst which the benches and tables of the feast were set. Many were the lamps, bowls on spears, which burned, and torches, too. And brightly glowed the long fire in the hall, over which tarsk and bosk, crackling and glistening with hot fat, roasted, turned heavily on spits by eager, laughing bond-maids.

"Svein Blue Tooth and I," said Ivar Forkbeard, rising, spilling Hilda from his lap, "have had our differences."

There was much laughter. The Forkbeard had had a price on his head. The Blue Tooth had sought his life.

"Doubtless," said he, "it is possible we shall have them again."

There was again much laughter.

"For a man, to be great, needs great enemies, great foes." The Forkbeard then lifted his mead to Svein Blue Tooth. "You are a great man, Svein Blue Tooth," said he, "and you have been a great enemy."

"I shall now," said the Blue Tooth, "if it be within my power, prove to be so good a friend."

Then the Blue Tooth climbed to the table's top and stood there, and the Forkbeard, astonished, climbed, too, to the surface of the table. Then the men strode to one another, meeting one another and, weeping, embraced.

Few eyes, I think, in the ruins of that hall, under the torchlight, beneath the stars, the height of the Torvaldsberg in the distance, illuminated in the light of the three moons, were dry.

Svein Blue Tooth, his arms about the Forkbeard, cried out, hoarsely. "Know this, that from this day forward, Ivar Forkbeard stands among the Jarls of Torvaldsland!"

We stood and cheered the fortune, the honor, that the Blue Tooth did unto the Forkbeard.

Ivar, no longer outlaw, now stood among the Jarls of the north.

Spear blades rang on shields. I stood proudly, strong in my happiness for the fortune of my friend.

But as the men cried out, and cheered, and the weapons clashed on shields, I looked to a place in the hall where, mounted on a great stake, was the huge, savage head of the Kur, which I had slain on the Skerry of Vars. For a man to be great, had said Ivar Forkbeard, he must need great enemies. I looked at the huge, somber, shaggy head of the Kur, mounted on its stake, some eight feet from the ground. I wondered if men, truly, knew how great their enemies were. And I wondered if men, in ways so weak, so puny, were adequate to such foes. The Kur, it seemed to me, in virtue of its distant, doubtless harsh evolution, was well fitted to be a dominant form of life. It would prove indeed to be a great foe. I wondered if man could be so great a foe, if he in his own terribleness, his ferocity, his intelligence, could match such a beast. On his own worlds, in a sense, man had no natural enemies, save perhaps himself. I regarded the huge, somber head of the Kur. Now he had one, a predator, a foe. Could man be a match for such a beast? I wondered on what might be the magnitude of man.

"Gifts!" cried Ivar Forkbeard. His men, bearing boxes, trunks, bulging sacks, came forward. They spilled the contents of these containers before the table. It was the loot of the temple of Kassau, and the sapphires of Schendi, which had figured in the wergild imposed upon him by Svein Blue Tooth in the days of his outlawry. Knee deep in the riches waded Ivar and, laughing, hurled untold wealth to those in the hall. Then his men, too, distributed the riches. Then, too, naked slave girls were ordered to the riches, to scoop up sapphires in goblets and carry them about the tables, serving them to the men, kneeling, head down, arms extended, as though they might be wine, and the warriors, laughing, reached into the cups and seized jewels. I saw Hrolf, from the East, the giant, mysterious Torvaldslander, take one jewel from the goblet proffered him, kneeling, by a naked, collared beauty. He slipped it in his pouch, as a souvenir. Ivar Forkbeard himself came to me, and pressed into my hand a sapphire of Schendi. "Thank you," said I, "Ivar Forkbeard." I, too, slipped the sapphire into my pouch. To me, too, it was rich with meaning.

"Ivar!" called Svein Blue Tooth, when the loot was distributed, pointing to Hilda, who, in her collar, stripped, cuddled at the Forkbeard's side, "are you not, too, going to give away that pretty little trinket?"

"No!" laughed the Forkbeard. "This pretty little trinket, this pretty little bauble, I keep for myself!" He then took Hilda in his arms and, holding her across his body, kissed her. She melted to him, in the fantastic, total yielding of the slave girl.

"Guests!" shouted a man. "Guests to enter the hall of Svein Blue Tooth!"

We looked to where once had stood the mighty portals of the hall of Svein Blue Tooth.

"Bid them welcome," said the Blue Tooth, and he himself left the table, taking a bowl of water and towel to meet the guests at the portal. "Refresh yourselves," said he to them, "and enter."

Two men, with followers, acknowledged the greeting of Svein Blue Tooth; they washed their hands, and their faces, and they came forward. I stood.

"We have sought you," said Samos of Port Kar. "I had feared we might be too late."

I did not speak.

He turned to regard the huge, shaggy head of the Kur, mounted on its stake.

"What is this?" he asked.

"Grendel," I said to him.

"I do not understand," he said.

281

"It is a joke," I said. Beside me, naked, in her collar, Leah shrank back, her hand before her mouth. I looked at her. "Yes," I said. She had been of Earth, a free girl, until brought as a slave to Gor. She understood my meaning. New understanding, new recognition, figured in her eyes. The wars of Priest-Kings and Others, the Kurii, were of ancient standing. I did not know, nor I suppose did others, outside the Nest, when the first contacts had been made, the first probes initiated, the first awareness registered on the part of Priest-Kings that there were visitors within their system, strangers at the gates, intruders, dangerous and unwelcome, threatening, bent upon the acquisition of territories, planetary countries. It seemed to me not unlikely that the Grendel of legend had been a Kur, a survivor perhaps of a forced landing or a decimated scouting party. Perhaps, even, as a punishment, perhaps for impermissible murder or for violation of ship's discipline, he had been put to shore, marooned.

"How is it that you have sought me?" I asked.

"The poison," said he, "that which lay upon the blades of the men of Sarus of Tyros, lurks yet in your body."

"There is no antidote," I told him. "This I had from Iskander of Turia, who knew the toxin."

"Warrior," said the man who stood with Samos, "I bring the antidote."

"You are Sarus of Tyros," I said. "You sought my capture, my life. We have fought as foes in the forests."

"Speak," said Samos to Sarus.

Sarus regarded me. He was a lean man, hard, scarred, with clear eyes. He was not of high family in Tyros, but had risen through the ranks to captainship in Tyros. His accent was not of high caste; it had been formed on the jetties of the island Ubarate of cliffed Tyros, where he had for years, I had learned, led gangs of ruffians; caught, he had been dragged before Chenbar, the Sea Sleen, for sentencing to impalement; rather, Chenbar had liked the looks of him and had had him taught the sword; swiftly, given his skills and intelligence, had the young, rugged brigand risen in the service of the Ubar; they were as brothers; there was, I was sure, no man in Tyros more loyal to her Ubar than Sarus. It was to him, as soon as Chenbar, freed of the dungeon of Port Kar, to which I had seen him consigned, had returned to Tyros, that the task had been given to hunt and capture the Ubar of Ar, Marlenus, and an Admiral of Port Kar, Bosk. Of these matters I have elsewhere written.

282

"The weapons of my men and myself, unknown to us, before we left Tyros," said he, "were treated with a toxin of the compounding of Sullius Maximus, once a Ubar of Port Kar." Sullius Maximus had been one of the five Ubars of Port Kar, whose reigns, dividing the city, had been terminated when the Council of Captains, under the leadership of Samos, First Captain of Port Kar, had assumed the sovereignty. The others had been Chung, Nigel, Eteocles, and Henrius Sevarius, the last of which, however, had ruled in name only, the true power being controlled by his uncle, Claudius, acting in the role of regent. Eteocles had fled; I had known him last to be in terraced Cos, an advisor to her Ubar, gross Lurius, of the Cosian city of Jad. Nigel and Chung were in Port Kar, though now only as powerful captains, high in her council. They had fought against the united fleets of Tyros and Cos and, without their help, doubtless Port Kar could not have won the great victory of the 25th of Se'Kara, in the first year of the reign of the Council of Captains, in the year 10,120 Contasta Ar, from the Founding of Ar. Claudius, who had been regent for Henrius Sevarius, and had slain his father, and sought the life of the boy, had been slain by a young seaman, a former slave, named Fish, in my house. The whereabouts of Henrius Sevarius, on whose head a price had been set, were unknown to the Council of Captains. The boy named Fish, incidentally, was still in my service, in Port Kar. He now called himself Henrius. Sullius Maximus, most cultured of the former Ubars of Port Kar, a chemist and poet, and poisoner, had sought refuge in Tyros; it had been granted him. "I swear to you that this is so," said Sarus. "We of Tyros are warriors and we do not deal in poisons. Upon my return to Tyros, Sullius inquired if our foes had been wounded, and I informed him that indeed we had struck you, drawing blood. His laughter, as if demented, he turning away, alarmed me. I forced the truth from him. I was in agony. It was to you that my men and myself, those who survived, owed their lives. Marlenus would have carried us to Ar for mutilation and public impalement. You were magnanimous, honoring us as warriors and sword brothers. I demanded an antidote. Laughing, Sullius Maximus, adjusting his cloak, informed me that there was none. I determined to slay him, and then take ship to Port Kar, that you might then, if you chose, cut my throat with your own hands. When my blade lay at the heart of the poisoner Chenbar, my Ubar, aroused by his weeping, bade me desist. Swiftly did I inform my Ubar of the shame

283

that Sullius Maximus had wrought upon the Ubarate. 'I have ridded you of an enemy!' cried Sullius. 'Be grateful! Reward me!' 'Poison,' said Chenbar, 'is the weapon of women, not warriors. You have dishonored me!' 'Let me live!' cried the poisoner. 'Do you, Sarus, retain the poisoned steel?' inquired my Ubar. 'Yes, my Ubar,' replied I. 'In ten days, wretched Sullius,' decreed my Ubar, 'your flesh will be cut with the steel of Sarus. On the tenth day, if you would again move your body of your own will, it would be well for you to have devised an antidote.' Sullius Maximus, then, shaken, white-faced, tottering, was hurried by guards to his chambers, his vials and chemicals." Sarus smiled. He removed a vial from his pouch. It contained a purplish fluid.

"Has it been tested?" asked Samos.

"On the body of Sullius Maximus," said Sarus. "On the tenth day, on his arms and legs, and twice, transversely, across his right cheekbone, that his face be scarred and his shame known, I drew the poisoned blade, drawing blood with each stroke."

I smiled. Sullius Maximus was a handsome man, extremely vain, even foppish. He would not appreciate the alteration of his physiognomy, wrought by the blade of Sarus.

"Within seconds," said Sarus, "the spiteful fluid took its effect. The eyes of Sullius were wild with fear. 'The antidote! The antidote!' he begged. We sat him in a curule chair, vested as a Ubar, and left him. We wished the poison to work, to be truly fixed within his system. The next day, when the bar of noon was struck on the wharves, we administered to him the antidote. It was effective. He is now again in the court of Chenbar, much chastened, but serving again as laureate and advisor. He is not much pleased, incidentally, with the scarring of his countenance. Much amusement on account of it is taken at his expense by his fellows of the court. He holds little affection for you, or for me, Bosk of Port Kar."

"He called you 'Bosk of Port Kar,'" said Ivar Forkbeard, standing near me.

I smiled. "It is a name I am sometimes known by," I said.

Sarus proffered to me the vial.

I took it. "There is, I discover, attendant upon its assimilation," said Sarus of Tyros, "delirium and fever, but, in the end, the body finds itself freed of both poison and antidote. I give it to you, Bosk of Port Kar, and with it the apologies of my Ubar, Chenbar, and those of myself, a seaman in his service."

"I am surprised," I said, "that Chenbar, the Sea Sleen, is so solicitous of my welfare."

Sarus laughed. "He is not solicitous of your welfare, Warrior. He is solicitous, rather, of the honor of Tyros. Little would please Chenbar more than to meet you with daggers on the fighting circle of Tyros. He owes you much, a defeat, and chains and a dungeon, and he has a long memory, my Ubar. No, he is not solicitous of your welfare. If anything, he wants you well and strong, that he may meet you, evenly, with cold steel."

"And you, Sarus?" I inquired.

"I," said Sarus, simply, "am solicitous of your welfare, Bosk of Port Kar. You gave, on the coast of Thassa, freedom, and life, to me and my men. I shall not, ever, forget this."

"You were a good leader," I said, "to bring your men, some wounded, from high on Thassa's coast to Tyros."

Sarus looked down.

"There is place in my house in Port Kar," I said, "for one such as you, if you wish to serve me."

"My place," said Sarus, "is in Tyros." Then he said, "Drink, Bosk of Port Kar, and restore the honor of Chenbar, and the honor of Sarus, and of Tyros."

I removed the stopper from the vial.

"It may itself be poison," said Samos.

I smelled it. It smelled sweet, not unlike a syrup of Turia. "Yes," I said, "it may be." It was true what Samos had said. It could be, indeed, that I held in my hand not an antidote, but a lethal dose of some unknown toxin. I thought of Turia, of its baths and wines. The plan of Tyros might thus, foiled upon the coast of Thassa, be in effect accomplished in the hall of Svein Blue Tooth, at least with respect to he known as Bosk of Port Kar.

"Do not drink it," said the Forkbeard to me.

But I had felt, after the battle, again in my body the effects of the poison, though briefly. I had little doubt but what it still lingered in my body. I had little doubt but what, in time, it would again force me to the blankets and chair of a recluse in a hall in Port Kar. If not countered, it would, eventually, doubtless, have its way.

"I shall drink it," I told Ivar Forkbeard.

The Forkbeard looked upon Sarus of Tyros. "If he dies," he said, "your death will be neither swift nor pleasant."

"I am your hostage," said Sarus.

"You, you called Sarus of Tyros," said Ivar, "you drink first."

"There is not enough," said Sarus of Tyros.

"Chain him," said the Forkbeard. Chains were brought.

"Sarus of Tyros," I said to Ivar, "is a guest in the hall of Svein Blue Tooth."

The chains were not placed on Sarus.

I lifted the vial to Sarus of Tyros. "I drink," I said, "I drink to the honor of Tyros."

Then I downed the contents of the vial.

22

I TAKE SHIP
FROM THE NORTH

Slave, girls, naked, carrying burdens, loaded the ship of
Ivar Forkbeard, the Hilda, moored at the wharf of the
Thing Fields. We stood on the wooden boards of the wharf.

"Will you not return to Port Kar with Sarus and myself?"
asked Samos.

"I think," said I, smiling, "I will take ship south with Ivar
Forkbeard, for I have yet to learn to break the Jarl's Ax's
gambit."

"Perhaps," said Samos, "when you reach Port Kar, we may
talk of weighty matters."

I smiled. "Perhaps," I said.

"I think," said Samos, "that I detect a difference in you.
I think that here, somehow, in the north, you have found
yourself."

I shrugged.

A seaman dragged Telima, by the arm, before us. She
was stripped. Her hair was before her face. Her wrists were
fastened behind her by the rude bracelets of the north. The
Kur collar, leather, some three inches in height, holding
her chin up, with its ring, was still on her throat. She had
spent the last five days chained in a small, log slave kennel.
She looked at Samos, and then, swiftly, lowered her eyes.

He looked upon the vulnerable, stripped girl with fury. He
knew well, now, what had been her role, her willing role, in
the plan of the Kurii.

"I will see that she is well punished," he said.

"You are speaking of one of my slave girls," I said.

"Ah!" he said.

"I will see that she is punished," I said. She looked at me.
There was fear in her eyes. "Put her on the ship," I said to

the seaman. He thrust her, ahead of him, stumbling, up the narrow gangplank, and put her on the ship.

In Port Kar I would remove the Kur collar and put her in one of my own. I would, too, have her beaten. Afterwards she would serve in my house, as one of my slave girls.

About my forehead I wore a Jarl's talmit. This morning Svein Blue Tooth, before cheering men, had tied it about my head. "Tarl Red Hair," had said he, "with this talmit accede to Jarlship in Torvaldsland!" I had been lifted on the shields of shouting men. In the distance I had seen the Torvaldsberg, and, to the west, gleaming Thassa. "Never before," had said Svein Blue Tooth, "has one not of the north been named Jarl amongst us." There had been much shouting, much clashing of weapons. Conscious I was indeed of the signal honor seen fit to be bestowed upon me. I had lifted my hands to them, standing on the shields, a Jarl of Torvaldsland, one who might now, in his own name if need be, send forth the arrow of war, summoning adherents; one who might, as it pleased him, command ships and men; one who might now say to the rough, bold seamen of the north, as it pleased him, "Follow me, there is work to be done," and whom they would then follow, gathering weapons, opening the sheds, sliding their ships on rollers to the sea, raising the masts, spreading the striped sails to the wind, saying, "Our Jarl has summoned us. Let us aid him. There is work to be done."

"I am grateful," said I to Svein Blue Tooth.

"I wish you well, Bosk of Port Kar," said Samos.

"Tarl Cabot," said I to him.

He smiled. "I wish you well, Tarl Cabot," he said.

"I wish you well, Samos," said I.

"I wish you well, Warrior," said Sarus.

"I, too, wish you well, Warrior," said I, "Sarus of Tyros."

Samos and Sarus turned about and left the wharf. They were going to the ship of Samos, on which they had come north.

Coast gulls screamed overhead. The air was sharp and clear. The sky was very blue.

I watched the girls loading the ship. Aelgifu, or Pudding, passed me, and then Gunnhild and Olga, bent under boxes carried on their backs. Pouting Lips and Pretty Ankles returned from the ship, down the gangplank, barefoot, to fetch more burdens. Hilda, bent over, a heavy sack of salt over her shoulders, staggered up the gangplank. Thyri returned down the gangplank, a yoke on her shoulders, from which dangled two empty baskets, on ropes. She had been carrying tospits and vegetables to the deck locker, to fill it. Wulfstan, once of Kassau, now of Torvaldsland, in charge of supplying the ship, leaned over the rail. "Fetch more tospits, Slave Girl," he called. "Yes, Master," said Thyri.

I saw Rollo board the ship. He carried a great ax, weapons, a sleenskin bag filled with gear. He was the first of the oarsmen to board.

Now came slave girls bearing skins of water. They walked slowly, bent over, placing each step carefully, that they not lose their balance, heavy skins, bulging and damp, across their shoulders. I saw Honey Cake among them, and the Forkbeard's golden girl, the southern silk girl, too, she laboring as any other bond-maid. I do not think that in the south she had been forced so to work. She staggered. "Hurry," said the girl behind her, "or we will be beaten!" The girl moaned, and staggered to the gangplank, and, slowly, foot by foot, her bare feet pressed by the weight deeply into the rough boards, climbed, carrying her burden, to the deck of the ship. Among the girls, too, I saw Bera, she one of the Blue Tooth's girls; one of several, who had been placed under the orders of Wulfstan to assist in the loading. She was naked. The other girls, resenting the tunic she had been given, had stripped her. Svein Blue Tooth had laughed. Masters do not interfere in the squabbles of slaves.

I looked up at the sky. It was very blue. For more than a day I had lain in fever, in delirium, while in my body had been fought the battle of poison and antidote. I had sweated, and cried out, and raged, but, in the end, I had thrown the furs from me. "I want meat," I had said, "and a woman." The Forkbeard, who had sat near me through the hours of the lonely contest, clasped me about the shoulders. He had ordered roast bosk and hot milk, and then yellow bread and paga. Then, when I had finished, Leah had been thrown to my feet.

I walked up the gangplank and stood on the decking, looking out to sea. There was a sweet wind on Thassa.

My delirium this time, interestingly to me, had been much different than it had when, long ago, the poison had first raged in my body. At that time I had been miserable, and weak, even calling out to a woman, who was only a slave, to love me. But, somehow, in the north, in Torvaldsland, I had changed. This I knew. There was a different Tarl Cabot than ever there had been. Once there had been a boy by this name, one with simple dreams, naive, vain, one shattered by a betrayal of his codes, the discovery of a weakness where he had thought there was only strength. That boy had died in the delta of the Vosk; in his place had come Bosk of Port Kar, ruthless and torn, but grown into his manhood; and now there was another, one whom I might, if I wished, choose to call again Tarl Cabot. I had changed. Here, with the Forkbeard, with the sea, the wind, in his hall and in battle, I had become, somehow, much different. In the north my blood had found itself, learning itself; in the north I had learned strength, and how to stand alone. I thought of the Kurii. They were terrible foes. Suddenly, incredibly, I felt love for them. I recollected the head of the giant Kur, mounted on its stake, in the ruins of the hall of Svein Blue Tooth. One cannot be weak who meets such beasts. I laughed at the weaknesses instilled into the men of Earth. Only men who are strong, without weakness, can meet such beasts. One must match them in strength, in intellect, in terribleness, in ferocity. In the north I had grown strong. I suddenly realized the supreme power of the united Gorean will, not divided against itself, not weak, not crippled like the wills of Earth. I felt a surge of power, of unprecedented, unexpected joy. I had discovered what it was to be Gorean. I had discovered what it was, truly, to be male, to be a man. I was Gorean.

Leah boarded the ship. She was barefoot. I had given her a brief, woolen slave tunic, which came high about her hips; it was sleeveless; it was split to the belly, belted with binding fiber. She carried, in a sleenskin bag, over her shoulders, much of my gear. I indicated to her the bench beneath which she might put it. She wore the black collar of the north. She turned and left the ship, going down the gangplank, to fetch more of my things. She walked well. She knew my eyes were on her, the sleek she-sleen. I enjoyed owning her.

I looked again out to sea. Last summer, in journeying to the forests, to attempt to rescue Talena, I had, in a tavern in Lydius, encountered a wench once known, Vella, Elizabeth Cardwell. She had made a delicious paga slave. I recalled her, licking my lips. Intent on the rescue of Talena, not wishing to be burdened by another wench, I had not yielded to the entreaties of the girl to buy her and free her. What a stupid request, I thought, to make of a Gorean male. It would have occurred only to an Earth girl. But if Elizabeth was stupid, or, more likely, naive, she was at least pretty. I thought then, too, of Talena. She had been disowned by

Marlenus of Ar. But she lived now in Ar, sequestered. She had insulted me in Port Kar. I smiled. I had left Vella, Elizabeth Cardwell, slave in Lydius. She had once, against my wishes, fled the Sardar, when I had wished, as a foolish Earthling, to return her to her home planet, for safety. Such a courageous act on her part had not been without its risks. She had fallen slave. I had met her in a tavern in Lydius. Gor is a perilous world, and particularly so, perhaps, for beautiful women. It is seldom that they, if not protected by a city and a Home Stone, escape the slave collar, the brand, the chains of a master. Elizabeth's act had been courageous. But she had lost her wager. I left her slave in Lydius, to the mercies of Sarpedon, the tavernkeeper, and his customers. It had been, as I now thought, a mistake. It had been a mistake because Elizabeth had been quite pretty. I would have been a fool to return so pretty a wench to Earth. When I returned to Port Kar I would arrange for an agent to buy her, if she had not already been sold to one who lusted for her and could pay her price. I would have been a fool to return so pretty a wench to Earth, I mused. Yes, I would, if it were commercially feasible, buy her, and keep her on Gor—as my own slave. I recalled that in my first delirium, fighting the poison, long ago, I had wept, and, in my fevered ragings, had begged for her comfort, that she love me. That seemed to me now incredible, but I recalled it, clearly. But I had changed in the north. This time, in my delirium, the wench, I recalled, had figured quite differently. No longer, this time, did I call out to her, or beg for her comfort, or love. This time it had seemed I had seen her on a slave block, naked, under torchlight, guided by the whip, turning for buyers. I dreamed in the delirium I had purchased her. "Do not return me to Earth," she had begged. "I will not," I told her. Then she had looked at me with horror, and I had, upon my return to my house, thrown her among my other slaves.

Ivar Forkbeard, with great strides, climbed the gangplank. Then, laughing, giggling, thrilled to be soon underway, approaching between two lines of seamen, came his slave girls. With them, less pleased, was the "golden girl," she with dark hair, and earrings. She dallied. One of the seamen took her by the back of the neck and thrust her, running, stumbling, half up the gangplank. She, too, then, weeping, boarded the Forkbeard's ship. "On your back," said a seaman to her, "and lift your legs, ankles crossed." The girl did so. He put the two-piece, hinged, double ankle ring on her. This is a simple fetter, without links, holding the ankles crossed.

It does not permit the girl to rise to her feet. When she had learned to be more pleasing, more radiant, her movements would be less restricted; I had little doubt that, by the time we reached Port Kar, she would be precisely what the Forkbeard wanted her to be. I looked at her. Our eyes met. She looked down, tears in her eyes. I had used her. She was quite good. But it had taken longer to arouse her than is common in a slave girl. The Forkbeard, I, and the crew, would improve her. The trip south would be long. Whereas it commonly takes a third of an Ahn to arouse a free woman, a female slave is often responsive from almost the first touch of the master. Why this should be I do not know. I suspect it is due, primarily, to two factors: the first is psychological. The collar itself, and the state of bondage, for no reason clear in my mind, commonly transforms even the tepid free woman into an orgasmic marvel of a slave. Perhaps they fear to be whipped if they are not pleasing? Perhaps, behaviorally, given no choice but to act as a passionate female slave, they find, suddenly, through simple psychological relationships, they, to their horror, have become only a passionate female slave. Perhaps it is the knowing that they are rightless, owned, dominated, which so deeply, so incredibly, triggers the profound web of yielding, piteously receptive, helplessly submitting reflexes; perhaps in the depth of their bodies lies the secret need to be sexually subjugated, totally, without which they cannot attain their full sexuality. I do not know. The second reason is presumably simple. It is merely that the female slave, abandoned, responsive, owned, constantly at her master's beck and call, ready constantly for his least pleasure, is frequently used. Female slaves are sometimes used, when the master's time permits, three and four, or more, times a day. It is not unusual to give an entire day to sport with a female slave, something unthinkable with a free woman. The slave girl, of course, has no rights. She may be used for hours. What counts is not her will, but her master's. Frequent use of the female slave, I suspect, keeps her body honed to submissive perfection. Whatever be the reasons, a common female slave, and one of no unusual heat for a slave, will be carried through a series of multiple yieldings, dozens, before the average free woman can be warmed. Then, when the master wishes, scorning perhaps her helplessness in his arms, despising perhaps, to her misery, her vulnerability to him, he takes ruthlessly, perhaps contemptuously, his delight with her. As a note, it might be added, that the slave female, in her master's arms, must, if he so commands, under the threat of the whip or death, vocalize her sensations, thus ventilating and reinforcing, multiplying, deepening, and increasing and intensifying them. Thus, cruelly, she is forced to help arouse herself and contribute to her own pleasures, and consequently, of course, those of the master. This command, sometimes implicit, sometimes a matter of the master's policy with his girl or girls, under which she is placed, to vocalize her pleasures, and abundantly, as well as, in her abandon, nudity, and beauty, manifest them physically, guides, accurately and surely, the master in the detailed exploitation of her weaknesses, in his depredations practiced on her body. She must betray herself. Do not blame her. No choice is given her. She is an instrument of passion on which he plays, delighting himself with the music of her expressions, her movements, her cries, even the wild, unrestrainable odors of her collared slave body. She is forced to contribute to her own sexual subjugation. Do not blame her. No choice is given her.

Following the last of the girls, carrying the last of my gear, came Leah, who stood, small, beside me. Ottar then, and Gorm, and the other men of the Forkbeard boarded the craft. Thyri, who had boarded earlier, stood near the bench of Wulfstan, where, already, he gripped an oar. Near the mast, chained to it by the neck, eyes down, knelt Telima.

Moorings were cast off. Poles thrust the Hilda from the wharf. Gorm held the tiller, mounted at the stern on the starboard side. The seamen brought their shields inboard, stowed their gear beneath their benches, grasped their oars. Slowly the tarnhead prow of the Forkbeard's sleek craft turned toward the sweep of Thassa. Then oars dipped slowly. The great red and white striped sail fell, opening, snapping, from the spar of needlewood. I turned back to the wharf.

The Forkbeard and I raised our hands, in salute, to the men there. We saw Svein Blue Tooth, the tooth of the Hunjer whale, stained blue, on its chain about his neck. He lifted his hand. Near him, kneeling beside her master, behind the line of his heels, was Bera, one of his girls. I saw, too, Bjarni, of Thorstein Camp, who lifted his spear to me, and beside him, too, the young man, his friend, he, too, lifting his hand, whom I had, it now seemed long ago, championed at the dueling field. There were many men there, armed, and wenches, too.

One of the seamen lifted the "golden girl," her crossed ankles in the fetter, that she might see. Then he threw her back to the deck, where, on her stomach, and elbows, head down, hair falling to the deck, she lay.

I saw Telima, standing by the mast, to which she was chained by the neck. I looked at her, harshly. Immediately she knelt, eyes down.

In my pouch there was a sapphire from distant Schendi. There, too, heavy and spiraled, was a ring of gold, which I had taken from the arm of the Kur I had slain. In the distance, as the ship moved to sea, the wind in its sail, oars dipping, I saw the bleak, white heights of the Torvaldsberg.

Hrolf, from the East, had agreed to return the war arrow to the Torvaldsberg.

We had given it to him. When he had left the ruins of the hall of Svein Blue Tooth I had run after him, and, a pasang from the camp, had stopped him. "What is your true name?" I had inquired.

He had looked at me, and smiled. It was strange what he said. "My name," he said, "is Torvald." Then he had turned away. I watched him return to the mountain. I thought of the stabilization serums, "My name is Torvald," he had said. Then he had turned away.

"Ho!" cried Ivar Forkbeard, striking me on the back, clasping me about the shoulders. "It is a good wind!" Then he turned away, to his duties on the ship.

I walked between the benches, to the prow, and, standing on the high decking, at the stem, put one arm about the prow and looked out to sea. Leah heeled me there. I turned to face her. I could see the lovely curves of the interior cleavage of her breasts, revealed in the parting of the rough slave tunic. I looked at the collar, her eyes. I pulled the tunic down from her shoulders, to her waist. "It is your girl's hope that she pleases you," she said. "Slip from the tunic," I told her. She untied the binding fiber, belting the tunic, and thrust it over her hips, to her ankles, and then stepped from it. "To my feet," I told her. "Yes, Master," she whispered. She lay on her side, her head on her arm. She did not look up at me.

I turned again to look out to sea.

I thought of many things, of Ar, of Marlenus, of Talena, with whom I was not pleased. When I had been crippled she had derided me; she had expressed contempt, pride; she had then held herself too good for me. I had had her returned to Ar. I wondered if, somehow, somewhere, we might once again encounter one another. Did we do so I thought now she might find me different.

I pondered trying chain luck in Ar. I wondered how she

might feel, the gag hood drawn over her head from behind, locked shut behind her neck, stripped, thrown on her back over the saddle of a tarn, bound, swept away, with a beating of wings, into total bondage. Publius, my kitchen master, I speculated, might find use for such a wench in his kitchens; after she had much pleased me, I would see that she was assigned to Publius. I had little doubt that the daughter, or she who had once been the daughter, of Marlenus of Ar, properly instructed by the switch, would make an excellent addition to the slaves of the kitchen. Perhaps, before I chose my wench for the night, one of her duties might be to scrub the tiles of my chamber.

I recalled how, in the forests, long ago, I had sought her. It had been my intention to repledge the companionship, and to become great on Gor, to raise high the chair of Bosk, climbing in riches and power to the heights of the planet, to become even, perhaps, in time, a world's Ubar.

Incredibly, perhaps, the values, wealth and power, which had driven me in the forest, when I had sought Talena, no longer seemed of much interest to me. The sky now seemed more important to me, and the sea, and the ship beneath my feet. No longer did I dream of becoming a Ubar. In the north I found I had changed. What had driven me in the forests seemed now paltry, irrelevant to the true needs, the concerns, of man. I had been blinded by the values of civilization. Everything that I had been taught had been false. I had suspected this when I had stood on the heights of the Torvaldsberg, on a windswept rock, looking upon the lands beneath, white and bleak, and beautiful. Even Kurii, on its height, stunned, had stopped to gaze. I had learned much in the north.

I looked again to sea, and to the sky. There were now white clouds in it. Somewhere, beyond the fourth ring, mixed in the belt of asteroids, intruding within the perimeters refused to them by Priest-Kings, were the patient, orbiting steel worlds. This I had from Samos. They were nearer now. Somewhere, above that placid sky with its swift, white clouds, closer now, were Kurii. I remembered the huge head, mounted upon the stake.

When I returned to Port Kar, I must speak to Samos.

I stood long at the prow. Then, after some hours, it grew dark. With my foot I nudged Leah, at my feet. She awoke. She knelt, and kissed my feet. "Take your garment," I told her, "but do not don it. Go to the waterproof, sleenskin sleeping bag by my bench. Spread it on the deck, between the benches. Then get within it and await me." "Yes, Master," she whispered.

I turned, in time to see her creep feet first, with a turn of her hips, into the bag.

I passed Telima, chained at the mast. The chain was attached to the large, sturdy, circular ring sewn in the locked Kur collar. She did not meet my eyes. She knelt, turning her head and putting its right side to the deck. I heard the chain touch the deck. I saw her hair on the sanded boards, in the light of the three moons. I passed her.

I removed my tunic. I thrust it beneath the bench. Then, wrapping my sword belt about my scabbard, the blade within, placed the weapon, belt and scabbard within the bag, that they be protected from moisture. I then slipped into the bag. "May your slave, Leah," whispered Leah, "attempt to please her master?" "Yes," I told her. She fell to kissing me, with the lascivious, wanton joy of the slave girl, given no choice but to reveal and liberate, and act upon, completely and with perfection, her deepest, most hidden desires, even though she might, in misery, scorn herself for possessing them.

Toward morning Leah slept, and I held her to me. I looked up at the sail, the stars over the mast.

I left the sleeping bag and drew my clothes about me, belting, too, to my side, the steel sword of Gor.

The Forkbeard was at the tiller. I went for a time to stand near him. Neither of us spoke.

I observed the sea. I looked up at the stars.

When I reached Port Kar, I would, I decided, speak to Samos.

Then, in silence, listening to the water against the hull, I considered again the stars, and the sea.